THE
UNSEEN
SISTER

ALSO BY ANDY MASLEN

Detective Kat Ballantyne:

The Seventh Girl

Detective Ford:

Shallow Ground
Land Rites
Plain Dead

DI Stella Cole:

Hit and Run
Hit Back Harder
Hit and Done
Let the Bones Be Charred
Weep, Willow, Weep
A Beautiful Breed of Evil
Death Wears a Golden Cloak
See the Dead Birds Fly
Playing the Devil's Music

Gabriel Wolfe Thrillers:

Trigger Point
Reversal of Fortune

Blind Impact
Condor
First Casualty
Fury
Rattlesnake
Minefield
No Further
Torpedo
Three Kingdoms
Ivory Nation
Crooked Shadow
Brass Vows
Seven Seconds

Other Fiction:

Blood Loss – A Vampire Story
Purity Kills
You're Always With Me
Green-Eyed Mobster

THE UNSEEN SISTER

A DETECTIVE KAT BALLANTYNE THRILLER

ANDY MASLEN

THOMAS & MERCER

Published by Thomas & Mercer, Seattle

www.apub.com

Amazon, the Amazon logo, and Thomas & Mercer are trademarks of Amazon.com, Inc., or its affiliates.

ISBN-13: 9781662511240
eISBN: 9781662511257

Cover photography and design by Dominic Forbes

Printed in the United States of America

For Jo. Always.

'I know you what you are,
And like a sister am most loath to call
Your faults as they are named.'

William Shakespeare, *King Lear*

CHAPTER ONE

Kat Ballantyne strode across Bowman's Common towards the trio of standing stones.

Her heart was racing.

It wasn't the exercise first thing in the morning. She was used to that, walking Smokey, her year-old cairn terrier. It was the call from Dispatch twenty minutes earlier that had spiked her adrenaline.

The call-handler's brief explanation – a dead body found in suspicious circumstances – had aroused two conflicting emotions in her. Excitement that she had another case to solve. Sadness that here was another soul gone from Middlehampton before their time. And this one wasn't coming back.

The morning had been going so well, too. Riley at a sleepover at a friend's house. A resulting extra half-hour in bed that she and her husband, Ivan, had made full use of. She smiled briefly at the memory.

Ahead, the Three Sisters loomed. Pitted grey faces scabbed with acid-yellow and sage-green lichen and weathered by millennia of wind and rain. Kat looked up at the tallest, known as Old Meg. At this angle, the topmost portion, undercut by erosion, appeared to be a nodding head.

Waiting for her in front of the stones, a figure. Fine white hair like thistledown. Bright blue eyes glinting in the sunshine. A crumpled bag in his left hand, into which his right dipped mechanically. By his side, a rangy black and white dog.

This was a surprise. She knew him. And his lurcher. Lois. They walked their dogs in the same places. Often kept each other company.

She frowned. 'Barrie?'

The old man, a retired beat cop with thirty under his belt, nodded a greeting to her. No twinkling smile today. No 'Morning, Skip', the nickname he'd bestowed on her the moment she told him she was a detective sergeant. He simply shook his head, mouth downturned.

'It finally happened.' His voice was flat, heavy. 'I'm the dog walker who found the dead body. I called it in. Told them you lived close. To get you out here pronto.'

In the distance, sirens fractured the silence shrouding the common. She looked past his shoulder, absent-mindedly ruffling the top of Lois's head as the dog nuzzled her thigh.

'Sorry, Lo-Lo,' Kat said. 'No treats with me today.'

She put her murder bag down and retrieved a pair of blue plastic booties. Slipped them on, plus a pair of purple nitrile gloves. She approached the dead woman lying at the centre of the standing stones among a scatter of gym equipment: brightly coloured kettlebells, mats, skipping ropes. A varnished wooden trolley with a red metal pull-along handle stood to one side.

People often came up to the common on fine mornings to work out. Kat shook her head. She didn't see the point. She played in the Middlehampton netball league herself. As much for the social aspect as the games themselves.

What was wrong with the woman's face? Kat moved closer to get a better view. It was swollen, like she'd had the mother and father of all bee stings. Lips so puffy they looked like a bad filler job. Only the tips of the eyelashes showed between inflated lids.

Anaphylactic shock? That's what it looked like. She dismissed it. Easy conclusions were for rookies and armchair detectives.

The woman wore black leggings and a tight turquoise Lycra exercise top that emphasised a flat belly and a small bust. Her arms were toned, shadows cast by the sun demarcating the different muscle groups. A half-empty clear plastic water bottle lay on its side nearby.

'Did you check for a pulse?' she called to Barrie over her shoulder.

He nodded. Tapped the inside of his wrist. Beside him, Lois had started whining.

Kat placed the backs of her fingers against the woman's forehead. The skin was cold to the touch. She pushed two fingers into the puffy flesh under the jaw where the carotid artery ran. Eyes closed, she felt for a pulse, altering the angle, position and pressure of her fingers. Better safe than sorry.

'Hi,' she said, even now hoping this was a false alarm. 'Are you OK?'

Knowing she was merely going through formalities, she shook the woman's shoulder.

'Hi,' she said again, louder this time. 'Can you hear me, lovely?'

Kat bit her lip as the woman's head lolled to one side.

Of course she couldn't hear Kat. She was dead.

CHAPTER TWO

Kat twisted round. A couple of uniforms were hurrying across the common towards her. Good. They'd set up a cordon. She'd already seen a couple of curious onlookers approaching, phones out, and had sent Barrie to keep them back.

She checked the rest of the body. The woman was holding something in her clenched right hand. A clear plastic tube with a yellow label just visible where it disappeared into her fist. What was that? A hypo? No, much too large. She peered at the label. The visible portion read 3 GET EMERGENCY MEDICAL HELP.

An EpiPen.

At best, Kat had a woman dead from a medical episode. At worst, it was homicide. She pulled out her phone and called Tom Gray, her bagman.

'Morning, Kat. What's up?'

'Dead woman on Bowman's Common. Suspicious. I need you to pull a team together and get out here.'

'Oh, right.' He sounded flustered. 'And by "team", you mean . . .'

'Come on, Tom, you should know this,' she said in exasperation. 'The pathologist. Darcy Clements—'

'—forensic coordinator, right—'

'—whoever's available in a marked car, and an ambulance.'

While she spoke to Tom, she unzipped the woman's gym bag. Beneath a towel, spare T-shirt, three energy bars and a rolled up electric-blue windcheater, she found what she was looking for. The tough black nylon wallet's Velcro strip parted with a rasp. She extracted a credit card and read the name. Jo Morris. Further ferreting produced a business card with a busy design of athletic silhouettes, rendered in black and lime green.

JO MORRIS

PERSONAL TRAINER AND FITNESS COACH

Kat had cleared the first hurdle: she had an ID. The upside was she wouldn't have to spend days or even weeks identifying the dead woman. The downside, however, was that later that day she'd be visiting the next of kin, arriving on their doorstep with a face frozen into a rictus of sympathy mixed with dread. Asking to come in, suggesting they sit, toughing out those moments when they insisted on standing. Then wishing they'd taken her advice when they collapsed, hopefully into the embrace of a sofa or armchair.

But all that was for later.

She rummaged deeper inside the bag, feeling around in the corners. That was odd. No phone. She checked the woman's clothing again. No armband phone holder, no rectangular bulge in the leggings. Another tick in the 'suspicious' column. Who went out these days without their phone?

The two uniforms arrived. Puffing. Red-faced.

'Dave, can you set up an inner cordon around the stones,' she said to the male PC, his bulk emphasised by his equipment belt.

'Aren't they listed or something?' he asked.

'Don't know, don't care. Just wind the tape round them, it won't do any damage.'

She turned to his partner, Deepika Mirza.

'Deep, can you move the gawkers back, please?'

The petite PC nodded. 'I'll do my best,' she said before striding towards the knot of spectators, arms spread wide. In a surprisingly resonant voice, she called out, 'OK, everybody. I'd like you all to take ten big paces backwards.'

While the two PCs organised the cordon, Kat squatted beside the dead woman.

At first sight it looked like she'd tried to jab herself with the EpiPen but the injector had failed. But what could have caused the reaction out here? An insect sting – like she'd first thought? Kat checked the visible areas of the woman's skin for a tell-tale raised bump or any visible redness, but found nothing.

Barrie called out to her. 'I'm off, Skip. They're taking my statement at Jubilee Place.'

She nodded. Waved a farewell.

A distant siren grew louder. An ambulance was bumbling across the undulating grass towards them. She scanned the horizon. The nearest houses were out of sight. No point in setting up door-to-doors. Or not yet anyway.

Tom was on the scene now, jogging over, his jacket flapping in the breeze. Some way behind him, clad in a lightweight beige trench coat that billowed in the breeze, the good-looking new pathologist at MGH, Jack Beale.

Kat stood, raised her hand in a brief wave.

Tom looked past her, towards the dead woman. He nodded sharply. Kat watched him gear up mentally. He had a way to go before he'd reach her old partner's standard. But Leah had a few more years under her belt, and Kat had to admit that Tom *was* shaping up nicely, despite the occasional brain freeze. Still had a rookie's weak stomach for autopsies, but that would pass.

'Dead of anaphylactic shock,' he said, shaking his head.

'Sure about that, are we?'

His features shifted restlessly for a second, a look that said, *This is a joke, right? You're testing me.*

'I saw the EpiPen. My cousin has one. With him it's peanuts. That's what they're for.'

'I know what they're for, Tom,' she said. 'I'm asking whether you're sure the cause of death is anaphylaxis.'

He scratched the back of his neck. Folded his arms and then, looking down and frowning, uncrossed them again and stuck his hands in his pockets.

'Is this where you make some crack about graduate fast-trackers and I bow to your superior experience in the field?' he asked.

'Let's just say, there's fast and then there's hasty. Did she manage to inject herself?'

'Well, I don't know, but—'

'Because if she did, was the EpiPen faulty? Maybe someone tampered with it.'

He held his hands up. 'I get it. I jumped to conclusions. Let me take over the interrogation. Right, Bambi,' he said, using the nickname the older cops bestowed on the newbies, especially if they carried a rolled-up degree certificate in their back pocket. 'Any petechiae on the whites of her eyes? Hard to tell, given the state of them. So she might have been strangled to death. How about injuries to the back of the head? No idea. Blunt force trauma still in play then, and—'

Kat let him off with a smile. 'That's enough. You're good. But let's give Jack a chance to do his job. We'll stick to investigating, eh?'

Jack had finished his preliminary examination and now joined them, peeling off his gloves.

'Morning, Tom. Morning, Kat.'

He smiled at her, holding her gaze a fraction too long.

'Morning, Jack. Can you do the ROLE?'

'Recognition of Life Extinct,' Tom said. Then frowned. 'Sorry. I'm Tomsplaining again.'

'She's dead. That's official. I'll know more after a forensic post-mortem.' Jack turned to Kat. 'If you think that's necessary.'

'I say it's suspicious.'

'This isn't me pushing back,' Tom said, brushing back a lock of dark hair that had blown over his eye. 'But can I ask why?'

'At the very least we need to know whether Jo managed to use the EpiPen and whether it worked properly,' Kat said. 'But more generally, we have a presumably fit and healthy young woman lying dead in the middle of a public park at seven forty-five in the morning.'

He nodded. 'OK, thanks.'

'I haven't finished. Where's her phone? Because it's not on her body and it's not in her gym bag, either.'

'At home?'

'Come on, Tom. Look at her. Even through that swelling I can tell she's no older than forty. No woman that age would come out to Bowman's Common without her phone. She just wouldn't.'

'So her killer took it.'

'Too quick again, Bambi,' Jack said. 'Anyone could have taken it. Maybe a member of our pharmaceutically dependent community saw her, thought she was asleep and pinched it.' He flashed a wink at Kat. 'If you're happy, I'll tell the paramedics to take her back to MGH.'

'Sure. Thanks, Jack,' she said tightly.

8

Arrogant twat! Like a lot of clever men who'd risen faster in their chosen professions than their age would suggest, Jack had a casual way of dismissing people he felt didn't come up to his standards. Now it was her bagman he was casually putting down. Presumably because he thought it would make him more appealing in her eyes. It didn't.

How could she have thought he was worth flirting with? Those first few weeks when he'd replaced old Dr Feldman had felt like a minor electrical storm every time their paths crossed, which was often, with young girls being murdered seemingly every other day.

'What do you want me to do?' Tom asked. If Jack's barb had caught in his skin, he was doing a great job of hiding his irritation.

She looked at the crowd of onlookers. Was a killer standing among them, watching the chaos their work had caused?

'Ask that lot if any of them saw Jo exercising inside the stones. Was she alone or with someone? If you get a vibe off anyone, make a note against their name.'

He nodded and strode away, gesturing at Deepika.

A white CSI van rolled to a stop. Darcy was close behind in an unmarked car. Kat stood back as the white-suited investigators documented the scene, laying out numbered yellow markers and clear plastic tread plates for the common approach path.

'Morning, Darce,' she said as the older woman came over.

'Morning. What have we got?'

'Young woman. Looks fit and healthy apart from the obvious. She's got an EpiPen in her right hand. No phone.'

Darcy nodded. 'Odd. We'll see if the assailant dropped it in a bin or something. ID?'

'Jo Morris.'

After leaving Darcy and her team to start the forensic sweep, Kat returned to her car. It took her forty minutes through the traffic to drive back home and then return to Jubilee Place.

Greeting her with a beckoning finger as she arrived in MCU was Stuart Carver – unaffectionately known as 'Carve-up'. His smug smile made her heart sink. What now?

CHAPTER THREE

Kat took her time weaving her way through the desks cluttering MCU's cramped accommodation. No harm in rubbing Carve-up the wrong way. She knew it was childish, but the prick deserved it.

'Yes, Stu,' she said, arriving in front of him.

Carve-up was known for his flashy clothes. Today he was rocking a royal-blue three-piece suit with a burgundy shirt and matching tie. He looked like a 1990s football pundit.

'I hear it was some dog walker found your DB this morning.' He smirked. 'You'll have to be careful, DS Ballantyne. You're turning into a walking cliché.'

'Speaking of clichés, how is your pride and joy? Is the motorised dildo still making you feel good about yourself?' she asked sweetly, quoting their boss DCI Linda Ockenden's jibe about Carve-up's scarlet Alfa Romeo convertible.

He scowled. 'Better an Italian thoroughbred than that heap you drive. Wouldn't hurt you to run it through the car wash once in a while. The image it gives off – Christ! You look like you're delivering Amazon parcels.'

'Yeah, but mine's German, Stu. When your pretty little sex toy is a pile of rust on your drive, my Golf will still be starting on the first twist of the key, getting me where I need to go.'

A couple of nearby detectives turned their heads as Carver and Kat's voices rose above normal conversational level. Neither could help it. Neither wanted to. And it wasn't as if their mutual loathing was a secret. Kat had even heard a rumour there was a sweepstake on when she'd take another swing at her line manager. The first time had earned him a bloody nose and a ruined shirt, and her a few days' administrative leave.

'And I suppose investigating an accidental death is getting where you need to go, is it? Good luck with that.' He sneered. 'Or are you going to try to parlay it into another serial killer case so you can go back to hogging the limelight while other hard-working detectives get on with the job?'

She took a step towards him. He retreated, banging an elbow into the partition wall marking his office off from the room.

'If you remember, you were all for Pulford being a copycat, Stu,' she said. 'I had to fight for every penny of extra budget, every extra warm body, every lab test, and you did nothing but obstruct me every step of the way.'

He shifted sideways to regain a little territory and squared his shoulders. 'All right, *Kitty-Kat*, calm down. You got your moment of glory. I'm just saying, don't expect every case you investigate to make you shine in front of Ockenden. You might be the golden girl now, but wait until a case goes cold on you. Because it'll happen.' He frowned. His eyes went distant for a moment. 'Believe me.'

She stared at him, breathing heavily, trying not to let it show. *Kitty-Kat*. They'd turned the trading of monikers into a martial art. Each seeking to wound the other with words sharper than the keenest edge. Stu: a schoolyard nickname for a DI who used his rank as a shield and a bludgeon all in one. Kitty-Kat: the name Kat's father had always used and which she hated almost as much as she hated him.

The two men played golf together every Saturday. Kat could detect her property developer father's corrupting influence in Carve-up's every utterance, every finely tailored suit, every pair of Gucci loafers. In the sophisticated scent of his aftershave and the petrol-rich exhaust fumes of his Alfa Romeo.

'I'm sure it will happen,' she said. 'And I'm sure you'll be there to offer your usual sympathy for a fellow officer up against it. But in the meantime, I've got a suspicious death to investigate, so you'll have to excuse me.'

He sighed, offering a patronising smile. '"Suspicious" according to the book, sure. But from what I've heard, you've got a gym bunny who probably ate a peanut by accident and carked it. There you are: case closed. You're welcome.'

She knew she shouldn't engage with him. That everything he said was designed to either provoke her or belittle her, or preferably both. Knew she shouldn't. Did anyway.

'I searched her bag. She had peanut protein bars. Hardly what you'd expect from someone with a fatal peanut allergy,' she snapped. 'Or do you think she took them up to the common to commit suicide?'

'So, a wasp stung her. Or a bee. Maybe she sat on a stinging nettle, I don't know. But it's obvious what happened,' he said. 'Tom told me her face looked like a blow-up doll.'

Shocked, Kat whirled round, searching for Tom among the bustling detectives. Couldn't see him.

'Was there anything else? Or did you just want to waste my time?'

'Do what you have to,' he said. 'Keep me posted. And try to resist the temptation to start grandstanding. We've all got cases we're working. Yours aren't any more important than anyone else's.' Shaking his head, he went back into his office.

Tom had just sat at his desk, a mug of coffee in his hand. Kat marched over.

'Hi, Kat. Coffee?'

'Yes. In a minute, please, Tom. Tell me, have you spoken to Carve-up this morning?'

Tom blushed. 'He grabbed me as soon as I got in.'

'What did you say about Jo Morris?'

'Just the basics. You know, she was dead, lying among her gym stuff. Face swollen, EpiPen in her hand,' he said. 'That's it. I didn't speculate on cause or anything.'

'Her face was "swollen". That's the word you used.'

'Yes, why? Should I have said "oedema"? Bit fancy for us working cops, isn't it?' he asked with a worried half-grin.

Her pulse slowing, Kat decided to come out with it. 'Carve-up said you compared her to a sex doll.'

Tom's mouth dropped open. 'I didn't! Kat, you have to believe me. I wouldn't be so disrespectful. I didn't need you to tell me not to call them "DBs". I already figured that out for myself.'

He looked stricken. Her internal jury foreman rose to his feet. *Not guilty, My Lady.*

'Don't worry about it. Just Stu doing what Stu does best. Shit-stirring like a pro.'

Tom glanced towards Carve-up's office door. Back at Kat. The half-grin called up reinforcements.

'Detective Shitspector Carver.'

She smiled. 'He's craptastic.'

Tom cackled, drawing Leah's attention. She came over.

'What's going on? Is this an open mic or is it just for you two?'

Still smiling, Tom filled her in on their little bit of stress relief. Leah snorted. 'He wears Poocci loafers.'

'And Poogo Boss suits,' Kat supplied, setting Leah off into a wheezing laugh.

'Stop, stop! My allergies are playing up,' Leah said, patting her chest.

The mention of allergies stopped the banter. Kat felt a rush of guilt. They were joking around, taking the piss out of Carve-up, while a woman lay dead in the morgue at MGH.

'Sorry, Leah,' Kat said. 'Tom and I just got a new case. A woman found up on Bowman's Common. Looks like she might have had some kind of allergic reaction.'

Leah nodded, serious now. Everyone joked around. It was a safety valve. Ambulance crews, firefighters, medics, they were all the same. But when reality hit you in the face it did tend to take the shine off those moments of black humour.

'You think it was an accident?' Leah asked.

Kat shrugged. 'Too early to tell.'

Too early, yes. According to the book. But what if Carve-up was right? What if Jo *had* died of anaphylactic shock? Either way, Kat was sure as hell not going to accept that explanation without a report from Jack.

She called him.

'When can you do the autopsy on Jo Morris?'

'For once my dance card is more or less empty. A report to finish and some teaching. I've got her scheduled for 2 p.m. today, if you'd like to attend?'

'I'll be there.'

'You need me too?' Tom asked once she'd pocketed her phone.

Such a simple question. Yet those four words were doing a lot of work, more than Tom suspected. Yes, he'd thrown up at his first autopsy. Not exactly a rare occurrence, but she knew he felt he'd failed a test. He needed to prove himself, even though he'd survived the other PMs he'd attended without a five-yard dash to the yellow plastic bin in the corner.

Jo's death was way off being confirmed as a homicide. So having him with her would be a distinct overcommitment of resources. She could say no and go alone. But then Tom would feel she was babying him. And there was another reason to take him. As a chaperone.

Oh, there'd be a mortuary assistant there, possibly a photographer if Jack could scare one up. If not, then his assistant would be taking the photos. A couple of CSIs, too. But ever since they'd flirted after he'd dissected a murder victim, Kat had felt uncomfortable being around Jack, especially after his smug put-down of Tom at the crime scene.

'Kat?'

She blinked. Tom was looking at her, eyebrows raised, waiting for her answer. And was that a ghost of a grin playing on Leah's lips?

Wanting a chaperone was tantamount to admitting she *needed* one. And she most definitely did not.

'No need,' she said, smiling at Tom's obvious relief.

Leah went back to her desk. Tom bent over his keyboard. Kat tried not to think about Jack Beale's bare arms as he scrubbed up for an autopsy.

Half an hour later, she and Tom drove over to Glover Street, part of the Hampton Hill estate, built in the early 2000s. The pavements were clean, the front gardens well-tended. Plenty of lollipop-shaped bay trees in ornate wooden planters, smart front doors in dark, sensible colours, glossy-leaved houseplants in downstairs windows.

Tom had identified Jo's next of kin. Her husband, Ian.

Standing on the doorstep, Tom flashed Kat a quick, nervous smile.

'You'll be fine,' she said.

He nodded, drew in a sharp breath and rang the bell.

16

CHAPTER FOUR

Kat looked up and down the street as she waited for Ian Morris to answer the door. Would he even be in?

It was mid-morning. There was every chance he'd be out at work. But a shiny black Audi sat on the drive beside them. It looked like the sort of car a man living in Hampton Hill would drive.

She could hear Tom breathing. In through the nose, hold, out through the mouth in a quiet hiss. He was practising some sort of exercise to keep calm.

She could have told him it wouldn't help. Nothing helped. Unless you didn't care about other people's pain, in which case you'd make a pretty crappy homicide detective. Maybe it helped if you'd felt that pain first-hand. Like she had all those years ago. When they'd come to tell her about her best friend, Liv. The fact that Liv had faked her own death in no way diminished the memory of that feeling of loss.

'OK?' she asked Tom.

'Yep.'

'Want me to do it?'

'Nope.'

The door swung inwards. The man holding it open towered over Tom and made Kat feel like a Lilliputian come face-to-face with Gulliver. The giant's face was a massy block of planes and angles. Dark eyes looked down at her from beneath a bony ridge crowned with thick, black brows.

'Ian Morris?' Tom asked.

'Yes. Can I help you? Are you police?'

Kat thought that was an odd question. Usually people assumed she was selling something. Double glazing, or possibly religion. She filed the observation away for the moment.

'I'm DC Gray and this is DS Ballantyne. May we come in?'

Ian Morris frowned. Scratched the side of his face. 'Sure. But what's this about? Is this about the parking ticket? I meant to pay it. But—'

'Perhaps we could come in first, Mr Morris. Then we can explain.'

Tom had himself under impressive control. Kat followed him in as Morris led them into a small sitting room dominated by a gigantic flat-screen TV bolted to the wall. She was trying to get a read on Morris. He'd seemed confused on the doorstep, but nobody really thought the police dealt with parking tickets, did they?

Her first boss's angular Belfast accent floated down the years to her. Sergeant Michael 'Paddy' McConnell had said to her, as they stared down at a woman's bloody body in her own kitchen, 'It's the husband.' Probationary PC Ballantyne had asked him why. And he'd said, 'Sure, it's always the husband, Kat.'

Once they were all seated, Morris making the springs of a black leather recliner squeak in protest, Tom looked him square in the eye.

'Mr Morris, I'm afraid I have some very bad news. This morning, we found your wife, Jo, dead on Bowman's Common. I am very sorry for your loss.'

Kat gave an inward sigh of relief. Tom had managed it without stumbling over the words. He hadn't waffled or used some ghastly euphemism. It was her preferred method and she'd taught it to him.

He'd asked her early on about the easiest way to do this kind of work. She'd corrected him immediately. Telling someone their wife, their parent, their child, God forbid, or their best friend was dead, well, there *was* no easy way to do it.

You could sugar-coat a poison pill, but sooner or later the coating was going to wear off. It was no kinder delaying the pain – theirs or yours. You might as well get it out there and then deal with their reaction afterwards. Hers had been catastrophic. She'd stumbled upstairs, fallen across her bed and wept for Liv until her eyes stung and her ribs ached.

Ian Morris's reaction proceeded in a series of discrete steps, as if he were choosing them from a menu. First, he simply stared at Tom, that heavy forehead knitting in confusion. Then he looked at Kat, eyebrows raised as if enquiring whether her sidekick was telling the truth. Finally, back at Tom.

He rubbed a hand over his blocky chin.

He shook his head.

'You've got it wrong. Jo's not dead,' he said with a crooked smile. 'She's at work.'

Tom glanced at Kat, eyes tight. A flicker of panic visible. She offered a tiny nod. *Keep going, rookie. You can do this. Just stick to the script.*

'I'm so sorry,' Tom said after a moment's hesitation. 'The woman we found had a wallet containing Jo's credit and business cards. I'd like to show you a photograph so you can tell us if you recognise her. I'm afraid her face is swollen. We think she had some sort of allergic reaction. Would that be all right?'

Ian shook his head. The movement didn't stop. His large bony hands were squeezed together between his knees.

'Mr Morris?' Kat prompted. 'Can I call you Ian?'

'Yeah, but this is wrong, I'm telling you . . . Jo? She's not dead. She can't be.'

Kat leaned towards him and made eye contact. 'Maybe you could just take a quick look at the photo for us, then we'll know, won't we?' she asked gently.

Except that was wrong, wasn't it? Because they'd shown Kat a photo, too. Of Liv. A shocking, grotesque photo. And then, after she'd finally made peace with her loss, and rebuilt her life, Liv had come waltzing back into it, telling tales of having to disappear to protect herself from a serial killer.

Ian held out his hand. 'Fine,' he snapped. 'Give it to me, then.'

Kat held up her phone. What a thing to have to do on a Monday morning. Show a man a photo of his dead wife's grotesquely distorted face and ask him to admit that, yes, this bloated body was the woman he married. The woman he loved. But, she chided herself, she was getting ahead of herself. Who was she to say he loved her? Who was she to say he hadn't killed her? *Sure, it's always the husband, Kat.*

Ian stared at the photo, dry-eyed for ten seconds. His head gradually slowed its metronomic motion. Then it stopped altogether. Kat watched him closely. No tears yet. That didn't necessarily signify anything. Shock made people do all kinds of things. Some dissolved into tears so copious there was a real risk of drowning. Others remained stoically dry-eyed, maybe only breaking down at the coroner's inquest, or at the graveside.

'Ian. I need to ask you. Is that Jo?'

'Yeah. That's her,' he croaked.

'I know this is hard, Ian, but it would really help us if we could ask you a few questions about Jo before we leave. Would that be all right?'

'Ask whatever you want. But I can tell you this for nothing. This wasn't an accident. Someone murdered Jo.'

'How can you be so sure? The path—' She caught herself in time. No sense in using upsetting words like 'pathologist'. The images they created were unhelpful, to say the least. 'The doctor said Jo looked as though she'd suffered a severe anaphylactic reaction.'

Kat already had a number of theories revolving in her head, but she wanted to hear what he'd say in response to this particular detail.

'She never went anywhere without her EpiPen. Not even to bed. She's got them all over the house. In her gym bag. Her locker at the leisure centre – she runs classes.' Ian made a fist and thumped it down on the top of his right thigh. 'Even if she did have a reaction, she'd have given herself a shot and she'd be fine. It's happened before. I've seen it. I mean it's scary but it's not fatal. She knows what to do.'

Kat nodded. In fact, his conclusion supported hers. So far she was leaning strongly towards homicide.

No way was it suicide. Hanging was by far the most common method for men and women, followed by either pills or exhaust fumes, assuming they didn't drive electric. Killing yourself by inducing anaphylaxis would be an excruciating way to die. And why include the performative element of doing it up on the common? That really looked like someone was making a point.

An accident? How? How would someone aware enough of their own allergies to carry an EpiPen fail to administer it correctly and save themselves? Answer, they wouldn't. But if the pen was tampered with? That would kill them for sure.

'Can I ask what Jo was allergic to?'

Ian nodded. Rubbed at his chin again as if he were trying to erase himself, starting with his jaw.

'Kiwi fruit. She got a seed on her lip once at a wedding,' he said, staring out of the window. 'We asked the waitress to check, and she said the chef didn't use them but there it was anyway. Jo collapsed. It was like she was struck by lightning, it happened so fast. But she still got her EpiPen in, even in that state.'

The insistent drumbeat got louder in Kat's head. *Murder . . . Murder . . . Murder . . .*

'How did Jo seem to you in the last few weeks? Had her behaviour changed in any way? Did she appear worried about anything?'

'Depressed, you mean? Listen, if you think she killed herself, you're wrong. Totally wrong,' he said, smacking one huge fist into his open palm. 'I've never met anyone with more positive energy than Jo. She's a force of nature. If she even *thought* she was depressed, she'd grab that black dog by the scruff of the neck and beat it to death.'

Kat nodded, though she wondered if his conception of depression would allow him to notice if his wife was suffering. But it was good he was talking, even if he seemed on the verge of exploding. In her early days in uniform, she'd once been picked up bodily and thrown out of the house by two brothers whose sister had been murdered.

The trouble was, Ian Morris's relative calmness, and his willingness to answer questions, counted for very little until he provided them with an alibi.

'Can you think of anyone who might have wanted to hurt Jo?' Tom asked.

Kat watched him closely. *Sure, it's always the husband, Kat.*

Morris shook his head. 'Impossible. Jo is this totally good person. She's all about helping people to overcome negativity, doubt, limiting beliefs. She thinks that physical fitness is like this golden path to making yourself complete. So you can achieve your life's goals.'

Kat was listening on two levels. To the words but also to the way he was using them. His refusal to accept his wife was dead came through in the use of the present tense. 'Jo *is*' not 'Jo *was*'. She'd heard it before, but never this consistently.

Ian looked across the few feet of carpet at her. She'd seen that stare in photos of shell-shocked soldiers. Blank. Uncomprehending. The brain in standby mode as the enormity of what had just happened sank in. Was his grief genuine? Or was he going to be up for a Best Supporting Actor Oscar?

'What's going to happen to her?' he asked, finally.

'Well, at the moment, we've taken Jo to the hospital. Middlehampton General.'

'I want to see her.'

'Of course.'

'Now.'

'That's really not a good idea. The pathologist will be conducting a post-mortem this afternoon. It would be better to wait until they've had a chance to make Jo look her best.'

In reality, she didn't want him touching the body and contaminating it with his DNA, but she held that fact back.

He opened his mouth to argue, then closed it again. Slumped back into the squeaking embrace of the recliner.

'Whatever.'

'Do you and Jo have children? We can arrange for you to collect them from school, drive you if you want.'

He shook his head. Didn't elaborate.

Back in Kat's Golf, Tom exhaled loudly. 'Does it ever get any easier?'

'Nope. I think it's like actors on first nights. You might have done it a hundred times before, but it's a new play, a new audience and there's every chance the stage will collapse with you standing right in the middle.'

'A cheering thought.'

She turned to him. 'You asked. Look, seriously, Tom, you're doing fine. Not just with the research and the digging and the endless bloody phone calls and emails. You've got the makings of a really good homicide investigator. Just keep at it and don't beat yourself up about it. Death knocks are bad, but even if you flub your words they're not mistakes.'

'Unless you go to the wrong house.'

'Yeah, well, that *would* be a mistake. Let's just try and avoid making it, shall we?'

She turned on the engine, put the car in gear and headed out of the estate.

Kat drove in silence until they reached North Street, with its bustle of morning traffic.

'What did you think of him?' she asked Tom.

Out of the corner of her eye she caught her bagman straightening in his seat. A tell whenever she questioned him on tactics or investigative procedure. The student eager to please both his lecturers and his pub-owning parents was still very close to the surface.

'Obviously, he was shocked. Not crying. I suppose that doesn't mean anything?'

'Correct. He could be sobbing his heart out right now.'

'He sort of idolised her, don't you think? He used all those phrases. Called her a force of nature, a totally good person.'

'To me, those phrases sounded a little bit rehearsed, if you know what I mean?'

'I do. Like something off Instagram. Nobody's that good, are they?'

'No. But then again, he had just been told his wife was dead in suspicious circumstances. Maybe it was his way of coping. Thinking of the good things they'd shared.'

'Could he have killed her, do you think? Or am I jumping the gun,' he added quickly. 'We haven't got cause of death yet. It could have been accidental.'

Kat slowed as they came to the tail end of a traffic queue at some lights.

'Here's what I think. We have a woman dead, apparently of anaphylactic shock. We have her husband's testimony that she never went anywhere without her EpiPen—'

'—which we know because we found it on her—'

'—and that even in the middle of an attack at a wedding, she was able to stick herself and avert a tragedy. So it seems unlikely this was an accident. I mean, she was holding it in her fist.'

'So what killed her then?'

Ahead, the traffic started to move. Kat put the car into gear and joined it.

'Honestly? I have no idea. But at two this afternoon, I hope to find out. And if Jack Beale tells me he thinks she was unlawfully killed, then I'll be launching a murder inquiry. And who do we put at the top of our list of persons of interest?'

'The husband,' Tom said. 'In the latest statistics, ninety per cent of homicide victims knew their attacker.'

Kat nodded. Yes, they did. And when it came to female victims, two in five were killed by an intimate partner. In Jo Morris's case, that meant Ian Morris.

She had a feeling she'd be looking in detail at his life over the next few days.

CHAPTER FIVE

Back at MCU, Kat called Darcy, wanting an update on forensics.

'We discovered three partial prints on Jo Morris's water bottle that aren't hers,' Darcy said. 'No match on the database. Sorry. Only hers on the EpiPen.'

Kat poked her head through Carve-up's door. He was talking to someone on the phone but covered the mouthpiece as soon as she spoke. She'd seen that expression on plenty of faces before. Usually on the other side of an interview room table.

'What is it?' he snapped. 'Can't you see I'm on the phone?'

She looked at the black receiver clamped in his fist. She toyed with a little wind-up. *Getting today's instructions from my dad, are you?* Decided against it. What Carve-up and her property developer father got up to between them was none of her business. Except when it got in the way of her doing her job. She smoothed out the scowl creeping across her face.

'You told me to keep you posted on the dead woman I found on Bowman's Common this morning.'

'Oh, right. Well?'

'Her name's Jo Morris. Positive ID from the husband. She had her own business as a personal trainer. No enemies, apparently, no signs of depression—'

'All right, DS Ballantyne. I don't need her life history. So it's accidental, yeah?'

'The post-mortem's at two. We'll know more then.'

He rolled his eyes. 'Fine.'

He resumed his call, murmuring into the handset as she left him to it. Who had he been speaking to? A senior officer? Possibly. Like a lot of bullies, Carve-up was a crawler.

But his tone, and the guilty look, had suggested less deference, more a shared secret. Had it been her dad after all? Was Colin Morton up to his usual tricks, trading money for information, or favours? She had no time to think about that right now.

She had a couple of hours before the post-mortem. She'd found that having something in her stomach helped with nausea rather than the opposite. She beckoned to Tom. He hurried over.

'Let's go and get a sandwich.'

The nearest decent cafe was on North Street. If it wasn't a 'fat jeans' day, Kat loved the crisp, nutty cannoli filled with lemon cream. They sat beneath a glass cover beside a small blackboard on which was written in multicoloured chalk:

Bi xêr hatî! It means 'Welcome!' in Kurdish. We short-ened it to Hatî for the name of our café.

John and Zerya

Not so long ago, she'd been at a table by the window, and made eye contact with a dead woman standing outside. Her best friend, assumed murdered back in 2008 by the Origami Killer, come back to life and ready to carry on as if nothing had happened.

Even though the entire experience of losing Liv had turned out to be a lie, the scars of her grief were too old and deep to be erased simply by the truth coming out. She was still trying to deal with the fact that Liv was alive, well, and living an apparently untroubled life on a commune in South Wales. So much time had elapsed. And although they'd both grown up since their teenage years, their lives were so different now that Kat was struggling with the whole idea of reconnecting.

She paid for lunch. Mozzarella, basil and tomato panini for her, plus an Americano. Ham and cheese toastie plus an extra-shot latte for Tom.

'I want you to start looking into Jo's background this afternoon,' she said, before biting into her sandwich. She snatched away a ribbon of burning-hot tomato skin that dropped onto her bottom lip.

'Wouldn't I be wasting time if Dr Beale says she died of natural causes?'

'You would, but I don't think he will. I can't see it, Tom. I've been thinking it through, going over all the angles. Allergy sufferers die when they *don't* have their injectors; it's the whole point.'

'So she *was* murdered, then?'

'It's the only explanation that makes any sense. So the sooner we can get started on victimology the better,' she said. 'I want to know everything about her. And despite what Ian said, I want to know the bits of her life that *weren't* so perfect. Did she have a falling-out with a client or a co-worker? Ian said she ran classes at the leisure centre. You could start there.'

'I'll go straight after this,' he said, holding up his half-finished toastie. 'What else?'

'Did she owe money? Was she having an affair? Did she have any addictions?'

Tom wrinkled his nose. 'Fitness coaches lead pretty clean lives in my experience.'

'OK, but maybe she liked her retail therapy, or she was into online gambling. Look for anything that might have brought her into contact with the wrong kind of people.'

'What about steroids? That's a big problem in the bodybuilding world. I bet there are a few guys who use the weights room who might be users. They get the old "roid rage" and fly off the handle.'

'Yes, good. Add that to your to-do list. Plus, we need access to her phone records and her bank accounts. We're looking for any unusual spending patterns or large withdrawals or deposits, especially in cash.'

'Got it. How about the neighbours? I could ask around, see if anyone saw a different side to her. Maybe heard her and Ian arguing?'

Kat finished half her sandwich and wrapped the other in a napkin.

'Yes. As you're on the fast track, I expect you'll be done by five. Shall we meet at Jubilee Place then and you can fill me in?'

He finished his own sandwich. Slurped his coffee.

'You kill me,' he said, getting up to go.

Kat checked her watch. Time she was on her way, too. Up to MGH and an appointment with Jack Beale.

Her phone buzzed: a text from Ivan, split into separate messages:

Can you pick up Riley from school tomorrow night
Have to work late at Marnie's (again)

Two little sentences. But they were doing a hell of a lot of work. He'd even added an eye-roll emoji. It didn't help.

Van hadn't ended the first sentence with a question mark. If it had been Riley, she'd have ignored it. Kids barely used any punctuation. Apparently, it made you sound 'old'. Basically, that meant over thirty. And therefore terminally uncool.

In Van's hands, however, it meant, *you* have *to take him, because I can't.* Fair enough. Kat had found it was a simple way to preserve her relationship with her son, which was changing so fast she found it hard to keep up. She frowned, nonetheless. Van had ducked out of a few recent things where he was supposed to be driving Riley somewhere. Leaving Kat to scrabble to rearrange her own schedule while he worked on his new client's website.

It was the second sentence she focused on. Why did he have to work at Marnie Pryce's *house?* OK, so his new client's business was home-based. But wasn't IT stuff all done remotely these days?

A wicked little inner voice piped up. *'Working late.' That's what they all say.*

She shook her head. No. Not Van. He wasn't the straying type. She'd never had a moment's doubt about him. He didn't even seem to enjoy flirting at parties or down the pub.

Yes, they'd married young. What had her mother said when she'd arrived home and flashed her engagement ring? *Darling, you're still a teenager!* Which was true. Just. Although they'd waited until they were both twenty-one before actually marrying.

She chewed on the inside of her cheek. Their marriage so far had been mainly the exhausting years of child-rearing. But now, aged thirteen, Riley was beginning to show some independence, despite the constant need for lifts here, there and every-bloody-where.

Had Van woken up one day and found he had time to look around? To see what he'd been missing. Was he finding it with Marnie Pryce?

'Miss?'

Kat looked up. A young waiter, rail-thin and fiddling with a black grommet distending his left earlobe, was standing a few feet away.

'I need to clear your table?'

'Sorry, miles away,' she said.

She headed out, preparing herself mentally for the post-mortem, squashing down thoughts of Marnie. She should take Van's text at face value. It was fine. *They* were fine.

The first time Kat had attended one of Jack Beale's post-mortems, staff shortages had meant she was the one taking the official photographs. Afterwards, he'd casually asked her out for a drink, smiling confidently, as if he knew she'd accept. Wow. Flirting within spitting distance of a dead body. That had been a first. Guilt struck her forcibly. Could Van tell? Had someone told him? Carve-up, maybe? Was Van paying her out in the same coin?

This time, the autopsy suite was crowded with gowned, masked and gloved figures.

Jack himself, of course. His assistant. A photographer. Two CSIs, one wet – for body fluids and tissue samples – one dry, for everything else. And Kat made six.

She looked at the dissection table and corrected herself. Seven.

'Let's make a start, then,' Jack said, looking straight at Kat.

Using red-handled trauma shears, he cut away the dead woman's gym clothes. Beneath the tight Lycra top and leggings, she wore a black sports bra and matching briefs. Her body was entirely free of tattoos, which Kat found surprising. She didn't have any herself, but when she walked around Middlehampton in the summer, it felt as though she was in a minority, certainly among women under fifty.

Kat inhaled sharply and pointed to the woman's belly, revealed as Jack cut away her briefs. At the top of her pubic triangle, a livid, lumpy, red weal the size of a fifty-pence piece blazed from the pale skin.

'What the hell is that?'

'Looks like she was burnt.' He bent closer. 'Make that branded. Recently.'

He motioned for the photographer to come closer and take a few shots. The mistreated tissue glistened in the cold, white light of the flash.

Kat moved closer and pulled out her phone. Up close, the wound resembled a crude figure eight. Did Jo's killer have a sadistic streak? She didn't like where that thought led her. She took a couple of pictures before resuming her place opposite Jack.

'How recently?' she asked, inspecting the dead woman's wrists and ankles. No ligature marks. Jo hadn't been restrained, then. Kat felt a whisper of relief.

'Judging by the lack of scarring and the inflammation, I'd say some time in the last twenty-four hours. Maybe less.'

'It looks so crude. Some sort of home-made branding iron. What did he use, do you think? A bent piece of wire?'

Jack nodded. 'Possibly. Two to three millimetres thick. OK, are we ready?'

'All yours, Doc.'

Jack lifted his head towards the mic suspended from the ceiling on its curly black lead. 'Deceased is female . . .'

Kat watched his capable hands working on the body, but gradually his running commentary faded. So did the sharp smell of menthol and thyme from the oil of camphor smeared under her nose. Even the sweetish stink of the corpse disappeared.

Her thoughts drifted away from the pungent dissection room. The brand on the woman's stomach bothered her. It couldn't be happening again. Not this soon after the Origami Killer. The odds were so small as to make an alien landing on the roof of Jubilee Place more likely. But then, what sort of person murdered a woman and then burnt a symbol into her flesh? She avoided even thinking of the obvious answer.

In any case, there was another obvious answer, wasn't there? And it came with a name. Ian Morris.

'Kat, you might want to take a look at this,' Jack was saying.

Her attention snapped back to the dissection room. Jack was pressing a gloved finger against the inside of the corpse's right thigh, ten centimetres below the groin. As she bent over the limb, he removed his fingertip.

Clearly visible in the shallow depression his finger had left was a small red puncture mark.

'From the EpiPen, I assume?' she said.

'It looks like that, doesn't it? Thing is, it appears to have entered the femoral vein.'

'Is that a problem? Doesn't it convey the adrenaline to the heart more quickly?'

'It does, but that can cause severe side effects, including spiking blood pressure, even a heart attack. That's why the makers always say to stick it hard into the top of your thigh. Here,' he added, poking the dead woman's quadriceps muscle and leaving another dent.

'She'd have known that, right?'

'You'd hope so. Maybe she was disorientated from the anaphylaxis.'

'But that would be a pretty accurate placement of the needle if she were struggling.'

He asked for a scalpel.

'This is officially unusual,' he said as he peered into the cut. 'There's no exit wound in the posterior wall of the vein, which I'd expect if she'd jammed it in, as the instructions tell you to.'

'It was inserted carefully,' Kat said. 'Which she couldn't have done if she was panicking or confused. Someone must have done it to her.'

'That's your department, not mine, but yes, that looks like the most likely explanation.'

Jack resumed his step-by-step dissection, keeping up the running commentary. Kat stepped away from the table, focusing inwards, trying to think her way into the mind of a killer who'd go to this level of extravagant planning to murder his victim, and who hated or despised her enough to brand her.

The killer hadn't just wanted Jo dead. He'd wanted to humiliate her.

So, yes, it felt like a homicide. But it was odd to place your faith in a side effect, however serious. There had to be something else.

CHAPTER SIX

At the end of the afternoon, after a quick catch-up with Tom, Kat drove over to Ian Morris's house again. Ian wanted to see his dead wife's body and there was now no reason to stop him. She'd offered to drive him, but he'd resisted, saying he'd take his own car.

The viewing room at the chapel of rest was painted in a muted blue. No external windows, but someone had chosen a soft lighting effect that managed to feel comforting without being funereal. Pleated maroon curtains covered the viewing window that gave onto the mortuary. She gestured for Ian to take a chair.

'Aren't we going to see her?' he asked in an emotionless voice.

'We usually do it via video. At least to begin with.'

Kat moved to a TV and switched it on. Jo Morris's shrouded upper torso filled the screen. The hands on the screen – she recognised Jack's long, elegant fingers – drew the sheet back.

Ian leaned closer and stared at the screen, which reflected as a tiny square in his eyes.

'It's her. Now can I see her?'

'Of course.'

She took him into the adjoining room. On stiff legs, he walked to the bed and stared down at his dead wife's face. He stretched out a hand and stroked his fingers down one cheek and then the other. He leaned over and kissed her forehead. Such a tender gesture. Could he *really* be the killer? Kat reproached herself for giving way to sympathy. Of course he could! In fact, the stats said it was *probably* him.

He turned away. 'Can we go now, please?'

Outside, standing by Ian's car, Kat explained that until they had the results of the autopsy, they couldn't tell him when he would have Jo's remains back. He nodded throughout her explanation, but she wondered how much he was really taking in.

'Ian, I'm going to arrange for you to have the support of a family liaison officer. They'll come to your house to help you deal with this awful situation. I have to go now but we'll be in touch. I'm sorry for your loss.'

He turned away, dragging his car keys from his jacket and sighing as they snagged on the lining of his pocket.

Kat seized this moment to ask the question she had to ask. 'Ian, before you go, there's just one last thing, and I'm sorry to have to ask.'

He swung round to face her. 'Can it wait?'

'Not really. Can you tell me where you were this morning between six and eight?'

He blinked, as if she'd just flicked grit into his eyes.

'What?' A hint of irritation in his voice. Understandable, really.

'Just to eliminate you from our enquiries. It's pretty routine.'

Still struggling to release his car keys, he swore, loudly, then, in a quieter voice, said, 'Home. Nobody was with me. I'm sorry.'

He yanked the keys and the pocket lining ripped audibly. Without saying another word, he climbed in his car and drove away.

The black Audi disappeared behind a stand of silver birches. Kat frowned. Was Jo Morris's murderer behind the wheel?

There it was again. That uncertainty. Before now, she'd always had a sixth sense when she was talking to a murderer, however good they were at hiding their true feelings. But there was something about this case that seemed to be mucking up her ability to think clearly about the Morrises' relationship.

Was it her own marriage? Was the fact she was worried about Van and Marnie interfering with her abilities as an investigator? She didn't want to explore that any further. Couldn't.

After all, it was entirely possible that Ian was one of those men who just couldn't express their emotions. Although he was a little on the young side for all that 'big boys don't cry' nonsense.

Her thoughts flew to her son. Riley had told her that crying at school was likely to get you a rep as a sissy, however right-on the times had become. But at home he was openly emotional. The death of his first pet, a hamster called Alice, had him weeping inconsolably in her arms.

Maybe Ian was on antidepressants. She'd heard something on the radio about how some varieties were supposed to blunt your emotions. Yeah, well, she wasn't about to open that particular can of worms with the grieving husband. He'd be straight on the phone to Carve-up making a complaint and wouldn't Carve-up just *love* that?

No. For now, she was going to play it by the book. Ian was a person of interest *at best*. No alibi, OK. But he'd admitted it immediately. In the absence of evidence placing him at the scene or having motive, she was going to go easy on him.

For now.

As she drove away from the hospital, another – even more uncomfortable – question intruded into her thinking about the case.

What if it was Liv causing the problem? Not in any practical way. She was safely tucked away out of sight in Wales. Somewhere nobody could discover that the Origami Killer's last original victim was alive and well; and able, for this fact alone, to wreck the case against him.

But Liv had fooled Kat into thinking she was dead. And she'd kept it up for over ten years before reappearing like a ghost, insisting on readmittance into Kat's life. What kind of a homicide cop wouldn't be able to see through that deception?

'I was only eighteen!' Kat shouted at the car in front. 'It wasn't my fault!'

Tears sprang to her eyes and she cuffed them away angrily. She was a good investigator, and she *would* catch Jo Morris's killer.

Tea that night was chicken korma and rice. Afterwards, Kat suggested she and her two men drive into town for a walk with Smokey. It was a beautiful evening and she wanted to show them both that she wasn't the absent-but-caring cop-mum Riley liked to portray her as when he needed a reliable wind-up.

To her surprise they both agreed. Though Riley's consent came, as usual, with strings.

'Can I have five quid? There's like this vintage market. There's a comic book stall.'

Kat fished a fiver out of her purse and handed it over.

As Riley grinned and reached for it, she gripped it tighter. 'This buys you being my sweet boy all evening, OK? No snarking.'

'Deal,' he said, still smiling, pulling the slippery plastic note through her fingers.

After parking in a side street behind the Bramalls, Middlehampton's permanent market, Kat threaded her arm through Van's. 'This is nice, isn't it?'

He checked his watch as he answered. 'Yeah. We won't be too long, will we?'

Kat forced herself to smile. 'Why? Got somewhere you need to be?'

'Just work,' he said.

She squeezed him tighter. 'It can wait. Let's see what they've got in the market.'

As the evening sun turned Middlehampton's brick buildings pinkish-gold, they wandered past the Butter Cross and into the market square. The granite-floored space was rammed. Half of Middlehampton seemed to have had the same idea.

They meandered among vendors selling everything from vintage clothes to vinyl records. Riley darted off to a stall selling American superhero comics, catching them up after a few minutes clutching a paper bag.

'*Annihilation 17*,' he said, triumph evident in his voice.

Kat caught Van's eye over Riley's head. Raised her eyebrows. *Any idea?*

He shook his head. *None at all.*

'That's great, Riley,' Kat said, smiling.

He looked up at her, lips twisted sceptically. 'You literally have no idea what it is, do you?'

'Of course I do!' She acted outraged. Hands on hips. 'It's the new, you know, *Annihilation* comic.' She caught his frown. 'Book. I mean. Comic *book*.'

'Yeah, it is. And it is well cool. I've got to not read it till we get home.'

As they were passing a stall selling ornately decorated hats – feathers, beads, veils and glittering metal chains abounded – a woman's voice cut through the chatter of the nearby shoppers.

'Van, love!'

The voice was deep. Rough-edged. So she was a smoker. Or she had a cold. Or, Kat thought with a twinge of jealousy, she'd been blessed with that mysterious, rasping tone that had men rolling over to have their tummies tickled.

To Kat's annoyance, the woman with the artfully tousled blonde hair who kissed Van lightly on both cheeks clearly wasn't a smoker. Her skin was too clear. And she wore minimal make-up: eyeliner and some clear gloss that emphasised naturally full lips.

Bloody hell! she thought as she assessed the other woman's appearance.

Van was smiling back. And then Kat had it. The identity of this sexy fortysomething who had interrupted her carefully curated evening out with her family. She was—

'Hi, I'm Marnie Pryce. Your darling husband looks after my website,' the bombshell husked, extending a tanned, slim-fingered hand Kat realised she was supposed to shake. 'You must be Kat. I mean, I know you are, obvs! I saw you on the telly at those press conferences you did.'

Kat hated Marnie on sight. She was dressed in tight white jeans and a clingy Wonder Woman T-shirt. Kat tried not to stare but it was a size too small, and Marnie knew it. Kat was wearing a baggy sweatshirt and only her second-best jeans. Definitely on the comfy side. She felt decidedly frumpy.

Beside her, Riley was sighing dramatically. Kat handed Smokey's lead to him.

'Why don't you take Smokes for a circuit round the market? Here' – she fished a two-pound coin out of her purse – 'buy yourself an apple or something.'

'An ice cream? I'll get strawberry. One of my five a day.'

Marnie laughed. 'Proper little charmer, aren't you?' she said, ruffling Riley's hair.

Kat smiled to herself, waiting for Riley to vent at this intrusion into his personal space. Instead, he grinned up at Marnie and . . . Jesus! Was he blushing? He was!

At that point, clearly self-aware, he dragged Smokey away, but not before bestowing a look of open admiration at Marnie.

'I have to go,' Marnie said with a smile. 'Lovely to meet you, Kat. Sorry I've been making such demands on your husband's time. He is a star, though. I don't know what I'd do without him.'

She turned on the rope-soled heel of her turquoise espadrilles and sashayed off through the crowds. Kat watched her go. God, she looked good in those jeans.

She turned to Van, expecting him to have his eyes glued to Marnie's perfect little bum. But he was looking at Kat with a crooked grin on his face.

'What?' she asked.

'You were looking Marnie up and down like some office perv.'

'No, I wasn't! I was just . . .'

His smile widened. 'Just what?'

She frowned. Yes. Just what? Checking out the opposition? Comparing herself to Marnie? Wondering if Van could see through the whole Jessica Rabbit act?

'Come on,' she said. 'There's a beer tent over there. You can buy me a glass of wine.'

As they strolled over to the bar, Kat replayed her encounter with Marnie. Bloody woman, holding out her hand like the pope expecting to have his ring kissed. She snorted. Liv always did say she had a filthy sense of humour.

She resolved to enjoy the rest of the evening. It was probably the last she'd have free for a while. And tomorrow she had to dig a little deeper into Ian Morris's life.

CHAPTER SEVEN

The next morning, Kat drove over to see Ian again. He opened the door smiling; then, when he saw it was her, pulled the corners of his mouth down and rubbed his eyes. It came off as fake to her. Another mark on the wrong side of the ledger headed *Innocent or Guilty.*

'Hello, Ian,' she said. 'Can I come in?'

'We're in the sitting room,' he said, then turned away from her. 'I'll be with you in a minute.'

Kat found the FLO she'd appointed checking his phone. DC James Porter was an empathetic detective with five years under his belt. He levered his lanky frame out of the sofa and nodded to Kat. He muted the TV and answered the question she hadn't needed to ask him – one reason she'd put him on the job.

'He's in shock, I think,' he said. 'We were just watching footie. Hasn't said anything off, though.'

Kat had had a mantra drilled into her by her first guvnor, and she did the same to her people now. *As an FLO, you* investigate *first, and* support *second.* The family, weaned on a diet of TV cop shows where the FLO would forever be dashing off to make cups of tea or choose films to watch on Netflix, thought it was the other way around.

So, occasionally, did FLOs themselves. Two had passed into Jubilee Place legend after the SIO found them wearing slippers bought for them by the family of a murder victim. She'd summarily rotated them onto other duties.

Ian came back in.

'How are you holding up?' Kat asked.

He sighed. 'I can't take it in. I can't believe she's dead. Who'd want to hurt her? She was an angel. She never made an enemy in her life.'

Kat nodded. 'I know. It's awful. But I want you to know I and my team are working flat out to find out what happened.'

It was a dance, she thought. An old-fashioned dance. Partners eyeing each other, matching each other, step for step. Keeping the regulation distance apart, taking care not to tread on each other's toes. The grief-stricken husband, blank-eyed, staring; professing total bafflement at his wife's murder. The sympathetic detective, brow furrowed; assuring him of her best efforts. At least one of them knowing that the odds pointed to him as the killer.

Kat tried to imagine what would happen if it was her lying in one of Jack Beale's refrigerated pod-hotel rooms? She pictured Van being questioned by DS Craig Elders, or maybe DI Molly Steadman, Kat's mentor. Feeling the unbearable pain of losing her yet being viewed as her potential murderer. She stopped herself. These were dark thoughts. She stuffed them back down.

Empathy had its place. But it had a conjoined twin: suspicion. And right now, in the absence of anyone else in the frame, that meant investigating Ian.

'Ian, would you mind if I had a look around?' she asked.

'What? Here?'

'I'm trying to build a picture of Jo's life. It would really help.'

He rubbed his palms on his knees. 'Sure. Knock yourself out.'

Leaving Ian and James to resume their conversation about football, Kat mounted the stairs. Ian's tone was off, that was for sure. *Knock yourself out?* Really? But her supplies of sympathy were pretty deep, and she'd continue to put his non-reaction down to shock. For now. Plus, he'd just given her permission to search his house. OK, not *search*-search. But you could do a lot if you knew how to look. And where.

The master bedroom resembled any of the dozens she'd poked around in over the years. Floral bed linen and pale pastel colours on the walls. Jo's taste, she assumed. She opened drawers, looked inside wardrobes, got down onto her hands and knees and peered under the bed.

She emerged with an impression of a married couple no different from her and Van. No weird stuff – pills, bondage gear, oversized butt-plugs in the nightstand. No drugs, as far as she could see. Ordinary books beside the bed: a sports biography on Jo's side, a thriller on Ian's.

She tried the other rooms. One was a non-descript spare bedroom dominated by an ironing board left up with the iron plugged in but not switched on. The third was more interesting. Obviously Jo's home gym. Not large, but spacious enough for a rowing machine, some smallish free weights and a couple of kettlebells.

Jo had pinned photos to a corkboard facing the business end of the rower. Mostly of her, either solo or with friends, engaged in all kinds of sports and outdoor activities. In one, Jo posed in a sludge-coloured bodysuit. Teeth bared in what might have been a smile. The caption: *Tough Mudder 2021. £9,200 raised for Emily's House Hospice.* Not a bodysuit, then. A head-to-toe slathering of Middlehampton's finest alluvial soil mixed with river water. In another, she was with a bunch of girls in bright pink bras worn over their tops. All grinning widely and raising glasses to the camera. *MoonWalk 2002. The Flaming C-Cups!! £14,215 for Cancer Research.*

The woman was a charity dynamo, combining her love of fitness with every kind of sponsored activity. Idly, Kat totted up the amounts in all the photo captions. Jo had raised almost a hundred grand. It was impressive. Then a less charitable thought posed for a photo dead-centre on the corkboard. Its caption: *What was she trying to prove?*

What had Molly Steadman said to her once, when she'd been teaching Bambi-Kat how to be a good detective?

Don't rely on intuition – you'll get further by knocking on doors and asking questions. But don't ignore it either.

Kat filed the thought away. For now.

Downstairs, she found James in the kitchen, spooning instant coffee into two mugs.

'How's he doing?' she murmured.

'He said he feels in limbo, like he can't process it until he knows whether it was an accident or not. Any news on that?'

'As soon as I get the post-mortem report.'

'What about you, though, Kat? Do *you* think it was an accident?'

'This isn't for Ian's ears, but no. By tomorrow I reckon we'll be launching a murder investigation. Tell me, does he go out at all?'

'Nope. Sits watching the telly. Talks about Jo sometimes.' Kat heard the suspicion in James's voice. 'What a fantastic woman she was, that kind of thing. Comes off a bit too try-hard in my opinion.'

'Do you think he'd come out with you if you asked him?'

'You need to have a snoop around on the QT,' he said. 'I'd love to say yes, Kat, but honestly? I tried already. Thought a change of scene might do him good but he point-blank refused. Said he couldn't bear the thought of meeting anyone he knew and having to talk about Jo.'

James motioned to the jar of coffee.

Kat shook her head. 'But could you stay in here for a minute or two? I want to ask Ian a few questions.'

As she turned, a flash of colour caught her eye. Where her own fridge door was plastered with slips of paper, receipts, photos, funny quotes clipped from magazines, and reminders, the Morrises' was pristine, apart from this one shocking-pink square. On the Post-it note, in curvy handwriting Kat assumed was Jo's, she'd scrawled, *ROZ? Discuss goals.*

She popped her head around the sitting room door. Ian was slumped in the recliner, eyes glued to the TV. A morning talk show.

Kat sat opposite him.

'Hey, Ian. Can I ask you a few more questions about Jo, please?'

He nodded without turning his head. 'If it'll help you find out what happened.'

'On the fridge, there's a Post-it, and it mentions someone called Roz. Does that ring any bells at all?'

'She had a new client. Could have been her,' he answered mechanically. 'I think they had a session booked yesterday.'

Kat made a note. Tracing this Roz was an urgent action. She might have been the last person to see Jo alive.

'I saw her photos upstairs. She was really into her charities, wasn't she?'

'Obsessed. When she wasn't working, it's what she did. Triathlons, trekking in some jungle or other, sponsored walks. You name it, Jo was collecting money for it.'

Was that resentment she heard, carried below the words like a coded message in a radio signal?

'I'd like to speak to as many of her friends as possible. We haven't found her phone yet. Do you know if she had a paper address book?'

'Why do you need to speak to her friends?'

'Just background. It's standard. Did she have a best mate?'

He wrinkled his nose, flicked a glance at the ceiling. Back to the TV screen. 'I don't know if she had a *best* mate, but there was a new friend she talked about a lot. A girl from the gym. Michelle, I think.'

'Michelle who?'

'Wilson.'

Kat groaned inwardly. Michelle Wilson. There could be dozens in Middlehampton alone.

'Do you know where Michelle lives?'

He seemed to have descended into a trance. She could see the bright rectangle of the TV screen reflected in his eyes.

'Ian?' Kat said. 'Sorry, could you maybe try to look at me for a second? I know you want me gone, but if you can think of Michelle's address I'll be out of your hair.'

She glanced at his shaved scalp. Poor choice of words.

His head rotated slowly until his eyes locked on to hers. 'Wheelwright Street, I think. I dropped Jo off there once. I can't remember the number, but they've got a boat in the front garden.'

Kat drove down Wheelwright Street, scanning the front gardens for a boat of some kind. Outside 179, a smart white dinghy sat on a trailer. Middlehampton was a good seventy miles from the nearest stretch of coastline – Southend-on-Sea on the Essex coast. But sailing clubs in Hertford and Broxbourne offered inland boaties the chance to mess around on lakes in the Lee Valley, a more manageable twenty-five miles south-east of the town.

The woman who opened the door was in her early thirties, wearing an orange apron dusted with flour. More flour had adhered to her high, domed forehead and the tip of her upturned nose.

'Yes?' she said, smiling.

'Michelle Wilson?'

'That's right,' she said, looking over her shoulder, clearly anxious to get back to her baking.

Kat produced her warrant card and introduced herself. 'I wonder if you'd have time to talk to me about Jo Morris?'

Michelle frowned. 'Is everything OK?'

'It's best if I come in.'

Once they were both seated at Michelle's kitchen table, Kat delivered her own version of the no-frills speech she'd trained Tom to give. 'I'm so sorry to have to tell you this, Michelle, but Jo was found dead on Bowman's Common yesterday morning. We're treating her death as suspicious.'

She waited. And watched.

Michelle blinked twice, rapidly. Swallowed. And then, shocking in the silence of the kitchen, she sneezed loudly.

'You're sure?' she said finally. 'She's got allergies. She might be in some sort of coma. You know, from anaphylactic shock.'

Kat shook her head. 'I'm afraid there's no doubt. Jo is dead. I'm so sorry for your loss.'

A sob erupted from deep in Michelle's chest. A horrid, broken sound. Her eyes overflowed with tears that plopped onto the tabletop. So different to Ian's buttoned-up response. Kat offered her a tissue from the packet she always carried. Michelle blew her nose noisily.

'How did she—?'

'We're not sure yet. But it does appear that she had some sort of reaction.'

Michelle turned reddened eyes on Kat. Accusing. As if it was her who'd caused Jo's death.

'But how? She never went anywhere without her EpiPen.'

'I'm trying to build a picture of Jo's life,' Kat said, leaning forwards to offer Michelle a second tissue. 'Could you help me identify her other friends? I know she was on various sports teams and she did a lot of sponsored charity activities. Treks and so on.'

Blotting her eyes, Michelle nodded. 'Of course. Do you need me to do anything now?'

'If you could give the names or addresses of anyone else who might have known her, that would be really helpful.'

Michelle disappeared from the kitchen and returned with an oversized Samsung. She transferred a handful of contacts to Kat's phone.

'I know this is going to sound harsh, Michelle, so forgive me, but I have to ask. I know she was on various sports teams and she did a lot of sponsored charity activities. Do you know if Jo had any enemies, or people who might want to hurt her?'

Michelle stared at Kat as if she'd just asked whether her friend was a child-killer. 'No! Of course not! Everybody loved Jo. I mean, she was one of those special people, you know? The stuff she did for others . . . I mean, I do *some* charity stuff. You might have seen me in a couple of the photos?' Kat nodded. 'But compared to Jo, I'm, like, this really lazy cow.'

'What about her marriage? How was it?'

Michelle frowned. Then she looked straight at Kat. A hunch might not be enough to break a case, but she had one now and it was telling her she was about to discover something interesting.

'This is off the record, isn't it? I mean, you asking me these questions? You don't tell other people?'

'I tell my colleagues, but nobody outside the police, no.' Kat leaned forwards, breathing easily, waiting. Hoping.

'Ian's' – Michelle snatched a breath – 'he's always on at her about money.'

'What do you mean?'

'We'd be out. Me and Jo, you know, gossiping, telling each other stuff about our husbands, nothing serious, just banter, you know? Lately she's been saying how Ian's pressuring her to lend him money. She inherited some from her parents, but she said it was for when they had kids.'

Kat said nothing. Sometimes leaving silence was more effective than asking questions. Especially when, as now, she sensed a witness wanting to unburden themselves.

'They've been trying for ages,' Michelle said, her floury fingers screwing the tissue into a ball. 'Ian made Jo get a test but it was fine. It's Ian, but he won't hear of it.'

'Why did Ian want her to lend him money?'

Michelle rolled her eyes. 'His precious business. He reckons he's this entrepreneur. He got made redundant two years ago and sank all his settlement into setting up this furniture website. Says he's going to import posh Italian leather chairs and that. But there's no market. Or if there is, he hasn't found it. He wanted Jo's inheritance money so he could buy more online advertising.'

'What did Jo think about that?'

'She said Ian had to follow his dream, but not with her money. I know that sounds harsh. Like, a wife should support her husband. But she started *her* business on her own.'

Kat nodded. A husband frustrated by, as he saw it, his wife's inability to conceive *and* by her refusal to bail out his failing business. Call it one and a half motives. Add in his lack of an alibi. And that weird, shut-down emotional response.

He was looking guiltier by the second.

CHAPTER EIGHT

At the end of the afternoon, James arrived back from Ian Morris's house. He came over to Kat's desk, waggling a notebook.

'Got some information for you. Ian's in shock but I did manage to prise two relevant facts out of him about Jo. Her parents died in a light plane crash. Names were Tasha and Connor Starling. So we have her maiden name too.'

She thanked him and added the details into her policy book. Jo shared a name with Middlehampton's MP. Were they related?

Next to stop by her desk was Tom.

'I was thinking of heading off. Is that OK?'

'Of course, but before you go . . .' Time to test the rookie on his local knowledge. 'Jo Morris was born Jo Starling. That surname ring any bells?'

He looked at the ceiling. 'Starling, Starling, Starling.'

'That's almost a flock.'

'Actually, the collective noun for starlings is "murmuration".'

'And we're back to Tomsplaining. I did know that, actually, but it sounds a bit pretentious out loud, don't you think? Like you're quoting poetry? Or' – she shuddered theatrically – 'writing it. Anyway, it's also, and slightly more relevantly, the surname of our local MP.'

'You think they're related? It's not that uncommon a name.'

'Maybe, maybe not. But he's an MP. I find that interesting. It might be nothing. But if it's something, my question is, why hasn't he come forward?'

◆ ◆ ◆

Kat arrived home to an empty house. Unable to pick up Riley from school as Van had asked, no, *demanded*, she'd arranged for Riley to go home with his friend Alfie Beckett. She and Alfie's mum, Jess, were long-time friends.

Kat called Jess.

'How are they?'

'Upstairs playing *Call of Duty*. I'm giving them pizza in a bit. Good day?'

'I've got a new case.'

Jess sighed. 'I don't know how you do it, Kat, I really don't. When you were CID, OK, fair play, I could see the attraction. But now? Investigating gory murders all the time? It would turn my stomach.'

'This, coming from a dental nurse.'

Jess chuckled. 'I do see some horrible sights, it's true. Today for example—'

Kat grimaced and shook her head violently. 'Nope. No, no, no. Don't want to hear it, thank you.'

'—you see, the patient needed a *lot* of work done,' Jess said.

Kat could hear how much Jess was enjoying herself.

'Please, Jess, I'll hang up,' Kat said. 'I mean it. I feel sick.'

'You're such a baby!'

'It's not my fault. Anyway, if you don't stop, I'll tell you what happens in an autopsy.'

'Truce. What time do you want to pick up Riley? Or shall I drive them both to footie, and you can take him home afterwards?'

Kat checked her watch. She needed to walk Smokey, make herself something to eat and, if possible, do a bit of work on the case. Jess's offer would give her an hour, at least, to try to reach some kind of conclusion about what had happened to Jo. But it would also mean missing the chance to spend some one-to-one time with Riley.

She and Van had noticed the difference in him since he'd turned thirteen the previous November. He was looking for an identity separate from his parents, and they wanted to give him room to find one without falling in with the wrong crowd. They'd already had a couple of scary moments just before his birthday, most recently when Van had discovered sexy photos of a friend's older sister on Riley's phone. That had turned out to be an innocent mistake – images shared on a WhatsApp group – but both Kat and Van had read him the riot act in their own ways.

Van had always done the bulk of the childcare. Being self-employed and working from home gave him the flexibility that Kat had never had, especially in her days as a uniformed PC. But he was busier than ever, and she knew he struggled sometimes to juggle his responsibilities. It was ironic, really, a man trapped by the parenting puzzle that usually affected women. Marnie's seemingly endless demands that he work at her house – not her office, her *house* – didn't help, either. Kat fought down the niggling worry that Marnie wanted Van for more than just his web-mastering skills.

A compromise presented itself. 'Can you take him?' she asked Jess. 'But tell him I'll be there as soon as I can after it starts?'

Freed from the immediate need to juggle her role as dog walker, mum and cop, she clipped Smokey onto his lead, stuffed a few poo bags into her pocket and headed out, down Green Lane towards the farm.

Barrie and Lois were out on their rounds, and Kat met them halfway round the big field locals called The Gallops. As far as Kat was aware, there was no connection to horse racing. But the side of the field furthest from town was bordered by a wide grassy strip – which, she supposed, she could imagine horses racing along early in the morning.

The evening sun was slanting low over the field, turning the wheat-stubble gold. It caught Barrie's baby-fine hair, making it glow like a halo. He offered Kat a crumpled white paper bag.

'Liquorice Allsort?'

She peered in at the multicoloured sweets and, carefully avoiding the brown ones, popped a squashy blue jelly into her mouth and chewed, releasing a delicious burst of aniseed.

'Thanks,' she mumbled around the sweet.

'Any news about that poor girl I found up on the common?'

'I was at the PM today. To be honest I'm not exactly sure,' she said, swallowing the Allsort. 'She'd had a severe allergic reaction to something, but her EpiPen was inserted into a vein, not the thigh muscle. It looks like that might have been what killed her.'

'Murder?'

'I think so, yes. If I tell you something, can you promise to keep it a secret?'

She felt bad for asking, but she had to, given she was about to share a detail she'd be holding back from the media.

He favoured her with a long look. 'I swear on Lois's life.'

Kat pulled her mouth to one side. 'No need for that level of seriousness, Barrie. A simple "yes" would have done.'

'They used to call me "the Shambles" at Jubilee Place nick back in the day. Know why?'

'Hopefully not your sloppy parade-ground style?'

He rolled his eyes. 'Cheeky! No, 'cause we're both one-way streets.'

'Cute. So, it looks like he branded her after he killed her.'

'Jesus! These sick bastards, where do they get it all from? I blame the internet.'

'I don't know, Barrie. Jack the Ripper didn't have Google, did he?'

He shrugged. 'How do you know it was after he killed her he did the branding?'

'I didn't see any ligature marks or skin damage on her wrists and ankles, so I don't think she was restrained. And even though it was pretty hideous, it looked like a clean impression. Like she was completely still when he did it.'

Barry frowned. 'Could she have undergone it voluntarily, do you think?'

Kat looked up into the sky, which was slowly turning a luscious pinkish-purple. Thinking. 'It's possible I suppose. But why?'

'Who knows?' Barry said. 'A sex thing, maybe? I stopped being surprised about what people do to their bodies years ago.' He handed first Lois, then Smokey a treat from his non-Allsorts hand, as the dogs circled back to him before racing off again. 'I mean, have you seen the kids nowadays? Holes here, there and everywhere. Young girls with more tattoos than a sailor on payday!'

Kat smiled. 'Careful, Barrie, you're starting to sound like an old fart!'

'I *am* an old fart, Skip. I'm entitled. But this branding thing. You want to know what it says to me?'

'It's why I asked you.'

'Assuming she was dead when he did it, I reckon he was making a point. Like, "I own you." That's what they mean, after all. Like slaves and so forth. Just turning her into a thing. Into property.'

◆ ◆ ◆

Back at home, Barrie's words circling in her head, Kat decided to conduct an experiment. She went in search of something a killer could turn into a branding iron.

The garage first. Van had installed a blocky timber workbench, complete with a vice, in the one decluttered corner. He kept a toolbox underneath it and had hung a few power tools on the wall above. A wooden shelf bore jam jars full of screws, washers, nuts and bolts, and an assortment of fixings he'd collected when dismantling old IKEA furniture. *I might need them one day* – his refrain whenever she challenged him on it.

He called the corner his 'workshop', and Kat was happy to indulge him. She knew he mostly used it to listen to heavy metal on his headphones, drink whisky out of a jam jar, and tinker with bits of old hi-fi equipment, hard drives and whatever else he had lying around at the time.

After fifteen minutes, she gave up. What wire she did find was too flimsy to shape, let alone impress into living tissue. Everything else was too thick, too inflexible or too combustible.

Inside again, she sat at the kitchen table and closed her eyes. Visualised the horrific burn on Jo Morris's belly. The curves, though crude, had been sinuous: no sharp corners. What would *she* use if she wanted to do something like that? The answer, when it came, was so prosaic it made her bark out a short ironic laugh. 'You have to be kidding,' she said to the empty room.

From her half of the wardrobe, she picked out a plain wire coat hanger. In the workshop again, she scrabbled through the toolbox until she found two pairs of pliers, one with thin, rounded jaws. She cut off the hook and straightened the hanger out. After clamping it in the vice, she bent and twisted the wire with the pliers until she'd fashioned a rudimentary branding iron, complete with a figure of eight at the end. She doubled over the bare wire at the non-business end and wrapped it in duct tape to make a grip.

Would it work, though? That was the question. Twenty minutes later, she was back in the kitchen, clutching a shrink-wrapped piece of belly pork she'd bought from the Co-op in the village. The skin was pale, except for some dark red numbers – 7,1,5 – inked onto one corner.

She picked up the branding iron, ignited a gas ring and held the figure of eight in the hissing blue flame. Pungent, oily smoke wisped away from the wire as the surface coating burnt off.

Once the brand was glowing scarlet, she took a breath, feeling suddenly anxious, and pressed it into the rind of the pork, which gave slightly, making her nose wrinkle in disgust.

The skin sizzled, crisped and blackened, and her nostrils filled with an unpleasant smell of burnt flesh. Even though she knew it was only meat, the action of branding something that had once been living tissue made her suddenly nauseous. She swallowed hard.

She pulled the wire free and peered at her handiwork. Impressed in the skin was a blackened and bubbling figure of eight. It could have been a twin for the mark on Jo Morris.

Christ, if Ian Morris *was* the culprit, he must have really hated his wife. Was it really only about money?

Kat couldn't shake the image of the burnt meat, even as she watched Riley's team fight grimly against clearly stronger opponents under the floodlights at the leisure centre. Beside her Jess was yelling encouragement and throwing the occasional salty remark in the referee's direction.

At half-time, while the boys milled around their coach eating orange segments and swigging water, Jess fetched her and Kat two teas from a nearby cafe.

'How's Van?' she asked Kat.

Kat ran a hand through her hair. She thought of all the time Van was putting in on Marnie Pryce's business. Sighed.

Jess frowned. 'Everything OK between you two?'

Kat took her time before answering. *Was* everything OK? On the surface, yes, of course it was. Then why was she obsessing over Marnie? Who at the end of the day was, simply, a client.

'He's got this new client. And she's, you know . . .' She bit her lip. Didn't want to say it out loud and give it oxygen. 'She's really sexy. I mean, *I* think it's completely overdone but you know what men are like.'

Jess rolled her eyes. 'Show 'em a couple of inches of cleavage and they turn into teenage boys.' Her face grew serious. 'But he's not, you know, interested, is he?'

'I don't think so. It's probably just me. But he has been working at hers a lot lately. He's there tonight, as a matter of fact.'

Jess frowned. 'Is that usual?'

'No. Normally he's on-site at some office or factory. But she runs her business from home.'

'Well, you can't blame him for that, then. Is he acting differently? Buying you presents? Acting extra-attentive?'

Kat didn't have to think long. Van was affectionate. But he'd never been the demonstrative kind, dragging her in for a snog in the middle of the street or wanting to do it anywhere and everywhere. OK, maybe when they'd been younger and backpacking round Thailand. But everybody did that. You couldn't keep it up into your thirties; you'd have a heart attack.

'No, he isn't. Oh my God. Should he be? Is that a sign he's losing interest?'

Jess smiled and put an arm round Kat's shoulders, squeezed her close. 'No, nitwit! But if a guy who's normally a bit laid-back suddenly starts showering his wife with gifts, or going all romantic, that can be a sign he's covering for an affair.'

Kat squinted at Jess. 'How do you know all this? Reece isn't . . . ?'

Jess shook her head. 'I've got him just where I want him. I just heard this psychologist on the radio talking about her new book on infidelity. She had this list of warning signs. But honestly, Kat, unless you actually suspect something, try not to get paranoid. It'll only make you see trouble where there isn't any.'

Kat nodded. Her friend was right. She and Van were good. They were fine.

Joyful shouts came from the pitch. Both women looked over. Alfie was racing in a wide semicircle, arms aloft, chased by Riley and the rest of his teammates, before executing a slide on his knees.

'That's going to take all the skin off,' Jess said. 'Not that he'll mind.'

Kat nodded, reflecting that half her job involved interacting with people hiding or disguising their pain. She'd interviewed two people so far about Jo Morris. Both had claimed to be in pain. Only one had shown any sign of that being true.

CHAPTER NINE

Jack's post-mortem report landed in Kat's inbox just before 9.30 a.m.

He'd concluded that the *manner* of death was homicide, as Kat had already decided.

Time of death was somewhere between midnight and 8.00 a.m., which Kat had narrowed down significantly to between 6.45 a.m. and 7.45 a.m., based on CCTV footage of Jo leaving her car before entering Bowman's Common, and Barrie's 999 call.

But it was the *cause* of death that held Kat spellbound. Under this heading, Jack had written: *Primary: intraparenchymal haemorrhage. Secondary: cardiac infarction (heart attack: a big one).* Then he'd gone into more detail.

> In a murder/manslaughter, I'd expect to see either an epidural, subdural or subarachnoid haemorrhage, all of which are often caused by either blunt force trauma (BFT) or penetrating injuries.
>
> *This* type of brain bleed is more typical in stroke victims or in cases of cerebral aneurysm. As far as I am aware, <u>it has never shown up as COD in a homicide.</u> (You have a 'first' on your hands!)

I have sent off blood and tissue samples for a full toxicological work-up.

Kat leaned back in her chair. Someone had gone to a lot of trouble to murder Jo Morris. But it didn't feel like the work of a serial killer.

Yes, the brand on the victim's belly was clearly sadistic. But from Kat's experience, which was limited, and her research, which was not, serials chose methods that were either more dramatic, or more controllable. Shipman had used the same *method* as Jo Morris's killer – lethal injection – but his chosen *poison* was morphine.

Whoever murdered Jo had to have known she had a fatal allergy to kiwi fruit. Had Jo mentioned it on her website? It seemed unlikely, but maybe she'd written a blog post. Then anyone could have read about it. Kat hoped not; it would blow the suspect-pool wide open.

Jo's site was only a few pages, and none mentioned her allergy. Nor did her social media profiles. Relieved, Kat moved on to the next step in the sequence of logic. If not web visitors, then who *would* know such personal details? Presumably her close friends would have known. Colleagues. Clients, maybe. Anyone who'd invited her and Ian round for a meal. Or to a wedding. Anyone she'd ever gone out for a meal with. Restaurant staff . . .

She groaned with frustration.

'What's up?' Leah asked.

Kat explained about Jo's allergy and the widening group of people who might have known about it. Given they had nothing concrete on Ian yet, she had no option but to widen out the investigation.

Leah shrugged. 'You want me to start tracking them all down?'

Kat was about to say yes, but she stopped herself.

'No. We need to be smart about this. There'll be dozens, possibly hundreds, and they'll be impossible to locate. Could be a kitchen porter from an agency or a student temping as a waitress who's gone travelling. Stick with whatever you're working on for now. I'll talk to Ian again. If I draw a blank, then we'll start looking at other lines of enquiry. Keep looking for this Roz character, too.'

One of Kat's lines of enquiry concerned branding. She wanted to know if people ever got themselves burnt on purpose. She was ninety-nine per cent sure Jo's killer had inflicted the brand on her, but what if she'd had it done voluntarily?

Fifteen minutes of reading fetish blog posts gave her the answer. Branding for sexual or body modification purposes was done carefully, precisely to avoid the type of deep tissue damage inflicted on Jo Morris.

Maybe to her more experienced colleagues, these outer-lying methods of expressing your personality weren't news. *Maybe*, she thought, looking around MCU, some of them indulged in the various activities described in words and pictures on the sex sites themselves. Because for sure, if Jo Morris wasn't a saint, nor were the hard-working men and woman charged with clearing serious crime in Middlehampton.

One of those people, though she immediately withdrew the adjective 'hard-working', stopped by her desk now. He squinted at her PC screen, on which a buxom young woman in goth make-up and extensive tattoos was trussed up in a kneeling position by a couple of hundred metres of rope.

'Porn, DS Ballantyne?' Carve-up asked. 'If you've got time on your hands, I've plenty of other cases you could help out on.'

'The woman I found yesterday – the *murdered* woman,' Kat added for emphasis, 'had a brand on her belly. I'm researching it.'

'Of course you are.' Carve-up resettled his suit jacket – soft, pinstriped and expensive-looking – on his shoulders. 'Might have been nice if you'd mentioned that at this morning's briefing. I'm not just here to greenlight your murder investigations, you know.'

'I only just found out, Stu,' she said, enjoying the look of annoyance that flickered over his face. 'But any investigative insights you could throw my way, obviously, I'd be massively grateful.'

He leaned down, looming over her, enveloping her in a pungent cloud of aftershave.

'It's not hard, DS Ballantyne. Guy brands her then kills her. Classic sadistic psychopath. You're welcome. Again.'

He straightened and wandered back to his office, pausing on the way to banter with the male detectives on his team.

Annoyed at finding herself agreeing with Carve-up, she held up her right hand, extended the index and middle fingers, thumbed back the hammer, sighted between his shoulder blades and pulled the trigger.

'Got a minute, Kat?'

A female voice. Composed of both authority and amusement. Not just any female voice. *The* female voice.

Guiltily, Kat whirled round in her chair to come face-to-face with the head of crime, DCI Linda Ockenden. Not a great look, caught in the act of murdering your DI.

'Sorry, Ma-Linda,' she said, in her flustered state, almost forgetting how she wasn't supposed to call the DCI 'Ma'am' but instead use her first name.

Linda snorted. 'Someone else can mop up DI Carver's blood. I want you in my office. Come on, pick your feet up.'

Kat hurried after Linda as she strode through MCU like an icebreaker through a frozen sea, deviating by not so much as a centimetre from the straightest path between Kat's desk and her office.

Kat's stomach was churning. She'd been found out. Her success in the Origami Killer case had been a one-off: beginner's luck. Or they'd discovered an irregularity in her application to join MCU. She was being booted out and sent back to CID.

Her career as a homicide investigator was over.

CHAPTER TEN

Two women, one in her sixties, the other perhaps ten years younger, sat at the small, round conference table in the corner of Linda's spacious, cluttered office. Kat didn't recognise the older woman. The younger, she did: Elaine Forshaw, the newly re-elected Police and Crime Commissioner for Hertfordshire.

Linda settled herself at the table, puffing a little as she squeezed in between the table and the glass panel behind her. She often prefaced their conversations with a jokey reference to her weight, but in the presence of visitors she was all business.

'You know Mrs Forshaw,' she said, nodding to the PCC, who offered a tight smile to Kat. 'This is Daniela Morris, Jo Morris's mother-in-law.'

Kat shook hands with both women before taking the last chair. It wasn't hard to see the chain of events that had led to this meeting. Ian Morris had had the unenviable task of telling his in-laws that their daughter had been killed, possibly murdered. They had friends in high places and had called in a favour, or maybe just thrown themselves on their doorsteps pleading for help. Either way, Elaine Forshaw had called Linda Ockenden, and here they all were.

Perhaps unconsciously, Daniela Morris was clasping her hands together tightly enough to drive all the blood from her fingers, which had turned corpse-white. Her nails were manicured, coated in a deep red metallic polish.

So, no, Kat wasn't about to be sent back to CID. But the pressure was going to mount all the same.

Linda took a breath and adjusted her glasses. 'Mrs Morris is—' She got no further.

'How did my daughter-in-law die, Detective Sergeant Ballantyne? Was it an accident, as my son claims? Or was Jo . . .' Her voice caught and she swallowed, tried again. 'Was she murdered?'

The front of Daniela Morris's black silk blouse was rising and falling rapidly. The poor woman was maintaining her calm by an act of will. Kat didn't answer immediately. There was a lot packed into that middle sentence – *as my son claims*. Did his own mother suspect him of lying? Did she know something about him that Kat didn't?

'I believe Jo was unlawfully killed,' Kat said carefully.

'What does that mean? Was she or wasn't she murdered?'

Linda held up a hand. 'DS Ballantyne is, correctly, being circumspect.' She nodded at Kat then turned to look directly at Daniela. 'Whoever killed Jo did so intending her to die, or at the very least suffer significant harm. But at this stage we can't officially say it was murder.'

Elaine Forshaw chose this moment to speak for the first time. 'Look, Linda, can we leave the legal language to one side, just for a minute? We all know it could be manslaughter, but it's not going to be infanticide or causing death by dangerous driving, is it? So she must have been murdered. What else could possibly have happened?'

'That's what I intend to find out,' Kat said.

'You'd better. I loved that girl like my own daughter,' Daniela said. 'I will not sit by while the police go through the motions and then say it was a tragic accident. Someone killed her and I won't rest until I know who.'

She banged the table, and the right cuff of her blouse slid back to reveal a delicate gold watch with a green enamelled face.

Elaine turned to her and laid a hand on her forearm. 'Daniela, nobody's going through the motions. I know Kat. She's one of the best detectives in Middlehampton. She'll get to the bottom of this. Won't you, Kat?'

Kat swallowed. Nodded.

Linda's PA, Annie, arrived with coffees. Over the clinking of teaspoons and the brief polite enquiries about milk and sugar or sweeteners, Kat tried to process what Elaine Forshaw had just said to her. It wasn't a threat. Not as such. Nothing so obvious, especially in front of Linda. But even softened by the endorsement of her investigative skills, the meaning was clear.

'Mrs Morris,' she said, waiting until she had Daniela's attention before asking a very sensitive question. 'Just now you said Ian "claims" Jo's death was an accident. What did you mean by that?'

Daniela's lips tightened momentarily into a bloodless line. 'Well, I didn't mean *he* did it, if that's what you're thinking,' she said with evident irritation. 'It's just a turn of phrase, isn't it? I just don't believe Jo would be that careless. It can't be an accident. It can't!'

The last two words came out in a half-sob. The tears that she had been holding back throughout the meeting formed in the corners of her eyes and she blotted them with a tissue, taking care not to smudge her mascara.

Once the two women had left the room, Linda motioned for Kat to stay seated.

'Sorry about that,' she said, shaking her head. 'And you thought it was all about blokes playing golf with the Chief Con.'

'Who is she? Or should I say, what is she?'

'Daniela Morris is all sorts of things. She's a businesswoman. Owns Morris's Chemists, yes?' Kat nodded. The firm had half a dozen branches in Middlehampton and several others in the neighbouring towns. 'She doesn't need to work on them much; they just tick over nicely, thank you very much. She's married to John Morris.'

'Would that by any chance be the John Morris who owns Middlehampton FC?'

'And who made a fortune in business before retiring to focus on playing real-life FIFA.'

'Let me guess. They're big supporters of Elaine Forshaw and they contributed handsomely to her campaign to get re-elected.'

'I can see why I promoted you,' Linda deadpanned. 'Long story short, and it's a familiar one, I'm getting leaned on to produce results. And just in case you think I should be able to stand up for myself against a mere elected official and a distraught parent, I also have the Undertaker breathing down my neck. Seems Daniela knows him, too.'

Kat sighed. Perfect. It was all she needed: having her every move scrutinised by Detective Superintendent David Deerfield. Although it did have a bright side.

'Does that mean I'll have more resources if I need them?'

Linda had a way of staring at you that made you feel like confessing, even if you'd done nothing wrong. As the seconds ticked by, Kat fought the urge to backtrack.

'It means you'd better sort this one ASAP, my girl,' Linda said finally. 'And when – *if* – you find you need some more pocket money, come and find me.'

Kat made her way back to MCU. Jo might have lost her own parents, but her mother-in-law was a force of nature, and with powerful connections to help turn her desires into action.

Leah hurried over as soon as Kat reached her desk.

'I know you said the brand wasn't a pro job, but I've been looking at the Middlehampton fetish scene,' she said, pulling her mouth into a comical quirk of surprise. 'It's amazing what you can get done in this fair town of ours.'

'Branding?'

'And the rest. Beading, scarification, implants, tongue-splitting. Jesus, Kat, it's like the Marquis de Sade out there. Anyway, I got a list of all the regulated places that offer branding. Thought I'd check them out, see if anyone had any insights into the significance of the design the killer used on Jo. Or maybe the tool he used.'

'And?'

Leah shook her head. 'They all said the same thing. Horrible amateur job. Might be a fetish thing, but most of those people know what they're doing. I mean it's bloody painful, obviously. And no idea about the symbol.'

'Good work, mate.' Kat hesitated. 'I'm not sure I really want to know the answer, but . . . beading?'

'They slit your skin and stick objects underneath. Beads mostly, hence the name. Apparently it's very popular with the guys.' She pointed towards her crotch. 'Makes sex more – you know? – exciting.'

Kat winced. 'Really?'

Leah grinned. 'I don't know, it could work. If he was on the small side or something.'

Both women cackled loudly, earning questioning looks from a couple of nearby male coppers.

'Could Ian have done it, do you think?' Leah asked.

'I mean, he *could* have,' Kat said, pulling her mouth to one side. 'But she wasn't bruised or scarred anywhere else. Abusive men like to hit women where it won't show. Breasts, belly, kidneys. I saw nothing.'

'And he wouldn't have gone straight to burning her?'

Kat shook her head.

She tapped the copy of the photo Leah had been showing around town. 'What *is* that, Leah? *Is* it a number eight?'

Leah swivelled the photo round by a quarter-turn so the numeral was lying down. 'An infinity symbol?'

Kat ran a quick internet search on 'infinity symbol'. A few seconds later she groaned. The results included dozens of websites and blogs offering to unlock, as one put it, 'the mystic secrets of the infinity symbol, from Kabbala to Hindu mythology, alien cultures to the Egyptian pharaohs.'

She swivelled the monitor round so Leah could see it.

The DC rolled her eyes. 'Excellent. So we have to go chasing down every woo-woo-believing yummy-mummy and UFO-spotting weirdo to see if they have a connection to Jo Morris?'

Kat shook her head. Pointed to one of the images in the results: an infinity symbol from whose wasp-waist rose a crucifix with two crossbars. 'Look at that. It's got a cross on top, but it says it's a satanic symbol.'

Leah's face, cracked with a grin just a second earlier, fell. 'Christ, I hope that's not right. If the media find out we've got a satanic murder on our hands this'll go viral.'

'Right. We keep this under wraps, OK? It's a burn mark, that's all.' Kat sighed. 'We're going to get all the usual loonies badgering reception, wanting to confess. This'll screen them all out.'

Tom came over. His face bore a greyish cast and his eyes were red. 'I've been going through Jo Morris's life. Financials, socials, everything,' he said in a dispirited tone. 'She never even had a Twitter spat with anyone. Woman's a bloody saint, after all.'

'Any sign of a Roz, or a Rosalind?'

He shook his head. 'Sorry.'

Like Ian, Tom had called Jo Morris a saint. Rather than reassuring Kat, it only worried her more. All Tom's initial research had shown was that the killer's motive was going to be hard to find. She remembered what Michelle Wilson had said about Jo's inheritance, and how she'd been refusing to lend it to Ian.

'So how much was in her accounts, then?'

'I've got the statements on my desk. Few hundred in her current account. A couple of thousand in her deposit account. Both with Nationwide.'

Kat frowned. 'No savings plans, ISAs, life insurance?'

'Not that I could find. I might have missed something. It's early days and I was trying to cover a lot of ground, so . . .'

'It's fine. Just keep on it. Thing is – her best friend said she'd come into money when her parents died. Apparently, Ian was bothering her for a loan, but she turned him down. I was expecting more than a couple of grand from the way Michelle was talking.'

'Could she have spent it all? Is that why she wouldn't agree to lend it to Ian?'

'You tell me. I didn't see much evidence at theirs when I had a poke around.'

He looked down at the photo of the brand and shuddered. 'What a sicko.'

Kat nodded. Then, realising something horrific, she turned the photo back to its original vertical orientation. She swallowed.

'What is it?' Tom asked.

'What if it's just an 8 after all? What if it means he's going to kill eight women?'

'Like, a countdown or something?' Tom asked.

She told Tom to keep digging, Leah to help him.

Kat stared at the photo. Praying she was wrong. Fearing she might be right. Yes, she could start interviewing everyone in

Middlehampton who'd ever posted about Wicca, or black magic, or got a devil tattoo. But she'd probably spend weeks chasing her tail – and possibly, given one explanation she'd seen online for the infinity symbol, which involved snakes, eating it as well.

So what did a sensible detective do instead? They did all the obvious things first, and well. It was cheaper, faster and, given the crime statistics, most likely to yield a result.

Kat drove back to Hampton Hill.

CHAPTER ELEVEN

As Ian led Kat into the sitting room, he explained that James was out buying milk.

'I have some news for you about Jo,' she said. 'From the post-mortem report, it does look as though she was murdered.'

Ian flopped back in the recliner. A single, cracked sob escaped his lips. He smothered it with a hand as if embarrassed to be caught showing emotion. Was she finally seeing the real Ian Morris? Or had he just sharpened his acting chops?

He looked at the windowsill, where wedding photos sat in silver frames. Kat followed his gaze. Saw Jo – tanned, beautiful, hair in a complicated up-do – beaming up at him. His hair was longer then, but not by much. Something occurred to her.

'How long were you married?' she asked him.

'It would have been our fourth wedding anniversary next month.' He scrubbed at his cheeks with both palms, reddening them. 'We got married at St Luke's, in Bradyfield. June, 2020.'

'I know it. It's such a pretty church,' Kat said, smiling at him as she worked the timeline back. Jo had been twenty-eight when she married Ian. 'Had either of you been married before?'

His head, which had been lolling back, exposing his Adam's apple, snapped forwards. She heard the click from one of his vertebrae, loud in the double-glazed room.

'What's that got to do with anything?' he asked dully.

'I'm just wondering about Jo's life before you two met,' she said, already sure that Ian was not Jo's first husband. 'If there's an ex-husband, I'd like to talk to him as well.'

'Jo was my first wife. I never found the right woman before her. She has an ex, though. Mark Knight.'

Kat nodded. Why hadn't Ian told James about the ex? He'd been in shock, mind you. And James had used the word 'prise' about getting information out of Ian. She let it go.

'Do you know why they divorced?'

'It was a no-fault thing. Incompatibility, I suppose. That's what she told me.' He scratched at his scalp. 'I met him once. Real snob. No wonder she dumped him.'

Kat made a note. Mark Knight had joined her list of people of interest. He'd be easy enough to track down. In fact . . .

'Is he local, do you know?'

'Runs an antique shop on Potten Walk. You should see the prices. Guy must be minted.' His gaze sharpened. 'You don't think he did it, do you?'

'It's too early to say. I just want to have a word with him. Ask for an alibi, things like that.'

She'd mentioned the alibi deliberately. Wondering whether it would unsettle Ian, who after all didn't have one himself. He stood up suddenly and went to the window. He picked up one of the wedding photos and stared at it. Without turning round, he started speaking.

'We had our problems, you know? We wanted a baby, but she couldn't conceive. Did you know that?'

Kat remained quiet. He was talking freely, and she didn't want to interrupt him, even with an answer to one of his own questions.

'She had tests,' he continued. 'Told me it must have been me. Low sperm count or something. I was embarrassed to go to the doctor. I don't mind admitting it. Old-school, I suppose. My dad was the same. Thing is, right? I *did* go and get tested. Just last week, actually. I'm fine. Normal,' he added, emphatically.

Now Kat did speak. Because this raised all sorts of questions. 'When was this, Ian? Did you discuss it with Jo?'

'I couldn't, could I? I only got the results yesterday. Bit bloody ironic, don't you think?'

'Can you think of any reason why Jo might have . . .' She didn't want to say 'lied', not to an apparently grieving husband. 'Why she might have got her own test results mixed up?'

'Search me. Maybe you should talk to the clinic. I can give you the name. It's the same one I went to. Middlehampton Fertility Centre.'

'Thanks, Ian, that's really helpful. Just to be clear, Jo didn't have children with Mark, did she?'

'No. They were only married for a year or so.'

Kat heard the front door open and close. James appeared in the sitting room doorway, holding up a pint of milk. He caught on fast and made his way into the kitchen without speaking.

She made another note. Then looked up at Ian. She was in a classic Catch-22 situation. She needed to search the house. But at the moment she didn't have reasonable grounds to apply for a warrant. But searching it might be the fastest way to finding something that pointed to Ian. There was, however, a tried-and-tested approach.

'One last thing. I'd like to hold a press conference. Jo was obviously well liked and had a lot of friends in Middlehampton,' she said with a smile. 'Would you be up for making a short appeal? Asking members of the public who were out on Bowman's Common on Monday morning to come forward?'

Ian's face twisted. 'Do I have to? I can't even face the thought of going out in public. James'll tell you.'

The compassionate thing to say would be: *Of course not. You just stay here and grieve for Jo. We can manage without you.* But right now, the instinctual, copper's side of her brain was in charge. The side that, in the long run, would find Jo's killer, whoever it might be.

'I understand it will be difficult for you, Ian, I really do,' she said. 'But it can make a massive difference if the next of kin asks the public for help. I'd be there with you. James, too, if that would help you feel more confident.'

'Would I have to speak?' he asked. 'Couldn't I just sort of sit there and you read out something I write?'

Which is when Kat saw – with a flash of intuition even Molly Steadman would have approved of – what the problem was. Like her – like pretty much everyone she'd ever come into contact with – Ian had a phobia of public speaking. Let alone the fact the occasion would be a police press conference in which he had the unlooked-for starring role.

But she really needed him to do the conference. One more try.

'Look, Ian, I know how stressful it can be. Public speaking, I mean. I'm a complete jelly when I have to do it. But I'll be there to support you. You won't have to improvise. Just read from a script we'll work up together. You don't even have to stand up or anything. Just sit behind a table. Nobody'll be able to tell if your knees go all wobbly.'

That was true, as far as it went. But Kat would be able to tell a lot from his behaviour. Speaking to TV cameras took so much energy out of you it left very little for maintaining a facade. She'd be watching Ian closely, not staring out at the journalists.

James came into the room with three mugs of tea.

Kat's initial flash of irritation at his timing evaporated as she realised how she could win Ian around. He needed a little push, that was all.

'Thanks, James,' she said, blowing on and then sipping the tea. 'I was just explaining to Ian how we help people when they want to do an appeal to the public. Even though it's hard.'

She shot him a meaningful look. But James was an experienced copper and he didn't need a push himself.

He half turned to Ian. 'It's over before you know it, mate,' he said. 'Tell you what: let's get it done and then go out for a bit. You've been stuck inside for days now. Bit of fresh air'll do you good. I might even buy you breakfast in Wetherspoons if DS Ballantyne here'll authorise the expenses.'

Kat smiled for all she was worth. 'Of course. Just keep James away from the black pudding. Gives him dog-breath.'

Smiles all round. Some genuine.

That was it then. Settled. They agreed to a press conference the following morning.

CHAPTER TWELVE

Kat made it home at just before 10.00 p.m. and found Van in the kitchen, his laptop open on the breakfast bar.

'Evenin' all,' she said, bending to kiss him.

He returned the kiss with interest.

'That was nice,' she said, pouring herself a glass of Pinot Grigio from an open bottle in the fridge, then faltering as she remembered Jess's point about straying husbands being over-affectionate. 'Want one?'

'I had a beer earlier. Got to get this done before I go up tonight or Marnie'll have my balls for earrings,' he said, pulling a face.

The thought of Marnie anywhere near her husband's balls had Kat's stomach clenching.

'Can't you tell her you need more time?'

Van actually laughed. 'Yeah, right. Not going to happen. How was *your* day?'

Kat pulled out the chair opposite Van.

'You shouldn't let her push you around,' she said, feeling a quick stab of jealousy. 'Or is it more like a lead she's got you on?'

He frowned. 'What? No! She's expanding her business and she needs some extra storage, the website improving, as well as bug-fixes to the new app. I'm sorting it all out for her.'

Kat frowned. What did Marnie *do*? When she'd asked, Van hadn't been evasive as such. He'd just said she ran an online network. *You know, a social thing.* Suddenly, she wanted to know.

'I never asked. What kind of social network *exactly* is it she runs?'

He grinned, but it looked to Kat like the expression a schoolboy would make if a teacher caught him watching porn on his phone. 'Promise you won't be appalled. Or cross or something.'

'Now you said that I can't, can I? Just tell me, Van, please. It's porn, isn't it? It's not some sleazy "barely legal" site, is it? Those things are just gateways for paedophiles. You know that, don't you? And what about all that business with Riley and those WhatsApp photos of his mate's older sister in her undies? Aren't you even *slightly* worried?'

Van stared at her. 'It's nothing like that. It's a dating site. Well, Marnie calls it "discreet introductions", but it comes down to the same thing.'

Kat sighed out of relief. 'Like eMatch or Tremble. One of those?'

Ivan pulled his lips to one side.

'Kind of.'

'What do you mean, "kind of"? Is it a specialist thing? Girls meet girls? Fetish enthusiasts? I don't know why you think I'd be appalled by that.'

Van closed the laptop lid and favoured her with a direct stare across the table. 'It's for married people.'

Maybe because she was tired, or because Van was being unusually cagey, Kat couldn't work out what he meant. Online dating was for *unmarried* people. That was kind of the whole point.

'What, like widowers?' she asked.

Ivan merely looked at her. Then, with a sound like Riley putting pans away as he unloaded the dishwasher, the penny dropped . . . from a great height.

'Oh no, Van! Really? It's for affairs? Please tell me it's not.'

'It is.'

'And you're happy about that?' she said, feeling her pulse bumping uncomfortably in her throat. 'She's basically ruining people's marriages.'

He shook his head. 'She's really not. They're doing that all by themselves.'

'But she's making it easier for people to commit adultery! I mean, why not just buy a hotel and advertise in the *Echo*? You know, "Fancy a shag with your bit on the side? Come to The Cedars. Rooms available by the hour."'

Perhaps unwisely, Van laughed. 'Come on, darling, you're being melodramatic. Although I quite like that tagline. If coppering doesn't work out, you could always go into advertising.'

She gulped some wine. 'It's immoral,' she said, hating the prissy tone in her own voice yet unable to get rid of it.

'It's lucrative is what it is,' Van said. 'Look, Kat, I get it – really, I do. But people will always find ways to have affairs whether Marnie's there or not. I mean, it's not as if it wasn't going on until the internet came along, is it?'

He stretched out a hand, reaching for hers. She snatched it back. No way was she letting him off the hook that easily. She could feel a very difficult conversation about fidelity creeping nearer and she really wasn't sure she was ready to have it yet.

'No. But it's just' – she wrinkled her nose – 'so sleazy, making your living that way.'

'Me or Marnie?'

'Both!' she said. 'If it was a brothel, she'd be the madam and you'd be the maid.'

Van waggled his eyebrows at her. 'Change your sheets, luv?' he said in a parodic cockney accent, like something out of a sixties sex comedy.

She tried not to smile; unwilling, yet, to let him off the hook.

'What's it called, anyway? PlayAwayFromHome? ShagPad? Don'tTellMyWife? CucksReunited?'

He opened the laptop and tapped a couple of keys, then swivelled it round to face her. Kat leaned closer, moving her glass out of the way. The site was irritatingly tasteful. Cream, grey and navy. She'd been expecting something tacky, tawdry; lots of black and red.

The logo mystified her.

'Dove & Charcoal? What does that mean?'

'Think about it.'

'If I wanted to think about it, I'd have thought about it.' She pushed the laptop away. 'Just tell me.'

'No! You're clever, work it out.'

She pulled the laptop back and stared at the screen. 'Oh, right. They're shades of grey. Like not everything's black-and-white,' she said. 'Marnie likes to think she exists in a morally ambiguous place, is that it?'

Van shrugged. 'More or less. Also, it looks suitably anonymous when it shows up on credit card statements.'

'Wow, she really has thought of everything, hasn't she?'

'It's just business, Kat.'

'No, it isn't! It's people's lives, Van. Their marriages, for God's sake. I wish you weren't working for her.'

She'd wanted to keep things light. Swapping increasingly silly names for the site or doing more comedy accents. But the pull of the issue at the core of Marnie Pryce's business wouldn't let her.

'You don't like her, do you?' Van said.

'I only met her that one time.'

'Yeah, but I could tell. It was like one of those cartoons, with little truncheons coming out of your eyes in a dotted line straight at her.'

Kat got up from the table and refilled her glass at the fridge door. 'I thought she was perfectly fine. A bit obvious, maybe, but basically, I didn't really take that much notice.'

Oops. She'd just shown her hand. What was it they said about alcohol? *In vino blabbermouth?* Something like that.

Van's eyes widened and he smirked. 'Oh, *now* I get it! You're jealous.'

'No, I'm *not!*' she said indignantly, one hand on her hip, the other raising her glass to her lips. *Yes, you are!* that sly inner voice piped up. 'I'm sure you and *Marnie* have a lovely time working out how to get more people using her site to cheat on their spouses. Sure you're not doing some field-testing?'

Shit! That had come out all wrong. Bloody Pinot Grigio.

'What? You think I'm having a thing with Marnie? Don't be ridiculous!'

Kat stared at him, pulse bumping in her throat. Here it came. The unavoidable question. She swallowed. It hurt. 'Are you?'

Van sighed. 'Of course not! I love you. I've *always* loved you. Look, maybe let's just park this, OK? We're both tired. We're not going to get anywhere; it's late and I still have some work to do.'

While she tried to decide whether she believed him, Riley wandered into the kitchen.

'Why are you and Dad arguing?' he asked.

'We're not arguing, darling,' she said, pasting a smile onto her face. 'Just talking.'

'Loudly, though.'

'I'm sorry, Riley. We'll keep the noise down, won't we?' she said, eyeballing Van.

'Come on, mate,' he said. 'Let's get you up to bed.'

Five minutes later, Van came back into the kitchen.

'Hey,' he said, holding his arms wide. 'You didn't tell me how *your* day went.'

She went over to him and let him hug her.

'I'm still looking at the husband.'

'That's usually the best bet, isn't it,' Van said, 'when a married woman's murdered?'

◆ ◆ ◆

Later, as Van snored beside her, the corners of his lips twitching in a sleep-smile, she wondered about Jo and Ian Morris's marriage. Jo's friend Michelle had said they'd argued about money. It was one of the most common motives for murder. But had sex played a part, too? That was even more common.

Maybe Jo had been having an affair, and Ian had found out. There would be an even more powerful, and primal, motive. Or had he been the one playing away from home? Jo had found out, confronted him, and he'd decided he needed to get her out of the picture.

Maybe one or both Morrises had signed up to Dove & Charcoal. Wouldn't that be convenient? Would Marnie play ball and let her have a look at her client list? Of course not! Her whole business was built on total discretion. But Van had backdoor access. Maybe she'd ask him to take a quick look for her in the morning.

The thought of the following morning's tasks reminded her that they were due to hold a press conference with Ian Morris. A flicker of anxiety ignited in her belly. Brilliant! Now she was wide awake.

She ran over the sequence of events, from her introduction to the forthcoming press conference at which Ian would ask witnesses to come forward. The questions from journalists and then wrapping it up and having James take Ian out for a long coffee or a late breakfast while she had a longer look around his house.

Because he looked good for it, didn't he? Money troubles, which his wife had refused to help with. Some issue about which of them was infertile. A buttoned-up, old-school approach to emotions, which she'd seen send men into violent rages before, when it all became too much for them.

CHAPTER THIRTEEN

Once Riley had left for school, slamming the front door so violently the glasses on the kitchen dresser tinkled, Kat turned to Van.

'I need to ask you a favour. Can you look up a couple of people on Marnie's client list for me?' Van's mouth opened – ready, she knew, to protest. 'It's literally just two names. I won't write anything down.'

He sighed. 'I'm guessing you've heard of the European data protection law.'

She had. Everyone had. Bloody GDPR. It was like a magic shield everyone from hospitals to big corporations could use to fend off police enquiries.

'I have, obviously. But this is a murder investigation, Van. I could always get a search warrant. But couldn't you just—'

His face darkened. 'Christ, Kat! Just leave it, will you? I'm busting my balls on her site and it's stressing me out and I'm not about to break the law, even to help you out.'

'Please?' she wheedled.

'I'm sorry, darling. I just can't. Get a warrant if you have to, but that'll be for Marnie to deal with, not me, OK? She's got lawyers but I'm sure she'll be as cooperative as she can be.'

Kat sighed. It had been worth a try. 'OK. I'm sorry, Van. I shouldn't have asked. I'm sorry.'

She grabbed her car keys from the hall table and shouted out a goodbye before leaving for the station.

On the drive in, Kat started to wonder whether her suspicions about Van were on the money at all – or so far off it she might as well give up being a detective altogether.

And then she thought of Jack Beale.

Oh God, was she projecting her guilt over Jack onto Van? She resolved to put her faith in her marriage and stop letting it interfere with the case. As to a warrant for Marnie's site, there were plenty of ways to conduct extramarital affairs that didn't involve online hook-ups. She decided to park it. She had a press conference to prepare for.

Waiting for the conference to start, Kat inhaled deeply, and immediately wished she hadn't. Sandwiched between Carve-up and Ian Morris, her nostrils filled with a heady, unpleasant mixture. Carve-up's cologne and Ian's body odour – a pungent, acrid reek that spoke of too many missed showers and an unhealthy blood-alcohol level.

She turned briefly towards Ian and smiled encouragingly. 'You'll be fine,' she murmured, keeping her head down, giving nothing away to any reporters who had mastered the art of lip-reading.

She nodded to James, Ian's FLO, who was standing at the back. Before the conference, she'd asked him to keep Ian out of the house for a couple more hours.

She nodded to a smartly dressed woman in her forties sitting in the front row. Auburn hair swept back from a high forehead. Soft features that belied the reporter's sharp nose for a story. Dawn

Jacobson, editor of the *Echo*. Kat went back ten years with Dawn, when she'd been a cub reporter on the paper and Kat was still in uniform.

Dawn smiled back, notebook open on her lap and pencil poised above it. Old-school: Kat liked that about her.

Beside her, Carve-up cleared his throat. The low murmur from the journalists subsided.

'Good morning, everyone. My name is Detective Inspector Stuart Carver, the senior investigating officer in this case.' He paused and looked round the room. Giving the reporters time to get his name and title down correctly. He needn't have bothered. They all knew. And, even if they didn't print it, they knew his nickname, too. 'Early on Monday morning, the body of a woman was discovered on Bowman's Common in Middlehampton. We believe she was murdered.'

As Stuart finished his introduction, Kat readied herself to give the statement she'd been preparing in her head half the night. Her heart was thumping in her chest and, as usual, her palms felt slippery with sweat.

The fresh-faced press officer, Freddie Tippett, had once offered her some advice, which was entirely in keeping with his reputation for telling the filthiest jokes in Jubilee Place. *Imagine your audience stark naked*, he'd said. *That or sitting on the toilet.* It hadn't helped. All that happened was she'd had a nightmare the day before a press conference in which it was she who sat, covering her chest with her hands, on the loo in front of a roomful of laughing journalists.

But Stuart wasn't handing over as Linda Ockenden would, telling the reporters *DS Kat Ballantyne will now make a statement.* He was outlining the details of the investigation himself.

'I want to ask members of the public who were out and about on the common during the early hours of Monday morning to make contact with the police. You may not realise it, but you may have seen the killer.'

As Carve-up continued, Kat made an effort to unclamp her jaw, which had tightened like a vice. He'd managed to patronise potential witnesses and was earning himself shakes of the head from the reporters with his flowery phrasing that he no doubt thought made him sound intelligent.

'I am now going to hand over to the victim's husband, Ian, who will read a short statement.'

Ian shifted in his seat and looked out at the ten or so journalists. Beneath the table, hidden by the Hertfordshire Police-branded vinyl drape, Kat gave his knee a quick nudge with her own. He looked round at her and tried to smile. He looked as though he might cry. She'd seen plenty of tricks from murderous husbands. Even real tears.

He picked up a single sheet of A4 from the table. The top edge fluttered, transmitting and amplifying the tremor in his hand. He cleared his throat.

'Jo was a wonderful woman. A loving wife, a successful entrepreneur, and a dedicated personal trainer.' His voice was quiet; Dawn Jacobson was leaning forwards and frowning, her head turned slightly to one side. Ian cleared his throat and tried again.

'She loved her work, and she loved this community. Whenever she could she tried to give something back. Now, some . . .' He tightened his lips. Kat tensed. In the rehearsal, Ian had lapsed into a stream of invective against his wife's killer. It was justified but wouldn't help at the actual press conference. '. . . some *person* has taken her away from me, from her friends, and family, from her clients, from this town.'

He sought out the video camera from the local BBC news team.

'Someone knows something. If you saw Jo with someone early on Monday morning, or you've heard someone talking about her murder, please come forward.'

Kat relaxed. He was back on script.

Ian leaned forward and pulled the slender black wand of the mic closer.

'And if you did it,' he said, his voice dropping into a threatening murmur, 'you'd better hand yourself in to the police. Because I've got friends in this town, and we'll make your life hell if we find you first.'

Kat's pulse, which had settled during Ian's appeal, skyrocketed. What the hell had just happened? She glanced behind Ian, to Carve-up. His eyes were wide, and he was alternately scanning the room and shuffling through the thin pile of papers on the table in front of him.

The room boiled with sudden noise. Dawn Jacobson's voice pierced the hubbub.

'DI Carver, did we just hear a call to arms? What's your view on vigilantism?'

Carve-up blinked. His mouth opened but Kat could see his brain was AWOL. It closed again, and he looked desperately at her. She hated doing it, but he needed rescuing.

'Mr Morris is understandably upset at the senseless murder of his wife,' she said, projecting her voice to the back of the room, where Freddie Tippett stood, nodding his approval. 'His remarks were made in the heat of the moment at what is obviously a very stressful time for him. Of course, Hertfordshire Police do not condone or encourage the general public to take the law into their own hands.'

'Do you have any suspects?' a reporter from a neighbouring town called out.

'We have a number of lines of enquiry. These are early days and I want to repeat Ian's heartfelt message to members of the public.' She found the BBC video camera and stared into its black eye. 'Did you see Jo on that fateful morning? Was she alone or with somebody else? Did you see anyone acting suspiciously on Bowman's Common, especially near the Three Sisters? However insignificant you think it might be, please call me at Jubilee Place police station or Crimestoppers.'

Kat took a few more questions, giving true-but-unrevealing, true-but-partial, or non-answers altogether: 'I'm sorry, but I'm unable to comment on the details of an ongoing investigation.'

When the reporters started repeating themselves, she decided enough was enough and brought the press conference to a close. The room empty, she thanked Ian and beckoned James to come over and whisk Ian away for a full English breakfast in Wetherspoons.

That left just her and Carve-up. She didn't like him, probably never would. But getting that rabbit-in-the-headlights feeling in front of the media was something she wouldn't wish on her worst enemy. Which, she thought wryly, was probably the man sitting next to her.

'You OK?' she asked him. 'Ian really played his joker on that one, didn't he?'

Carve-up sneered. 'Oh, you loved that, didn't you? Watching me lose it in front of the vermin.'

She reared back. 'What? No! Ian practically announced he was forming a lynch mob. Anyone would've struggled to come back from that.'

'Don't patronise me, DS Ballantyne.' He got to his feet. 'I'm still the SIO on this and you'd better start bringing me some results soon.'

Scowling, he stalked off, leaving Kat open-mouthed. She parked her resentment at her line manager. She had somewhere to be.

While James was plying Ian Morris with a full English and a pint of ale, Kat and Tom entered Ian's house. Tom was still hesitant, despite Kat's assurances. She didn't know how long James would be able to keep Ian occupied, so they had to move fast.

'Gloves on, please,' she said.

'Don't we need a warrant?'

Kat shook her head. 'James had Ian sign a consent form yesterday.'

'What if he withdraws his consent? We covered this on my course. A warrant is always the safest course of action.'

'Let's cross that bridge when we come to it. Warrants take time.'

And executive approval, which I don't have.

He shrugged. *Your funeral*, he seemed to be saying. 'What are we looking for?'

'I saw a laptop in the lounge last time I was here. Why not start with that?'

Leaving Tom to poke around in the lounge, Kat headed upstairs. With the luxury of time, she didn't have to scoot from room to room. She could work down below the surface a bit. The master bedroom first, then.

Kat sat on the double bed, resisting the urge to straighten the duvet out and plump up the pillows.

The chest of drawers housing Jo's clothes yielded nothing of any value. A few sets of matching lacy underwear among the sports bras and everyday knickers. Hardly proof of an affair.

She rifled through Ian's clothes in the wardrobe, checking the pockets of all the jackets and trousers. Apart from a few paper tissues, fluffy with age, they were empty.

'What next?' she muttered.

She moved to the laundry hamper, a dark brown wicker drum with a hinged top. It was overflowing with dirty clothes. One by one she plucked out the garments inside and held them up to the light. Nothing out of the ordinary. Men's underpants, a soft white bra, some high-leg knickers, some racerback vests of Jo's, a handful of men's shirts in white, pale blue and pink. Such a conservative choice of colours – and exactly the same as Van's. *Men!* A pair of stone chinos, too.

Just as she was about to return the clothes, she spotted a triangle of pink fabric almost hidden beneath a sagging fold in the dark brown cotton lining of the hamper. She reached in and pulled it free: another of Ian's shirts.

As it came out it brushed past her face and she caught a whiff of something light and floral. Roses and jasmine. Aftershave? It seemed unlikely. Way beyond what she'd expect even the most metrosexual man in Middlehampton to wear. And that description certainly didn't apply to Ian Morris.

She inhaled deeply and tried to place the scent. Saw Jo's perfumes arranged in a little row on the dressing table. Tested each of them. Here it was. That same floral aroma. J'adore by Dior.

Maybe Jo had used one of Ian's shirts as a nightie. She shook it out, and gasped. Dark red droplets fanned out from a point just below the collar, extending down almost to the midpoint of the shirt.

Kat had washed enough spaghetti Bolognese drips out of Riley's tops to know that this was not a food stain. A word sprang to the front of her mind, in flashing neon scarlet.

Spatter.

CHAPTER FOURTEEN

Kat placed the bloody shirt in an evidence bag, which she sealed and labelled before hurrying downstairs.

Tom was in the lounge, peering at the laptop.

'You got in, then?' she asked.

'No password. Which, by the way, I find interesting. It says they trusted each other.'

'Good point. Whose is it, his or hers?'

'Looks like hers. Lots of stuff about fitness, training, nutrition, all that.'

'Anything point to an affair?'

He shrugged. 'I'm not really sure what I'd be looking for, but there's nothing in her emails.'

'She could have been using an online service.' *Like Dove & Charcoal.*

'Yeah, but we'd need to take this away with us and have digital forensics look at it. I haven't got the skills to do that from here. Or the time, probably.'

Kat grinned. 'Sorry, Tom, what did you say?'

He frowned. 'I don't have the time.'

'No. Just before that. Something about skills, was it?'

He screwed his mouth over to one side. Then he rolled his eyes. 'Oh, *I* get it. Very funny.'

Kat held her hands up. 'No, no. I'm just impressed that you feel comfortable enough around me to admit to weakness.'

He grinned back at her. 'Do I detect the merest hint of sarcasm there, DS Ballantyne?'

She widened her eyes and fanned her fingers across her front.

'*Moi?* Not at all. I, on the other hand, did find something.' She held up the shirt in its paper evidence bag. 'A bloodstained man's shirt.'

'Really? That's amazing!' Then Tom's face fell. 'Hang on, though. She was poisoned, not stabbed.'

Kat let her arm drop to her side. 'I may have oversold that a little. We're not talking buckets of blood. But if it's Jo's and it's on one of Ian's shirts, which she appears to have been wearing, that's interesting, don't you think?'

Tom pointed at the bag.

'She's got his shirt on. They have an argument.' He clenched his right hand. 'He hits her. Maybe gives her a nosebleed or something. That's evidence of domestic violence. Could show he had it in him to kill her.'

'Yes, it could. Or it could show she had a spontaneous nosebleed, and for all we know, Ian rushed off to get a cold flannel from the bathroom.'

'Did you find a bloody flannel?'

'Good point. No. Not in the laundry basket, anyway.'

'Maybe it's in the utility room.'

The washing machine door was open and more dirty clothes were stuffed into the drum. But after pulling them all out and sorting through, then turning his attention to the tumble dryer, Tom looked round at Kat, shaking his head. 'Nothing. Unless he threw it away.'

'Why throw it away if he was using it for an innocent purpose? Actually, you know what? That doesn't matter. What matters is we have a bloodstained man's shirt that we need to get tested.'

'So, what now? Can we leave with it?'

'We just need to ask Ian if he's OK with us taking it away.'

Tom frowned. 'You said he signed a consent form.'

'He did, and I'm still banking on that being enough. But if this comes to something, his defence will say we took it without making it clear what evidence we seized.' She mimed throwing the shirt away. 'Ten-to-one the judge would rule it inadmissible.'

Ten minutes later, the front door lock clicked. Kat got up from the sofa and gestured for Tom to do the same. James came into the lounge first, nodding to Kat, then Tom, with Ian behind him.

If Ian was surprised to see two detectives waiting for him in his own sitting room, he didn't show it. He pointed at the bag held in her left hand.

'What's that?'

This was the tricky bit. She needed to explain what she had, why she wanted to take it and get Ian's renewed permission. But she also needed to absolve James of any blame, as Ian might see it. No sense disrupting the relationship James had been working so hard to establish.

'I was looking for more of Jo's clothes and I found one of your shirts in the laundry basket,' she said. 'It's got some blood on it and I want to send it off to the lab to be tested for DNA. Would that be OK, Ian?'

He put his hands in his pockets and, in a move worthy of a police officer, answered her question with one of his own. A deceptively simple one.

'Why?'

'Well, I'd like to know whose blood it is, for one thing. And how it got there.'

He nodded, as if he'd been expecting this answer.

'Is it the pink one?'

'Yes.'

'Jo liked to wear my shirts as nighties. That was the last one she wore before . . .' He looked down at the ground, then at James, who nodded sympathetically. 'Before Monday. I put it on last night because it smells of her, but I got a nosebleed and . . .'

'So you're saying it's your blood?'

His eyes flashed. 'Of course I am! Why? Do you think when my nose bleeds, someone else's blood comes out?'

'No, of course not. But I would like to have it checked out by our lab, just to get everything clear.'

He folded his arms. 'And if I don't want you to take it?'

'Well, you'd be well within your rights to say that,' Kat said carefully. 'But what I would do then is sit here and call my DCI and tell her I want a search warrant. I think, given I'm investigating a murder, she'd agree. Then I'd call a magistrate. Once I had the warrant, I'd seize this shirt' – she held up the evidence bag – 'anyway.'

Ian looked at James.

'Can she do that? I thought you were here to support me?'

'He is, Ian,' Kat said, quickly, before James could answer. 'But as the case officer for Jo's murder, this is my decision. It's nothing to do with James. This is on me.'

'You can't just *get* a warrant,' he said, still resisting. 'You have to have grounds.'

Had he been preparing for just this moment? Kat had her answer ready.

'You're right. And my grounds would be that I suspect you of having carried out an assault on your wife, causing the blood spatter on this shirt,' she said, keeping her voice level, but firm. 'In fact, I could arrest you on that suspicion and then, under three different sections of PACE – that's the Police and Criminal Evidence Act – seize it quite legally. But I'm sure neither of us wants to go down that road, do we?'

Ian underwent a complete change of mood. He smiled, which Kat found disconcerting.

'It's fine. Sorry. I'm just so mixed up. Look, take it. But there's something I need to tell you.' His eyes flicked left and right; he was finding it difficult to look her in the eye. A classic tell. He was confirming her suspicions. He had a guilty conscience. And now the evidence was piling up, he was floundering. 'I didn't have a nosebleed.'

'Then how did your blood get on the shirt?'

'It's not mine,' he said with a curious little nervous grin. 'It's Jo's.'

'OK, so how did *her* blood get on one of your shirts?'

'It's a bit embarrassing.'

Kat sat down, motioning for the other two detectives to do the same. With three people performing the same action, Ian followed their lead. Once they were all seated, Kat smiled at Ian. Internally, she was . . . not rejoicing, not exactly. This was a murder they were talking about. But she felt it. The sense of a hunt coming to its end.

'Look, Ian. I know you're going through a horrible time. And the last thing I want to do is pile any more pain on you,' she said. 'But if a little embarrassment will save us all a lot of wasted effort when we're trying to catch Jo's murderer, don't you think that's a small price to pay?'

Now he did look her straight in the eye. He sighed, rubbed his hands on the tops of his thighs.

'It was on Sunday night. We'd had an early night, you know' – he dropped his voice – 'for sex?'

Kat nodded, wondering where this was going. 'And then what?'

'Afterwards, she put my shirt on, and I made a sort of joke out of grabbing her, saying something like, "Hey, that's my best shirt." I mean, it's not, but I just said it, you know? For a joke?'

Suddenly Kat saw the destination this drawn-out little tale was heading for. And she understood why Ian had been so reluctant to part with the bloody shirt.

'So, you're both, what, tussling a little bit? Like play-fighting?' she asked.

No need to worry about leading the witness; they weren't in court, yet.

Ian grabbed onto Kat's words like a drowning man reaching for a lifebuoy.

'Exactly. Play-fighting. Only she twisted away, and I lost my grip and then somehow my fist caught her in the nose.' He turned to James, who was sitting there stony-faced. 'I mean, dead centre. And she said something like, "Oh, you idiot, now look what you've gone and done. You've given me a nosebleed." I got her cleaned up and then I threw the shirt in the laundry basket. It's got nothing to do with her murder, though. I mean, you believe me, don't you? If I'd killed her, I'd hardly be so stupid as to leave it where anyone could find it, would I?'

Kat wanted to tell him that people did all sorts of stupid things after committing murder. Soon after joining MCU, she'd worked on a case where the culprit had bought the murder weapon, a claw hammer, for cash, but then used his Tesco Clubcard to collect the points. Probably just force of habit, but it had cost him his liberty.

Instead, she said, 'Thank for clarifying that, Ian. If you're happy for me to take this shirt, can you just sign a new consent form for me?'

Tom was already fishing in his briefcase. A couple of minutes later, Kat had the relevant paperwork signed and dated, permitting her to seize the bloody shirt.

What she needed now was a fast turnaround from the DNA lab. Unfortunately, that meant asking Carve-up to sign-off on her request. Would their mutual loathing really lead him to deny a course of action that could see a murderer put behind bars?

No, and she knew why. He'd been smarting ever since Ian had blindsided him at the press conference. She'd give him Ian Morris on a plate, and he'd be only too eager to help.

CHAPTER FIFTEEN

Kat went to see Carve-up in his office. He was working in his shirtsleeves. The cuffs were secured with gold links in the shape of handcuffs.

His suit jacket, the forest-green one he never failed to mention was Versace, hung on a hook on the wall behind him. Typical Carve-up, she thought. To have expensive clothes but then not to look after them properly.

He looked up and frowned. 'Yes?'

I love you too, Stu.

'It's about the Jo Morris murder. I need—'

'Yeah, I've been thinking about that. Sit down,' he said, baring his teeth. After a moment or two, Kat realised he was smiling. She sat and watched as Carve-up put down the fat Montblanc pen he was holding, aligning it north-south on his desk, and looked across at her. 'Clearly, what we're dealing with here is a stranger-murder. Remote location, no witnesses. Bizarre MO. In fact, I think you were right all along. We've got a serial on our hands.'

'Sorry, Stuart,' she said, so wrong-footed she used his given name. After all, she hadn't suggested anything of the kind. 'Why are you thinking that? You were convinced it wasn't.'

'I've been reading the file. Looking at the crime scene photos. It's obvious.' Carve-up picked up the pen again and tapped out points on the desk. *Tap* – 'Death by kiwi fruit. Weird.' *Tap* – 'Infinity symbol branded onto vic's belly. Weird.' *Tap* – 'Location, freakiest place in Middlehampton. Weird.' *Tap* – 'Vic's phone taken, clearly a trophy. Weird.' *Tap* – 'Finally, vic had no enemies. So clearly chosen because she fits some physical type. Weird.' He sat back, with a smug smile. 'You're welcome.'

She stared at him in utter disbelief. How one man could read the same file as her and come to so many bad conclusions was breathtaking.

He mistook her open-mouthed expression for one of admiration. 'I may be nothing to you but a glorified pen-pusher these days, but I do, just, remember how to interpret evidence. So what is it you need? A task force? A big press conference – get the nationals in? Operation name? Extra budget? I'll stay as SIO of course, but I'll make sure you get your full share of the credit when we catch this guy.'

And then she saw it. The reason behind Carve-up's bewildering change of opinion. Having missed out on what he no doubt saw as the glory last time round, he was going to make damn sure he was front and centre of this investigation. Probably planning which suits he'd wear for the various press conferences as the operation progressed. No doubt he'd stand in front of a full-length mirror at home, and practise introducing himself as DCI Carver.

Time to burst his little bubble. 'It's not a serial killer.'

His eyes popped wide. 'What?'

'It's not even a stranger. It's someone she knew.' She leaned forwards and fixed him with a hard stare. 'At the moment I'm looking at Ian Morris. But if it's not him it's definitely someone Jo knew. It's what I came to tell you. I found—'

'Are you crazy? How could you say that, Kat?' Now it was Carve-up's turn to revert to using a name that didn't wind the other person up. 'You saw the way he reacted in the press conference. OK, he totally got under my skin, I admit it. But I can't see a guy who's killed his wife issuing threats like that.'

She shook her head. 'Classic distraction tactic.'

'Respectfully, I have to disagree. Look, I was slow to get behind you on the Origami Killer case, but that was just my naturally cautious approach. I have to think of things above your paygrade like budgets and performance metrics. But I supported you in the end, and we caught the guy.'

Kat heaved in a breath. This was reinventing history on a grand scale. He hadn't supported her; he'd undermined her at every turn, including siccing his tame Sky reporter onto her. Never mind. Time to set him straight now. She didn't have a fancy fountain pen to use as a conductor's baton, so she counted off rebuttals to his points on her fingers.

'One, I know serial killers get their rocks off devising horrible ways to kill people. But kiwi fruit? No, it doesn't feel right.' Carve-up opened his mouth to interrupt. She didn't let him. 'And that's because, how would a stranger know Jo had a fatal allergy to the things? Two, I agree the brand is weird, but on its own it could just indicate rage at something Jo did to the killer. Plus, I'm not even sure it *is* an infinity symbol.

'Three, yes, the Three Sisters is beloved by our pagan community, but it's also remote, out of sight of CCTV, and with dozens of paths in and out, not to mention unfenced bits you can just walk through. Four, maybe the killer took the phone not as a trophy but because we'd identify all her contacts from it, including the killer. And five, nobody gets to their mid-thirties without rubbing at least one person up the wrong way. I'm looking at her past and that's where we'll find the person who murdered her.'

Carve-up studied her for a few seconds. 'I'm at a loss,' he said. 'Last time you were hot for it being a serial killer. Now we've got another one and you're telling me it's, what, a domestic?'

Finally, he'd given her the opening she wanted. 'I'm saying let's follow the evidence. On which subject, I found a bloodstained shirt in their laundry basket. Ian lied, then spun me this tale of sex-play gone wrong and him *accidentally* giving Jo a nosebleed. It could point to evidence that he's ready, willing and able to use violence. I want a 24-hour DNA screen on it.'

Carve-up looked disappointed. Like Riley had done as a little boy when she'd told him it was time to stop watching *Thomas the Tank Engine* and get ready for bed. An almost-pout.

'Well, if that's your take on it, DS Ballantyne, you're the case officer. I'll approve it. But when he does another one with the same MO and signature, you and me are going to have words.'

She left his office feeling, once again, that talking to her line manager was like talking to someone with multiple personalities. One minute sneering and scowling. Then bending over backwards to accommodate her, to the point of calling her 'Kat'. Belittling her and professing not to understand her. Before finally reverting to type and threatening her.

She knew why. It was all a game to Carve-up. If he'd ever cared about solving crime for its own sake, that was long ago. Now it was all about the *metrics*. And DI Stuart Carver's laser focus on his own career. It was a miracle he kept his suits so clean given how hard he strove to climb the greasy pole.

CHAPTER SIXTEEN

Opening her mouth wide to stop herself grinding her teeth over Carve-up's behaviour, Kat called the office of Reuben Starling, MP. The phone was answered by a young-sounding woman with a brisk but bouncy voice – a dog trainer crossed with a nursery school teacher.

Kat introduced herself and said, 'I'd like to make an appointment with Reuben Starling.'

'Reuben's in the House today, DS Ballantyne. He has a surgery tomorrow here in town, though.'

Kat envisioned a queue of people waiting to bombard their elected representative with complaints about potholes, dog waste on the streets, his avowed support for Britain's nuclear deterrent, Britain's treatment of migrants, broken traffic lights, and teenagers daubing graffiti on the railway bridges.

'That's not going to work for me. I'm investigating a murder and I need to see him urgently.'

'I could call him. Give me your number and I'll call you straight back.'

Ten minutes later, her phone rang.

'DS Ballantyne, it's Holly? From Reuben Starling's office? He says he's got an hour free this evening between 6.30 and 7.30. If you could possibly get to the House of Commons, he'll meet you in the lobby.'

It was a three-hour round trip including the meeting. She could be back in Middlehampton by 8.30 p.m. Maybe a little later depending on the traffic. She checked her calendar.

'Tell him I'll be there,' she said. 'Thanks, Holly, you've been really helpful.'

Kat had only been to the House of Commons once before. Her Politics A-level teacher had made a yearly trip with her senior classes. During her year's outing, Kat and Liv had sat at the back, along with the rest of the rebels who couldn't wait to leave school and start 'livin' it large', as Jason Franklin had boasted during the trip. They'd spent the journey singing Kylie hits and giving the thumbs-up to drivers following the coach. Or, if they didn't respond in kind, the middle finger, before collapsing into giggles.

The fun had ended the moment they'd stepped down from the coach in Parliament Square. A few of the politics nerds – Eric Clark, Philip Montgomery and their little gang – had practically wet themselves as they entered through the black iron gates under the watchful eyes of armed coppers. Everyone else slouched around, hands thrust in pockets, competing for the most bored facial expression.

Now, as she showed her warrant card to the machine-gun-toting cop on the gate, she felt things differently. Despite being here on official business, she craned her neck to stare up at Big Ben. Eric Clark's nasal voice floated down to her over the years. *Actually, Big Ben's the bell inside. The tower is called—* The rest of his pronouncement had been drowned out by jeers from Kat's own crew.

As promised, Reuben Starling was waiting for her in the ornate tiled Central Lobby of the House itself. He waved, before disappearing behind a knot of young besuited men and women, walking, almost running, through the crowded space, all yammering into their phones, messaging, or flipping papers over on clipboards. She recognised a couple of faces from the TV: a minister at the Home Office; the deputy leader of the opposition.

Kat negotiated the throng before arriving in front of Starling. He held out his hand.

'DS Ballantyne, it's a pleasure. I'm a great supporter of your work.'

'Thank you. I didn't know you took an interest.'

He grinned – a boyish smile that made him look younger than his sixty years. 'Sorry. I just lapsed straight into politico-speak. I was talking about the police in general. I'm on the Home Affairs Select Committee. Just came out of a meeting, so I'm still on autopilot. But I did follow the Origami Killer case closely, as you'd expect. You did do a fantastic job.'

'It was a team effort. I was supported by some really hard-working officers.'

'Of course. Tea? Or something stronger.'

'I'm driving. Tea would be fine.'

As she followed him through a maze of identical corridors, Kat wondered how anyone could ever become comfortable working here. Rookies often had a little trouble finding their way round Jubilee Place. But the feeling passed after about a week. She imagined she'd still be needing a trail of breadcrumbs after years working in this Victorian rabbit warren.

They emerged, finally, into a surprisingly modern cafeteria that opened out onto a terrace overlooking the Thames. Starling bought her a tea and himself a large glass of red wine. Seated at a table by the balcony, he raised the glass to his lips. In the sunlight, she saw he had a boozer's red nose and thread veins spreading their scarlet webs over his cheeks. Silver stubble glinted on his jaw.

He smiled, drawing crow's feet around his eyes. 'Cheers!'

She took a sip of the tea, which was the best she'd ever tasted. 'That's good.'

'House of Commons' own brand. So, DS Ballantyne, what can a lowly MP do for a member of Hertfordshire Constabulary?'

She wondered how best to begin. Although she'd tried out various openings during the drive down from Middlehampton, none had felt quite right. Was it odd he didn't know? Surely an MP would know what was happening in his constituency? But then, maybe there was simply too *much* to know.

She decided on the direct approach. Asking questions like a good copper. 'Have you seen the news this week? The *Echo*'s website, maybe?'

He shook his head then took another mouthful of the wine, which had already stained his lips a dark purple. Must be strong stuff.

'It's been somewhat frenetic here since Sunday. Late-night sittings. Committee work, meetings with my minister. Correspondence with constituents. Bloody lobbyists who sink their little curved teeth into you like leeches and won't let go.'

She nodded. Smiled. Best to keep him happy. But his complaining sounded like self-pity mixed with self-importance. Her elected representative was clearly a boozer, happy to swill subsidised wine on the taxpayer's pound. And the duties he'd listed? Wasn't that just the job?

Kat didn't pay much attention to politics unless they appointed a new Home Secretary. She couldn't decide who were worse. The hard-nosed bastards who wanted to arrest teenagers in hoodies on sight, or the liberals who thought rapists and child-molesters should get therapy. What she really wanted was someone who'd actually pay to recruit more coppers.

Starling was clearly winding up for a longer speech, so she cut him off. 'A young woman was murdered sometime early Monday morning. On Bowman's Common. Her name was Jo Morris,' Kat said, watching for a reaction.

A flicker of concern altered his features. Just for a moment.

'OK,' he said cautiously.

'We've been looking into her past, obviously, and we discovered that her surname was originally Starling.' She withdrew a photo from her bag and placed it on the table, between his wine glass and her white bone-china teacup. 'I wondered whether you were related?'

Starling glanced at the photo. Then back at Kat. In that moment, Kat knew he *did* know Jo Morris. Nobody took that brief a look at a picture of someone they'd just been told was dead unless they recognised them straightaway. What would he say?

His eyes bulged and a cough burst free from his clamped lips, along with a fine spray of wine that had Kat rearing back from the table. People at neighbouring tables turned to see who was dying of TB. Reassured it was only a fellow patron having trouble with his drink, they smiled and returned to their own conversation.

Wiping his eyes then lips with a cotton handkerchief he fished from a pocket, Starling apologised in a croak.

'Sorry. Went down the wrong way.'

'How did you know Jo?' Kat asked.

He sighed out a breath, then inhaled slowly until he had his breathing under control. 'Jo was my niece. One of them, anyway. My brother's daughter.'

'First of all, Reuben, I'm sorry to have to come here and bring you such bad news,' she said. She took out her notebook. 'What's your brother's name?'

'His name is . . . was Connor.' He grimaced and took a careful sip of his wine. The glass was almost empty. 'He and his wife, Tasha, died in a light plane crash ten years ago.'

'I'm so sorry,' Kat said. 'It was near Luton, wasn't it?'

'Yes, well remembered. You're a Middlehampton girl, then. Sorry, woman. Mustn't forget my progressive credentials, must I?'

She smiled. 'It's fine. My bagman's just the same.'

'Connor had his pilot's licence. They were coming back from a trip to France. Nobody knows exactly what happened. He lost control. He and Tasha were killed instantly.'

Kat gestured at his now-empty wine glass. 'Can I get you a refill?'

'It's the Merlot. Large one, please.'

The service was efficient, the queue at the bar short, and Kat returned a few minutes later to find Reuben busy on his phone. He took the glass with both hands, as if she were a priest offering communion.

'Thanks.' He took a healthy swig and set the glass down with a rattle.

'What can you tell me about Jo?' Kat asked, finishing her tea.

He dragged a hand over his stubbled cheeks. He turned from her and stared across the Thames to the stark rectangular block of St Thomas' Hospital on the far bank. He sighed. Had grief just kicked in? Or was he finding it as hard to answer as she'd found it to ask her original question? Finally, he faced her.

'I haven't seen Jo for many years,' he began, appearing to choose his words carefully, spacing them evenly as if reading from a script. 'So what she was like in adulthood, I'm not sure. Losing her parents like that must have been a real wake-up call.'

Kat leaned forwards and clasped her hands on the table. Trying to draw Reuben out by focusing all her attention on him, hoping she could make the rest of the cafe fade away.

'Wake-up call from what?' she asked.

Reuben gulped down his wine. Fixed red eyes on her.

'In truth, Kat, when I knew her,' he slurred, before draining his glass, 'my niece was a pedigree bitch.'

Kat hadn't been expecting that. However much a grieving relative had misgivings about the dead, they were usually far more reticent.

'Could you expand on that for me, Reuben?'

'Where shall I start?' He picked up the empty glass, and for a second Kat thought he was going to ask for a second refill. But he just twirled it around by the long narrow stem, looking at the small flecks of black grit in the bottom. 'Tartrates. Also called "wine diamonds" if you didn't know. Perfectly harmless. Unlike my niece.'

'What did she do?'

'In simple terms, she was a bully. But she took things to extremes. Connor told me some of it. He couldn't do anything with her, and Tasha just brushed it off. Said it was being blown out of proportion. But quite frankly, Jo was a monster.'

Kat was scouring her memory for girls talked about in those terms. Even though she and Jo had gone to different schools, she felt sure someone that fearsome would have been notorious well beyond the school gates.

'That's pretty strong language,' she said.

'It was pretty strong meat, DS Ballantyne,' he said, falling back on her formal title, perhaps feeling it was more appropriate given what he was divulging.

He had little more to impart, and after a few more minutes of small talk, he made his excuses about having to prepare for his next appointment.

On the drive back to Middlehampton up the M1, she pondered Reuben Starling's damning verdict on his niece. As the wine had loosened his tongue, he'd shed any inhibitions he might have had sober and painted a succinct but compelling picture of Jo Morris.

At school, she'd been a monstrous queen bee, supported by her mother, who had indulged her daughter, showering her with money and gifts. Complaints had been waved away as inconveniences or made to vanish by the liberal application of money from her property development business.

Kat wondered whether her own father had ever crossed paths – or swords – with Tasha Starling. It was another, personally unpleasant, line of enquiry she needed to pursue.

CHAPTER SEVENTEEN

The next day, Kat took her first coffee of the morning back to her desk, to find a package waiting for her.

Leah appeared at her shoulder. 'Courier dropped that off for you.'

Kat opened the padded envelope. It contained a letter. An honest-to-goodness letter. Cream envelope. And her name and address in handwriting. Stamped in smudgy, blood-red ink: PRIVATE & CONFIDENTIAL. *What the hell?*

'I see the 1980s are trying to get in touch,' Leah said.

Kat frowned, turning the silky envelope over in her hands. 'I know, right? Who writes letters these days?'

'Serial killers?'

Kat shook her head. 'Handwriting's too nice.'

Smiling, Leah went back to her desk.

As she slit the flap with her thumbnail, Kat experienced a sudden jolt of adrenaline. What if it *was* to do with the case? She hastily pulled on a pair of nitrile gloves before extracting the letter. The stationery matched the envelope, although the enclosure – a single folded sheet of A4 – was the cheap copier paper everybody used. She put it to one side and read the handwritten note.

Hi Kat,

Here are the results of the DNA scan you requested on the bloody shirt related to the Jo Morris murder.

Given the rather surprising conclusion in section 2, I thought I'd send this to you by courier. Wouldn't want anyone reading your emails by mistake.

I know you'll have questions, but let me assure you, the results are in no doubt. I double-checked everything personally. There's no mistake.

Best regards,

Vaughan Brown (NDNAD)

'"Curiouser and curiouser," said Alice,' Kat muttered as she laid the letter aside and unfolded the report.

Why would the National DNA Database lab write to her personally? And what was so 'surprising' about the results that they felt the need to send them without any possibility of someone else seeing them? A move that had cost valuable hours.

Too excited to read patiently, she scanned the page, picking up section 1's conclusion: the blood on the shirt belonged to Jo Morris. That was good. Then she took in the heading of the second section.

Other matches

She read on. The DNA from the sample matched one other record in the National DNA Database. Not completely: by 25 per cent.

Jo Morris had a half-sibling. And that half-sibling had a name. Kathryn Ballantyne.

A wave of heat rolled up from the front of Kat's shirt. Sweat broke out all over her neck and face. She felt light-headed and was aware that she was breathing very fast. She scrubbed a fist over her forehead and stared down at the piece of paper quivering in her grip.

There had to be some mistake. A mix-up. She'd submitted a reference sample from a case and somehow it had been swapped with Jo's. But then the two samples would be 100 per cent identical, not 25 per cent. And the DNA from the bloodstain wouldn't match. Or it was a different Kathryn Ballantyne.

Pulse racing, she read on. A note confirmed that the sample was her own. It had been submitted as part of the protocol for all serving police officers in case their DNA should contaminate a crime scene.

The paper fluttered in her fingers. She squeezed her eyes shut and rubbed at her right temple, where her pulse felt as though it might burst through the thin bone. Tried to steady herself with some deep breaths. But it just made things worse. Nausea rose in her throat, and she swallowed hard to prevent herself throwing up. Shaking, she got to her feet and rushed from the room, making for the Ladies.

She burst through the door and locked herself into the first empty cubicle. Let her head drop between her knees and hang down until, little by little, the feelings of shock and panic ebbed away. She raised her head and waited for the little white sparks to stop worming around the edge of her vision.

Someone came in as the groan issuing from her throat died away.

'Kat?' It was Leah. She sounded worried. 'Are you all right?'

Kat unlocked the cubicle door and joined Leah by the sinks. She opened her mouth to speak. Normally, she didn't mind sharing with Leah. They went back a long way and had never kept secrets.

When Leah's previous boyfriend had cheated on her, it had been Kat who'd comforted her over a couple of bottles of Pinot Grigio.

The trouble was, she couldn't think how to explain that something impossible had just happened. Should she just show Leah the report? Her arm extended towards the frowning DC. Seized with a sudden panic, Kat stopped it. How could she tell anyone at work she was related to Jo? She'd be off the case that instant. Talk about a conflict of interest!

'I'm fine. Must've eaten something that disagreed with me.'

Ignoring Leah's frankly sceptical expression, Kat splashed cold water onto her face, then went to find Tom.

How could her dad have had another family? Why had she never suspected? What kind of a detective was she? First Liv, now this.

She shook her head. This new information would see her summarily removed from the case. No way could she allow that to happen. She opened a door in her mind and shoved the information about her and Jo inside. Slammed and bolted it shut.

The discovery of her complicated family had at least yielded a prime suspect in the murder of her newly discovered half-sister. DNA evidence linked Ian Morris to an assault on his wife. Enough for an arrest.

CHAPTER EIGHTEEN

Despite Kat's misgivings about Ian's likely reaction, not to mention his size, he'd shown no resistance, physical or verbal, when she'd arrested him at just after 10.00 a.m.

If anything, his reaction had been one of bemusement. It was the first time she'd really wondered whether she had the right man in custody. But a bloodstained shirt was a bloodstained shirt. Not arresting him wasn't an option, especially with his mother and the PCC scrutinising her every move.

After being booked in at 10.30 a.m., he'd asked for a duty solicitor and Kat had an hour before one would be available.

She left MCU and headed for a nearby patch of grass. Calling it a park would have been a stretch, even for Middlehampton's image-conscious council. But it had a few benches and, at this time of day, was empty apart from a clutch of scruffy-looking urban pigeons.

It was the first spare moment she'd had since learning about her and Jo's blood tie.

Who the hell could she talk to? Van? In easier times he'd have been the obvious choice. But the whole business with Marnie felt unresolved. Would he be as supportive as she needed him to be while she kept niggling at him for proof of his fidelity?

Jess? Maybe. But Kat wanted, needed, to keep this in the family for now. Which led to the man at the centre of this mess: her dad.

But confronting him about Jo would give him the one thing he valued above all else in his relationships. Power. He could take the information straight to Carver – a big favour to a man he knew hated his daughter. And that would be Kat off the case. Oh, she'd talk to him at some point. She just needed to find a way to neutralise the threat. He'd kept it a secret this long, so maybe – *maybe* – he wanted it to stay that way. It was a huge gamble, but she couldn't see she had any other choice.

A pigeon hopped close to her foot, one of its own disfigured by disease or injury, twisted into a scaly pink fist. She shooed it away then let her head fall back. If she didn't talk to somebody, she'd burst. But it had to be kept a secret.

Her head snapped forwards. Who was so good at keeping secrets, she'd even kept the one that she was alive?

Liv answered on the first ring. 'Kat! How are you? Working another big case, I see. I watched your press conference.' Her voice bubbled with enthusiasm.

'I'm good. Listen, I haven't got long. Are you doing anything tomorrow?'

'What? Er, no. I mean, chores, the usual. Why? Are you coming over again? That's great! I can take you into town. We can get a drink. Oh, there's this great new Chinese restaurant that's just opened. We could—'

'Sorry, Liv, I just don't have time, what with the case. I was hoping you could get over to Middlehampton. There's something I want to talk to you about.'

'Ooh, mysterious. But yeah, of course. Mid-morning? Eleven?'

'Perfect.'

'Cool. I'll see you then. Love ya.'

'Love you, too.'

◆ ◆ ◆

The tape recorder finished its tooth-loosening screech. Kat looked across the table at Ian. He sat forward. Not tense, not exactly. Watchful, she decided. Alert. A charitable interpretation would be 'eager to help'. Next to him, one of the duty solicitors. A young woman Kat had met before, with whom she'd, if not exactly hit it off, at least exchanged looks of mutual respect.

Tom sat back, keeping still, as Kat had asked him to.

'Ian. We've had confirmation that the blood on your shirt was Jo's. Can you explain how it got there?'

'I already told you.'

'Yes. But you are now being interviewed under caution.' She nodded at the tape recorder.

'Well, like I said to you before, me and Jo were play-fighting and I caught her across the nose with my hand. It started a nose-bleed. Which I helped clean up.'

Kat nodded. Consulted her notebook. 'You caught her across the nose with your *hand*.'

'Yes! I just said that, didn't I?'

The solicitor leaned forward. 'My client has already answered that question, DS Ballantyne.'

Ignoring her, Kat looked at her notebook then back at Ian. 'At your house, when I asked you, you said, "somehow my fist caught her in the nose".' She waited for a count of three. 'Which was it, Ian. A fist, or a hand?'

'Look, it was an accident, all right? Yes, it was my fist.'

'OK, glad we've cleared that up. So, you punched your wife in the face hard enough to cause a nosebleed. Did that happen often?'

'No!' He reared back. 'I know what you're trying to do here. But I swear to you, I never hurt her. It wasn't me. You should be out there' – he jabbed a thick finger at the wall – 'catching whoever actually killed her.'

'And we are investigating every line of enquiry, trust me. How's business?'

Back to that conversational tone again, as if they were mates meeting in the pub for a catch-up.

He blinked. 'Business?'

'Yes. Your furniture importation business. Italy, isn't it? Luxury leather recliners, that type of thing?'

'I haven't really been thinking about it. Bit too much going on – in case you'd forgotten.'

'Is it profitable?'

'It's early days.'

That was interesting. He'd switched back to giving short answers. No attempt to weave a narrative.

'So, not profitable then?'

'I'm at the investment stage. Building the brand.'

'And you have the money to do that?'

'I manage.'

'Ever ask Jo to help out? Lend you some cash to pay for advertising?'

He scowled. *There!* He knew she knew. Not necessarily how. But he was back on the hook.

'No comment.'

'I see. How would you react, Ian, if I told you that I'd spoken to someone who informed me that Jo had told *them* she'd turned you down for a loan?'

He ground his jaws together, so the muscles at the back of his cheeks bulged.

'No comment.'

She closed the folder and suspended the interview.

◆ ◆ ◆

With no need of a search warrant now Ian was under arrest, Kat went back to the house in Hampton Hill.

She entered the kitchen. On her previous visits, she hadn't noticed any kiwi fruit. None in the fruit bowl, no bulging net bag on a counter.

She shuddered at the thought. Why anyone would even want to eat them was beyond her. Horrible, hairy little things. They reminded her of the most unlovely part of a man's anatomy.

Assuming Ian had disposed of any evidence that he'd used kiwi fruit, she started opening cupboard doors looking for the waste bin. Or, judging by the gleaming surfaces and modern style of the units, the separate compost bin. She found it just to the right of the sink. Two plastic bins, one behind the other. Black, lined with a white bag, for general waste at the front. Blue, unlined, at the back, full to overflowing with vegetable matter and fruit skins.

She lifted the front bin out then pulled the compost bin clear of the shiny steel frame. A dozen or so small, black fruit flies rose from its multicoloured contents and flew silently around Kat's face.

'Get off me!' she said, swatting ineffectually at the slow-moving creatures, before plonking the bin on the floor.

There was nowhere in the kitchen where she could examine the bin's contents. She found the back door key on the ring she'd borrowed from the custody suite and took the bin into the garden. The small suburban plot was mostly laid to lawn, with a narrow flowerbed down each side. At the far end stood a small shed, still with the vibrant burnt-orange stain it must have come with. They had a compost bin, stood to reason they'd have a compost heap, too. Or maybe a green-lidded wheelie bin from the council.

Kat carried the overflowing bin down to the end of the garden, wrinkling her nose at the sweetish smell of rotting fruit that enveloped her.

Behind the shed was a small heap of organic waste including eggshells, apple cores, yellow melon rinds emitting the sharp pear-drop stink of acetone, blackish-brown avocado shells and what looked like fresh hedge-clippings. She upended the bin onto the beaten-flat earth at its front edge and kicked the debris apart with the toe of her boot. A slimy brown banana skin stuck to her instep, and she sent it flying onto the heap with a deft flick of her foot.

Squatting, she scanned the mess of vegetable waste for that tell-tale skin. Brown and bristly on the outside, a vivid green within. But there was nothing. Maybe he'd been a little smarter, then. She looked around for something she could use to poke through the heap itself. Found what she needed in the shed: a long-handled rake.

She dragged the prongs through the compost, working back and forth until she'd reduced the heap to a wide patch of half-rotted organic matter spread over a square metre or so. 'Come on,' she muttered, as she hooked at the reeking slurry of skins, peels, seeds and leaf fragments, 'where did he put you?' She knew she'd fallen into a trap. Wanting evidence to be where she needed it to be to justify her theory. What if it wasn't? Did that exonerate Ian? No. Not at all. But it would set her investigation back.

Her eye caught on a flash of green. That was it! No. It was the wrong shade. Then she looked again. Stepped closer, and then, heedless of the muck now squelching up around her feet, leaned right down until her nose filled with the sweetish stench of rot and fermentation.

She poked her finger into a clod of brownish-green muck and pulled the topmost piece of . . . whatever it was . . . aside. And there it was. A brown, hairy egg cup, its innards scooped out but

121

leaving a few traces of that distinctive jade-green pulp and a few tiny black seeds.

This was what she'd been waiting for. A break in the case. Smiling grimly to herself, she took an evidence bag from her pocket, reversed it like she would a poo bag for Smokey, then clawed her fingers around the kiwi-fruit cup and sealed it inside.

Ian Morris had some more explaining to do.

CHAPTER NINETEEN

Kat smiled across the table at Ian. The room was so quiet she could hear Tom breathing beside her.

'I found kiwi fruit in your compost heap, Ian,' she said conversationally. 'Pushed right down at the bottom. I'm not really much of a gardener myself' – a smile – 'my husband does most of it. But by the state of it, I'd say it must have been there a while. Maybe a week. Can you tell me what it was doing there?'

Ian swallowed audibly. 'I know what it looks like. I'm not stupid.'

She clasped her hands softly in front of her. 'What does it look like, Ian?'

'Like I must've put some in her food or whatever. You know, to . . .' He gulped audibly.

'To what?'

'To kill her,' he whispered.

'And did you?' she asked, easily, as if she'd merely enquired whether he'd erected the garden shed himself.

'No! Of course I didn't! I loved her. I told you that.'

'How did it get there?' she asked. 'The kiwi fruit in your compost heap, I mean?'

His shoulders dropped. Resignation. She'd seen this before. That moment in an interview when it all became too much. When the subject had too many balls up in the air, and one fell to the ground and pretty soon there were blood-red rubber spheres bouncing here, there and everywhere.

'I put it there, but it's not what it looks like.'

'Yes, you said that before. And then you said it looks like you killed Jo.'

'I buy them sometimes. They're packed with antioxidants. They're a proper superfood.'

For the first time, Kat lost her cool. 'And your wife had a fatal allergy to them! Could you not have got antioxidants from somewhere else?'

He shrugged. 'I just love them. I know it sounds stupid, but it almost stopped me asking Jo to marry me. When I found out, I mean. I didn't know if I could live my life without ever eating another one. I used to eat at least three every day.'

'Well, frankly, Ian, yes, that does sound strange. Why couldn't you have them when you ate out? Or just buy some from the market and eat them on the spot? Why did you have one in the house, when you knew it could have triggered anaphylactic shock in your wife?'

He sighed out a breath and held his hands up, making a T with two index fingers. 'Time out. I need to tell you what happened, so please can you just let me talk without interrupting?'

The solicitor was writing copious notes as her client spoke, presumably on the point of confessing.

'Of course. Take your time, Ian,' Kat said. 'I'm not going anywhere.' *And neither are you if you admit to killing your wife.*

'First off? I only bought it on Monday afternoon. After she was dead. And I couldn't do any of those things you just said, because Jo's allergy was so severe, if she'd even kissed me after I'd eaten a kiwi, it would've triggered an attack.'

Kat shook her head. She wasn't sure whether it was because she didn't believe his cockeyed story or because she did. Time to test it a little further.

'Let me get this straight, Ian, because I have to say, I am finding all of this really hard to wrap my head around. Literally on the day your wife is found murdered, with kiwi fruit the likely murder weapon, your first thought is, "Oh, well, now she's dead, at last I can go up the Co-op and buy myself a kiwi"?'

Tears were forming in the corners of Ian's eyes. He brushed them away with a surprisingly delicate motion of the tips of the fingers so recently demanding time to get his story straight.

'I was in shock. I can barely remember what I did that day. But you can check, can't you? The Co-op will have CCTV, won't they? I paid with my phone. There'll be a record, won't there?'

It was a good point. Beside her, Tom made a note. For the first time since the interview had begun with a nails-down-a-blackboard screech from the tape recorder, she felt she was hearing the truth. Except . . .

'Why did you bury the skin so deep, Ian? Why not just leave it in the bin, or chuck it on top of the compost heap?'

He sniffed and wiped more tears away. 'Why do you think? Because it would look bad, wouldn't it?'

'Me finding the murder weapon hidden on your property? Yes, it would look bad.'

'But I didn't kill her! I swear.'

Kat forbore from telling him that if she had a pound for every time a villain who was later convicted had sworn to her they hadn't done it, she'd be a rich woman.

Wanting to do more digging – of the figurative type this time – she ended the interview. The PACE clock hadn't run down yet, so Ian was heading back to the cells.

CHAPTER TWENTY

At 9.00 a.m. on Saturday, Kat drove into the station. The PACE clock had run down on Ian Morris's twenty-four hours of detention without charge, and she had no option but to release him. Under investigation, but still.

On the off chance he'd woken up in a good mood, she called Carve-up and asked him to authorise another period of detention.

'You got anything concrete to hold him on, DS Ballantyne?'

'No, but if—'

'Yeah, that's what I thought. Request denied.' Then he shouted, clearly at someone else, 'I'm coming. It's just a work call. Nothing important.' His voice lowered again; he addressed Kat. 'Sorry about that. I'm on the golf course. Enjoy your weekend, *Kitty-Kat*.'

Back home, she made a coffee then went back to working on her laptop. Sometime later, the doorbell rang. Sighing, Kat got to her feet. Another Amazon delivery for Van? Or Riley? She couldn't ask them. Riley's team were playing away to a Watford team, so she was alone in the house.

Smokey raised his head off his forepaws and gave her a droopy-eyed look of enquiry. *Trouble, boss?*

'It's fine, Smokes,' she said. She held her palm out towards him. 'Stay.'

Reassured, he settled back down to his snooze, grunting as he rearranged his squat little body. She checked her watch: 11.05 a.m. Of course. Liv. She hurried to the door. The blurry figure on the other side of the glass waved. Mostly they just texted, plus the occasional call. But Kat had been over to the farm once, and Liv had made a flying visit to Middlehampton.

'Hi, Kat,' Liv said, enveloping Kat in a hug and a cloud of patchouli.

Her hair, blonde and cropped when she'd reappeared in Kat's life the previous September, had grown out now, back to her original dark brown.

Kat's butterflies were in full flight. She had no idea how Liv would react to her news. Part of her worried she'd go storming over to Kat's parents' house to have it out with Colin.

'Coffee?' she asked, forcing herself to smile.

'I'd love one. I've been on the road since six. The M4 was murder.' She grinned again. 'Oops! Poor choice of words.'

Smokey roused himself and trotted over to Liv to give her ankles a sniff.

She bent to scratch behind his ears. 'Hey, Smokey. How are you doing, little guy? I do love your funny little winky eye.'

Kat gave herself time to think by filling the kettle and going through the rituals of spooning coffee into mugs and fetching milk from the fridge. Heart beating far too fast, and not really needing caffeine to push it into even higher gear, she handed a mug to Liv and gestured for her to sit at the table. Kat joined her, clapping the lid of the laptop shut.

Liv sipped her coffee. 'So, what's this big mysterious secret you can't talk about over the phone?'

Kat felt tears pricking the corners of her eyes. Her throat felt thick, as if the words might stick there. 'I . . . The woman whose murder I'm investigating . . . she . . .' Kat inhaled sharply. 'I found out she was my half-sister.'

Liv frowned. 'I thought Diana was your *full* sister? Anyway, wasn't the dead woman's name Jo something?'

'It is. Was. We did a DNA test. That's what I'm trying to tell you. Jo was my half-sister.'

Liv reached across the table and took Kat's hands in hers. Squeezed. 'Oh my God, Kat. That's so awful. To find out you had another sister and to lose her all at the same time. How are you even coping?'

Kat laughed, a cracked sound that set a couple of wine glasses ringing on the dresser. 'Coping? Er, not very well, actually.'

'What did Van say?'

'I haven't told him yet.'

'Why? I thought you two were total soulmates.'

Kat sniffed. Feeling the tears coming and letting them. Liv scurried round the table and knelt beside her. Enfolded her in her arms.

'Hey,' she murmured into the side of Kat's neck. 'It's OK, whatever it is. Going through a rough patch, are you? I'm here for you. Always and for ever, remember?'

It was their catchphrase. A line lifted from *Thelma and Louise*, the film they'd watched so many times as teenagers they knew every line off by heart.

Kat sniffed back tears and snot. 'I think – thought – Van was interested in this woman he's working for. It's all right now, I think. But you know, I'm—'

'—not sure you want to load this onto him as well. I get it, Kat, I really do. Look,' she said, leaning back and smiling, 'why don't you tell me more about Jo?'

Kat dried her eyes and, chest heaving with the aftershocks of her crying, told Liv as much as she could about her dead half-sister.

'Have you spoken to your dad?' Liv asked, when the story ended at the trio of standing stones on Bowman's Common.

Kat shook her head. 'He's mates with my boss. I can't risk it getting back to him. He'd boot me off the case.'

Liv nodded. Scrubbed fingertips through her hair. 'Yeah, but you have to.' Her eyebrows drew together. 'So, good old Colin's got leverage over you 'cause he's friends with, whatsisname, Carver? Right. Well, all you need is leverage back.'

'Yes, but how?'

Liv crossed her eyes. 'Er, hello? Your mum? I bet she doesn't know, right?'

'I'm pretty sure my dad would have kept this a secret.' She saw it, then. Such a simple plan. 'I tell him if it reaches Carve-up, it reaches Mum the same day.'

Liv's eyes were crinkled with a broad grin. 'Bingo!'

They hashed out a few more details, and by the end Kat felt more relaxed than she had since discovering her connection to Jo. As soon as she had some time, she'd go and have it out with her dad.

Liv pointed at Kat's laptop. 'Is that the Three Sisters case?'

'Yeah. You said you read the *Echo* online?'

Liv smiled. 'I do, but I've got an even better source. It's this podcast – *Home Counties Homicide*. You'll never guess who runs it. It's—'

'—Mutt-Calf!'

They said it in unison, then both laughed. They'd been at school with Ethan Metcalfe. Already widely regarded as a 'right creep', he'd tell anyone who'd listen that he was going to marry Kat one day. After the second time he'd repeated his weird claim, Liv had bestowed the moniker 'Mutt-calf' on him – *because of how he's always slobbering after you.*

Smokey had wandered over and was standing by Liv's ankle. She reached down to scratch him behind the ear.

'Hey! We should go for a walk. Take Smokey.'

Kat was about to refuse, citing work, but then changed her mind. She found she did want to spend time with Liv, and maybe a walk out to the farm would kill two birds with one stone. Give them time to catch up, and keep Liv out of the centre of town where it would be Sod's law they'd run into Carve-up.

It turned out that Sod's writ ran, like that of the Common Law, into the countryside as well as the town. As they walked into The Gallops, Smokey was joined by his own best friend, Lois. The two dogs ran off through the crops, barking joyously and setting thirty or more rooks rasping into the air from a stand of beeches.

They'd be meeting a copper after all. Barrie was approaching from the other end of the field, coming out of the sunlight so his baby-fine white hair glowed like a dandelion clock.

Kat's mind raced as she worked out all the possible implications of him meeting Liv. In the end, the multiplying scenarios defeated her, and she just had to wait to see how things played out.

'Hi, Barrie,' she said, forcing a smile as he joined them.

'Skip. Lovely day for it.' He turned to Liv. 'Hello.'

'This is my friend,' Kat said, hesitating. 'Louise. She lives in Wales.'

He turned to Liv, proffering a crumpled white paper bag. 'Liquorice Allsort, Louise?'

Liv placed a hand on her chest and batted her eyelashes at Barrie. 'Oh my God! These are literally my favourites. You're not single, are you?'

'I'm happily married,' he said, his eyes dancing with good humour. 'But if the old girl kicks me out some day for insufficient attention to the dishwasher, maybe you could give me your number.'

'Maybe if you'll save me the coconut ones, I will,' she said, plucking out a pink and black cylinder.

Surprised to find herself jealous of Liv's flirting with Barrie, Kat leaned forwards and peered into the bag of multicoloured sweets. Leaving the brown ones she couldn't bear, she picked out a blue aniseed jelly.

'Whereabouts in Wales do you come from, Louise?' Barrie asked.

'Little village called Summerleaze near Cardiff, but I'm actually from here.'

He smiled. 'Thought you didn't sound like a sheep-shagger.'

Liv widened her eyes in mock outrage. 'Racist against the Welsh!'

She laughed. A raspy sound that reminded Kat of the rooks Smokey and Lois had just disturbed. And of Marnie's husky voice.

'What took you from Middlehampton to Wales?' Barrie asked. 'Did our fair town lose its lustre?'

Barrie had an ex-cop's unerring ability to ask exactly the right question. Kat held her breath. What would Liv say now? But maybe Liv was a little more street-smart than Kat gave her credit for.

'A friend of mine runs this little hippie commune on a farm out there,' she said, sliding Kat a conspiratorial look. 'He invited me, and I said yes. Simple as that.'

Kat felt the tension leave her. 'We're kind of on a mission, Barrie,' she said. 'Visiting a few old haunts. We'll push on if that's OK?'

'Of course! Me and Lois have a date with the duck pond.'

He bowed to Liv, adding a saucy wink for good measure. 'My lady.'

After he'd gone, Liv turned to Kat. 'You didn't have to use a fake name. Though I liked your choice. Did you really think I was going to blab about what happened back then? I'm not an idiot, Kat. It's Liv here, yes? Sharpest mouth and lightest fingers at Queen Anne's, remember?'

'Sorry, lovely. I'm still trying to process the fact you're alive, I guess. But it's best we don't use your real name here. Especially around ex-cops with inquiring minds, like Barrie. As far as everyone in Middlehampton knows, you're dead, *remember*?'

Liv threw her arms around Kat again, squeezing hard. 'It's me who should be apologising,' she said fiercely into Kat's hair. 'I did a terrible thing to you.'

Kat squeezed back. Maybe they could make it work, after all. Liv had really changed the way she looked, putting on a few kilos in the intervening years. Gone was that spiky, sharp-elbowed teenager with flashing eyes full of pent-up resentment and aggression. In her place, a softer version who looked more comfortable in her skin than a lot of the women Kat saw on a daily basis.

'Let's forget that,' Kat said, releasing herself from Liv's embrace. 'Ancient history.'

'So, tell me about the case instead?'

'I can't say much more than you already know, and . . .' She stopped walking and turned to Liv, seeing a way to get a little closer to the victim. 'You used to hang around with some kids from Middlehampton College, didn't you?'

'Sometimes. A couple of the other girls at Shirley House went there.'

'Jo's maiden name was Starling. Did you ever come across her? She was—'

'—literally this massive evil bitch.' Liv's cheeks had turned blotchy and pink. 'I'm sorry to say that, what with her being your half-sister, but, Kat, she really was. I mean, one of my mates from the home – Keisha, her name was – she was mixed-race, OK? She told me Starling and her psycho mates tied her up and said they were going to lynch her.'

Liv had just confirmed what Reuben Starling had told Kat.

'Do you remember the others' names?'

'God, it's been so long. I need to think.' Liv stared up at a couple of the rooks still wheeling overhead. 'Yes! Keisha said Starling's sort of second-in-command was called Elise something.'

'Did she say what her surname was?'

Liv shook her head. 'Sorry, no. Is that no good, then?'

'No, it's great. Thanks.'

A sly expression stole over Liv's features. 'Is someone taking revenge on them, then? God, I hope so.'

Kat pulled her head back. 'Really? You're pleased?'

'Oh. Well, I mean, obviously not *literally* pleased. But, you know . . .' She waggled her head. 'I mean, they do kind of deserve it.'

Kat frowned. The delicate thread connecting them that had been thickening as they spoke felt suddenly in danger of snapping.

'They really don't, Liv. Nobody does.'

Liv scratched her forehead. 'No, you're right. Obviously, it's terrible.'

Kat's emotions churned. She'd spent half her life grieving for a dead friend who'd turned out to be alive. Now she had a half-sister she'd known nothing about, who really was dead before Kat could even say, 'Hi, sis.'

◆ ◆ ◆

After the walk, Kat apologised but told Liv she had to work. In truth, she'd enjoyed seeing Liv again. She could even see a way to re-establishing their friendship on an adult footing.

'That's OK. I thought I'd look up a couple of the girls from Shirley House while I was over,' Liv said with a shrug and a smile. 'One lives in Hemel Hempstead now. Married with a kid and a nice little house.' She grinned wickedly. 'Don't worry. I won't go and introduce myself at the police station.' She put on a posh voice that reminded Kat a little of Tom. 'Yah. Hi. I, like, actually faked my own death to escape a serial killer? And I pointed the finger at, like, this totally innocent guy? But we're cool, yah?'

Kat sniggered nervously. It was going to be all right.

Keep telling yourself that.

CHAPTER TWENTY-ONE

Just before 9.00 a.m. on Monday, Jack forwarded Jo Morris's toxicology screen report to Kat. One line in his short covering email stood out.

Check out the third para. Happy to discuss over a coffee if that would help?

Kat frowned. Was Jack's offer of a coffee innocent? Colleagues working on homicide investigations could reasonably be expected to meet informally to share ideas. Or was he the sort of man who took 'no' as a challenge? Not that it mattered. She wasn't interested in Jack Beale and his arrogant self-belief.

But, from a place inside herself less perfect than she'd care to admit, another thought sidled up and whispered in her ear. *It's only a coffee. And look at Van. If he's working late at Marnie-the-sexpot's house, and it's as innocent as a kid's playdate, surely you can have an Americano with a good-looking pathologist?*

She tapped out a quick response, her stomach fluttering. Irritation? Or excitement? She didn't know, and that bothered her.

Thanks, Jack. Good thinking. Let me read it then I'll call you.

The toxicology report ran to a single page. Jo had traces of alcohol in her system equivalent to a glass of wine consumed within the previous twenty-four hours. She was negative for all prescription drugs and also for oral contraceptives.

The headline news was contained in paragraph three, as Jack had said. Jo's bloodstream was loaded with enough epinephrine – aka adrenaline – to get a dead horse over the finish line at Middlehampton Racecourse. No surprises there. That was what the EpiPen was for, after all. But what had Kat's pulse ticking up and her eyes skittering over the sentences was a single line, reading:

Significant concentrations of 1P-LSD.

In a footnote, the report's author explained that the drug was a fully synthetic form of the commonly available Class A drug. Kat squeezed her eyes closed and tugged on both earlobes – a habit she had when she was thinking – as she tried to make sense of it all. What the hell?

Had Jo been using LSD? It seemed highly unlikely. Especially on a work day. People took all kinds of drugs at the weekend, and even apparently clean and sober people might test positive for weed, coke or ecstasy on a Monday morning. But she was a personal trainer and, to judge from her blog posts, a true believer in the old line 'my body is a temple'.

So had her killer administered it? Was it to disorientate her before causing a brain haemorrhage with the EpiPen?

She called Jack. He picked up immediately, almost as if he'd been waiting, phone in hand, for her call.

'Interesting, isn't it?' was his opening comment. His second: 'Coffee? I'm really pushed his morning, but there's a charmingly terrible cafe on the ground floor here.'

God, the man was arrogant. His busy job meant they should meet at MGH. No thought that a homicide detective's work might also mean a meet near work would be convenient.

'Let's meet in town. Do you know the new place on North Street? Hatî?'

'*Herî baş li* Middlehampton!'

What had he just said? She asked him to repeat it.

'It's Kurdish. It means best in Middlehampton,' Jack said, the smile evident in his voice. 'John and Zerya are friends of mine.'

He knew the owners *and* he spoke Kurdish. Of course he did.

'Great. See you there in about' – she checked the time – 'fifteen minutes. If you're not too pushed.'

'No probs. I can just shuffle a couple of things around. My clients tend to be quite patient people.'

Was it a joke for her benefit? Or was he being sarcastic? She cursed herself again for not being able to read him. What she needed was a poster like those in the shift office. Mugshots and brief notes on Middlehampton's known villains: 'nominals' in officialese. 'Frequent flyers' in unofficialese. Jack's would read:

Jack 'The Knife' Beale.

MO: cuts up dead people; flirts with married detectives.

Distinguishing marks: gorgeous arms.

Notes: arrogant, annoying, sexy-as-hell.

Frowning, Kat went back to pulling on her earlobes.

◆ ◆ ◆

Kat was pleased to see she'd beaten Jack to the cafe. It meant she could order a coffee without having to engage in a little pantomime about who paid. She had a feeling he was the sort of man who'd profess his feminist views while simultaneously insisting on paying.

She ordered an Americano and took it to a table. Sat with her back to North Street but facing the door. Jack arrived a few minutes later, flashed a smile at her and joined the queue.

Once he was seated opposite her, he dipped his croissant into his cappuccino and took a huge bite – another man, like Tom, who didn't need to worry about what he ate.

'Jo Morris's killer gave her LSD, then injected her with epinephrine in her femoral vein, causing a brain haemorrhage,' she said, giving Jack a chance to finish his mouthful.

He nodded, swallowing the coffee. 'God, that's good. Yes, that's what it looks like to me. The LSD is like strapping a turbocharger onto the epinephrine. It turned the risk of death from intravenous injection into a racing certainty.'

He had a smear of chocolatey milk foam on his top lip. Without thinking, she reached over and brushed it away. It was what she'd have done with Riley, or Van for that matter. But as she pulled her hand back, she was horrified. It was far too intimate a gesture.

He carried on. If he'd noticed her blush, he wasn't saying anything.

'I did some reading. It's vanishingly rare as an accidental combination. I only found one reference in the literature.' Jack took another sip of his coffee, more carefully this time. 'This poor kid at a festival took 1P-LSD. He used his EpiPen after eating a veggie curry with peanuts in it. Death was instantaneous.'

'Same cause? An intra— sorry, how do you pronounce it?'

'Rhymes with Karen-Thymol. And yes. An intraparenchymal haemorrhage. Exactly like Jo Morris.'

Kat sipped her own coffee. She was glad it was black and therefore carried no risk of a milk moustache – and a reciprocated gesture from Jack the Knife.

'How would anyone know to do that?' she asked. 'It's hardly a run-of-the-mill MO.'

'That's more your department than mine. But it's specialist knowledge. I did run a few trial searches, though,' he said, wolfing down another bite of the croissant, showering buttery flakes on the table, which he swept onto the floor. 'Just to see. You can't get anywhere near it by googling "what combined with epinephrine causes brain haemorrhage".'

'So our killer already knew that LSD would ramp up the effects of the EpiPen to fatal levels?'

'I assume so, yes.'

Kat finished her coffee. 'I have to go, Jack. Need to see a man about a tab.'

He rose from his chair. 'It was nice to see you without a dead body playing gooseberry,' he said, then he frowned and seemed to be struggling to find the words he needed. 'Listen, tell me if I'm imagining things, but you seemed a bit, I don't know, pissed off with me at the crime scene last Monday. I hope I didn't do something to offend you.'

'No, nothing. Well' – she put her finger to the tip of her chin – 'not unless you mean putting Tom down like he was one of your students.'

'Did I?' He looked up for a second. 'Oh. Calling him a Bambi. It was that, wasn't it?'

He looked genuinely sorry, and she was tempted to brush it aside. But Tom was her bagman and deserved her loyalty.

'Yes, it was that, Jack,' she said. 'I know it gets slung around at Jubilee Place, but it's a cop thing. We do it affectionately.' She thought of Carve-up and some of his canteen buddies. 'OK, most of us do. But it was pretty snarky, what you said.'

'Right. I'll apologise next time I see him. I honestly didn't mean it, Kat. I'm mortified.'

Kat gave him a hard stare. Looking for a tell. A flicker of an eyelid that would suggest he was still playing games. No. He did, genuinely, look upset. She awarded him a small tick on the credit side of the ledger.

Maybe there was hope for him yet.

After walking briskly back to Jubilee Place, struggling to fit Jack Beale into a conveniently labelled compartment in her brain, Kat found Tom at his desk, head in hands, a half-drunk mug of cold coffee at his elbow.

'How's your research going?' she asked him.

The look he bestowed on her was eloquent. A long, bored stare. Eyes red from peering too long at a monitor without blinking.

'That good, eh? Get your jacket, we're going to the pub. Time for some proper police work.'

Smiling to herself, she spun round, leaving Tom to hurry in her wake.

CHAPTER TWENTY-TWO

Kat glanced up at the text above the Hope and Anchor's forbidding front door, thick with many coats of gloss black paint and armoured at its foot with a dented steel plate.

FRANK AND SUE STRUTT, Licensed to Sell all Intoxicating

Liquor for Consumption on or off These Premises

The pub also served as an *unlicensed* clearing house for all kinds of other intoxicating substances, and much more besides. She pushed through, Tom at her heels, into the dim interior of the Hope's public bar.

Kat liked pubs. When she and Van got the chance, they'd head into town for a quiet pint and a glass of something cold down by the river or on the 'golden mile' on a buzzy Saturday night. And there was plenty of choice for those who worked or lived in Middlehampton. Chic wine bars. Gastropubs. And 'family-friendly' establishments, where the kids could run riot in the soft play area while their parents enjoyed a drink.

Rumour had it a punter *had* once ordered a glass of wine in the Hope. In 1999, so the story went. Said punter's fellow patrons had bestowed on him an evil eye so ferocious he'd left without taking a sip. Probably just as well. The bottle was alleged to have sat, unopened, in a warm cupboard for ten years before that.

As for the food: certainly, you could eat. Crisps, peanuts, pork scratchings. Grey-green gherkins swimming in cloudy vinegar. A jar of monstrous pickled eggs like milky eyeballs. All were firmly, and permanently, on the menu.

And, yes, the Hope was definitely family-friendly. In fact, it was owned by a member of one of Middlehampton's friendliest families. If by 'friendly' you meant willing, for a price, to supply your heart's desire from a wide and occasionally changing menu of illegally grown, manufactured or acquired merchandise.

Drugs, mobile phones, DVD players, tablets, laptops, upmarket cars no bank manager in her right mind would lend you the money for, compliant migrant labour easily cowed into working for slave wages: if you needed it, the Strutts could provide it. Their criminal activities made her dad's dodgy property dealings look like a kid cheating at Monopoly.

It would have been an exaggeration to say the bar went quiet as the two cops entered. The fruit machine kept up its frenzied siren song for the addicts clustered around its jukebox lights. A dart thunked into the well-worn board in the corner. And the till drawer rattled as the barman made change for a punter old-school enough still to be paying for his drink with cash.

'Morning all,' Kat called out cheerily. 'Don't mind us.'

Heads that had turned in their direction returned to their tables, drinks, newspapers or betting slips. Except for one.

In a dark corner, opposite a heavily bearded biker, sat a short, soft-looking man, pale eyes jittering behind gold-rimmed spectacles. Kat felt a wave of irritation mixed with a single strand of pity.

She wasn't sure what Ethan Metcalfe did for a living, had no reason to care. But what she *did* care about was his podcast. Mainly because he used it as an excuse to insert himself into MCU cases under the guise of 'investigative journalism'.

Adult-Ethan wasn't a stalker. Not quite. But he made her uncomfortable, and that was enough.

'Kat!' he called out, waving frantically. 'Over here. It's Ethan.'

As if she couldn't tell. She could hear Liv's mocking tones in her head. *It's Mutt-calf!* The man with Ethan looked over and then, after hurriedly finishing his pint of Guinness, stood up and moved to an even darker corner of the pub.

Tom glared in Ethan's direction. 'It's Middlehampton's favourite citizen journalist. Want me to get rid of him?'

'Hold your horses, Rambo. He's well within his rights to have a drink in the Hope. Wait here.'

Kat walked over to Ethan's table and stood over him. 'What are you doing in here, Ethan?'

He smiled up at her. 'Probably the same as you. Investigating the murder on Bowman's Common. My listeners have a right to know. They *demand* to know.'

She nodded in the direction the biker had taken. 'Who's your friend?'

He tapped the side of his nose. 'A journalist never reveals his sources.'

She sighed. 'Ethan, he's literally sitting over there. I could just go up and talk to him.'

He pushed the glasses higher on his nose, which was sheened with waxy-looking sweat. 'I was asking him if he knew Jo Morris. He said he did, but I think he was just using me to get a free beer.' He sipped his own. 'So, any theories? Because I think it's fairly obvious what we're dealing with here. Another serial killer.'

She needed to squash this down now. It was bad enough Carve-up raising the subject, even if only to put her down. But if Ethan started putting the theory out on his podcast and website, it would only spread panic.

'OK, Ethan? Firstly, "we" aren't dealing with anything. *I* am dealing with a live homicide investigation. *You* are getting in my way.'

'But, Kat—'

'Secondly, there's zero evidence it's a serial offender. You'll be making yourself look stupid if you go with that on your podcast.'

He was shaking his head vigorously. 'You're wrong, Kat. I have it on good authority that's precisely what we – you – are dealing with.'

'What good authority?'

He beckoned her closer and, reluctantly, she dipped her head. Close enough to smell his unpleasant, tobacco-smelling breath and see the individual droplets of sweat beading his nose.

'Let's just say a senior police source and leave it at that,' he murmured.

She straightened, furious. Because who else could it be but Carve-up? What the hell sort of game was he playing?

Of course! The same game he *always* played. Messing around with Kat's investigations, sowing mistrust, leaking details of the case – anything, as long as it gave him a little bit of leverage.

There was nothing to be gained by prolonging the conversation. Ethan would carry on regardless. She'd just have to hope his podcast had as little reach as she imagined.

She rejoined Tom and led him over to the bar.

'Morning, Frank,' she said to the stocky, broken-nosed forty-something polishing a pint glass. 'Nice to see the boss putting in a shift.'

'I like to keep my hand in. What can I get you, Kat?' he asked, flipping the red and white glass cloth over a beefy shoulder.

'Lime and soda for me, please. Tom?'

'Make that two.'

Frank Strutt poured cordial into two glasses, then filled them with soda from the bar-gun. In his hairy paw it looked a lot more like its namesake than it did a soft-drinks dispenser.

'Who's your friend?' he asked, nodding at Tom.

'This is my new bagman, DC Tom Gray.'

'What happened to Leah?'

'She's still around. Working with Craig these days.'

Frank smiled amiably at Tom as he dropped ice cubes into the glass with stainless-steel tongs, added a wedge of lime, and placed it in front of him.

'Pleased to meet you, Tom. You'll learn a lot from Kat, if you're smart enough to keep your ears open and your trap shut.'

Tom flushed, and below the level of the bar Kat saw his right fist clench. *Easy, tiger.* Frank Strutt liked to rile rookies the way other landlords liked to joke with regulars or paper the back of the bar with foreign banknotes.

She fished out her phone to pay.

Strutt shook his head. 'On the house.'

Kat shrugged, holding out her phone. 'I can afford it.'

'It's only cordial and fizzy water.'

She waggled her phone. 'So it won't even put a dent in my bank account.'

With a sly smile he held out the card machine.

'Is Isaac in?' she asked, as the machine bleeped.

Frank inclined his head towards a door, above which a sign pointed to the beer garden. Kat led Tom out through the door and along a narrow brick-floored corridor.

'You know him, then?' Tom murmured.

'Frank's the oldest child of Joe and Anna Strutt. The Strutts are one of Middlehampton's finest crime families. Joe's more or less passed the reins to Frank now. He and I go way back.'

They emerged into bright sunlight, making Kat blink after the gloom of the bar.

Behind her, Tom made a disparaging noise. 'Huh. Some beer garden.'

The concrete yard had just enough room for four close-packed picnic benches. A bird-crap-encrusted yellow beach umbrella rose from the only occupied table. In its shade sat a thirty-something man – scrawny, dressed in black Adidas sportswear, with a wispy ginger moustache-and-beard combo. Before him, a quarter-full pint of lager. He was engrossed in his phone and failed to notice the two detectives until Kat sat opposite him.

The man's head elevated slowly as though an invisible hand was winding it up on a pulley. His pupils were the size of pinholes. He rubbed at his top lip. 'Hi, Kat,' he slurred, smiling lopsidedly.

'Morning, Isaac,' she said. She nodded at his glass. 'What's that?'

'Carlsberg.'

Kat looked up at Tom. 'Can you get Isaac a pint of Carlsberg, please, Tom?'

Isaac laid a hand on his concave belly and winced. 'Haven't had breakfast yet, Kat. I could murder a cheese sandwich.'

'And a cheese sandwich,' she added.

Tom failed to conceal a scowl. She knew why. He hated being treated like a skivvy, pandering to this lowlife's bodily needs. Ah, well. She'd told him he was about to do some real policing. Time to learn what that meant.

'I didn't see a food menu,' he said.

'Tell Frank I asked for it.'

With his lip still curling, Tom turned on his heel and stalked off, back to the interior.

'Who's he?' Isaac asked, rubbing at his moustache again.

Kat smiled at Isaac. Full name, as recorded regularly by the custody sergeant at Jubilee Place, Isaac Amos Handy. His mum was a very religious woman, and her son's chosen career caused her enormous shame and guilt that she tried to expiate every Sunday at All Saints over in Grove Park. His father, a street preacher, no doubt drew on his son's life to inspire his more bloodcurdling passages about hell and damnation.

'My new partner. DC Gray. You might want to be nice to him.'

'I'm nice to everyone, Kat, you know that.'

It was true. More or less. Low-level drug dealers had any number of people to please, placate or pacify, up and down the supply chain. Customers, obviously, got the full-on obliging salesman routine.

'How's business, Isaac?'

He raised a hand to his moustache again. 'Business?'

'Look, I don't know if you heard, but I'm Major Crimes now. You know, rape, arson, murder, that sort of thing. Your nefarious activities aren't my concern anymore.'

His bony shoulders dropped by a few inches. Some of the wariness left his pinholed eyes. He shrugged. 'I get by.'

Cagey. Admitting nothing. But acknowledging the truth they both knew, especially since Kat had arrested him for dealing at least twice before.

'Sold any acid recently?'

His wiry eyebrows knitted together. 'That's Class A. I don't—' He caught himself.

Kat laid a hand on his forearm. Just a hint of pressure. Not menacing, just enough to show him she wasn't about to take any nonsense. With a more switched-on punter, that action would have meant filling in a use-of-force form. With Isaac, she felt she could safely ignore the rule.

'I'm not here to bust you, OK? I'm investigating a murder.'

His eyes widened again. 'Wow! Cool.'

'It's really not,' she said, wondering just how much of his current special offer he'd personally consumed before she and Tom appeared to take the shine off his high.

'Oh, no, of course. Murder. That's bad.'

'Sell anyone any tabs recently? Pills? Windows?'

He began twisting one end of his moustache. 'No. On my honour. I don't deal in that anym—' He looked defeated. 'OK, maybe I do have the occasional line of naughty stuff in my inventory. But acid? No. Not since those Albanians came to town. They're trying to control it all now. We all got the same message. Weed, Molly, Chester, Special K, all that? It's fine. Anything heavier goes through them. Or they go through you. Not sure Frank and his family are very happy about it, mind.'

Tom appeared with a pint of lager and a thick sandwich made with what looked to Kat like homemade bread. She tried to picture Frank Strutt elbow-deep in a big mound of dough. Failed. Sue, then. Although even that was a stretch. It would take her longer to get her heavy gold rings off than to make the stuff in the first place.

'Cheers, Tom!' Isaac said, then bit off a mouthful and chewed noisily.

'Isaac's been filling me in,' Kat said to Tom. 'Apparently Middlehampton's LSD trade is under new management.'

Tom nodded. 'Do we know who? Should we question them?'

Isaac swallowed noisily and slurped at his lager. 'That's a really bad idea,' he said, staring at Tom, head jerking. 'No offence, but those guys? They're not, you know' – he trailed off, looking up at the underside of the umbrella – 'very friendly.'

'Albanian,' Kat said. 'That means organised crime, unlike our resident freelance peddler of joy here.'

'Can we talk to the drug squad?' Tom asked.

'Later.'

'So, who got murdered? That girl up on the common?' Isaac asked, speaking around another mouthful of sandwich. 'I saw something in the *Echo*.'

Kat caught a glimpse of his brown, crumbling teeth and felt her stomach turn over.

Still thinking he might have sold Jo some LSD, she pulled out a copy of the website photo Tom had downloaded and showed it to Isaac. 'You recognise her by any chance? Her name's Jo Morris.'

He looked at her, eyes narrowed. 'Actually, Kat, now I come to think about it, business *hasn't* been so good recently. I even had to go to the food bank last week.'

Kat opened her wallet and extracted a tenner. Placed it on the slatted wood in front of Isaac. He reached for it, but she pushed her fingertip down to fix it in place. There were rules. Isaac knew them just as well as Kat did.

He sighed. 'She looks like a girl I knew at school.'

'Which school was this?' Tom asked, checking via raised eyebrows that he should continue, and receiving a nod of encouragement.

'Middlehampton College.'

'*Looks* like her or *is* her, Isaac?' Kat said.

He tugged on the tenner. She maintained the downward pressure.

'OK, fine. It's her. Bit older obviously, but it's her all right. Kind of hard to forget.'

'What can you tell me about her?' Kat asked, wondering whether there was a current Isaac Handy in Riley's cohort of students at the school.

'Back then? She wasn't Jo Morris. Jo Starling, that was her name.'

'What was she like at school?'

'I don't know, do I? We moved in different circles.'

Kat lifted her finger off the tenner, which disappeared into the pocket of Isaac's stained tracksuit top.

They left Isaac to finish his sandwich, going out via the back gate rather than through the pub.

'Frank say anything to you when you were getting Isaac's pint?' she asked Tom.

'He was singing *your* praises,' Tom replied. 'Let me guess, you went to school with him and, even though he was one of the bad boys, you had a sneaking regard for his entrepreneurial approach to life.'

'You're *half*-right. We both went to Queen Anne's. But not at the same time. He's ten years older than me. Which, by the way, I'd have thought you might have noticed.'

'Sorry. Anyway, your lives went in opposite directions. But this is Middlehampton, so you run into each other from time to time, especially given your respective professions.'

Kat grinned at him. The rookie was catching on fast. '*Exactamente.* How we do things is more than just cop and CI, though. It's more of a mutual-respect thing. This isn't the Met, Tom: yes, I went to school with some of the villains here. Played netball against others. We drank – drink – in the same pubs, buy our groceries in the same supermarkets. It's natural in a place like this. I've always tried to treat the people I go after as human beings, and I expect them to return the favour. I don't fit people up, ask for kickbacks or give them a beating somewhere there's no CCTV. And I expect them to help me when I need a little whisper.'

'And it works?'

'Not all the time. But, yeah. It works. They *are* criminals, and when we catch them out, we arrest them and off we go,' she said. 'But they also know what's happening where nice people don't go, and that tends to be where we get answers. Treat them with respect and they return the favour. Sometimes with interest.'

'But surely they expect something in return? Aren't we opening ourselves up to undue influence?'

Kat snorted. 'Now *there's* a phrase straight out of the College of Policing's manual! Well, yes, technically we could be. But these *criminals'* – heavy emphasis – 'they are, or ninety-nine-point-nine per cent of them are, just ordinary human beings.' They reached the car, and Kat unlocked it and slid behind the wheel. 'People like being treated with respect. Even common courtesy works. They still want to help, even if they are on the wrong side of the street.'

'It's the bit of the job I struggle to get my head round.'

Kat sighed. Tom was being more than usually innocent today. But at least he was being honest. Maybe she could help him out. 'What's our job, Tom?'

'Well, to investigate—'

'—forget your criminology degree. Just tell me in plain English.'

'Fine,' he huffed, sounding more like Riley than he'd be pleased to know. 'To catch bad guys.'

'Exactly. Not to judge them. Not to weigh their morals in the balance. Not to pronounce sentence. We just catch them *when they do something wrong*. And funnily enough, talking to other bad guys is often a good way to do that.'

Tom folded his arms. 'You think I should wear out more shoe leather, don't you?'

Kat braked as an old lady pushing a white Scottie dog in a shopping trolley stepped off the kerb without looking.

'I'm just trying to open your eyes a little. People like Isaac are useful,' Kat said, smiling at the old woman and waving her across.

Five minutes later, she turned into the Jubilee Place car park, thinking hard. Thanks to Isaac, it was now confirmed that Jo had gone to school at the pride of Middlehampton's state sector: Middlehampton College. Riley's school.

Kat felt it then. A door opening in the case. She didn't know where exactly it would lead, but it was going to take her one step closer to solving Jo's murder.

But before she went any further with her investigation, she had an appointment with the man without whom Jo would never have existed. Her father.

Their father.

CHAPTER TWENTY-THREE

Palms sweaty on the Golf's steering wheel, stomach churning worse than before a big press conference, Kat drove across town to her father's office.

He could very easily have run his property business from the house; it was certainly large enough. But he'd once told her that the people who mattered would never take him seriously unless he had offices in the centre of town. It made sense, even though he also liked to complain – boast, she often thought – about the running costs.

For the police, like everybody else, parking in South Lane, Middlehampton's business and financial district, was usually a case of circling the NCP looking for a space. Or leaving your car on a double yellow and risking a ticket. But not if your father ran a successful company there. Then you just rang his PA and booked yourself one of the visitor spaces in their own small car park.

Kat had known Suzanne 'Suzy' Watkins her whole life. As a child visiting her dad's office, Kat had always looked forward to dipping a hand into the jar of sweets that Suzy kept on her desk. They'd met at social events over the intervening years, getting on fine despite, or perhaps because of, the fact that both knew his flaws as well as his strengths.

Because her father did have virtues; something Kat had always recognised. He was successful in business, generous to employees and, in his way, a devoted father. Clearly his devotion to his wife had been built on shakier foundations.

Morton Land's offices occupied a single floor in a tower block that still retained some of its eighties glamour. Cobalt-blue tinted glass glittered in the sunlight. Pink granite-a-like arches, columns and pediments gave the place the vague feel of a classical temple, as built by a toddler with too many cylinders and triangles and not enough rectangles in their brick box. It was a breezy day and pigeons careered around the north-west corner where some fluke of the architecture had created a vortex.

She made her way to the fourth floor.

'Hi, Kat,' Suzy said with a smile, as Kat pushed through the double doors into reception. 'Go on through, he's expecting you.'

If the building's exterior suggested a Greek temple, the interior, at least as evidenced by Colin Morton's office, was an altogether more clubby affair. A bottle-green leather Chesterfield sofa and matching armchairs. A Turkey carpet in rich reds, browns and oranges. Mahogany bookcases and a chrome drinks cabinet straight out of a 1920s speakeasy.

An assortment of modern art prints adorned the walls, which were papered in green and white Regency stripes above a carved wooden dado rail. Clubby, yes. But a club for people who found the idea of decor from a single historical period too limiting.

Colin rounded his vast aluminium and toughened-glass desk and came towards Kat, arms wide, having first flipped open the single button on his suit jacket so it wouldn't pull.

'Morning, Kitty-Kat, what an unexpected pleasure.'

He enveloped her in a hug, which she returned, though with less pressure. His aftershave – the scent he always wore, Aramis – flooded her nostrils, making her feel like that little girl visiting Daddy's office all over again.

But this time it was adult business that had brought her here. And she wouldn't be bought off with sweets. Oh, there'd be some emotional horse-trading all right. But she was pretty sure she'd emerge the victor.

Releasing Kat from his embrace, Colin gestured to the armchairs. 'Take a pew. Suzy'll be in with some coffee and biscuits in a minute or two. Then we can find out what's brought you to my office, can't we?'

Kat took the chair with its back to the picture window, an instinctive choice that put her with the light at her back. Her heart was racing, and her palms were clammy.

It was taking all her self-control not to either blurt out what she knew or bolt for the door. She clenched her stomach muscles in an attempt to quell the riot taking place down there. It didn't help. Now she wanted to use the loo.

Once Suzy had delivered the coffee and Colin had poured two cups, he looked at her appraisingly.

'Not like you to pay me a visit during the working day.' He sipped his coffee and gently replaced the cup in its saucer. 'Or any other time, come to that.'

She tried her own coffee. The caffeine intensified her anxiety. She felt like throwing up.

'You know why, Dad,' she said.

'Not really. I know why you think you need to keep some sort of air gap between us,' he said. 'But, as I've said many, many times before, it's all in your head.'

'So, if a team of forensic accountants went over your books, all they'd find is neat columns that all added up. Every pound in, traceable to a bank loan, an investor or a property sale. Every pound out, to a legitimate contractor.'

He sipped his coffee, smiled. 'It seems you've already been over them yourself, Kitty-Kat.'

Enough of this. If he used that hated nickname one more time, she'd either throw her coffee over him or fluff what she needed to say. She needed to be calm. OK, calm *enough*.

Lying awake in the small hours before dawn brightened the bedroom curtains, she'd tried out dozens of different ways of broaching the subject of her half-sister. None had sounded right. She opened her mouth, wondering what was going to come out. At the last minute, she decided.

Play it cool.

'Did you ever meet another property investor called Tasha Starling?' She watched his reaction, looking for a tell. A tightening of the lips. A blink. A twitch. A hand reaching out to pick a non-existent piece of lint off a trouser leg. Or maybe a bit of face-acting? Wrinkling that tanned forehead.

His face was immobile. 'Why do you ask?'

'Did you?'

'It sounds like you think you know the answer already.'

'Just tell me. Don't make me turn this into an interrogation.'

'Then, yes. I did. A long time ago now. We were joint investors on a project together.'

A great many sarcastic responses presented themselves to Kat at this point. But she kept to the plan. 'But your relationship was more than just business, wasn't it?'

A hooded look came into his eyes, then. She knew why. He'd been thinking this was going to be another of her attempts to uncover some dirt on his business dealings. He could bat those away all day without breaking a sweat. But now she was veering onto personal territory. A place Colin Morton guarded very carefully indeed.

He smoothed a hand over his hair. 'I'm not sure I know what you mean, Kitty-Kat.'

There. She knew it. She'd rattled him. He was jabbing back into that sore place where he could be sure of getting a rise out of her, of distracting her. Maybe provoking a blow-up he could use to close the whole conversation down.

'Let me spell it out, then.' She leaned forwards in the chair, feeling her jeans sliding over the shiny leather seat cushion. Her pulse stuttered like a nervous suspect in an interview room. 'I think you and Tasha Starling had an affair.'

Well, you're the expert on that subject, her subconscious whispered maliciously.

Her father was making a decent fist out of appearing calm, but she knew she'd got through his defences. It wasn't anything as specific as a particular muscle twitching. She was just his daughter, that was all; it was enough. She *knew* him. And right now, he was radiating a mixture of curiosity and wounded pride. Caught out, but also intrigued. So Tasha clearly hadn't told him about Jo.

For perhaps the first time in her adult life, Kat felt she had something over her father. A weird feeling. To be savoured, even as the knowledge of what he'd done gnawed at her.

'You're wrong. I love your mother,' he said in a deep, level voice. 'I would never do anything to hurt her.'

The words were the right ones. It was the tone she found unconvincing. *Fine, have at it, Dad.* Her blood was up now; he'd squandered all the chances she'd offered him to come clean.

'Perhaps you didn't consider screwing Tasha Starling on the side would hurt her.'

Something strange happened to his face. Fleeting expressions chased each other across his smooth, perma-tanned features as if driven by a sudden squall. Teeth bared. Brows knitted together. Eyes narrowed. Lips tightened then relaxed into a guilty, millisecond smile. Blink and you'd miss it. Kat missed none of it. Knew she'd poked a bruise.

'How dare you speak to me like that,' he said in an eerily calm voice. 'You might be a detective, a sergeant at that, but you're in *my* office, in *my* company, in *my* building.' He must have caught her own shocked expression. 'Oh, yes, Kitty-Kat, I own it. So when I tell you I did not have an affair with Tasha, that's it. End of.'

Kat's heart was pounding. Her throat hurt. 'How dare I, Dad? How *dare* I? How about because while you *weren't* having an affair with her, *she* got pregnant with a child you fathered on her?'

He shuddered as if an unseen torturer had affixed electrodes to his genitals. Gripped the armrests of his chair. Despite the awfulness of the situation – after all, she was about to tell him he had four children, not three, and deliver a death knock in the same breath – she experienced a rush of pleasure.

'You don't know that,' he hissed. 'You can't!'

'I know Tasha named her Jo. I assume she didn't tell Connor. They brought her up as their own. And last Monday, she was murdered. Her DNA sparked a partial match with mine. That's how I found out I had a half-sister.'

He palmed sweat from his brow. His mouth worked, but no sound emerged. Beneath the sunbed tan, his skin looked pale, giving his cheeks a greenish cast. Was he going to be sick? She looked around for a wastepaper bin.

No need. He drew in a breath and expelled it again through his teeth, as if in pain so great he needed to scream but wouldn't give in to the urge.

'What are you going to do?' he asked in a distant tone.

'Catch her killer, of course. What else?'

'No, I mean are you going to tell your mother? Are you going to tell Nathan and Diana? You can't. It will wreck everything I worked so hard for. This family, Kat, it means everything to me. You can't spoil that.'

There. He'd given her the opening she needed.

'*I* can't spoil it? Jesus, Dad! It wasn't me in bed with Tasha Starling, was it? Anyway, don't you think they have a right to know? Oh, no, wait. Of course you don't. Otherwise you'd have told them yourself by now.'

'Kat, please. It would devastate the family. *Our* family. Think what it would do to your mum.'

Several responses jostled for primacy right then. But Kat stuck to her plan. She looked him straight in the eye. 'You like making deals, don't you, Dad? Land, planning permission, loans, all that?'

He blinked. 'What are you talking about? Of course I do. But I fail to see—'

'I'm offering you a deal now. You don't tell your golf buddy Stuart Carver, and I don't tell Mum.'

He looked blank. But only for a second. Colin Morton was a man used to calculating angles. As his mental geometry set supplied the answer, he smiled thinly.

'Well, well. My little girl's all grown up. Stuart would kick you off the investigation, wouldn't he, if he found out you were related to the victim?'

She aimed for a casual look. A quick shrug. Lower lip pooched out for a second.

'Maybe, maybe not. But I don't want to take the risk. And you have no idea what Mum would do. Maybe she'd kick you out altogether. Sue you for half of the business. Whatever she did, it would ruin your public image as one of Middlehampton's leading citizens, or however your PR department describes you in the press releases. As for Diana and Nathan, well, it might turn them against you, too. Bang goes your dynasty.'

Her dad leaned back in his chair. Steepled his fingers under his nose. She knew it was all for show. She'd won.

'Fine,' he said. 'This stays between us.'

She didn't bother asking if he meant it. Or offering her hand. This was one deal Colin Morton would never try to wriggle out of. But she still had questions. And now the ground had firmed beneath her feet, she wanted answers.

'Did you even care about Jo while she was alive?'

'Tasha thought it was best if we ended things and pretended it had never happened,' he said. 'I offered to pay for an abortion, but she was determined to keep it. Her, I mean. To keep the baby. She had her own money. More than I did back then. Wouldn't take a penny.'

'Is that true, Dad? She didn't ask you for child support? She didn't try to screw you back? Get money out of you in exchange for not telling Mum?'

He shook his head sadly. 'Why are you dragging this up now? It's ancient history. You said yourself, Jo's dead. Tragically, but all the same . . . And so are Tasha and Connor. What's to be gained by raking over the coals again?'

Tears pricked her eyes. 'She was my sister, Dad! You never told me.'

'Half-sister.'

Her mouth dropped open. She launched herself across the gap between them and slapped his face. Her palm stung and the crack was sharp and bright in the muted interior of the office. His own

160

hand went to the insulted side of his face and cradled the reddening flesh. But his eyes were hard. Unforgiving.

Without waiting for him to tell her, she spun round and marched out, slamming the door behind her with as much force as she could muster. Riley would have approved.

Suzy was heading for her boss's door as Kat left the office.

CHAPTER TWENTY-FOUR

Back from her confrontation with her dad, Kat was opening yet another case document when her phone rang. No caller ID.

'Hi, Kat, it's me. Isaac.'

She'd have recognised his whiny voice without the introduction. 'Yes, Isaac, what do you want?'

'Don't be like that, Kat. I'm calling with information.'

She breathed in and out quickly, forcing herself to smile in the hopes he'd hear it even if he couldn't see it.

'Sorry, just been in a trying meeting. What have you got for me?'

'Something juicy. Probably worth more than a pint of lager and a cheese sandwich, if you catch my drift.'

'Why don't you tell me what you know, and if it's decent, I'll slip you another tenner.'

She heard a loud sniff and wondered whether he was literally doing a line while he spoke to her. Or was it the sudden release of pressure from a nitrous oxide canister – what people like Isaac called 'whippits'.

'Come on, Kat, I wasn't born yesterday. This is related to that murder case you're working. You're going to want to hear it, I promise. Can you come and meet me? I don't want to talk on the phone.'

She sighed. It could be nothing, it could be something. But Isaac had always come through for her in the past.

'Where and when?'

'Like, now? How about down by the canal. Near the old paper mill.'

◆ ◆ ◆

Much of the land either side of the towpath had been redeveloped. Chichi apartments that overlooked refurbished narrowboats turned into funky cafes. Bits of the old industrial infrastructure tarted up to enhance what the town's planners liked to call 'Middlehampton's urban waterside'.

But not the depressing bit of scrubland where Isaac Handy was waiting for her.

A hollow shell of steel girders and fractured asbestos roofing panels occupied the spot where a thriving paper mill had once stood. The machinery that had once churned out millions of miles of paper long-since sold off for scrap. Now nothing remained but a vast cracked asphalt and concrete floor, punctured by gangling weeds topped with acid-yellow flowers. Old truck tyres, empty wooden reels as tall as a person, and the smashed panes of thousands of windows added a finishing touch to the bleak decor.

Standing on the towpath with the ruined factory behind him, Isaac looked like the last man alive in some post-apocalyptic thriller. Although, in his pristine Adidas tracksuit, red and white this time, clearly one who'd raided a branch of JD Sports.

Kat walked over to join him. The wire carcasses of shopping trolleys poked out of the green water, which smelled bad. Kat pictured rotting . . . things . . . lying invisible beneath the rainbowed surface of the canal.

'So?'

Isaac scratched at a spot on his chin. He looked like an adolescent. He stared into the murky water. 'I was thinking, this has got to be worth, like, fifty at least.'

'Pence?' she said. 'Yeah, I could run to that.'

His eyebrows shot up. 'Pounds!'

She wondered whether he *had* taken something. 'Please don't take the piss, Isaac,' she said. 'You're strictly a tens and twenties guy. Now, let's hear it, and we'll decide which of those is your lucky number.'

He turned to face her, and she caught it, then: the greedy glint in his eyes, coupled with something else. A confidence she'd not seen before. Maybe he did have something worth a little more.

'Give me twenty and I'll tell you half of it. But the other half's gonna cost you thirty.'

She smiled at him. Took a step closer, which had him backing up.

'Isaac, we go back, don't we? I mean, I've arrested you at least twice. But I've always been respectful to you, haven't I? Treated you properly. Not called you names like some of the male coppers do. Always throwing their weight around, aren't they?'

He grimaced as if his guts were griping. 'You're OK, Kat,' he agreed, raising his hand to pick at the spot again.

She fished a tissue out of her pocket. 'Here, you've made it bleed.'

Dabbing the tissue against his cheek then inspecting the evidence, he thanked her. 'Forty?'

'Have you met my DI? Mr Carver would carpet me if he knew I was throwing money around on unregistered informants. It's not worth it, Isaac. I'll just have to carry on without your info.'

She turned as if to go and, because Isaac was nobody's fool, started walking.

'Wait! How about thirty and a lift somewhere after we've finished talking.'

Kat smiled to herself, then adjusted her features into a neutral expression, turned and went back to him. On the whole she preferred Isaac to 'Mr Carver'. At least Isaac was an honest crook.

'Lift where? I'm not taking you to meet one of your suppliers.'

'It's nothing like that. I'm going to visit my mum. She's on chemo up at the hospital.'

Was he being serious? Or was this just another ploy? She took in the quiver of his lower lip.

'I'm sorry to hear that, Isaac. I mean, not that she's having chemo, but about her cancer. Where is it?'

'The doctors found a shadow on her left lung.' He looked away for a second. 'She smokes, see. I'm always telling her those things'll kill her, but she won't listen.'

Maybe he was too stoned to see the irony in a drug dealer telling his mum off for smoking. It didn't matter. That was between the two of them.

'Yes to the lift and yes to the thirty. Now, tell me what you know.'

'Thing is, Kat, I might've not been entirely honest with you in the Hope.'

She frowned. 'I think we'd better just have it.'

'You know you asked me if I sold acid, and I said no? Well, I do still sell the odd bit,' he said, at least having the good grace to look shamefaced. 'Not a lot, 'cause it's true what I said about those Armenians—'

'You said they were Albanians before.'

'Oh, did I? I thought it was, like, you know, the same basic country. Like those other ones, Slow-something.'

Kat's patience was running out. 'Slovenia and Slovakia. Can we get to the point, please? Or not only am I not going to spot you thirty quid, but you can get the bloody bus up to MGH.'

He looked panicked. 'I saw the press conference you did. And that bloke who was with you. The husband, right?'

'Yes. Ian Morris,' she said, feeling that maybe Isaac was going to come through after all.

'He bought some off me. Tabs,' he added, as if he couldn't believe Kat would be capable of following his train of thought.

'When?'

Isaac shrugged. 'My memory's not that reliable. But definitely this year. It was cold out, so I'm thinking . . . January? February maybe?'

'And it was definitely him? You're sure?'

'That I *am* sure about.' He tapped his forehead. 'Got an excellent memory for faces.'

'You'd swear to that in court?'

Isaac looked as though she'd just asked him whether he'd admit to being a nonce in the Hope's public bar on a Friday night.

'Would I have to? I mean, it's not good—'

'—for your reputation. Look, Isaac, as far as it goes, this is golden. But nobody's going to hold it against you if you help put a violent man who murdered his own wife behind bars, are they? It's nothing to do with your line of work. If anything, it might earn you some extra kudos.'

Isaac frowned, mulling it over. He shrugged. 'Maybe you're right. Anyway, if I *literally* had to? I guess so.'

Kat passed him two twenties. He looked at the notes in surprise.

'But I thought—'

'Get your mum a present. Some books to read, flowers, whatever'll take her mind off the chemo. Now, come on. Let's go back to my car before I change my mind.' She started walking. 'And if you tell anyone DS Ballantyne's dishing out twenties like sweets, I'll cut your balls off.'

Isaac laughed as he trotted to keep up with her. 'Scout's honour.'

The image of a school-age Isaac in a khaki uniform, complete with necker and woggle, dealing baggies of weed behind the Scout hut made Kat smile. But it didn't last as she processed the implications of this new piece of intelligence.

She had evidence Ian Morris had bought both the components of what was, effectively, the murder weapon used to kill his wife. OK, so he'd bought the kiwi fruit Kat had found in the compost heap *after* she died, but maybe he'd already procured one without leaving a paper trail.

Time to bring Ian back in for a chat.

CHAPTER TWENTY-FIVE

Kat called Van to tell him she'd be late home. For once, he didn't seem bothered about having to take on all her jobs along with his own.

'It's fine, honestly,' he said when she asked him if he was sure it was OK. 'I've already taken Smokey out and Riley's over at Alfie's. I was only going to be working anyway. You're probably better off at the station than here.'

'Working?' she echoed, trying to keep her voice light. 'Marnie again?'

'The back end's playing up.'

'I'll see you later,' she said, picturing Marnie Pryce's own perfect little back end in those tight white jeans and hating herself for doing it.

'Wake me up when you come in,' Van said. 'Whatever time it is. Love you!'

Kat fought down an irrational stab of irritation. Why shouldn't Van be working on a client's website? Especially since she'd been the one to call him with the news she'd be creeping in late. Marnie's lightly tanned face swam into view. Glossy lips stretched in a winning smile. *We're ever so discreet*, ghost-Marnie purred. *Your spouse will never know.*

'Everything all right, Kat?'

She looked up. Tom was standing by her desk with a mug of coffee. He put it down by her elbow and slumped into a chair. She took a sip of the coffee and grimaced. It had better have lots of caffeine in it because there was nothing else to recommend it.

'That good, eh?' he asked with a grin.

'Not even.'

She left the foul brew on her desk and went to find Linda Ockenden. Going over your line manager's head was bad form, but when said manager was a dickhead of biblical proportions, it was allowed. At least in Kat's rulebook it was.

Two minutes later, Kat was asking Linda's PA if there was any chance of a quick meeting with her boss.

'She's chock-a-block until next week, I'm afraid.' Then Annie Brewster lowered her voice to a theatrical whisper. 'Although she does have a soft spot for you, so if it's urgent?'

Kat nodded. 'It is.'

Annie grinned. 'Don't tell me, you've drunk one too many cups of station coffee and you need a cup of Linda's special stash? You'd be surprised how many senior detectives just drop by hoping I'll make them some. I'm surprised nobody's tried to lift the whole bag.'

'Oh my God, she'd be on *Crimewatch*. "I would urge members of the public to be on the lookout for the Coffee Thief,"' Kat said, in a wickedly accurate parody of Linda's 'media voice'.

Linda's office door opened and the woman herself stood there, one eyebrow raised, arms folded beneath her bust. Kat blushed, while Annie stifled her laughter.

'That's odd,' Linda said, eyeing first Annie then Kat. 'I thought someone must've had the telly on replaying one of my press conferences. But all I find is you two' – she aimed a finger at each woman in turn, thumb cocked like a revolver – 'having a laugh at my expense. Come on, then. "If it's good enough to tell, it's good enough to share", as my mum used to say.'

'Kat was—' Annie began.

'—going to give you an update on the Bowman's Common case.'

'I'll bring you both a coffee,' Annie said, with a wink for Kat.

'No, you get off home. I'll do it,' Linda said. 'I think it's just about within what our dear HR department are pleased to call "senior management core competencies".'

Coffees made, Linda motioned for Kat to sit at the round conference table occupying half of her office.

'I found out today the husband, Ian, bought LSD from Isaac Handy earlier this year,' Kat said. 'Jo Morris's tox screen came back positive for traces of the drug.'

Linda pulled a face. 'Please call it toxicology, Kat. I hate the way every cop in Middlehampton talks like an American these days.' She grunted. 'Probs showing my age.'

'Sorry, Ma-Linda,' Kat said, earning a chuckle from Linda, who waved away the apology.

'Isaac Handy, eh? I had no idea the little scrote was still alive. I thought he OD'd.'

'He did. April of last year,' Kat said, taking a sip of the coffee and sighing with pleasure. 'For better or worse, the doctors in A&E brought him back from the brink.'

'If he's sharing info like that, it's probably for the better.'

'Over and above any statistical likelihood that Ian did it, this really puts the spotlight on him,' Kat said. 'We know the killer used LSD to boost the effects of the adrenaline he injected into Jo's femoral vein after he gave her kiwi fruit. Ian's been released under investigation, but I want to bring him back in.'

Linda nodded. 'OK, and you're asking me instead of DI Carver – why exactly?' Then she wrinkled her nose. 'Don't answer that. Fine, go ahead. What about motive?'

Kat relaxed, just a little. One hurdle cleared. 'A friend of Jo's told me Ian had been pestering her to lend him some money for his business. She said no, apparently.'

Linda nodded. 'Husband goes to his wife for cash. She turns him down flat. "Sorry, babe, it's your business, you make it work." He loses it, does her in, inherits the money anyway. Alibi?'

'Nope. Home alone, allegedly.'

'This is good work, Kat. I had Daniela-bloody-Morris on the phone today, bending my ear about the case. At least next time she calls I'll have something to tell her. Keep me posted, yes?'

Kat knew a dismissal when she heard one. She nodded and was back at her own desk a few minutes later. The taste of Linda's coffee lingered in her mouth; she pushed the cold mug of station swill as far away as possible without actually tipping it off the desk altogether.

Tom was still hard at it, bent over his screen. When he looked up and saw Kat was back, he scooted over on his swivel chair.

'I've been doing more digging. Found a guy we should definitely talk to. His name's Tyler Bolton. Works at the leisure centre as a fitness instructor. According to the receptionist there, he had a thing for Jo, but it was all one-way.' He checked his notebook. '"If he's not a stalker, he's the next best thing", quote, unquote.'

Kat tugged on her left earlobe, thinking of Ethan. Given her growing certainty that Ian had killed Jo, this was a complication she could have done without. She couldn't afford to ignore it, though. She wasn't one of those cops who got tunnel vision about a case, ignoring new evidence just because it didn't fit the picture they'd painted in their head.

'Got an address?'

'And landline, mobile, email, Instagram and Twitter. I got the feeling people might be happy to hear we were coming to talk to Tyler.'

'DC Gray, I'm impressed! What did you do, sit on the corner of her desk and flutter your lovely long eyelashes at her? Or did you ask her out?'

He let his jaw sag and pressed spread fingers to his chest, imitating one of Kat's trademark gestures. 'Ooh! So many sexist assumptions in one innocent-sounding question. That I'm not a good enough copper to get information without using sexual flirtation. That the receptionist was a woman. And that I have beautiful eyelashes.'

Kat grinned. 'Sorry, mate. Although I didn't say they were beautiful. Just lovely and long. Half the women in this nick would kill for them.'

Tom nodded. 'Apology accepted. I'll tell Eleanor when we have dinner.'

Kat's eyes flashbulbed, and she grinned widely. 'You pig! You enjoyed that, didn't you?'

'You take your fun where you can find it. So, I was hoping I could have Sunday night off?'

'Of course. You know, you can have more than that, Tom. I know we all get so immersed in cases we don't want to miss anything, but you are allowed to rest.'

'I know that,' he said, smiling. 'And mostly this is where I'd rather be. It's just, I've been having a bit of a dry spell recently, so . . .'

'It's fine. I get it. So, Eleanor, eh?' Kat put her finger to her chin. 'Hmm. She must be bright if *you* asked her out. Mid-twenties. Athletic build. How am I doing?'

'Not bad. Have you ever thought about becoming a detective?'

'Nah, mate. Too much like hard work. Pretty?'

'Lovely! Red hair. Blue eyes. Freckles.'

'Sounds like you might have a type.'

Tom looked away, then. Kat caught a look of profound sadness in his eyes in the couple of seconds when he avoided her gaze. She felt a pang of regret. Had she just trodden on an emotional corn? Was there another redhead at the far end of Tom's dry spell? She didn't get the chance to ask.

'Her name was Janis. She was from San Antonio. That's in . . .' He stopped himself, grinned guiltily. 'You know where San Antonio is, don't you?'

Kat smiled. It felt good to be sharing some history with Tom. She'd never tell Van this, but sometimes she loved being at work when everyone else had gone home. Pulling a late, or even an all-nighter; bantering with your bagman, or woman when she and Leah had been a team.

'Ten points for not Tomsplaining.' She leaned towards him, forearms resting on top of her thighs. 'What happened?'

'We broke up after a fight. We decided we weren't compatible.'

'It sounds like you really miss her.'

He shrugged, and his gaze flicked away for a second time. '*C'est l'amour.*'

Kat decided not to push it. But his offhand declaration – *That's love* – rang hollow. He'd loved the girl. He might as well have had it tattooed on his forehead.

Three hours later, she yawned so widely her jaw cracked with the sound of a distant double-barrelled shotgun. She rose from her desk, groaning as her back resumed a vaguely normal human configuration.

'Time to go home, Tom,' she said.

'I just want to finish a few things off.'

'It'll all still be here in the morning. Make sure you're not.' She stifled another yawn. 'Without going home for a few hours shut-eye first.'

'Thanks for Katsplaining.'

'Cheeky sod!'

Kat drove home through virtually silent streets, planning more urgent actions. Top of which was a visit to both the home and the workplace of one Tyler Bolton, Jo Morris's almost-stalker.

CHAPTER TWENTY-SIX

At 7.45 a.m., accompanied by PCs Dave Tyrell and Deepika Mirza, Kat re-arrested Ian Morris on his doorstep.

'Is this a joke?' he said as Dave folded him into the back of a marked Astra, which suddenly looked way too small for two such big men. 'I'm literally not even allowed to bury my wife and you're f—' He caught his breath. 'This is police harassment. You're persecuting me. I'm an innocent man!'

This time, a duty solicitor was available immediately, meaning Kat was able to begin the interview within the hour. No opening pleasantries this time. The direct approach was called for.

'Have you ever used LSD, Ian?'

He reared back. 'What? No!'

'No? Never bought any from a drug dealer here in Middlehampton named Isaac Handy? He's quite distinctive. Got the whole Tony Stark goatee thing going on, only Isaac's is a very fetching shade of ginger.'

'No. Absolutely not. Look, cards on the table. Yes, I smoke the odd bit of weed, but that's it.'

'You're telling me Isaac's lying when he says he sold it to you?'

A muscle under Ian's left eye had started flickering when Kat asked him about the LSD. It was a minuscule movement, but under the harsh light of the overhead neon tube, each tic produced a tiny smudge of shadow on his pale skin. Someone was lying, but it wasn't Isaac Handy.

'He's a drug dealer, yes?' Ian had regained a little of his former confidence. 'Of course he's lying. He's scum.'

'Why would he lie, Ian?' she asked. 'What possible motive would a drug dealer have for telling me he'd sold drugs to someone he hadn't?'

'How should I know? Maybe he's involved somehow.'

'So you think Isaac might be implicated in Jo's murder. You could be right, at that. We'd have to arrest him and really work on him.' She smacked one fist into the other palm. 'Phone records, that type of thing.'

She waited. Without any help from her, Ian had just dug a hole and jumped into it with both feet. He looked at the door, as if wishing he could make a run for it.

'LSD is Class A, right?' Ian asked. His cheeks took on a pink tinge. 'I know a little bit about that scene.'

'It is. But I need to remind you, Ian, I am a homicide detective. My colleagues down the hall might be interested in what you get up to in your spare time, but' – she leaned forwards, fixing him with a stare – 'all I care about is finding the person who murdered Jo.'

She sensed it. One of those moments when a suspect coughed.

He sighed, swiped his forehead with a palm no doubt already greasy with sweat.

'Yes, then. I did buy some tabs off Isaac. Back in January. It's just a recreational thing. I hardly ever do it these days, but Jo was at some conference and I just fancied it, you know?'

'Thanks for clarifying that, Ian,' she said, making a note. 'Interview suspended.' She turned to the uniformed PC standing in the corner. 'Take Mr Morris back to his cell, please.'

At 9.32 a.m. Kat and Tom strolled into Middlehampton Leisure Centre's foyer. The double-height space reverberated to the sounds of cups and saucers clinking from the cafeteria beyond the reception desk. A gaggle of kids in navy and grey Middlehampton College uniforms were lounging around several tables shoved together. Their banter and occasional bursts of laughter raised the noise to new levels.

The receptionist looked over at them and smiled, rolling her eyes towards the schoolkids. She was very pretty. Red hair, blue eyes and freckles.

'Hello . . .' Kat peered at the girl's name badge. Oh, so *this* was Tom's new squeeze. 'Eleanor. We're looking for Tyler Bolton.' She held out her warrant card.

'The gym's down the corridor, on the left,' the receptionist said with, what, a faint smirk?

As Kat strode towards the gym, Tom called out to her. 'Won't be a second.'

She turned her head to see him leaning down, talking to Eleanor. It was hardly the time for flirting, even if he had been going through a dry spell.

Kat pushed through the double doors that led to the gym. She wrinkled her nose as the smell assailed her. Mainly sweat, plus a tang of body odour. Plenty of people already working out on the machines, split roughly fifty-fifty men to women. What looked like a couple of staff in turquoise and black tracksuits, holding clipboards as they watched or encouraged their charges to 'smash it', as one young woman urged.

Kat wandered over. 'I'm looking for Tyler. Is he around?'

The girl swept a hank of hair away from her eyes. 'He's just getting changed. Should be out in a sec.'

'Which way to the changing rooms?'

The girl smiled. 'We call it the "changing village" now. Gender-neutral. Out the way you came in and first on the left. Our section is through the door marked "staff".'

Kat met Tom just outside the door and together they entered the changing facility. It was the unisex variety, with separate cubicles and showers. Men and women wandered to and fro in gym kit. A twenty-something girl walked past Kat in just her undies, offered a quick, confident smile. Kat reflected that if she had a body like hers, she'd probably smile, too.

She nudged Tom, whose head had swivelled to follow the gym-bunny. 'Put your eyes back in, DC Gray. This is official business.'

'Sorry, guv,' he murmured, earning himself a quick grin.

They went through the door leading to the staff area.

'Tyler Bolton?' Kat called out.

A man's head appeared from one of the cubicles. Shaved scalp, thick neck, pale blue eyes fringed with black lashes.

He scowled. 'That's me. But this area is staff-only. If you want to book a session you have to do it through reception.'

His tone bordered on aggressive. She found it odd.

'Police, Mr Bolton. Can we have a word?'

He frowned, then withdrew his head. A moment later he left the cubicle and came to stand in front of Kat and Tom, arms folded across a massive chest. He wore black shorts with a turquoise stripe down the sides, and a loose strappy gym vest in matching technical fabric. Bands of tribal tattoos around vast biceps. More encircling his calves. Script running down his right forearm that read *No Limits*.

Kat had never thought of herself as a fan of muscle. But Tyler was a prime specimen of a very particular sort of masculinity. The guy was *jacked*. Powerful bulges, sculpted planes, thick ropes of veins wriggling beneath the skin. She put his age at around twenty-five.

He towered over Kat. And even Tom, who was a six-footer himself, gave away a couple of inches to Tyler. Kat fought to keep her eyes on his face, but they seemed to have a will of their own and skittered over his chest and arms.

'What's this about?' he asked.

'We're investigating the murder of Jo Morris,' Kat said, all at once aware that here was a man with the strength to overpower anyone, let alone a woman probably half his size.

And wasn't it a little odd that he hadn't followed his question up with a rhetorical *Is it about Jo?* They'd worked together, after all. It was like carrying a placard reading, *Guilty Conscience!* She waited him out, wanting to see how he'd react.

He adopted a stricken expression. 'Oh God, yeah, of course. I mean, we're all in shock, obviously.'

Obviously? Well, the way he replaced all the alpha-male posturing with this theatrical sad-face came off as pretty obvious to her. It screamed 'faking it'.

'Can I call you Tyler?'

'Sure! Of course!'

'Thanks, Tyler. Can you describe your relationship with Jo for me?'

He blinked. Said nothing. Swallowed, his Adam's apple just visible through the column of muscle.

'Tyler?' Tom prompted. 'Detective Sergeant Ballantyne asked you a question.'

It was a nice little move. The way Tom used her rank to startle the big guy. Kat was, again, impressed with her bagman.

Tyler inhaled: a quick, sharp breath. Kat knew he was about to lie to them.

'Colleagues, obviously. But you already know that,' he added. 'Otherwise? Nothing, really. We didn't socialise outside work.'

Interesting. He hadn't lied after all. Or not by commission. But by omission? Yes. That he *had* done. She nodded, as if approving of his no-nonsense recounting of some *obvious* truth.

'So, you didn't fancy her, then?'

He blinked. She'd already come to think of it as a tell.

'Well, yeah, obviously she was fit. You know, attractive and everything. But I don't know if you know this yet . . . she's married.' Blink. 'Was, I mean.'

'You can fancy someone who's married, though, Tyler,' Tom said with the verbal equivalent of a blokeish wink.

'Not me.'

'Jo not your type, then?' Kat asked, starting to get a feel for the rhythm between her and Tom. Enjoying it.

'Not really. I prefer curvy girls.' Blink. 'I'm not gay, if that's what you're implying.'

'I'm not implying anything. Not that it would bother me if you were. We're just trying to get to the truth, aren't we, Tom?'

'The truth,' Tom repeated. 'About Jo Morris's murder. So, she wasn't your type, you didn't fancy her, you never asked her out or pestered her, and if we were to look inside your locker we wouldn't find – oh, I don't know, what wouldn't we find, guv?'

Kat shrugged. 'Photos printed out of Jo in her gym kit? Maybe a couple of upskirts. Or sneaky shots of her in the shower?'

'Nothing like that!' Tyler blurted, stepping back as if Kat had physically pushed him.

'Then you won't mind showing us,' Tom said.

'What? No! I mean, yes, I *would* mind.' He folded his arms again. A defensive pose this time. 'That's my private property. You've got no right. You need a search warrant.'

'You're half-right,' Tom said. 'The property *inside* is private, but the locker belongs to Middlehampton Council. The centre manager just gave me permission to look inside. And Eleanor on reception gave me a master key. So, if you wouldn't mind pointing out your locker, we'll just have a quick peek to satisfy our curiosity.'

Tyler was breathing heavily. His face was white. He jabbed a finger in Tom's face. 'This is harassment. I haven't done anything!'

Kat watched him. He'd just used the same word as Ian Morris when she arrested him. It was a common-enough accusation villains loved to throw out. But still, it was a coincidence that two suspects in the same case would react the same way.

Tyler's blinks were rattling out a couple of times a second. He was stressing out. Was he about to attack Tom? She tensed. Ready to move. *Against that?* an inner voice asked. *You'll be lucky.*

'It really isn't harassment, Tyler,' she said calmly. 'We're asking you perfectly reasonable questions, to which, I have to say, you seem to be avoiding giving straight answers. Now, I think we'd better see your locker, don't you?'

Tyler said nothing. He turned away. Kat thought she saw his hand going for a key in his pocket. *Like women use on dark nights*, she had time to think, before Tyler, screaming 'I said NO!', spun all the way round, a fist the size of a Sunday roast steaming in to deliver a good-sized punch to Tom's face.

Tyler's meaty paw sailed past Tom's right cheek. Kat could have sworn she felt the breeze it made. Heart racing, she jumped back, reaching behind her for her baton – which was in the boot of the car.

There was a smacking sound like a stick breaking, and a deep, explosive gasp as Tyler doubled over. Tom had just punched him in the solar plexus. A single blow like a piston shooting out of a cylinder. He danced back, out of range of the bigger man's counterattack.

But it was a needless precaution. Tyler collapsed, rolling onto his back, hands clasping his wounded abdomen. His mouth formed an almost comically round 'O' as his temporarily paralysed diaphragm fought to suck air into his lungs.

Tom heaved him onto his belly and, as Kat watched with wide eyes, snapped on a pair of cuffs.

'Locker number?' Tom asked.

'Nine,' Tyler gasped.

'Stay there,' Tom barked.

He stepped over Tyler's prone body and found the triple row of staff lockers. The master key slid home and he opened the tall steel door.

Standing beside him, one eye on Tyler, Kat glanced inside. The sight that greeted her reminded her of an American high-school movie where the nerdy kid has stuck up photos of the prom queen. Or maybe a war film where a fighter pilot's locker is plastered with pin-ups.

Tyler Bolton's locker door was decorated with photos of Jo Morris. Most looked like selfies grabbed from her Instagram. Smiling into the camera in her gym kit. Working it on a resistance machine. Her non-phone hand curled round a kettlebell the size of a water melon. But one, clearly a candid shot, a little pixelated, showed her in a white bra and knickers bending to retrieve something from the changing room floor.

Kat turned to Tyler. Feeling disgust and anger mingling in her breast. 'Tyler Bolton, I am arresting you on suspicion of murder.'

The rest of the caution completed, she motioned for Tom to help her haul the unresisting Tyler to his feet.

CHAPTER TWENTY-SEVEN

Tyler had insisted on a lawyer as soon as he'd got his breath back enough to form coherent sentences. It took thirty minutes to track down one of the duty solicitors, and another thirty for him to hold what he pompously called 'a conference' with his client.

Given that said client had just attempted to deck a police officer and had a stalker's wet dream of a photo display in his locker, Kat thought 'conference' was over-egging it. Just a little.

The interview room stank of disinfectant. The last person to be interviewed in it, an arrest of DS Craig Elders, had claimed to suffer from claustrophobia. When Craig had, mildly, suggested that she was merely delaying the inevitable, she'd shaken her head, emitted a sharp bark of a cough, and emptied her stomach onto the floor.

'So, Tyler,' Kat said, staring at the over-muscled fitness instructor whose tanned skin looked grey under the harsh light from the fluorescent tube above his head. 'Where shall we start? OK, why did you assault my colleague, DC Tom Gray? Maybe you're taking anabolic steroids. Did you get a flash of the old roid-rage?'

'I didn't assault him. I missed.'

'You swung a punch, which you clearly intended to connect. That's assault. Why?'

'I thought he was going to hit me. It was self-defence.'

Kat nodded, as if she were taking his ridiculous assertion seriously.

'We might come back to that. Bearing in mind that I was standing right there, I'd love to hear what evidence you had, or thought you had, that led you to that conclusion.' He opened his mouth. She cut him off. 'But not now. Tell me about the photos of Jo Morris in your locker.'

He shrugged. 'There's no law against it.'

'Ever hear of upskirting, Tyler? You had a photo of Jo in her underwear taken in the changing rooms at work. That is illegal under the Voyeurism (Offences) Act, which came into force on 12 April 2019. Why did you take it?'

Tyler blinked.

The solicitor leaned over and spoke behind his hand in a low murmur.

Tyler nodded. Smirked at Kat. 'No comment.'

'At the gym, you said Jo wasn't your type.' She turned to Tom. 'What did he say, Tom?'

Tom made play of consulting his notebook. 'He said, "I prefer curvy girls."'

Kat nodded, smiled. 'There you go, Tyler. Your exact words. Why collect photos of a woman who, by your own admission, you didn't fancy? That's a bit odd, isn't it? I mean, it's a bit like me fancying Jack Reacher, but having photos of Tom Cruise on my phone.'

He blinked again. 'No comment.'

'You've got illegal images of a co-worker you claim you didn't fancy in your locker. We have a witness statement that you were pestering the same co-worker, Jo Morris, for a date, which she repeatedly turned down. At the moment, while we're having our little chat in here, my colleagues in our digital forensics team are having a good old rummage through your phone. Messages, photos, socials . . . well' – she spread her hands – 'everything, basically.

184

And they're making me a list of every time you attempted to contact Jo. And her replies – if there were any. You could save everyone a lot of time if you'd just tell the truth and explain your interest in Jo Morris.'

Kat had heard older detectives talk about 'interview time': how hours could go past in a flash, where seconds might drag out to hours. While she waited to see whether Tyler would answer with anything more than a 'No comment', she watched the red sweep second hand on the wall clock make one full revolution. As it brushed past the '12', he spoke.

'Fine! I did ask her out,' he blurted. 'I mean, you saw the photos. She was totally fit, and I got the feeling things weren't all that rosy in the marital department, if you get my meaning. But she just looked down her nose at me. Like I was some sort of pond life.' He leaned across the table. 'Girls like her, they think they're so special. She said I only got ripped by using steroids. Said my cock – her word, by the way, not mine – was probably shrivelled away to nothing.'

'Wow. That must have really pissed you off,' Kat said.

'Yes, it pissed me off!' Tyler said, ignoring the warning hand his solicitor had just raised. 'That's why I had the photo of her in her underwear. I liked to look at it and think, "Well, you might think you're too good for me, but I've seen what you've got to offer and, believe me, it's not all that."'

Somewhere in this frenzy of self-pity, misogyny, contradictory testimony, and an admission of breaching the upskirting laws, Tyler was telling the truth, Kat was sure of it. He hadn't blinked once. She suspected the steroids had blunted whatever smarts he might once have possessed.

But that left the way open to a more direct line of questioning.

'Tyler, thank you for telling me all that. I'm sure it felt good to get it off your chest.' He nodded, chest rising and falling steadily.

Kat continued. 'Can you tell me where you were last Monday, between 6.00 a.m. and 8.00 a.m.?'

'Pardon?'

'I'd like you to give me your whereabouts early on the Monday morning.' He still looked puzzled. 'Where you were?' she clarified.

He scratched his head. 'At home. Getting ready for work.'

'Anyone confirm that? A flatmate? Your mum?'

He shook his head. 'My parents both leave early for work.'

'You've just told us that you made an unwanted sexual advance to Jo Morris—'

'I asked her out, that's all! Christ! I didn't try to rape her.'

'I think, when our digital forensics team come back with their report, we're going to learn that it was more than just a single request for a date, but let's leave that. You asked her out. She said no and humiliated you into the bargain. By your own admission, her refusal pissed you off. Enough to take a candid photo of her in her underwear, which you stuck onto the inside of your locker. To me, that looks a lot like a motive to murder her. You also have no alibi. So, as well as a motive, you also had an opportunity. Did you kill Jo Morris, Tyler?'

'No!' he practically screamed. 'No,' again, in a quieter voice. 'I absolutely did not.'

'Did you know about her allergy to kiwi fruit? And' – she held up her hand – 'before you answer that, I want to remind you that you're under caution. I'm sure your solicitor has explained to you exactly what that means.'

The lawyer nodded, before turning to Tyler and whispering behind his hand.

'Yes, I did. But so does everybody else. It's part of our training. We all have to fill out a form, same as the clients. In case a gym-user goes into anaphylactic shock or whatever. We're all trained in first aid. I mean everything. Cuts, like, serious ones. Drowning. CPR. The defibrillator. Administering EpiPens.'

Her pulse ticked up at that last admission. 'Have *you* ever had to inject someone with an EpiPen, Tyler?'

'Me?'

'Yes. Has anyone ever had a bad reaction to something at the gym, or actually just in town, and you witnessed it and decided to help them?'

'No, I have not,' he said carefully, shaking his head.

'Sounds to me like you have.'

'Well, I haven't.'

'I see. Does the leisure centre keep records of medical episodes that occur on the premises?'

'Well, yeah, but—'

'And if we ask for a copy stretching back to your first day of employment there, will we find a record of you having to administer an EpiPen to save a client's life?'

This time, Tyler didn't bother waiting for his lawyer to offer any more whispered advice.

'No comment.'

Blink.

◆ ◆ ◆

That night, as Kat and Van sat up in bed reading, she cleared her throat. Her stomach was jumping, and she'd not taken in a single word since she'd opened the book.

'I got the results back from a DNA test on some evidence a couple of days ago,' she said in a quiet voice, half hoping Van wouldn't hear her.

'Anything useful?' he asked, without lifting his eyes off the page.

A wave of anxiety engulfed her. She couldn't find the words to tell him about Jo, even though she'd already told Liv and her father. She found she wasn't even sure she wanted to. Somewhere along the line, the uncertainty about Van and Marnie had dented Kat's faith in their marriage. And now she wasn't sure she could open up to him. It could wait. She needed more time – and space – to find the right words.

'Just confirming something we already suspected, that's all.'

'That's still good, isn't it?'

'Yeah, yeah, still good.'

She turned away and put her book on the nightstand. Switched off her bedside light and slid down beneath the covers.

As she lay there, waiting for Van to join her, she tried to imagine how she could break the news to him. Nothing sounded even half-realistic.

CHAPTER TWENTY-EIGHT

Kat woke at 3.41 a.m. By 5.35 a.m., she'd reread all the key case documents.

Maybe Ian and Tyler *were* connected to Jo's death, but she would have a hard time proving it. Tyler was unpleasant, but, apart from the illegal image of Jo, she had nothing solid on him. What evidence she had on Ian was circumstantial, even if it was high-quality circumstantial. Any defence lawyer worth the name would demolish the kiwi-fruit-and-LSD line she had on Ian.

'Your Honour, the Crown seeks to prove that my client murdered his wife because they found kiwi-fruit skin in his compost heap. By that token, I am surprised Middlehampton police haven't turned up at the doors of half the people in this courtroom.'

The court laughs. The judge smiles behind a raised hand.

'As for the LSD. I would remind the court that we only have the word of a convicted drug dealer that my client did indeed purchase the drug. He has since retracted his admission that he bought it and blames heavy-handed interview techniques employed by DS Ballantyne.'

She shuddered. *No.* The more she thought about it, the more it seemed to her that the key to the whole case lay in Jo's background as a school bully.

Liv hadn't been able to remember the other girls' names, although she'd said Jo's right-hand woman was an Elise someone. Maybe Isaac would know.

His phone rang forty-five times before he answered. No voicemail. Obviously, he felt his customers would be wary of leaving messages.

'H'lo?' he mumbled, his voice drugged with sleep, and who knew what else.

'Isaac, it's Kat. I need to ask you about Jo Morris and her little gang of bullies.'

'Oh, right, yeah. Sorry, it's a bit early for me. What time is it?'

'Six on the dot.'

'Bloody hell, that's cruel and unusual right there.'

'OK, anyway, do you remember the names of the other girls in Jo's gang? Maybe an Elise?'

'Oh, right. Let me think.'

'I need to know, Isaac. Come on, I've played fair with you on this, haven't I?'

'I'm not asking for money, Kat. I really am thinking,' he protested.

'Sorry.'

She listened to him breathing. She heard a catch.

'Yeah! There *was* one called Elise. I remember 'cause her second name's quite unusual. Got a pen?'

'I'll remember.'

'It's Burrluck. That's two Rs. Elise Burrluck.'

◆ ◆ ◆

Before she left the house, Kat wrote a note reminding Van to sign a permission slip for a school trip and write a cheque for the deposit.

She stuck it on the fridge, then left for work. She felt a pang of guilt that she wouldn't see Riley, and another for avoiding her husband.

Once her computer had woken from its slumber, she ran a couple of database searches to find Elise Burrluck. While she waited, she googled her and found her social media profiles.

She had her contact details inside two minutes and was calling her mobile number shortly after the final results popped up on her screen.

'Elise Burrluck?'

'Who is this? Look, if this is one of them scam callers, you can just do one, yeah? I ain't got time for this crap. I got up early to do a new shoot, OK? I'm an influencer? Instagram? TikTok? Do you even *have* them in your country?'

'My name is Kat Ballantyne. I'm a detective sergeant with Hertfordshire Police. Can I come to see you? I'm investigating the murder of a woman – Jo Morris. You might have known her as Jo Starling?'

In the silence that followed, Kat could hear Elise's breathing. Then a muffled sound that might have been a sob. Was she crying?

'Sorry, but why are you telling me this? Are you trying to give me depression or something? I mean, my fans expect me to project a certain image. Like, I am this really upbeat, sunny person. People love that about me. I can't be all weepy or red-faced or whatever.'

Kat frowned. Was she in shock? It might explain her reaction, which was decidedly off.

'I'm sorry, Elise. But I would really like to talk to you.'

'No! This is not going to affect my life, OK? Me and Jo? That was years ago. School, for Christ's sake.'

'I understand if you want to put all that behind you, but—'

'I'm sorry? Put all *what* behind me?'

A hard tone had entered into Elise's voice. Kat felt the ground beneath her feet sliding. The last thing she wanted to do was antagonise a potential witness.

'Were you and Jo close at school? Friends?'

'No! Like I said, that's all ancient history. What sort of saddo even thinks about school? I have to go.'

'Please don't hang up!' Kat said sharply. What if Liv was right? What if someone had planned to take revenge, not just on Jo Morris, but on her lieutenant too? 'Look, Elise, even if you don't want to see me, can I just ask you to be careful about talking to people you don't know well. Don't answer the door without checking who's there.'

This time Elise actually laughed. 'What the hell? I'm a bit old for stranger-danger, don't you think? Goodbye.'

◆　◆　◆

Two hours later, Dispatch called Kat. 'Kat, got an odd one just now. Thought you might want to check it out.'

'Go on.'

'A woman's just called 999 saying she's been poisoned. Paramedics are towards.'

Kat's pulse jumped. 'What's the address?'

'It's 14 Canterbury Road.'

Dreading the answer, Kat asked, 'What's her name?'

'Elise Burrluck.'

Kat looked around. Saw Tom. Waved frantically at him. 'Come on. We've got to go.'

The killer *had* come for Elise. If they could get to her in time, maybe she could identify her attacker.

CHAPTER TWENTY-NINE

Kat drove fast through Middlehampton, blue lights flashing their semaphore on the dash, swerving around cars too slow to pull over.

Reaching Elise's address – a new-built townhouse, three storeys, yellow brick – Kat knocked loudly on the front door. When she got no response, she squatted down and called through the letterbox. She peered in. A woman's body lay on its side, oddly contorted.

'I can see her on the floor. We need to get in.'

Tom nodded and began checking the windows. 'They're all locked,' he shouted.

A siren made Kat turn. The ambulance screeched to a halt outside the house and two paramedics jumped out. She recognised them. Rosemah Abang, a short, dynamic Malaysian woman, and Ryan Meade, tall, blond, gangling.

'Sorry we're late,' Rosemah said. 'We got the shout when you did, but the stack is a nightmare this morning. Too many jobs competing for too few ambulances.'

'There's a woman lying in the floor in there,' Kat said. 'Clear and immediate risk of loss of life. Have you guys got a method-of-entry kit on your van?'

Rosemah nodded. 'Hold on.'

She ran back to the ambulance and returned with a heavy crowbar. With a piercing crack and a splintering of wood, the door gave way. They were in.

While Ryan checked the woman's neck for a pulse, and Rosemah began CPR, Kat stared down at the body.

The woman's back was arched so severely that her heels were touching her behind. And her face was distorted into a horrifying grin – lips pulled back so far that all her teeth were showing. Even so, Kat recognised Elise from her Instagram pictures.

'What do you think, Rosie?' Ryan asked, straightening. 'She's had some kind of seizure. There'll have to be a post-mortem for sure.'

'There will,' said Rosemah. 'But I could save Dr Beale a lot of trouble. It's rat poison.'

Kat's eyebrows shot up. 'Really? I thought that was banned nowadays.'

Rosemah shrugged. 'I don't know about that. But in Kuala Lumpur this one time? I saw a man who died with that exact same expression on his face. It's called *rictus sardonicus*. His body contorted the same way, too. He took rat poison after his wife died. It was in all the papers.'

As the senior paramedic, Rosemah pronounced recognition of life extinct, meaning there was no possibility of reviving the woman. It was official. Kat was investigating two murders.

She crouched beside Elise. She looked like she'd died in a lot of pain. The call had come in while Ian and Tyler were both still at Jubilee Place. She'd have to release both men. Even though she'd been doubting their guilt, it still hurt to lose both her prime suspects simultaneously.

Kat eased down the front of the soft grey velour joggers and plain black knickers and drew in a quick breath. Burnt into Elise's lower belly was the same ugly figure of eight. Beside her, Tom muttered an oath.

She was sure Jo had been known to her killer, and it followed the same was true for the woman lying contorted in death in front of her. A pang of regret surged through her. If she'd only tried harder, maybe Elise wouldn't have opened the door and would now be filming her new product endorsement.

There were no signs of forced entry until Rosemah had crowbarred the door. Somebody had simply walked up the front path, rung the doorbell and waited for Elise to open it. Then they'd blitzed her in an attack, administered the poison, branded her and disappeared.

Jack Beale arrived. She stood up as she heard him talking to the paramedics. He must have told them he'd take over the medical aspects from here because seconds later the ambulance's high-mileage engine roared into life and they took off, on to the next poor soul needing help.

'Morning,' he said, all business now he had a corpse to deal with. 'What have we got?'

'Morning.' She moved aside, giving him room, pleased she felt nothing but professional curiosity as he worked. 'Looks like a second victim. Poisoned, branded.'

Jack knelt at the woman's shoulders, made a few cursory but efficient checks, and nodded. 'OK, I am certifying her dead at' – he checked his watch – 'call it 11.35 a.m.'

'When can you do the autopsy?'

'Does now work for you?'

'You've got a slot?'

'I'll make one. Listen, Kat, this looks horribly like a pattern.' As she had done, he hooked a finger into the waistband of the joggers and pulled them down, exposing the ugly burnt-on design. 'Correction. It *is* a pattern. You need to catch this guy before he does another one. Because if that happens, we'll be back to fending off reporters with a mucky stick.'

Normally, Kat didn't take kindly to people, especially men – especially confident, attractive men like Jack Beale – telling her what she *needed* to do. But maybe because she could feel the same dread he was experiencing, she let it pass. Because he was right, wasn't he?

Patterns meant more bodies. She had to catch the killer fast. And her two prime suspects were currently locked up tight at Jubilee Place.

Somewhere in Middlehampton, the killer was walking free. And maybe already targeting another victim.

CHAPTER THIRTY

As soon as she got back to Jubilee Place, Kat had Ian and Tyler released. The former looked grateful. The latter as arsey as he'd been when he'd tried to deck Tom. He left, threatening legal action. Kat hoped it was just a jacked gym-rat venting.

By the end of the day, she had cause of death for Elise Burrluck. She'd died from asphyxia caused by paralysis of the nerves that controlled breathing. Cause of asphyxia: acute strychnine poisoning, which they knew for sure after Jack leaned on the toxicology lab for a same-day screen.

The dose was huge. Far more concentrated than might be expected in rat poison, from which strychnine had indeed been banned as an ingredient in 2006. The strychnine had been delivered via inhalation, probably of an aerosolised liquid form of the poison.

The blunt-force trauma injury to the back of her head, in which fragments of dirt were embedded, had been caused by contact with the hall floor, presumably when she fell backwards in the seconds after being attacked. A bruise had begun forming on her upper chest. Kat pictured her assailant shoving hard over the breastbone.

Thanks to the emergency call, they could pinpoint time of death as between 11.05 a.m. and 11.25 a.m., when she and Tom had arrived on the scene. Jack had told her that the onset of symptoms of strychnine poisoning typically occurred after ten to twenty minutes. So the murderer had to have been at Elise's address by 10.45 a.m. at the latest. Death normally took two to three hours, but in this instance had occurred much more rapidly, owing to the high concentration of poison.

But above all these facts, Kat had observed something during the post-mortem that had totally reshaped her understanding of the case.

When Jack had cut away Elise's briefs, he'd revealed a small tattoo on her right hip. No more than three centimetres long, and perhaps two across, it comprised a rose-pink 'S' superimposed on a turquoise '3'. And in outline, the combined characters almost exactly matched the livid mark burnt into the skin on her lower belly. The brand wasn't an '8'. It wasn't an infinity symbol, either. It was a crude, homemade replica of the tattoo Elise already had needled onto her skin.

Kat didn't know what 'S3' signified for Elise Burrluck, but whatever it was, it meant something to the person who had murdered her and Jo Morris.

Then it hit her like a flash of lightning. She'd been fooled temporarily by the way the tattoo artist had applied the inks. It wasn't 'S3' at all. It was '3S'. And where had she found Jo Morris?

At the centre of the Three Sisters.

She screwed her eyes tight shut and tugged on her earlobes. There it was again. 'Sisters.' Ripples were spreading out through the case: everyone they touched seemingly linked by that relationship. Kat and Jo, her half-sister. And now Jo and Elise.

The following day, Jack called to confirm that Jo Morris had had no tattoos of any kind. So although the symbol linked the two victims, only one had felt the need or desire to have it inked permanently onto her body.

The murder wall had been expanded and now contained two networks centred on photographs of the two dead women. Kat had written *Three Sisters* in the centre, arrowing connections to the standing stones and the pair of victims plus a blank rectangle with a question mark at its centre.

At 9.00 a.m. Carve-up convened a briefing to run through what they knew. Heading into the big conference room in MCU, Kat's guts were squirming. She knew what was coming from Carve-up. And she was only half convinced she knew how to counter it.

The room was packed. It did nothing to ease Kat's nerves. Getting chewed out by your boss was never pleasant; experiencing the event with an audience made it ten times worse. And Carve-up, she knew, wouldn't miss the chance to perform.

He'd stopped shaving around his mouth and chin recently. The fledgling goatee put her in mind of Isaac Handy. She wondered which man was the bigger criminal. Although she had nothing so formal as a dossier on Carve-up, she had a few lines of enquiry. One, as a uniformed PC he'd shared crime scene photos with a friend of Liv's. Two, he'd been part of a trio of detectives who'd extorted sexual favours from prostitutes in exchange for not arresting them. Three, and the most damning of all, as far as Kat was concerned, he was a regular golf partner of her father's.

'DS Ballantyne,' he said, breaking her chain of thought, 'you were first on scene yesterday. What can you tell us?'

She ran through the details of the crime scene. Projected photos onto the wall. Summarised the results of the post-mortem and the toxicology report. Outlined possible lines of enquiry and urgent actions. Waited for the blow to fall.

Carve-up held back for a full five seconds. Another of his cheap tricks.

'A second dead woman. Murdered in her home. Poisoned, in fact. Branded as you showed us, on the exact same spot on her body, with the exact same symbol as Jo Morris. And while Ian Morris, your prime suspect, and Tyler Bolton, were actually . . . remind me again?'

God, he was actually enjoying himself. Her cheeks aflame, she answered, 'In the cells downstairs.'

'Forgive me here, but that kind of does rule them both out as suspects in Elise Burrluck's murder.' He smirked. 'We have a second victim now. Same MO.'

'It's not the same at all.'

'Really? Oh, well, maybe you could enlighten us as to how two women dead by poisoning with identical brands above their pu—' He caught himself just in time, she thought. '—on their abdomens – are not the work of the same killer? The same *serial* killer.'

Time to fight back. To claw back a little respect. 'Serial killers are classified as stranger murders. I don't believe either Jo or Elise were killed by a stranger. We have witnesses who've said Jo was a nasty piece of work at school. And that Elise was her second-in-command. I think our killer is somebody they picked on at school. So that's where I'm looking next.'

'What witnesses?' Carve-up demanded.

Kat thought fast. No way could she admit Liv was still alive. It risked exposing Kat for her part in withholding evidence during the Origami Killer investigation.

'Reuben Starling MP and Isaac Handy,' she said firmly.

At the mention of the second name, groans rang out.

Carve-up pounced. 'Great. So, a politician and a convicted drug dealer. Neither profession exactly a byword for honesty.'

'Which is why I'll be following up the tips in person,' she retorted.

'What about Elise, Kat?' Leah asked. 'Any sign she knew her attacker?'

Kat wished she had a better answer than 'Not at this point. There were no signs of forced entry, so it's my working assumption the killer just rang the doorbell and sprayed poison into her face.'

'So it *was* a stranger, then?' Carve-up said triumphantly.

'It could have been, yes,' Kat said. 'But attacking someone in her home is a lot different from out on the common, and we know serial killers have very fixed patterns. Even a change of attack strategy or venue is massively significant. It can rob the killing of the necessary elements to be meaningful for them.'

'I didn't realise we had such an expert in our midst,' Carve-up said.

But as he looked around the room for answering winks or chuckles, she saw that she was winning the others round.

'Then we have the method of death,' she said. 'Strychnine. That's very different from kiwi fruit and LSD.'

'Sounds like we're in the middle of a bloody Agatha Christie book,' one of the older detectives said – to a low burble of chuckles. 'I mean, who can even get hold of strychnine? Hasn't it been banned for years?'

'Since 2006,' Tom said. 'It was used in rat poison until then, but the EU banned it because it caused undue suffering, and all supplies were recalled. Last reported case of strychnine poisoning occurred in 2009. You can still buy unlicensed rat poison online, though.'

For once, Kat was grateful for the Tomsplaining. She shot him a quick smile and mouthed a *thanks, mate*. He nodded back.

'I wish we could cause some of the toerags we get in here undue suffering,' Carve-up said, but his attempt at humour cratered.

Kat outlined her working theory that Jo and Elise had been two-thirds of a gang of bullies and that one of their victims was now, for reasons unknown, out for delayed and very final revenge.

'But the satanic symbol!' Carve-up protested. 'That points to a serial.'

Kat picked up again. Time to put Carve-up back in his box once and for all.

'It's not satanic at all.' She projected a photo of Elise's tattoo. 'Our second victim had this inked onto her right hip. It's "3S". I think it stands for the Three Sisters. It was where Jo Morris was found, after all.'

Talking about sisters brought the shocking fact of her relationship to Jo Morris storming back to the front of her mind. She had to push it away, almost with a physical effort, as she struggled to maintain her composure.

'Looks more like "S3" to me,' Carve-up said.

'Audi do an S3,' someone said. 'Doesn't half go. Lovely little motor.'

Kat could feel herself losing it. Why couldn't they see it? And why couldn't they shut up while she groped her way in some sort of meaningful direction?

Struggling to keep her voice level and feeling the butterflies in her stomach mounting a full-frontal assault, she tried again.

'Listen! We've got *two* possibilities. Either Elise Burrluck was so in love with some sporty little Audi she had the model number inked on her hip. Or it's linked to the literal name of the place where I found Jo Morris. But before we go haring off looking for a serial killer with a thing for prestige cars, a library full of Agatha Christie novels and a medieval torture chamber in his basement, I think we should follow the evidence and do some basic policing and look deeper into their pasts. Because I'm telling you, somewhere we will find skeletons in both these women's closets, and when we do, I think we'll find the murderer there as well.'

Hands on hips, she threw a challenging glare around the room. Heart bumping against her ribs.

'Am I *literally* the only person here who sees it? Come on, people! They were in a gang of bullies. They pushed someone over the edge. Now it's payback time.' Inspiration struck her with the force of a well-aimed baton. 'Wait! *They* were called the Three Sisters! Elise's tattoo. It wasn't the name of the *stones*. It was *their* name. Their logo.'

Maybe her tone had put people on notice, but she got through the rest of the meeting without any further interruptions.

Afterwards, she called Isaac. Maybe she could prod him into remembering another name. No answer. No way to leave him a voicemail either.

Time for some basic policing of her own. Because maybe it *was* all about the bullying. But she still wanted to close down every other line of enquiry.

And that meant talking to Jo's first husband.

CHAPTER THIRTY-ONE

Mark Knight Antiques occupied a prime spot on Potten Walk, a cobbled street running east-west in Three Hills. The large display window to the left of the front door contained a single object in front of a folded wooden screen. A Chinese vase standing on a simple dark wooden table.

Antiques weren't really Kat's thing, but as she peered at the intricately painted ceramic, she could appreciate the detail and the simplicity of the shape. Then she saw the price on a small computer-printed card to one side.

'Ten grand?' she said indignantly. 'Maybe I'll buy two.'

Tom smiled. 'Win the lottery, did you?'

'Don't do it.'

'That would lower your chances of winning, I suppose.'

She pushed the door open, setting a small brass bell tinkling on a blued-steel spring. A young woman who might herself have been Chinese looked up from the tablet she was working on. She smiled, revealing delicate wire braces with sparkly blue stones in front of each tooth.

'Welcome to Mark Knight Antiques,' she said in a beautifully precise upper-class voice. 'I'm Tamsin. Can I help you with anything in particular? I saw you admiring our display item. It's a Famille Rose "Immortals" vase. Six characters and of the period 1736 to 1795. Extremely rare.'

Kat flashed her ID. 'We're here to see Mark Knight. Is he in?'

'Mark's upstairs with a client. I expect he'll be finished in a few minutes. You're welcome to wait here.'

Kat nodded. 'Can you let him know we're here, please?'

'Of course.'

Perhaps Tamsin was used to fielding requests from detectives. Either that or whichever university or finishing school she'd attended had furnished her with a bottomless supply of sangfroid along with the cut-glass accent.

While Tamsin picked up the phone and spoke to her boss, Kat motioned for Tom to join her further into the shop.

'Have you clocked these prices?' she murmured after they'd wandered around the display cases for a few minutes. 'Our Mr Knight's a cut above the average Middlehampton antiques dealer.'

'I'd like to think so,' an amused male voice said from the other side of a tall mahogany cabinet inlaid with mother-of-pearl roses.

The man who appeared from behind the cabinet grinned, revealing sharp-pointed canine teeth that gave him the appearance of a suave vampire. A shock of dark gleaming hair swept back from a high forehead emphasised the look, though it was undercut by the deep tan. At some point he might have had an athletic figure, but a layer of fat, the result of good living no doubt, had smoothed out some of the angles.

'Who do you sell this stuff to?' Kat asked, wondering whether a search of her parents' house would reveal any items bearing an MKA label on their backs.

'Am I being investigated, Detective Sergeant?' he asked, his dark eyes twinkling. He waved his own question away. 'Joke. Yes, we do specialise in the more, ah, rarefied end of the market. We have a few members of the Middlehampton FC first team who buy on an occasional basis. Investments, mostly. And businesspeople. Some of the older families in the outlying villages, too.'

As Knight chuntered on good-naturedly, Kat wondered how he and Jo Starling, as was, had got together. On the face of it, they seemed an unlikely match. She believed that, given the right circumstances, love could cross any divide, whether of money, class, occupation or outlook. *Could.* Just didn't. Or not very often. Not in Middlehampton, anyway.

But then, something about the way he pronounced a French phrase gave her pause. She didn't know what it meant but he'd stumbled over the unfamiliar word. Beneath his cultured tones, she'd heard – just for a split second – a hint of the accent she always mentally referred to as 'Old Middlehampton'. It was a cross between cockney – a legacy of the post-war working-class exodus from London – and a more rural Hertfordshire twang.

Despite his surname, maybe Mark Knight wasn't so noble after all.

'We're investigating the murder of your ex-wife,' Kat said, interrupting him mid-sentence. 'We'd like to ask you a few questions.'

'Oh, right, of course.' The easy smile slipped off his face like polish being wiped from a gleaming piece of wood. 'Perhaps you'd like to speak in my office.'

Once they were seated, and an offer of coffee had been made and politely refused, Kat got down to it.

'Can you tell me why you and Jo got divorced, Mark?'

He frowned and shifted in his chair. 'Is that relevant?'

Interesting. Kat distrusted members of the public who answered questions with questions. It wasn't natural. It was the sound of somebody giving themselves time to think.

She offered him a smile. 'We're trying to build a picture of Jo's life. It's called victimology. Find out how somebody lived, and you find out how they died. And, more importantly, why.'

He shrugged. 'I suppose it's on record anyway. The marriage had, as they say, irretrievably broken down.'

Kat nodded sympathetically, as if happy to accept Mark's glib answer. Saw him relax. Good. Time for the follow-up.

'Yes, but that's basically the *requirement* for a divorce, isn't it? What I'm interested in is the *grounds*. Also who petitioned for divorce in the first place. Was it you or Jo?'

It was a valid, if personal, question. But there was a deeper level of interest. She craved information about her half-sister. Who she was. What she was like. Was being a bully the whole story? What about the charity work? Was she trying to atone for a misspent youth?

He shifted in his chair. Glanced at the clock on the wall. 'I don't understand what this has to do with Jo's murder. Isn't it always about sex, or money or something? Something in the victim's life *now?*'

'People commit murder for all sorts of reasons,' Tom said. 'Sex. Money. Drugs. They can all be factors. In Jo's case we're wondering whether the killer's motive lay somewhere in the past. What was the reason for your divorce?'

Beneath the deep tan, Kat saw a flush on Mark's cheeks. The reason seemed fairly obvious. He'd had an affair. Jo had found out and pressed the nuclear button. Game over. Good for her.

'We were separated for two years,' Mark said, eyeballing Kat as if reading her mind. 'Mutual consent. Not quite a no-fault; they didn't have them back then. But it was amicable enough.'

Kat looked around the office. Took in the antique clocks, the Chinese porcelain, the watches, fine furniture and oil paintings. Apart from watching the occasional episode of the *Antiques Roadshow*, she didn't have a clue about his line of business. But Mark Knight clearly had several hundred thousand pounds' worth of stock here, let alone whatever he had in warehouses or lockups. That suppressed Old Middlehampton accent came back to her. And with it, another line of questioning.

'What's *your* background, Mark?'

His eyes widened. 'Pardon?'

'I'm just wondering how an ordinary Middlehampton lad got his start in the antiques business?'

The jab was well-aimed. He blinked, looked at Tom, who merely stared back at him, then glanced at the clock again, as if someone, somewhere, might ring a bell and declare the round over.

'I, er . . . I've always had an interest. I used to watch the *Antiques Roadshow* as a kid.'

There! The voice. He was struggling to hold on to his posh manner. She'd rattled him.

'Me, too!' Kat said, beaming. 'I bet you did, too, Tom, didn't you?'

'Every Sunday night,' Tom said. 'Family tradition.'

Kat nodded. 'And how did you go from watching the telly to having your own shop stuffed with gold clocks and ten-grand-a-pop vases, Mark? I mean, that's quite a step up, isn't it? Did you take out a business loan? Borrow from friends? Come into an inheritance?'

His lip twitched on that last word.

Tom leaned forwards. 'We can easily check. But given we're investigating a murder and time is precious, you'd be really helping us if you just told us now.'

Mark swallowed. Kat could see the guilt written on his face as clearly as the maker's name on the white dial of the clock sitting atop the mantelpiece.

'It wasn't me,' he said. Then, realising how that sounded to two homicide detectives, he added quickly, 'I mean it wasn't me who came into an inheritance. It was Jo.'

'From her parents,' Kat said. 'Connor and Tasha Starling.'

She fought down an urge to blurt out, *Except Connor wasn't her father. That would have been my dad, Colin-bloody-Morton.*

'They weren't her parents. Well, Tasha was her mum, obviously, but Connor wasn't her father.'

'Go on,' she managed, pinching the web of skin between her thumb and forefinger to try to fight off the nausea that threatened to overwhelm her.

'Jo told me once, when she was drunk. Tasha had a brief affair in the 1980s. She got pregnant and decided to keep the baby. That was Jo.' He sighed, even more deeply than before. 'Anyway, turns out I had the same character flaw as Tasha Starling. Jo caught me out playing away from home and asked for a divorce. Said she'd take me to the cleaners.'

Kat was thinking about Jo's inheritance. Saw where Mark had got the money for his shop from.

'But you threatened to reveal the truth about her parentage, and for some reason that was enough to stop her in her tracks. You blackmailed her and she handed over her inheritance to you in exchange for a mutual-consent separation.'

Mark at least had the good grace to blush properly, so that his tanned cheeks took on a tawny hue.

'I'm not admitting to blackmail.'

'Let's say you negotiated,' Kat said. 'You said, "Give me the money you inherited, and I'll keep quiet about your unconventional family background." That about it?'

Mark nodded.

Kat's mind was spinning. Michelle Wilson had told her Jo had refused to lend Ian Morris any money. And Tom had discovered no real evidence of a biggish sum in her bank and savings accounts. It was simple. Jo didn't have any money to lend.

'You cleaned her out,' she said.

'Look, I'm not proud of what I did. But it was a long time ago,' he said. 'And poor Jo's dead now, so whatever happened between us isn't going to affect things, is it?'

'It might if she decided to confront you over the blackmail and demand the money back,' Tom said. 'Did she call you? "Mark, if you don't give me my inheritance back, I'm going to the police about you blackmailing me." Something like that? We haven't got round to analysing her phone records yet, but what if we find a message like that? It would put you in the frame for her murder. I mean, what a motive! Kill her or lose this amazing business you've built up. Not to mention your reputation.'

'That's outrageous! I would never do anything like that.'

Kat held up a hand. Her bagman had the makings of a brilliant interviewer. The way he'd avoided admitting they didn't even have Jo's phone was masterly. She nodded fractionally at him. But he'd missed the obvious question.

'Maybe we're getting ahead of ourselves,' she said. 'Where were you last Monday morning between 6.00 a.m. and 8.00 a.m.?' •

Mark pulled his head back. Checked the clock again, as if all the answers he needed would magically appear on its silvery-white face.

'Probably in bed. I'm a late riser.'

'Alone?'

'Yes, alone,' he snapped. 'Oh, God. You think I *did* kill her, don't you? Well, I didn't, OK? I loved that woman.'

Mark's chest was heaving, and his right hand gripped his own throat as if he wanted to strangle himself – or perhaps simply prevent any incriminating words tumbling out. His smooth upper-class tones had vanished, replaced with a full-bore Middlehampton accent, from which time had sanded some of the rougher edges.

'Apparently not enough to prevent you having an affair,' Kat said.

'I screwed around!' Mark blurted. 'That makes me pond life, not a murderer!'

Kat frowned. 'Sorry, Mark. Why did you just call yourself "pond life"?'

'It was one of Jo's phrases. That's what I am, isn't it? What you think of me? I see you're married,' he said, nodding at the ring finger of her left hand. 'You despise me.'

'You've got me all wrong, Mark,' she said. 'I don't despise you. I just want to understand you. I mean, yes, if you were a paedo, I'd probably struggle to stay neutral, but in our line of work we meet a lot of people who've committed murder. As for adultery, well' – she shrugged, once again fighting the impulse to visualise Van and Marnie together – 'that's between them and their consciences. And their lawyers, I suppose. And here's the thing. Ninety-nine per cent of the time, people who've committed murder, they're just ordinary people like you and me. They're not slavering monsters chopping people into bits and barbecuing them on a Saturday night. They're husbands, wives, brothers, sisters' – she gulped – 'sons, daughters. Everyday people who just, for a single moment, snap. Now, what you have to understand is that we are not going to stop digging into Jo's background. Tom was right. We're going to look under every stone, inside every locked cupboard, every device, every private journal, right back to her birth certificate if we have to. So any little secrets she was keeping – or you were keeping – they're all going to come out. So, why don't you save yourself, and us, all that trouble and just tell us the truth. Was Jo making trouble for you over the money?'

He ran a hand through that luxuriant dark hair. Wiped sweat from his top lip. He was going to break. She could feel it. The only question was, what was he going to cop to?

CHAPTER THIRTY-TWO

Mark glanced from Kat to Tom and back again. He chewed his lip as he did so.

'I don't know if I should say anything else without a solicitor,' he mumbled.

'Tell me why you think you might need a solicitor.'

'If I told you something that would make me look bad. Like you said, that I had a motive . . .'

'Are you saying she did contact you about the money?'

'Look, I don't know why she suddenly changed her mind. But yes, all right, she sent me a message. I can show you if you like?'

'Yes, please.'

Mark fiddled with his phone then held it up for Kat to see.

I want my money back. I need to help Ian. You're doing OK now so it shouldn't be too hard. End of the month or I tell the police you blackmailed me out of my inheritance.

'How much money are we talking about, Mark? I forgot to ask,' Kat said.

'Two hundred thousand.'

Kat raised her eyebrows. 'OK, that is a lot of cash. And she was willing to pass it all over to you just to avoid people knowing she was the result of an affair?'

He stared at her for several seconds. She sensed it. Another, deeper truth was about to break the surface like a whale breaching.

'It wasn't about that. Not really.'

'What was it about?' Tom asked.

'It went back to her school days. Jo was a bully. There were three of them.'

Kat kept her face still. But her mind was whirling. The theory she'd blurted out in the briefing was spot on. Three of them. Three sisters. The tattoo on Elise Burrluck's hip. The name of their gang. The standing stones.

'Does the name Elise Burrluck mean anything to you?'

'I don't know. Should it?'

'You don't read the *Echo*, then?'

'I try not to. Why?'

'Tell me about the bullying.'

'Mostly it was low-level stuff. But something they did went way too far. She was bitterly ashamed of it. So, when we got into the argument about my affair, I brought it up again. I said I'd go public with it. I mean, you've seen her social media stuff. The woman painted herself as a bloody saint! Well, I said to her that if she was a saint, I was the pope.'

'Could you have paid her back?' Tom asked. 'Have you got a spare two hundred thousand pounds knocking around you could have given her to stop her going to the police?'

Mark started stroking his hair again. *It must make him feel calm*, Kat thought.

'That's just it, isn't it? All this?' He waved an arm around. 'It looks impressive. But I don't own most of it. It's on consignment or I've borrowed against future sales. I have advertising costs, and the rent on this place is astronomical. Yes, I make a good living, but nothing like the kind where I could just write a six-figure cheque.'

Kat clasped her hands on the gleaming wood-topped desk. 'That's why I feel troubled by your story, Mark.'

'But it's true! Every word!'

'I'm sure it is. But . . . look at it from my point of view. You blackmail your ex-wife out of her inheritance.' She held up a hand to forestall his protest. 'Sorry, you *negotiate* her out of it. You build up a thriving but not *mega*-thriving antiques business, dealing with all sorts of celebrity customers. Then, claiming she needs to help husband number two with *his* business, Jo texts you, demanding her money back or she comes to us. You can't pay her back. You panic. You're going to lose everything if she makes a formal complaint. You have no alibi for the morning of her murder.'

He was pulling his fingers through his hair so forcefully it was as if he wanted to drag it right out of his scalp.

'I didn't kill Jo,' he said in a breathless voice. 'You have to believe me.'

'Did you kill Elise Burrluck?' Tom asked.

Mark swung round to stare wild-eyed at Tom.

'What? No! Of course I didn't! I told you, I'd never even *heard* of her until you mentioned her.'

'Can you provide your whereabouts for yesterday, between 10.45 a.m. and 1.00 p.m.?'

'Wait! When? Yes. Absolutely I can. I was visiting a recently bereaved lady to discuss her husband's collection of military medals. After leaving here at about 10.00 a.m., I went home to pick up a couple of things. Then I was with Mrs Levinson from roughly 11.00 a.m. until noon, and then I drove back here through extremely heavy traffic, some sort of roadworks again – bloody council, always digging up the roads – and I was back at the shop just before 1.00 p.m., which Tamsin can confirm.'

Kat made a note of the times and stages of his journey, underlining the gaps.

'OK, Mark, that's all for now. Thank you again for your time and your cooperation. We'll see ourselves out.' She turned at the door. 'One last question. Did you and Jo have any children?'

'No. She said she never wanted to have them. I wasn't fussed, so that was that.'

◆ ◆ ◆

'What did you make of him?' Tom asked over coffee ten minutes later.

'Apart from being a slimeball who blackmailed his wife out of her inheritance after *he'd* had an affair, you mean?'

Tom grinned. 'Yeah, apart from that.'

'He's got motive for Jo and no alibi. And he could easily have found enough time in his little antiques-buying trip with Mrs Levinson to attack Elise at home.'

'But why would he kill Elise? I don't see a motive.'

Kat took a sip of her Americano. Time to try out the new theory that had been coalescing in her brain while they'd been talking to Mark Knight. It still related to the bullying, but maybe it wasn't a victim after all.

'OK, here's a story for you. Jo and Elise were two-thirds of a gang of bullies at Middlehampton College back in the noughties. They called themselves the Three Sisters. Elise was so proud of it, she got a tattoo of their logo. They went too far one day. Jo was ashamed of it and in adult life tried to make amends by doing all her charity work. That's why she gave in to Mark over the money. Shame. It's a powerful human emotion.'

Tom was nodding. Now he grinned. 'And again with the Katsplaining.'

'To continue, if I may?'

Tom nodded, still grinning.

'Elise finds out somehow – maybe Jo tells her – and decides she wants a slice of the action, too. Maybe they reform the gang to put more pressure on Mark. He has a can't-pay-won't-pay moment and decides to murder them both.'

Tom swigged the last of his extra-shot latte. 'You paint a compelling picture. Do you think the third member of the gang is in danger?'

Kat finished her own coffee. 'I don't know. If it *is* Mark, and member number three is in the dark about the blackmail, I don't think so. Plus, now he knows we're looking at him, he'd have to be crazy to attempt it.'

'He didn't *strike* me as crazy. Pond life, yes. A nutter, no.'

'Exactly. But if it's *not* Mark, or Ian, then I want to find this person they bullied to extremes. Because that's a big motive. And it would mean they're probably going after all three "sisters".'

He looked at her. 'Back to school?'

She nodded. 'For me. I want you back at Jubilee Place. I need that connection between Mark and Elise.'

'I'll have a chat with digital forensics. See if they've got into her phone or laptop yet. All we need's one message.'

Kat nodded, already lost in thought. Would a woman really pay a cheating husband a couple of hundred thousand pounds to have her school exploits kept quiet? Had she really been that bad?

With a murderer on the loose and a third potential victim in the frame, Kat knew she had no time to lose.

CHAPTER THIRTY-THREE

Kat crossed the playground at Middlehampton College, memories of her own schooldays at Queen Anne's swirling around in her head. Her and Liv gossiping, or snarking about the nerdy kids. Skipping lessons to smoke forbidden cigarettes at the distant end of the playing field. Bunking off completely to wander around town, maybe, or catch a bus to St Albans, Hemel Hempstead or Watford.

The tarmac yard was painted with multiple overlapping sports courts in different colours. It teemed with kids in sizes from dots just moved up from primary school to gangling six-footers, maintaining carefully calibrated distances from each other according to some unspoken but clearly understood code.

A fleeting image from a nature documentary she'd watched with Van and Riley some weeks earlier popped into her head. A tropical reef: with the sharks as the sixth-formers, and the colourful little clownfish and scarlet shrimps as the year-sevens.

She scanned left and right, looking for Riley. She'd already decided that if she saw him, she'd play it cool. A quick nod at most. No waving. And certainly no calling out or hugging. God, he'd cringe. If not actively beat her off. Having your mum come 'up the school', as it was still called, was social death.

Just as she reached the main entrance, she saw him. He was standing with a couple of other boys, one with a ginger afro. Their lips were moving yet they weren't looking at each other; their phones held their attention. Suddenly desperate for him to notice her, she lingered, one hand on the door.

As if sensing her, he did look up. His forehead crinkled. Was he going to scowl at her? Then he flashed her the briefest of smiles. Her heart soared. Feeling unreasonably happy, she returned his grin and then went inside.

Once she'd explained why she was there, the school secretary – or *Administration Coordinator*, as her desk sign declared – couldn't have been more helpful. Within minutes, Kat was being escorted up a flight of stairs, along a corridor floored in polished parquet, to an office door with a wooden sign laser-cut with the words *Henry Randle, Headmaster*. Kat knew the name, of course, but hadn't met the man personally.

The secretary knocked then pushed open the door. 'DS Ballantyne for you, Headmaster.'

Tea offered, accepted and promised, she left.

'Please, take a seat,' Randle said, indicating she should sit facing him across the desk.

He looked too young to be a headteacher. Clean-shaven, with short, white-blond hair. Blocky features and a questing look in his ice-blue eyes that suggested someone more used to making a living outdoors – possibly at the helm of a Viking longboat – than running a secondary school.

'Thanks for seeing me at such short notice, Mr Randle,' she said.

'Call me Henry, please.' He smiled apologetically. 'I know I look too young to be running a big school like the College. But it's all on merit, I assure you. For my sins, I'm what they like to call a super-head. Maybe I should get myself fitted for a cape.'

It sounded like a rehearsed line. She suddenly felt sorry for him. Probably having to explain himself at every off-site meeting, conference and course. Give him a shaggy haircut and a slouchy posture and he could pass for one of the sixth-formers lounging about outside.

'And not a can of spray paint?' she said.

His mouth quirked upwards. 'How did you know my nickname?'

'"Randle the Vandal"? My son's just gone up to year eight. It was one of the first things he told us when he came here last year. When I was at Queen Anne's we used to call our headmistress "The Dragon". Her surname was Waggon. Not very inventive, but then, that's kids for you.'

'I quite like it. I have a little off-the-cuff lecture about the real Vandals. They sacked Rome in AD 455 and then proceeded to . . .' His pale cheeks flushed pink. 'Which you didn't come here to listen to. I'm sorry. Has something happened involving one of our students? Or is this part of your community outreach work. If you do it? I mean, maybe you're too senior. Are you?' He gulped. 'Sorry. Talking to the police makes me nervous. Must have a guilty conscience.'

She decided to put him out of his misery. 'You're not the only one. But I'm not here about the current student body. I'm investigating two murders. Jo Morris – her maiden name was Starling – and Elise Burrluck. They were students here from around 1995. You have records, I'm hoping.'

'Yes, of course. Some still on paper, but yes, we'd have a record of any student who attended the College right back to its formation in 1953, when—' He paused, smiled. 'Again, not relevant to your visit today.'

She warmed to this super-head with the puppyish demeanour. The clash between his obvious abilities and easily flustered nature was interesting, but maybe the hint of vulnerability made him seem more human to the kids. Although, she thought, at Queen Anne's, they'd have chewed him up and spat out the bones by lunchtime on his first day.

'Is there anyone on the staff now who'd have taught either Jo or Elise?'

He looked up at the ceiling, as if he had the names of past and present teachers painted up there. Then back at Kat. He looked pained. 'Part of my job when I arrived was to . . .' He cleared his throat. 'To . . . ah, *refresh* the teaching staff. Some of the older members of staff had been, frankly, coasting. I had to make quite a few changes.'

'That would be a no, then?'

He shook his head.

'Not entirely. Two members of staff made the cut,' he said. 'Nigel Jenkins is head of maths. He's fifty-three. An outstanding educator. And Vera Maidment is one of our chemistry teachers. She's a few years off retirement.'

'Are they both at school today?'

'They should be. Let me check.' He swivelled his chair round and opened a sleek silver MacBook. Tapped a few keys. 'Oh. Nigel's on holiday. He'll be back next Monday. But Vera's here, and she's got a free period. She's probably in the staffroom. Let me take you. I can introduce you then leave you to it. Unless you'd like me to stay?'

Kat smiled. 'I think I'll manage.'

She followed him down a short corridor and into a large, comfortably furnished room that smelled, just faintly, of tobacco smoke. It must have been baked into the walls. She pictured the staffroom at Queen Anne's. A dark and mysterious place that one only visited under duress. Sunlight spearing through a vale of blue cigarette smoke. Different times.

Vera Maidment put down a copy of the *Times Educational Supplement* and smiled when Henry introduced Kat. She patted her hair, a uniform reddish-brown that suggested she'd coloured it herself. Or maybe she was one of the poor women with alopecia who had to wear a wig. Behind silver wire-framed glasses, intelligent eyes gazed at Kat as if looking directly into her soul.

She had a corner of the large room to herself, a pile of homework on the armchair to her left, a worn brown leather briefcase on the other side. Clearly a woman used to staking out her territory.

'What can I do for you, Detective Sergeant?' she asked, folding small, fine-boned hands in the lap of her skirt – a soft tweed in sage-green and heather.

'I'm investigating two murders: Jo Morris and Elise Burrluck. They came here in the mid-nineties. I wondered whether you ever taught either of them. Jo's maiden name was Starling.'

Vera wrinkled her nose. She might simply have been thinking, but to Kat the expression reminded her of Smokey smelling something disagreeable.

'One teaches so many children. And that was a long time ago.'

Kat smiled. 'I know, but can I be persistent and ask you to think hard? It's very important.'

Vera closed her eyes. Beneath the lids, her eyes wandered left and right, up and down. As if she were dreaming. She opened them again. 'I *do* remember. At different times, yes, I taught both of them. I was also Jo's form tutor in year ten.'

'I've spoken to a couple of people about Jo,' Kat said. 'And there's quite a big difference between the adult woman, who did all kinds of things for charity, and the younger version who went to school here. Bullying was mentioned. Could you shed any light on that for me?'

Vera looked away. Beneath her dark purple blouse, which picked up the heather in her skirt, her chest was rising and falling noticeably. 'Every school has its fair share of bullying, although theirs went far beyond the usual.' She frowned. 'Wait . . . Ballantyne? You're Riley's mum, aren't you?'

'Yes.' Kat felt suddenly nervous. 'I'm sorry that I don't get to as many parents' evenings as I'd like to. You're not saying he's a bully, are you?'

'No, no, nothing like that. Riley's a lovely boy. High-spirited, maybe, but boys will be boys. Not that we're allowed to say that sort of thing anymore. Henry would send me to a workers' re-education camp if he heard me, but there we are,' she said, a mischievous grin revealing uneven grey teeth. 'I'm too old, and old-fashioned, to care. No, I just recognised the name, that's all. Anyway, he might have told you the odd story, and yes, we try to stamp it out. But it's low-level. Name-calling, some stuff on their phones.'

'Was it different back then?'

Vera nodded. 'I'm afraid Jo and Elise made a great many children's lives a misery while they were here.'

'Was there anyone in particular they picked on?'

Another nose-wrinkle as she pondered the question. 'I wouldn't say so. Not really. They were, shall we say, democratic in their attentions.'

'So there would be records? Of people who complained?'

Vera shrugged her bony shoulders. 'There might be. But where you'd find them, I have no idea. There have been so many changes here over the years. It wouldn't surprise me if somebody hadn't thrown the lot in the incinerator. Maybe his nibs did it.' She nodded in the direction of the headmaster's office. 'You know, fresh start, new broom, clean sweep, all that?'

'I'm working on the assumption that Jo and Elise were joined by a third girl in their gang. I think they called it the Three Sisters. Would you remember a name?'

Vera shook her head. 'I'm afraid not. It was such a long time ago and my memory's not what it was.'

Kat handed Vera a card. 'If you think of anything else that might be helpful, call me.'

'I will.' She sighed. 'You know, I'll be leaving at the end of this year. Henry's suggested I take early retirement. I think he wants to see the last of the old guard disappear so he can finally remake the school in his own image. I can't say I'll be sorry. I went into this profession with such high ideals.'

'Meaning what?'

Vera looked at the ceiling. 'Oh, I don't know, just that I wished I'd done more, that's all. So many children I could have helped if I'd had more time. I remember them all, you know.' She frowned. 'Ignore me. I'm closing in on retirement and I have a horrible feeling it's not just the teaching profession I'll be saying goodbye to.'

Was she ill? Was the wig to cover hair loss caused by chemotherapy? Kat let it pass. None of her business. She'd met the same blend of resignation and wistfulness about the past in older coppers who hit their thirty and handed back their warrant cards.

Before leaving the school, Kat sat in her car to think. Vera had been willing to help, just not able. Who else could Kat turn to for help in keeping the flickering flame alight in her bullying theory? Reuben Starling? Clearly no love lost there between uncle and niece. But she didn't fancy another meeting with the borderline alcoholic MP. Then she smiled. Maybe she didn't need to.

'Isaac, it's Kat,' she said, relieved that this time he *had* answered his phone.

'I'm a bit busy right now,' he said, sounding flustered.

She pictured him counting blue pills or packing tight little green bundles into baggies.

'How's your mum?' she asked.

If he hesitated, she'd know he'd played her the other day.

'Better. I got her flowers like you said. That was decent, what you did the other day. Giving me the extra for her present. She can't have chocolates. Says they make her feel sick, what with the chemo and everything. They've given her a wig, too, but it's all wrong, like something out of the drama cupboard at school.'

Isaac's remark reminded her of Vera Maidment's unnaturally thick hair.

'Yesterday, you said Jo Starling and Elise Burrluck were in a gang, yes?'

'OK,' he said, hesitantly, like he was expecting her to spring a trap.

Sure now that she already knew the answer, she asked, 'Did it have a name, this gang?'

'They called themselves the Three Sisters, like the stones on Bowman's Common. They used to go up there at night and smoke weed. Do crazy stuff. I don't exactly know what.'

'Do you remember the name of the third member?'

She held her breath. Isaac had been pretty fuzzy the last time they'd spoken. But he seemed sharper today.

'Hayley Edwards. She was a nutter. Used to love inflicting pain on people. Took pride in it.'

Kat released the breath and made a note of the third name. *The third sister.* Now for the killer question. Literally. 'Did they ever pick on anyone in particular?'

He answered immediately, like he'd been waiting for her to ask him.

'Her name was Goneril Pickering. And before you say anything, she was this really nice girl. Bright, friendly, the whole package. It's just . . . her idiot parents gave her that name. I mean, what were they thinking? You can imagine what she got called. Mostly that's as far as it went, but those three, they just saw it in her, you know? Vulnerability. They never let up.'

'What happened?'

'I don't know. Not for sure. But she disappeared from school before her A-levels and never came back. The rumour was she tried to kill herself.'

'Thanks, Isaac, this is really useful.'

She heard the grin in his voice. 'Don't make a habit of it. It's back to cash for questions next time.'

'Fair enough. Say hi to your mum from me. Tell her I hope she's feeling better soon.'

On the drive back to the station, Kat's mind took each victim in turn. Jo Morris, the former leader of the gang, had remade herself as a charity superstar. She'd priced the distance between her new image and her former exploits at two hundred thousand pounds. *And she was your half-sister*, the insistent voice in her head screamed at her. She blocked it out.

Elise Burrluck, so proud of the fact she belonged to the Three Sisters she'd had their logo, or whatever it was, tattooed on her hip.

Both murdered. It wasn't hard to figure out the reason for the MO. Poisoned for their toxic pasts. Jo's body had been posed at the centre of the Three Sisters on Bowman's Common. A message from the killer. *This is for what you did to me.* And now she had the name of the third member of their evil little gang. Hayley Edwards.

Hayley was in real danger if Isaac's memory was working properly. Shame Vera's was so spotty. But if Isaac *was* right, then Kat had a confirmed motive. Revenge. And a new prime suspect. Goneril Pickering.

CHAPTER THIRTY-FOUR

After she and Tom had exhausted all the standard, and a few of the more creative, sources, Kat had to admit defeat. She could find no trace of Goneril Pickering. Unusual, but not impossible. All it needed was a name change. Lord knew the woman had reason.

She switched her focus to the parents. Both were lecturers at the university: Grahame in English, Stephanie in Drama.

Not knowing whether academics spent all day on campus, or worked from home, Kat decided to try the house first.

The Pickerings lived in a handsome Victorian villa. Decoratively carved red brick – Tudor roses and ivy leaves – surrounded the wide front door. The door was a beautiful object in its own right, its two upper panels glazed with stained-glass panels.

Kat rang the doorbell and stood back. The door swung inwards, revealing a bearded man in his late sixties wearing faded jeans, a crumpled chambray shirt and battered sheepskin slippers. Intense dark eyes blinked from behind black-rimmed glasses.

'Yes, what is it?' he snapped, looking her up and down. 'I'm right in the middle of something, so whatever you're selling, the answer's no.'

Kat was tempted to ask him why he'd bothered coming to the door if he was so busy. Instead, she took control of the conversation in the simplest way possible.

'Grahame Pickering?'

'*Professor* Grahame Pickering, yes. And you are?'

She held up her warrant card. 'Detective Sergeant Kathryn Ballantyne. I'd like to ask you a few questions about your daughter, Goneril. May I come in?'

'I haven't seen her for years. I don't know what I can tell you.'

Kat stood her ground. He scratched his beard and looked away. 'Fine. You'd better come in then.'

He didn't offer coffee or tea. Just led her to a book-lined study. He swept a long-haired cat off a leather armchair and flapped a hand at it. He took a wooden swivel chair by the window and stared at her, the sun behind him shining through his thinning hair and creating a halo. An effect, she felt surer by the second, that was entirely unwarranted.

How best to begin another awkward conversation? The way she always did. By being polite but straightforward. Just ask the question and deal with the fallout afterwards.

'I'm sorry to have to bring up something I'm sure you'd rather not talk about. I'm investigating two murders. During the course of the investigation, it's been suggested that after a campaign of bullying at school, Goneril might have tried to take her own life. I just wondered whether that was true or not?'

He scratched his beard again and looked longingly at the book-and-paper-strewn desk.

'Yes, it's true. She took some pills,' he said, finally. It was interesting that he showed no interest in who might have been murdered. Typical head-in-the-clouds academic. 'I'm not sure what else I can tell you.'

'Was there anyone who seemed particularly affected?'

'I suppose her sisters would have been.'

'Sisters?'

More sisters! she wanted to scream.

'We have *three* daughters. Goneril's the oldest, then Regan, then Cordelia.'

Kat frowned as she wrote down the names. The ripples from that original lobbed rock seemed to be getting larger, not smaller, the further they spread from the original point of impact. And then there were those names. She looked up at Grahame. He was smiling.

'You're thinking that's a lot of baggage with which to saddle a child.'

'Not at all,' she lied.

'Do you know your Shakespeare, DS Ballantyne?'

'We did *Macbeth* at school.'

'Ah, then allow me to enlighten you,' he said in a patronising tone. 'You've heard of *King Lear*, I assume?'

'The mad one,' she said, unable to resist the temptation to wind him up, even though the pompous academic was a potential witness.

His lips pinched together as if he'd been served some less-than-wonderful wine at a university dinner.

'Well, it's a little more nuanced than that, but anyway, Lear has three daughters. Goneril, Regan and Cordelia. We thought they would be' – he paused – 'distinctive.'

Kat nodded. He'd got that right.

'How about a boyfriend?' she asked.

'There *was* a boy, I think. I can't remember his name. Stephanie would know. She's much better with names than I am. Real names, I mean,' he said with a smile. 'I could list you the principal characters in any Shakespeare play in alphabetical order, if you'd like.'

Unsure whether the offer was serious – he did seem to be waiting for permission to go ahead – Kat tried to keep him focused.

'Stephanie would be your wife?'

'That's right. She's an associate professor in Drama and Performing Arts. She's up there now.'

'And how about you?'

'I'm the Head of the English Department. I specialise in contemporary fiction, but I maintain a soft spot for the greats. Chaucer, Shakespeare, obviously, Dickens and so forth.'

'You said you thought Goneril's sisters were affected by her attempt to end her own life. I can't begin to imagine how awful it must have been for all of you. Can you tell me *how* her suicide attempt affected them?'

'Well,' he said, scratching his beard again. Kat was seized with an irrational urge to find a pair of scissors and start chopping it off. 'Before we get to that, we must ask ourselves, was it really a serious attempt? I mean, she did it at home, in an unlocked room. I found her. It was more of a cry for help, perhaps even just attention-seeking.'

Kat took a steadying breath. Was he for real? His poor, bullied daughter had been driven to a despair so extreme she'd tried to kill herself, and he was analysing it coldly as if it were a scene in some play he didn't rate.

'Did either Regan or Cordelia ever talk to you about wanting to hurt the girls who'd been bullying their sister?'

He pursed his lips, inhaled slowly, then spoke on the outbreath. 'No. I don't believe they did. They probably forgot all about it. You know what teenage girls are like, I assume, Detective Sergeant.' He looked her up and down. 'Having been one yourself.'

Kat felt her temper fraying. Breaking all of her own rules about losing it with a witness, she snapped at him. 'I know that if my older sister had been bullied to the point she tried to kill herself, I'd be pretty bloody angry. Is that what you mean, Professor?'

He blanched. Perhaps he was more used to doe-eyed students fawning over him than suddenly irritable homicide detectives giving it to him straight.

'My daughters have each, for their own reasons, decided to maintain a distance from us. I have no idea why, precisely. You should talk to Stephanie,' he said. 'Emotions are rather more her department. Literally.'

'And I will definitely do that. Do you know where your daughters are living now, even if you don't have any contact?'

'Now that I *can* answer. Cordelia is in Australia. She's working on a sheep station, as far as I know. Took what you might call a different path to the one we'd envisaged for her. Regan lives in Middlehampton. We get a card at Christmas, but she has made great efforts to prevent us making contact. As for Goneril, she, ah, well, let's just say she moved away, shall we?'

'Moved where?'

'Talk to Steph. She'll fill you in. Now. If you have no more questions, I really do have to get on. I'm writing a book. On contemporary resonances of classical—'

'Thank you,' Kat said. 'I'll see myself out.'

She found Stephanie at the university in a small, black-painted rehearsal space lit by theatre-style spotlights secured to matt-black steel beams overhead.

Her abundant dark hair, curly enough to be called frizzy, was pulled back into an unruly bun and speared with a pencil. Her large, round green eyes seemed surprised and delighted by everything around her, like a child newly released into a garden after years of being kept in a locked room.

A small group of students were sitting cross-legged on the floor watching their leggings-and-denim-shirt-clad professor raptly. She was talking about the joy not just of inhabiting one of Shakespeare's characters but 'infusing them with your own life force'.

It all sounded a little woo-woo to Kat, but she was here as a homicide investigator, not a theatre critic. She pushed the thought away. Irrelevant, unnecessary and quite possibly disrespectful to another woman's profession.

Looking over at her new visitor, Stephanie smiled. 'I'll be with you in a moment.'

Kat held up her warrant card. 'Police, Professor Pickering. Can I have a quick word?'

Stephanie looked shocked, just for a second, then hurried over.

Where her husband had been offhand, irritable – a typical university don in Kat's experience – his wife was the complete opposite. Warm, effusive, touch-feely, setting multiple silver bangles ringing as she shook Kat's hand so thoroughly she feared Stephanie might draw her into a hug. The effects of being a drama faculty professor, she assumed. All that barely adult emotional energy sloshing around her classes like so much cheap wine.

'Of course I can help you, Kat,' she beamed once Kat managed to introduce herself. 'Just let me finish this class. We're almost done.'

After a couple more minutes, she dismissed the group of adoring students with a blown kiss and an injunction to 'look deep into your inner being and find *your* Romeo, *your* Titania, *your* Caliban'.

Kat was expecting to be led to a private office lined with copies of Shakespeare plays and decorated with macramé plant-holders and vintage theatre posters. So she was taken aback when Stephanie folded herself into a cross-legged seated position on the bare black stage. Kat joined her, wincing as her left knee popped. Grateful, though, that the occasional game of netball she still managed to find time for meant she wasn't too stiff to cross her own legs in front of Stephanie.

'I've just come from speaking to your husband,' Kat began. *Your arsehole husband.* 'I'm investigating the murders of two local women who I believe were involved in a campaign of bullying against your oldest daughter.'

She waited, then. She hadn't asked a question, but that was deliberate. In her experience, most people found silence, space, uncomfortable. They'd rush to fill it, sometimes with unexpected revelations. Confessions, even.

Kat was starting to see suspects everywhere. *Even the parents of a girl driven to the point of suicide?* Kat knew the sorts of feelings she'd harbour towards anyone who did that to Riley.

Stephanie scratched the side of her nose. An echo of the tic her husband had displayed as he rummaged around in his beard for some sort of comfort or solace.

'What did he say?' she asked. 'About Goneril? About what happened?'

'Actually, not a great deal. He mostly suggested I talk to you.'

Stephanie rolled her eyes and huffed out a breath. The effect was stagy. Kat suppressed a smile. Perhaps that was an occupational hazard of lecturing in drama. *Everything* you did started looking like a performance.

'Sounds like Grahame,' she said. 'I'm afraid he's always found books more interesting than people.'

Kat nodded, as if that sort of husband were a common experience. 'By the way, do you mind if I record our conversation? It's so much easier than taking notes by hand.'

'What? Oh, no, go ahead. Nobody takes notes these days, do they? Grahame's always complaining how his students all set their phones on their desks and just record the whole lecture.'

'I asked Grahame about whether Goneril had a boyfriend. He seemed to think there might have been someone,' Kat prompted.

Stephanie nodded, smiled. She took the pencil out of her bun and commenced to fiddle with it.

'There *was* a boyfriend. Her first. And only, as far as I know, at least at school. Mark was such a lovely boy,' she said with a wistful smile. 'He took it hard, what happened to her. In the end, he drifted away from us.'

Kat's ears pricked up at the name. 'Mark? Do you remember his surname?'

'Knight. He's doing very well for himself these days. He has a rather upmarket antiques shop in town.'

Kat didn't need to make a note. She'd be going back for a second chat with Mark.

'And when you say he took it hard, can you tell me what you mean by that?'

Stephanie heaved another sigh, setting the tiny silver bells on the neck cords of her blouse tinkling against her chest.

'After Goneril took the pills, Mark barely left her side. He came to live with us. He was like a full-time carer. When he wasn't at school, obviously. But then, after she left, he just changed. He became moody, withdrawn, sulky. Eventually he had a blazing row with Grahame. Said these awful, unspeakable things. How Grahame didn't really love Goneril. How we should have gone to the police. He said – and believe me, Kat, I can remember those lines he spoke as if they were printed on a page in front of me right now . . . Anyway, he said, "If you were a real man, you'd get a gun and you'd kill those bitches." He was overwrought. He didn't mean it. But after that he moved out and we've never really seen him since. Not in the flesh at any rate. I did see him on the TV a few months ago. *Antiques Roadshow.*'

Kat had to adjust her position. Her right foot was tingling with pins and needles and one of her hips felt like it might never unfold again.

'What do you mean, "after she left"?'

'Goneril never came back to us after the overdose. I think she blamed us for what happened to her. She even told us we'd done it on purpose, giving her that name. That we'd painted a target on her back. She left home, lived with friends, started taking drugs. I heard a rumour she'd even started selling herself. Sex work,' she added in a theatrical whisper, just in case Kat hadn't understood the euphemism. 'She moved to London in the end. We haven't heard from her since.'

Stephanie's voice cracked and she swallowed noisily. Wiped her sleeve over her eyes.

'I'm sorry,' Kat said, meaning it. 'And for pushing you to think about these painful memories. Do you remember what sort of pills Goneril took?'

Stephanie shook her head and sighed. 'Some sort of tranquiliser. The doctors said they were too degraded by her stomach acid to positively identify. Benzodiazepines, they said.'

'Were you or your husband on any prescription medication at the time?'

'They weren't ours, if that's what you mean. We've both had our fair share of troubles, but we don't believe in medicating the human condition, Kat.'

Kat nodded. She'd never heard taking tranquilisers described like that before.

'Grahame also told me your middle daughter, Regan, doesn't really speak to you either. Why is that?'

Stephanie turned reddened eyes on Kat. 'She also blamed us for what happened. As soon as she could she moved out, too. Even Cordelia couldn't wait to get away from us.' She sniffed. 'She went as far away as she could manage. Australia! Works on a sheep station of all things. Why would she do that?'

Feeling Stephanie was expecting an answer, Kat aimed for something suitably vague yet relatable.

'It sounds like she needed to find herself.'

'You're right! She did. I just wish it could have been a little closer to home.' Stephanie stretched out a hand and grasped Kat's in a hot grip. 'Honestly, Kat, it's positively Shakespearian, don't you think? All we need's for Grahame to murder me before having his head cut off by a jealous suitor, and then we'd have all three acts.'

Kat waited for a wink, or a knowing smile. But none came. Stephanie Pickering was in earnest. She literally saw her life as a theatrical production. It explained a lot. Feeling that the Pickerings' story was all too much like real life, no playwright needed, Kat gently disengaged Stephanie's hand.

'Do you have an address for either Goneril or Regan?' she asked.

'I'm sorry. I know how this sounds, but I don't.' She laid a hand on her breast. 'I grieve every day for my lost daughters, but they've made their wishes abundantly clear.'

'How about Cordelia?'

'Oh, yes. There at least I can help you.'

Stephanie produced a phone and transferred a mobile number to Kat's.

She had one more question before leaving and going to see Mark Knight. It was intrusive, and perhaps not strictly relevant, but Stephanie herself had given her the opening.

'Stephanie, I have to ask, when Goneril said you'd put a target on her back, giving her that name, what do you think she meant?'

'Oh. Well, I'm sure you know the story of Lear.'

Kat smiled. 'Pretend I don't.'

'They weren't very nice women, the two older daughters. Goneril felt we'd saddled her with more baggage than a name should come with.'

'That's all?'

'Yes – why, what else would there be?'

Could Stephanie really be this naive? Did she really not hear the similarity to the name of an STI? No point hammering the point home.

'Sorry to ask, but did you always plan to go with all three names?'

Now it was Stephanie's turn to smile. The expression brought crow's feet to the corners of those large, green eyes.

'No, of course not! But when our first child was a girl, we thought it would be appropriate for both our specialisms to go with Goneril. I mean, one hates to see one's child's first classroom and all those little coat pegs labelled with the same names. At least our daughter wouldn't be mixed up with anyone else.'

'And the other two?'

'When Regan came along, the name just seemed to suggest itself. Naturally, when I had a third girl, we had no choice. Grahame was rather pleased. I think he saw himself as this old king, possessed of three daughters competing to demonstrate which loved him the most.'

To Kat it sounded like so much academic BS, but she kept that opinion to herself. Two women were dead, and she had to find their murderer. And now, in Mark Knight, she had a person of interest who'd been married to the first victim, who she suspected was threatened with exposure by the second, and had been the first boyfriend of the girl they'd almost bullied to death.

CHAPTER THIRTY-FIVE

After the dark of the drama studio, the bright light outside made Kat squint until her eyes adjusted. Around her, students wandered along paths between patches of grass.

She felt a pang of regret as she remembered her own, all-too-brief, stay at Nottingham University. How would she have turned out if she'd graduated with a law degree instead of fleeing her demons after just one week? She reproached herself for daydreaming. She didn't have the luxury.

She glanced up at the huge red-brick clock tower that dominated the campus. It was 11.55 a.m. What time would that make it in Australia? She stopped. Realised she didn't even know which bit of Australia Cordelia Pickering was working in. They had more than one time zone, didn't they?

She checked on her phone. Cordelia Pickering would be somewhere between eight and ten hours ahead. So between 7.55 p.m. and 9.55 p.m. She thought it might work in her favour. Surely sheep-shearing – or whatever the youngest Pickering sister was doing for money – would be over for the day. Finding a quiet spot amongst some slender birch trees, far away from any of the students, Kay tapped in the country code and then the number.

The phone was answered almost immediately.

'Yeah, who is this, please?'

The girl from Middlehampton had acquired an Australian accent.

'Is that Cordelia Pickering?'

'It's *Judith* Pickering. Jude. Who is this?'

The young woman sounded hostile. Kat needed to win her confidence, and fast, before she hung up.

'Jude, my name is Kat Ballantyne. I'm a detective sergeant with Hertfordshire Police. I'm based in Middlehampton. I'm investigating two murders that I believe are linked to your older sister's attempt to take her own life. Can we talk?'

'I need to put my beer down, hold on.'

Kat became aware of the background noise. Noisy. Laughter. Some rock music that sounded like AC/DC. She pictured a pub somewhere in a red-dust town under an endless blue Australian sky, battered pickups parked outside, their white paint turned tawny.

'OK, I'm back.'

Jude's voice was clear and there was silence behind it. Kat saw her standing at the back of the pub, nothing beyond her but thousands of square miles of red earth. Or was that the interior? Sheep presumably had to graze on something.

'Who's been murdered?' Jude asked.

'The victims' names are Jo Morris and Elise Burrluck. Jo Morris was originally called Jo Starling.'

The pause on the line stretched out for several seconds. A faint tinkle of breaking glass and a burst of male laughter was all Kat could hear.

'Well, well, well. Karma's a bitch,' Jude said, finally. 'How did they die? Painfully, I hope?'

'They were poisoned.'

'Whoa! That had to hurt, right?' Jude's Australian accent had grown stronger as she'd become more emotional.

'Jude, have you heard from either of your sisters recently?' Kat asked.

'Ali not for years. She never got it together again after what those bitches did to her. Last I heard she was in London. Misha's still in Middlehampton, though. Wait, you don't think one of those two killed them, do you? I'm not helping you if you're trying to pin this on them. They wouldn't. I know it!'

'I'm not trying to "pin" anything on anyone, Jude, I promise. But I do need to talk to . . . Misha, did you call her?'

'We made a pact. We swore we'd never use those dreadful handles our parents saddled us with. We used our middle names instead. Goneril became Alison – well, we all call her Ali. I became Jude and Regan became Misha. Short for Michelle.'

Kat's brain was flashing like a lightning storm. *Misha equals Michelle. Equals . . .*

'Is Misha married, Jude?'

'Yes. Couple of years ago. Stan's a diamond.'

'What's her married name? Surname, I mean.'

'Wilson.'

'And do you have a number for her? An address even?'

'Of course I do! But you have to promise me you won't try and put all this on her.'

Kat inhaled. Let the breath out slowly, carefully. She wasn't going to lie. But she really wanted the middle Pickering sister's contact details. If it was on Wheelwright Street, and the house had a boat outside, then she and Michelle Wilson would be speaking, at length. And probably at the cop shop.

'I can't promise you that, Jude. I'm a detective. I just ask questions and follow the evidence. But I could also do some more digging and find her details anyway. You'd just be helping me save some time.'

'Why should I, though? If I help you catch the murderer, that's not going to help me and my sisters, is it?'

'It might not even be Michelle. Or Alison,' Kat said. 'It could be all sorts of people. Those girls bullied lots of other people besides your sister, didn't they?'

Jude paused again before answering. In the silence, Kat pictured sheep in the centre of that red-dirt road, wandering, miles from the ranch, or farm, or whatever they called the places where those millions of animals roamed. Fancied she heard a distant bleat.

'And you just want to talk to her?'

'That's all. I promise.'

It was a promise Kat felt she could both make and keep. Even if the talking in question was reciting the official caution and asking whether Michelle understood what she'd just been told.

'Hold on.' Another, longer pause. 'One-seven-nine Wheelwright Street.'

'Thank you, Jude. I have to go.'

She called Tom on her way back to the car park. 'Meet me at Mark Knight's shop in fifteen minutes.'

'I haven't found anything out yet,' he said.

'No, but I have. Mark Knight went out with Goneril Pickering.'

'You've got a lead, then?'

'I've got a lot more than that, mate. I've also got a stronger motive for Mark to have murdered Jo and Elise, and I've tracked down the middle sister. She was born Regan Pickering, but after her sister tried to take her own life, they all switched to their middle names. She's married now. Her name is Michelle Wilson.'

'Jo Morris's new friend.'

'Exactly. So I'm wondering whether she'd got close to Jo without Jo realising her true identity.'

'How? Wouldn't Jo have recognised her from school?'

'They probably never mixed. A couple of years difference in age doesn't mean a lot to adults, but it's like a forcefield for teenagers,' Kat said, remembering the playground at the College. 'You must remember from your own school. And maybe Michelle has changed a lot physically. It happens. Or she could have deliberately changed her look to fool Jo.'

'Could she be working with Knight?'

'I think we need to ask more questions, don't you?'

Kat drove towards the centre of town filled with renewed optimism that she was going to solve the case. Tom was waiting for her outside Mark Knight's shop. Hands in pockets, he was bending forwards from the waist to scrutinise the Chinese vase in the window. Grinning to herself, Kat stole up behind him.

'It's a fake,' Kat said loudly, right into his ear, making him jump back.

'You sod!' he exclaimed.

'Relax, Tomski, could have been worse,' she said, still smiling. 'I could've Tasered you. Then you'd really be hopping.'

'Tomski? I like that.'

'Just been talking to Jude Pickering, or Cordelia if you prefer.' She frowned. 'Talk about dysfunctional families. Those poor girls.'

'What do you mean?'

'I'll tell you later. We'll get Leah out for a quick drink. Let's go and talk to Mr *Antiques Roadshow* again.'

Dressed in a peony-pink linen shirt and navy chinos, Mark was talking to a middle-aged couple in a corner of the shop, gesturing at a grandfather clock with an ornate, gold-tooled face. He saw Kat and frowned momentarily. Once the couple smiled and moved away, he came to join Kat and Tom.

'Hello again,' he said with a broad smile. 'Back so soon?'

'I wonder whether we could have a quiet word in your office, Mark,' Kat said.

He pulled his cuff back and checked his watch. Stainless-steel case and bracelet, blue and red face. Nautical-looking. Like something James Bond might wear.

'I am rather pushed for time this afternoon, Detective Sergeant. Can it wait?'

'I'm afraid it can't.'

His eyes flicked over to the couple, who were now running appreciative fingers up and down the clock's highly polished case.

'I'll be with you as soon as I can,' he called over.

'Mark, we do, really, need to speak with you,' Kat said.

'This is the middle of the business day,' he countered. 'You can see what's going on.'

The bell above the door jangled and two more obviously well-heeled Middlehamptonians wandered in, nodding at Mark as if they knew him before wandering deeper into the shop.

Kat nodded, smiled. 'Of course I can, Mark. But right now, what's going on for us is a double murder investigation.'

'I can't. I'm sorry. If you'd like to come back later, or make an appointment with Tamsin, we can find a mutually convenient time, I'm sure.'

He folded his arms and made to walk away, as if this pronouncement settled matters. Kat nodded to Tom.

'Mr Knight,' Tom said, in an assertive tone. Not over-loud, just authoritative. Knight turned back. His new customers also turned at the sound. 'Would you perhaps feel more comfortable being interviewed under caution at Jubilee Place police station? That is also an option.'

Mark's eyes widened. 'Are you arresting me?'

'Not at all. An interview under caution is entirely voluntary. You'd be entitled to legal representation, which we can provide if you can't afford your own, and you'd be free to leave at any time.'

Kat kept her face immobile. Inwardly she was full of admiration. Tom had got that all-so-damned-reasonable tone of voice down to a tee.

'No, no need for any of that. I've got nothing to hide. I already gave you an alibi.' He looked over to where the lovely Tamsin, today wearing her hair up in an elegant chignon, was hunched over a laptop. 'Tam, I'll be upstairs. Keep an eye on everything for me. And be ready if the Westcotts need help with anything.'

With that, he led Kat and Tom up to his office. This time he skipped the offer of coffee.

'What's this all about?' he asked, eyes flicking from Kat to Tom and back again.

He was trying to smile, but the muscles around his mouth were too tense to permit it. The effect was of a corpse whose expression had been teased and tweaked into place by a mortician's fingers.

'Mark, did you have many girlfriends when you were at school?' Kat asked.

'Why on earth is that relevant? It was years ago.'

Kat scrutinised that tanned, well-fed face. The furrowed forehead. The tightened lips. The skittering gaze. He was hiding something.

'Did you, though?'

'One or two, I suppose.' He shifted in his chair, as if its comfortable padded leather cushion had been filled with marbles while he'd been downstairs. 'I wasn't a player – if that's what you're asking?'

'Anyone special?'

'Not really. You don't at that age, do you?'

'Did you go out with Goneril Pickering?'

244

The effect was startling. He swallowed, causing his prominent Adam's apple to bob beneath the skin of his throat. The blood giving his smooth-shaven cheeks a ruddy tinge beneath the tan drained out so fast it was like watching a sped-up film of the tide going out.

'Who?' he gulped.

The attempt at feigned ignorance was pitiful.

'Goneril Pickering,' Kat said. 'She was one of your ex-wife's victims. I would have thought you'd remember her. Apparently, you nursed her back to health after she took an overdose.'

'That was a long time ago,' he said shortly. 'I wasn't even eighteen.'

More dissembling. What the hell was he playing at? Was she looking at a double murderer?

'But you resented what they did to her, didn't you?'

'I don't remember.'

'Let me help you, then. You said to Goneril's dad, and I'm quoting her mum here, "If you were a real man, you'd get a gun and you'd kill those bitches." You were never tempted to go after them yourself?'

He shook his head violently, setting a lock of hair flying loose. 'That was just a teenage boy venting. Look, I went out with Goneril, and I loved her. Well, I thought I did. It was very intense. *She* was very intense. After they did what they did to her . . .'

He pulled out a snowy-white handkerchief and blew his nose.

Sure she knew the answer, Kat asked a question that would take them a huge step forward.

'Mark, did they do anything specific to Goneril? Something that left a scar?'

Wiping his eyes before replacing the handkerchief, Mark sniffed loudly, then nodded. 'They branded her with the logo of their gang. Can you believe it? They actually burnt a stupid symbol into her skin. I mean, what kind of sadistic monsters do that?'

'Where?' she asked softly.

He touched his belly, just below his belt buckle. 'That was when she took the pills. I came apart. I think, at that time, if you'd said you could wave a wand, or a truncheon, I suppose, and they'd be dead and it wouldn't come back to me, I'd have said, go ahead. Do it! Did I kill Jo and Elise? No. Like I said before. I didn't. And I proved I couldn't because I was elsewhere. That's literally what "alibi" means, isn't it?'

'It is what it means, Mark,' Tom said. 'But we've identified a couple of time periods during the morning when you say you were visiting your elderly widow when your whereabouts can't be accounted for. No CCTV picked you up. No credit card transactions in shops along the way. You would have had time to get to Elise's house and still make your appointment.'

Mark's mouth worked. Then he clamped his jaws together. The muscle at the angle bunched as if he were chewing.

Kat leaned forward. 'Something's not adding up for me here, Mark. How did you go from wishing Jo Starling dead to marrying her?'

He hesitated before answering. 'This is going to sound strange. I bumped into her in the street years afterwards. I really laid into her and instead of defending herself, she just burst into tears. Well, we were right in the middle of town, and it was embarrassing. I ended up taking her to the pub for a drink. We got talking and I realised how much she'd changed. How much she regretted, and I mean *bitterly* regretted, what she'd done. I saw a different woman and I was attracted to her. One thing led to another.' He trailed off and shrugged.

'I see. Love is blind. Is that what you're telling us? Actually, don't answer that. Instead, can you answer my last question, about whether you murdered Elise Burrluck?'

'I think I'd like you both to leave,' he said, folding his arms across his chest. 'I didn't murder either Jo or Elise. If you want to ask me any more questions it's going to be at the police station, with my solicitor present, and it won't be voluntary, either. You'll have to arrest me.'

Before Tom could speak, Kat gave him the most minute of head shakes. She needed silence to reign, just for a second. Mark had made a bold move. *Put up or shut up*, essentially.

Asking to be arrested in no way denoted innocence. No more than avoiding it signalled guilt. All it did was reflect one individual's emotional reaction to being questioned by detectives about a serious crime. Psychopaths might enjoy the game of cat-and-mouse. A self-righteous blowhard, sure of their own innocence, might do it to score points.

She got to her feet and thanked him for his time. Tom followed suit. Glancing at her. She shot him a look she hoped he'd interpret correctly. They needed evidence, not just connections.

CHAPTER THIRTY-SIX

Leaving Tom at Jubilee Place, Kat drove to Wheelwright Street. It was just past four in the afternoon, meaning the streets were clogged with parents – mainly mums – on the school run. As she drove, she turned one aspect of Judith Pickering's statement over in her mind. It wasn't what she'd said, but what she hadn't. Specifically, even though she'd delighted in the news that Jo and Elise were dead, she hadn't mentioned Hayley. It seemed an odd omission.

This time, Michelle Wilson answered the door without apron or flour-dabs on her nose. The domestic goddess had been replaced by an altogether more stylish woman. Expensive-looking jeans, a simple teal cotton sweater with three-quarter sleeves, and matching green gemstones at her ears and throat.

She smiled when she saw Kat on her doorstep.

'Come in. Tea? I've just made a pot.'

'Yes, thank you, that would be great,' Kat said, following Michelle inside.

Kat took in the open laptop on the table, the pile of printed-out sheets beside it covered in flowcharts and tables of numbers.

'What line of work are you in?'

'I'm a research chemist. I work up at the Bohrheim factory on The Campus. I mean, I'm working from home today, obviously.' Michelle poured the tea. 'So, what brings you back?'

Kat parked the connection that had just sparked in her brain. Both victims had been poisoned, one with a banned substance, the other with a synthetic Class A drug. And Michelle Wilson was a professional chemist.

'It's about your sister,' Kat said. 'Goneril.'

Michelle's eyes flashed. She started breathing heavily. 'Don't call her that! OK? You do *not* call her by that name. She's Ali. Or you can call her Alison – if it's more official.'

'I'm sorry. My mistake. Why didn't you mention her when I came to talk to you about Jo Morris having been killed? I should tell you, I've spoken to your parents. I know what happened. I know what those girls did to Ali.'

Michelle took a gulp of tea and swore as the hot liquid burnt her. She stared at Kat. Not with animosity, she felt, but as if judging whether she could truly understand what she and her two sisters had gone through together.

'I didn't tell you because I assumed you'd put two and two together and arrest me for murder.'

'*Did* you kill Jo Morris, Michelle? I would understand if you just snapped one day. You had reason enough to hate her.'

The expression of empathy was genuine, as far as it went. Kat could easily understand a person suddenly losing it badly enough to lash out and kill someone.

The problem with the murders of Jo Morris and Elise Burrluck was that there was nothing sudden about either of them. Both had required a lot of planning. Gathering resources, research, surveillance, subterfuge even. It spoke of premeditation. Something juries took against almost every single time the Crown Prosecution Service barrister presented them with it.

'It wasn't me,' Michelle said. 'I hated them. All three of them. But I would never kill them.'

'Do you know who *did* kill them?'

Michelle's facial expression was a picture of innocence. The forehead lightly creased in puzzlement. The gaze level. The muscles at the corners of the mouth relaxed. The lips curved upwards just enough to sketch a smile.

'No. Of course I don't know who murdered them.'

The face said she knew nothing. She was innocent. Trustworthy. Without guile.

She might as well have yelled, *I do know! But I'll never tell you.*

Her eyes had betrayed her. As Kat asked the question, they'd flickered over to the fridge.

Her hands had refused to play their part, too. The right had risen to her throat and was clutching her neck as if to stop her saying anything else. Kat didn't need an expert in body language to tell her that here was a woman fighting hard to suppress the truth. Being an inquisitive, observant homicide detective was enough.

Kat rose from her chair and crossed to the fridge. She bent to peer at a photo in the centre of the colourful mishmash of children's drawings, postcards and novelty magnets.

Posing in front of the brightly lit helter-skelter from the annual town carnival, Michelle was hugging an older woman who bore such a close resemblance to her it had to be Alison. She was gaunt, and Kat saw that the age difference was exaggerated by her pallor and the straggly greying hair around her face. It looked very much as if she hadn't managed to kick the drugs her mother had spoken of.

'Is that Alison?' Kat asked.

Michelle looked round and nodded.

'Have you been in regular contact?'

'She's my sister. I love her. Of course I have.'

'When was the last time you saw her?'

Michelle rubbed the tip of her nose. 'Two weeks ago. No, three. I remember because Dickie, he's my son, got a prize at school the day before and I told Ali about it.' She checked her watch. 'He'll be home from school soon. My husband's collecting him. Is this going to take long?'

'I'll be as quick as I can. I need to speak to Alison. Do you have an address for her?'

Michelle looked panicked. 'You can't! She's very vulnerable. She wouldn't be able to cope.'

'I promise you I will be sensitive to her situation, Michelle. But I really do need to speak to her urgently.'

Michelle shook her head from side to side. 'You can't possibly . . . She wouldn't . . . She's not strong enough.'

'Wouldn't what, Michelle? What wouldn't she do?'

'Anything! That's what,' she exclaimed, spreading her hands wide. 'She can barely dress herself some days. I hardly think she could get all that poison together and murder two women.'

'What poison?' Kat asked mildly.

'The, the . . . poison that killed them! It was in the *Echo*. Jo Morris was poisoned to death. So was Elise Burrluck.'

Kat shook her head. 'Jo Morris died of a brain haemorrhage brought on by a misplaced injection of adrenaline from her EpiPen. And we haven't released details to the media of the way Elise died. How did you know? Did Alison tell you?'

'No! Absolutely not. It wasn't her. I know it.'

Kat maintained a neutral expression. But she was rejoicing. This was it. The break in the case that had eluded her so far. Michelle knew more about the murderer's MO than anyone not intimately involved had a right to.

'Then tell me where she's living at the moment. I can go and talk to her, and we'll find out, won't we? If she's innocent like you say, well, you've nothing to worry about, have you? I need to remind you that I'm conducting a murder investigation. That gives me all sorts of legal powers that I'd rather not use. But, Michelle, believe me when I say I'll use them all if it helps me catch a murderer.'

'It's a convent.'

Surprised, Kat frowned. 'She's a nun?'

'No. The nuns there run a halfway house for recovering addicts, people with different vulnerabilities. It's their mission. They're called the Anglican Sisters of Saint Gertrude. It's in Clemmows Hall.'

Kat knew the place. A rambling stately home that had, at some point, been willed or gifted to the nuns as a way of offsetting estate duties. It sat in vast grounds on the western edge of town. A peaceful place for someone with a troubled life to try to recover.

Michelle bit her lip. 'The nuns are helped out by care workers. There's one in particular who's made friends with Ali. Really helped her, you know? Her name's Mercy Kipyego. Ask for her.'

Kat left with Mercy's mobile number. Apparently, the sisters were a very modern order who saw mobile telecommunications as yet more evidence of God's power to make his children's lives easier. It worked for her.

What she wanted, more than anything, was to jump back into her car and drive straight out to Clemmows Hall. She was acutely aware that one of the Three Sisters was still out there, alive, and, if she'd caught the news, possibly terrified she was going to be next. But Kat also had a family. And she desperately wanted to spend a couple of hours with Van and Riley, not to mention Smokey.

She called Mercy and made an appointment to see her and Ali at 10.00 a.m. the following Monday – the earliest possible time, apparently, since Ali had gone away for a couple of days – then drove back to the station.

She'd barely had time to check her emails before Carve-up swaggered over to her desk. She caught the flash of his sickly chartreuse-green tie in the corner of her eye and looked up. Great. The perfect end to the day. He wasted no time.

'I treated myself to some new Apple AirPods,' he began, perching on the corner of her desk. 'Fantastic sound quality. Thought I'd check out a couple of podcasts. See what all the fuss is about.'

Now she understood. Because what podcast could Carve-up possibly be referring to if it wasn't *Home Counties Homicide*?

'Have you caught any of Ethan Metcalfe's shows, DS Ballantyne? He's very insightful.'

'I'm not sure about that, Stu. My dog's got more insight into murder than Ethan.'

He smiled. 'Give the guy a break. Although I have to say, he doesn't seem to return the favour. Anyway. I have to be off. Got an evening golf game. Playing the top half up at the country club with the Undertaker. Make sure I have a full report on my desk by 9.00 a.m., yes?'

Kat watched Carve-up's retreating back, visualising a standing stone toppling over and squashing him beneath it.

CHAPTER THIRTY-SEVEN

Kat walked through her own front door at 7.30 p.m.

Silence.

She called out, 'Anyone home? Mum-slash-wife looking for a little company!'

'We're in the kitchen. Stop shouting!'

Riley's voice cracked on the last word. His voice had just started to break a couple of weeks earlier. Now, every few sentences it would soar up an octave then plummet into his boots, leaving him red-faced. Whether from anger, frustration or embarrassment, she couldn't tell.

Smokey at least was pleased to see her. She heard his claws clicking on the floor before he arrived, pink tongue poking out, his lazy eye with its permanent wink making her smile.

She crouched beside him and scratched behind his ears. 'Hey, Smokes! Didja miss me, huh? Didja miss your mummy? We'll go for a walk later. See if we can find Lois and Barrie, eh?'

Kat detoured to dump her bag and laptop in the dining room and went through into the kitchen. Smokey trotted along behind her and curled up in his bed in the corner.

The sight that greeted her stopped her in her tracks, even as she headed for the fridge and a much-needed glass of wine.

Riley and Van were facing each other across the kitchen table, a chessboard sitting between them. Judging from the haphazard groups of pieces at their elbows, the game had been in progress for a while. She'd never played, but it had to be nearing the end.

'Who's winning?' she asked, perching on one end of the table. She raised the glass of cold Pinot Grigio and took a decent mouthful.

'Shh!' Riley hissed. 'Can't you see we're playing?'

Kat glanced at Van. He smiled but shook his head, too. *Keep quiet or risk an explosion.*

Feeling ignored and not liking it, despite knowing that she only had herself to blame for not having been home earlier, she slid off the table and went to the stove. An orange Le Creuset casserole, its base and sides blackened from much use, sat on the hob. She lifted the lid and smiled.

Van had made a big batch of one of his Bolognese sauces. No slow-cooked shin of beef and fresh herbs for her boys. Here was 'the Dad way' in all its glory. Steak mince, tinned tomatoes, tomato purée and dried herbs.

She bent her head and inhaled. It may have been simple, but it smelled divine. She ladled two scoops into a pasta bowl and stuck it in the microwave. While it hummed and clonked, the edge of the offset bowl catching the inner wall every few seconds, she sawed off a slice of bread and buttered it thickly.

Moments later she was spooning the scalding sauce onto a corner of her slice of bread and blowing frantically so she could get the fragrant mixture into her mouth. Her stomach growled in readiness, making Riley turn his head and grin at her.

That smile lifted her heart more than any amount of cold white wine ever could, and she reciprocated, mouthing, *I hope you win.* She was enjoying watching her two boys facing off over a small wooden board rather than one of the verbal boxing matches they usually preferred.

As she mopped up the last few smears of deep red sauce with a saved crust, Riley leaned back and punched the air.

'Yes! Checkmate, Dad. You snooze, you lose.'

Van studied the board for a few seconds longer, then sat back, shaking his head.

'If I'd been snoozing it would have been easier to bear. Well done, mate. That was a class ending.' He turned to Kat, an eyebrow raised as he nodded at her sparkling white pasta bowl. 'Hungry?'

'Not anymore. That was vintage Ballantyne. You should Instagram it.'

'What? And have every Tom, Dick and Harriet stealing my old family recipe? It goes all the way back—'

'—to 2015,' Riley piped up, grinning at Kat.

She held out a closed fist. 'Nice one.'

She held her breath. He bumped back. This evening couldn't get much better.

'How's the seedy underbelly of Middlehampton, Mum?'

Apparently it could.

'"Seedy" . . . Where on earth did you get that from?'

He shrugged. She gave it a solid seven on the RBIS – the Riley Ballantyne Insouciance Scale. 'History. It was in one of Winston Churchill's speeches. It just sounded cool.'

She raised the glass to her lips. Found the glass was empty. Put it back again.

'Well, I have a strong feeling we're getting close to finding the person who murdered those two ladies.'

Riley snorted.

'What?' she asked, fearing she'd made another 'old person' linguistic misstep. She was correct.

'When you say "ladies" it makes you sound so old-fashioned. Like, from the eighties.'

'OK, women, then. Better?' He nodded. 'So, you know there's not much more I can talk about.'

'Yeah, yeah, yeah, details of ongoing investigations are totally confidential. I know. Is that why you were in school today? Is it one of the teachers?' His eyes popped wide open. 'Oh, my God, is it the Vandal?'

'No, silly! I was just trying to find someone to talk to about the case. Both victims went to the College.'

'But you're OK? I mean, you're going to catch him?'

'You think it's a man?'

He frowned. 'It usually is, though, isn't it? That's what you always say.'

'I do say that, and yes, it could well be a man. There are some men we're looking at who could be him. But there are ladies— women, too. It's a very sad story. It seems like it all goes back to bullying at school.'

She hesitated, unsure how to continue with what she wanted to say. Went to the fridge and refilled her glass, tipping the neck of the bottle towards Van with her eyebrows raised.

He pointed at the half-full beer bottle beside the chessboard.

She sat again, looked into Riley's eyes. Strove to keep her voice light. 'Is there bullying at the College now?'

'Some.'

'Like, how much?' she asked, slipping into Riley's way of talking.

'I don't know. People just do it, don't they?'

'Yes, but I mean, do you ever see it?' *Do you ever* do *it?* she wanted to ask, knowing there was no way she could.

He shot her a sly look. '*I'm* not doing it, if that's what you're asking.'

'Oops!' Van said. 'Caught red-handed making unfounded accusations.' He turned to Riley. 'Got your brief on speed-dial, mate? You might need him. This cop's got it in for you.'

Kat pulled her head back in mock-horror. 'No I haven't! It's just, this woman who was murdered. The first one, I mean. Everyone who knows her now thinks she's such a good person, but in her past, she'd done these terrible things.'

Riley nodded. 'Yeah. We did that in RE. Like, can a good person do bad things, and can a bad person do good things? It's the problem of evil,' he added.

Kat and Van burst out laughing together.

Riley scowled, all trace of his good humour from a moment ago vanished.

'What?'

'Oh, darling, you sounded like this, sort of guru. Like you were a hundred years old, not thirteen,' Kat said.

His face darkened further. Kat recoiled. Had she just tipped him over the edge? Moments like these tended to end in pyrotechnics. And with his unpredictable hormone levels, those fireworks could be as devastating as a pipe bomb.

Riley took a huge breath and let it out in a dragged-out grunt.

'I love you, Mother. And now I have homework to do.'

Riley left the table and walked, as if balancing a book on his head, to the door.

'Wait, what just happened?' Kat asked.

He turned at the kitchen door. 'We did Buddhism in RE, too. "Conquer anger by non-anger. Conquer evil by good." Laters.'

Kat stared at the empty doorway. Half-shocked, half-impressed by her son's iron self-control, she could only shake her head.

'Impressive, isn't it?' Van said from behind her.

She turned round. 'Has he done that to you, too?'

'Oh, all the time. I think he gets a kick out of seeing our faces.'

'Well, if it keeps him from exploding a nuclear warhead in our home, I'm all for it,' she said.

An almighty bang from upstairs shattered the calm. The Art Deco pendant lamp above the table swayed on its chains. Smokey whined and poked his snout under his foreleg. Only one object in the Ballantyne household made that distinctive crash. Riley's bedroom door.

Kat grinned guiltily at Van. He winked. She felt the laugh build inside her like an incoming tidal wave and stifled it in the crook of her elbow just in time. Shoulders shaking, she waited for the paroxysm to pass, then looked up at Van. He was wheezing with silent laughter and pointing at the ceiling. She looked up. A hairline crack had appeared in the paint, emanating from the lamp and zigzagging towards the back door for a metre or so.

'Fifty megatons, minimum,' Van said, setting Kat off again.

When she'd regained at least a measure of control he came closer and took one of her hands.

'How *is* the case going? Are you conquering evil by good? You haven't been around much lately, so I've not been able to ask.'

She leaned forwards and rested her head on his chest. She spoke into his denim shirt, which smelled, deliciously, of him.

'I think so. But, Van, these women, or girls. The stuff they did at the College. They drove Goneril Pickering to attempt suicide and they threatened to lynch this mixed-race friend of Liv's. Who even *does* that?'

'They sound like psychopaths.'

'I know! And I'm just struggling to get my head round it.'

She was also struggling with the fact she was related to one of them. The stress of keeping it from Van was getting too much. She'd have to tell him soon.

'I thought getting your head round psychopaths was part of the day job.'

'I suppose so. But these girls were just . . .'

'Normal?'

'Maybe. But there's bullying and then there's bullying. We had it at Queen Anne's when Liv and I were there, but it was just the usual. Name-calling. The odd fight. Girls being ostracised. But those three, they went to extremes.'

'Have you got someone in mind? Beyond the "person of interest" level.'

'You know I can't say, darling. But put it this way, although Riley was right about the likelihood it'll be a man, I have a strong suspicion I'll be knocking on a woman's door when it comes to the crunch.'

She'd been fiddling with a mother-of-pearl snap on his shirt while they'd been talking. Now, using her thumbnail, she prised it open with a satisfying little click.

He looked down at her, the corners of his mouth curling upwards.

'Can I *help* you?'

Click went another of the snaps. She slid her hand over his chest and found his nipple. It tightened under her palm.

'Yes, you *can* help me,' she murmured, her voice thickening suddenly. 'Because this case has been stressing me out and I need to relax.'

Click.

CHAPTER THIRTY-EIGHT

Kat rolled over and looked at the digital clock on her nightstand. Groaned inwardly. It was 4.28 a.m.

She lay on her back. Closed her eyes and tried to remember the names of everyone in her graduating class from the police training college in alphabetical order. Fifteen minutes later, sighing, she was still wide awake.

This case was getting to her. So many sisters. The three Pickering sisters. The three sisters in *King Lear* after whom their unworldly parents had named them. The vicious gang of bullies who'd named themselves the Three Sisters. And the standing stones on Bowman's Common that had presumably given them the idea.

Something tickled at her cheek. She brushed at it and her finger came away wet. She felt a weight in her chest; she knew what, or rather who, had put it there.

Thanks to her father, there was a fourth sister to Jo Morris, Elise Burrluck and Hayley Edwards. Kat herself. Oh, she could split hairs about half-sisterhood all she liked, but she was related to one of them by blood. And it didn't make her feel good.

Hating herself for it, she rolled towards Van and lay against him, hoping he might wake naturally. He muttered something that could have been a word and shuffled away from her.

'Van,' she whispered. 'Are you awake?'

'I am now. What is it?' He turned over to draw her inside his arms.

It was time.

'I found something out when we were profiling some DNA evidence. It's about me. My family, anyway. I didn't tell you before because I couldn't find the right moment.'

'Are you about to tell me you were left on Colin and Sarah Morton's doorstep in a rush basket?'

'Please don't joke, Van, this is serious.'

'OK. But you've got me worried. What is it? What's wrong?'

She took a quick breath. 'The first victim was my half-sister.'

He pulled himself upright, dislodging her so she bumped her nose on his hip. She sat up beside him and turned to look into his eyes, just visible in the dim light sneaking into their room from the hallway.

She laughed. A cracked, crazy sound in the darkness. 'Imagine that! I just found out I have a half-sister, only I can't talk to her because she's been murdered.'

Van twisted to face Kat. He placed his hands on her shoulders. 'Kat? Look at me and just take a long, slow breath.'

'We were practically the same age,' she said, trying to steady her breathing. Failing.

'You mean your dad—'

'Had an affair, yes. Her name was Tasha Starling. She got pregnant and the baby – my half-sister – turned into a monster who tortured Goneril Pickering until she attempted suicide. She grew up to be Jo Morris. And now she's dead. As is her mother.'

Tears were running down Kat's cheeks as she spelled out, in these few, stark sentences, the awful connection between her and the woman whose murder she was investigating.

'My God, darling. Why didn't you tell me as soon as you found out?'

Trying not to sob, which she worried would wake Riley, Kat buried her face into Van's neck.

'It's the case. I haven't had time to think since I found out.'

His eyes widened.

'Haven't had . . . Come on, darling, it's not like you've been stuck in some hotel somewhere. You've been here every night; there's been loads of time.'

'OK, but I just, I mean, I didn't feel able to.'

'Why? I'm a good listener, aren't I?'

Here it came. The moment when she'd have to share her fears about him and Marnie. She felt ridiculous even saying it. But at least it would be out in the open between them.

'It was when I thought you were having an affair with Marnie,' she whispered. 'It's just been bothering me.'

'Kat, I thought we'd put that one to bed. Sorry, bad choice of words, it's a bit early for me. Look, Marnie likes to make people feel special. With women she flatters them. Compliments their clothes, their hair, whatever she thinks will work. With guys, well, you said it yourself, she's a bit more obvious.'

'She's like a bloody baboon in heat, waggling that bum of hers.'

'Don't forget her boobs!'

She slapped his bare shoulder. 'How could I? They're out to here!'

Laughing, he drew her back into his arms. 'Come here, you.'

She felt so different. Softer, relaxed. Despite the pressure from the case, things were better between them than they had been for a while.

Van's next questions put a spike of anxiety right through that warm place in her chest.

'Have you spoken to your dad?'

'Yes.'

'How did that conversation go? I bet he wasn't pleased you'd found out?'

Kat nodded. *He was even less pleased when I forced him into a pact of mutually assured destruction.* 'Let's just say my Christmas present this year might not be quite as nice as Diana's.'

'That good, eh? Have you told her? Or Nathan?'

This time Kat shook her head, relieved she could tell Van the truth on this one.

'No. And I'm not going to.' She got out of bed and put a dressing gown on. 'You want a cup of tea?'

'Yeah, go on, then. I'm awake now.'

While she padded around the kitchen, Smokey watched her from his bed in the corner. She smiled at him. Imagined his doggy thoughts.

What's the boss up to? Now she's cleared the air with Mr Boss, is she going to finally crack the case?

CHAPTER THIRTY-NINE

The weekend saw Kat in the office for a few hours, and swapping phone calls with Tom as he shared his research into Michelle Wilson. On Monday morning, she drove up to Clemmows Hall. She rolled her car to a stop on the gravelled circle in front of the house, pea shingle crunching and popping under the tyres.

Like her parents' house, the parking area was centred on a statue. But where the Mortons had opted for a gold-leaf reproduction of Eros at Piccadilly Circus, the Walbrooke family had stayed within the confines of classical statuary. A white marble reproduction of Canova's *Three Graces* stood, arms around each other, in the middle of a stone basin in which bright orange fish flickered.

A sign beside the heavy, studded front door welcomed visitors to the community of the Anglican Sisters of Saint Gertrude.

Through prayer, charity and work, we serve God.

She tugged the long, stirrup-shaped bell pull that ran alongside the door through iron hoops driven into the ancient brickwork.

A bell chimed inside. A pleasant, warm sound that made Kat want to be among people who she imagined never experienced the sorts of troubles she and her team were called on to investigate. She corrected herself. Why was she here, after all?

After a short wait, the door swung inwards. She felt disappointed that it didn't creak. Perhaps nuns these days knew about WD-40.

The woman standing in front of her had shining dark skin, and wide-spaced, smiling eyes. No habit or veil.

'I have an appointment to see Mercy Kipyego,' Kat said.

The woman nodded. 'That is me, Detective Sergeant Ballantyne. Please, come in.'

She held the door wide, and Kat stepped over the threshold into a cool hallway floored with worn black and white tiles. At the far end, a scrawny young man in jeans and a crumpled grey shirt was pushing a mop across the floor. In the oblique light, the wet tiles gleamed as if made of polished steel.

Mercy held an arm out to the side. 'Will you follow me, please?'

Her voice held the cadences of East Africa. Perhaps she hadn't been in England long. Kat asked her.

'Oh, no, I have been living in Middlehampton since 2010. But I like to keep home close to me,' she said, 'and my voice is where it seems to like residing. And you? Is this your home town?'

'Born and bred, for my sins.' Kat blushed. 'I mean . . .'

Mercy laughed. 'Please, do not worry. We have a phrase for it around here. We call it "Religious Tourette's". People come here and then all they can say is "Oh, God" this, and "Jesus" that. It is quite funny.'

She led Kat into a simply furnished sitting room. A far cry from her dad's opulent, if confusingly decorated, office. A two-seater sofa covered in a multicoloured crocheted throw. A couple of low armchairs, similarly clad. A basic wooden coffee table, much ringed by carelessly placed mugs. A houseplant in a

Chinese-patterned chamber pot with its handle missing. Probably not worth ten grand.

'Alison should be joining us shortly,' Mercy said. 'I told her you were coming, and she seemed pleased to know you wanted to speak to her. Would you like some tea while we wait?'

'Yes, please. That would be lovely.'

A few minutes later, Mercy appeared with the tea. She frowned. 'Is Alison not here yet? That is a puzzle. I specifically told her the time and not to be late.' She smiled. 'Some of our residents have a shaky grasp of the concept of punctuality. They'd be quite at home in Kenya.'

A worm of doubt squirmed in Kat's belly, making jerky figure-of-eights. She had, after all, given a person of interest in a double-murder investigation advance notice that she'd be coming to talk to her. She supposed she could have turned up unannounced, but the aura surrounding the community, and the language of its website, had persuaded her that politeness would yield more results. Not a mistake she'd make again.

'But Alison is definitely here this morning?' Kat said, wishing it had come out sounding more like a statement than a plea.

'Well, I haven't actually seen her. I was working in the garden early this morning and missed breakfast with the others.'

She frowned and Kat's anxiety notched up a level.

'Where might she be if she's forgotten our appointment?' she asked.

'I do not know. Maybe her room? Residents can move freely around the Hall and grounds, DS Ballantyne. This is not a secure unit.'

'No, no, of course,' Kat said. 'But could we maybe go and see if she's in her room?'

'Of course. Follow me.'

Alison's room was the last on a narrow corridor on the second floor of the main house. Mercy bent her head towards the simple wooden door and then rapped with the second knuckle of her index finger.

'Alison? Are you in there? DS Ballantyne is here to see you. Did you forget?'

There was no answer. By now, Kat would be opening the door and entering, but this was Mercy's home and she forced herself to move at the other woman's pace.

She knocked again, but when nothing happened, she shrugged and twisted the brass doorknob. Kat followed her inside and bit down on a swear word.

The bed was neatly made. In fact, it didn't look as though it had been slept in. The door of the plain wooden wardrobe was open. All it contained were a few wire coat hangers. Her person of interest had just elevated herself to the status of suspect. Unfortunately, she'd achieved that by doing a moonlight flit.

Knowing the answer before she asked, she turned to Mercy. 'Do you have CCTV here?'

'I am afraid not. As I said, this is not a secure unit. In any case, why would we? Our residents live here because they want to. Nobody would dream of keeping tabs on them.'

'When did you last see Alison?' Kat asked, pulling out her notebook.

'Last night. We played cards together, whist, from after dinner till about nine. Then I had work to do and Alison said she was going to bed early.'

Kat thanked her then ran back to her car. She pulled away so violently, she sprayed gravel up from her tyres as she swung out from the circle in front of the hall. Goneril Pickering had several hours' head start on her. She could be anywhere.

As soon as she arrived in MCU, Kat gathered the team around her.

'Goneril Pickering is in the wind,' she said. 'That makes her our prime suspect. Tom, any news from Michelle's employers? Would she be able to do private work in one of their labs?'

'They said it would be possible. She's very senior. As long as she followed protocols, she'd have a pretty free hand.'

'God, those names,' one of the uniformed cops said, staring at the whiteboard. 'I mean, what a millstone to have round your neck your whole life. What were the parents thinking?'

'It's what the girls thought, too,' Kat said. 'That's why they all made this pact to never use them. Goneril's Alison, Regan's Michelle and Cordelia's Judith.'

'At least they sound normal,' the cop said. 'Why aren't you looking at Judith, too?'

'She's in Oz,' Kat said. 'Probably the best alibi of the three of them.'

Then she stopped dead. Her train of thought jumped the tracks. How did she know? Because she'd called Judith's mobile and used the Australian country code. But that didn't mean anything at all, did it? Calls just bounced around all over the world, using phone masts the way a monkey used trees, to swing from one cell to another until they reached their destination.

What if Jude wasn't in Oz at all? What if she was right here, in Middlehampton? What if it was Jude who'd been Jo's last client?

'What is it, Kat?' Leah asked.

Kat rushed across to the whiteboard and snatched up a blue marker. 'Jo Morris's new client. The one on the pink Post-it note on the fridge door. I don't think it was "Roz" at all. I think it was

"R" – for a pseudonym Judith chose at random – then a space, then "Oz", question mark. Because of her accent.'

She scrawled up *R OZ?* on the whiteboard, trying as best she could to imitate Jo Morris's loopy scrawl.

'What are you saying, Skip?' someone asked.

'I'm saying, suppose all three Pickering sisters are in Middlehampton? I'm saying they might all have conspired to murder the members of the gang that drove Goneril to attempt suicide. Maybe the care worker, Mercy Kipyego, is involved, too.' It was a big what-if, but it didn't materially change her course of action. Just increased the suspect pool. 'Right, urgent actions. Leah, stay on the search for Goneril. Right now, she's our prime suspect. Check CCTV at the railway station, ANPR on the roads leading to the M1, every traffic car, every response vehicle. You might catch her hitching a lift.'

'If we get a hit, do I arrest her?'

'You do, but you get her down on the ground and immobilised first. Use force if necessary.'

'Isn't that a bit heavy-handed?' Tom asked, frowning.

'She's got access to poison. We know that for a fact. She might have some on her hands. I don't want you taking any risks, Leah. You wear gloves when you cuff her, and you put an anti-spit mask over her head as well.'

Leah nodded. 'Got it.'

'I want Cordelia's phone traced. Darcy, can you get digital forensics onto her phone. It must've used a mobile mast somewhere in Middlehampton in the last week or two, maybe longer.'

Nodding, Darcy made a note of the details.

'I want everyone else looking for Cordelia Pickering, aka Judith,' Kat said. 'Someone find a photo. Try the parents. Right. Go! I'm off to see Michelle.'

Kat had barely made it to her desk when her phone rang.

'Yes!'

'Kat, it's reception. I've got a woman on the phone, she's very distressed, says she thinks she's going to be murdered. Name's—'

'Is it Hayley Edwards?'

'Yes.'

'Put her through.'

The line clicked.

'Hello? Is that the detective?'

'Hayley, this is DS Ballantyne. Can you tell me where you are, please?'

'I'm at home. I just got back from holiday, and I was flicking through the *Echo*,' she said breathlessly. 'Jo Morris and Elise Burrluck, right? They've been murdered. Well, I know this is going to sound strange, but I think I'm in danger. I'm next! You have to do something!'

'Hayley, can you breathe for me, please,' Kat said, feeling short of breath herself. 'I just need to confirm something. Can you tell me why you think you're in danger of being murdered?'

'At school, we were in a gang. I mean, looking back, it was disgusting.' There was a long pause. A sigh. 'I'm ashamed, to be honest. I don't know if I can talk about it.'

'Please go on.'

Another long pause, during which Kat could hear the other woman's breath coming in short gasps.

'We picked on this girl called Goneril Pickering. I mean, we were really cruel to her. I think she's taking revenge on us. Jo, then Elise, and obviously I'm last. Can't you put me in protective custody or something? I'm terrified they're coming for me next.'

'I'm working on it, Hayley. Right now, though, this minute, I want you to stay indoors. Make sure all the windows and doors

271

are locked and don't answer the door to anyone. Nobody, OK? Not even if you think you recognise them.'

'But what are you going to *do*? I can't stay in here until you catch her.'

Kat's mind was racing. Because Hayley had asked the big question. What exactly *was* she going to do?

'Just sit tight for now. And tell me your address.'

'It's 17 Masons Road in North End, near the playing fields.'

'The ones with the allotments at the back? All right. I know where you mean. I'll call you again when I've got something more to tell you. But you're safe at home.'

Kat hung up. She hoped she hadn't just lied to Hayley.

She went to see Carve-up. Much as she hated to ask for his authority for anything, only he could agree the expenditure necessary for protective custody.

She knocked on his office door. He looked up, saw it was her, and smirked as she entered. 'Yes, DS Ballantyne?'

'The surviving member of the original Three Sisters just made contact. She's here in Middlehampton and she's in fear for her life.'

He rolled his eyes. 'This the gang of psycho-bitches who drove that poor girl to try and kill herself? Shame we can't tell her you reap what you sow, eh? Should have thought of that when they were branding that poor girl like a cow.'

Carve-up wasn't the first detective who'd volunteered that opinion. Different phrasing, but the same basic attitude. *Serves them right.*

Kat had to disagree. Because you couldn't start making judgements about whose murder deserved to be investigated and whose didn't, could you?

Maybe it would be a vicious bully one day and everyone would agree. Then the next, someone who'd battered his wife. Or a paedo.

No contest, he had it coming. But what if the next victim had posted something online that had offended half the town? Did *she* deserve to be murdered? Should they do the bare minimum, then move on and add it to the cold-case pile?

No. In her opinion, murder was murder. You investigated without fear or favour. Let the courts decide who was guilty. Her job was just to catch them.

'Can we put her up in a hotel?'

'For how long?'

'I don't know,' she said in frustration. 'Until we catch the killer.'

'Oh, right. And how long's that going to take? By close of play today? End of tomorrow? End of the week? End of the month? Next month? Next year? Never?'

He was about to swing the invisible baseball bat marked *Budget* and knock her request over the roof and into the next street.

'We're close,' she said. 'I've got multiple suspects and they're all known to us. I've got addresses for two of them.'

This was true, although Goneril no longer lived at hers.

'What's your risk assessment for this third woman?'

'She's at home right now and I've told her to stay put. I don't think there's a risk of the killer breaking in to get to her. It's not the MO. Jo was murdered out of doors and Elise opened the door to her killer. I've told Hayley not to answer the door to anyone.'

Carve-up smiled triumphantly. 'There you are, then. She can call someone to do her shopping, it'll be just like in lockdown. You get a wiggle on and catch whoever's appointed themselves a one-woman vigilante squad and we won't have any need to spend money we don't have on putting her up at the Premier Inn.'

'Can I at least put a car outside her house?'

'Why? You just said she's locked up nice and tight. And you said you've got a prime suspect and you know her address. Just get after her, give her a tug and, bish-bash-bosh, everyone's a winner.'

She left him to it. She'd have more luck winning the money she needed on the lottery than prising it from Carve-up's hands.

And she had a suspect to arrest.

CHAPTER FORTY

Kat briefed Tom on the upcoming arrest of Michelle Wilson, who Kat had now started thinking of as Regan Pickering. Then she called the head office of Bohrheim, Michelle's employer. She'd googled them ahead of the call. The company specialised in repurposing natural poisons into therapeutic pharmaceuticals.

Today was one of Michelle's 'in office' days, meaning she'd be on-site at the factory on The Campus for meetings until at least 6.00 p.m.

Tom drove, while Kat ran through the procedure with him.

'No need for protective gear for this one. She won't be expecting us. And if she's at work, shaking hands and whatnot, she can't be coated in arsenic or whatever she plans to use next.'

Tom nodded, signalling and changing lanes to take the ring road out to The Campus. He'd really been studying the street map of Middlehampton, and she liked the way he always knew which route to take depending on the time of day.

'Can I carry out the arrest, please?' he asked, all humour gone from his voice.

Kat straightened. 'Sure. You've made arrests before, I take it?'

'Yes, of course.' He paused. 'You know, minor stuff, but an arrest's an arrest, right?'

'Just follow procedure and you'll be fine. As we're doing it at her work, let's keep it low-key, though. No need for cuffs. We just go in, arrest her, walk her to the car and bring her in. No theatrics.'

'But what if she makes a run for it?'

Kat flashed on Tom decking Tyler Bolton. She didn't want any more drama like that. Not in a presumably crowded office with dozens of witnesses, all ready with mobile phones to capture the moment two Middlehampton detectives roughed up a suspect. Although the more she thought about Tom's agile footwork at the gym, the more she wondered where he'd learned to fight like that. Certainly not on the police unarmed defence tactics course.

'If she runs, which I doubt she will, you go after her while I call in backup. She won't get far, though. The Campus is ringed by main roads and there's no public transport.'

'What if she jumps in her car?'

'Relax, mate! This isn't *The Fast and the Furious*. Call Traffic and give them her reg number.'

They arrived outside the Bohrheim HQ building ten minutes later and took one of the staff-only parking spots. Kat placed a laminated A4 sheet on the dash. It read *On Official Police Business*. It had no legal force, but it might stop some officious security guard from making trouble and slowing them down.

Inside, she approached reception and smiled at the twenty-something woman at the desk sitting behind the pale wooden riser above the desk.

'We're here to see Michelle Wilson. Where is she, please?'

'Do you have an appointment?' The receptionist smiled, but she made no move to pick up a phone or consult the screen in front of her.

Kat and Tom whipped out their warrant cards.

'We're police' – Kat peered over the desk – 'Maya. Can you just tell me where to find her?'

The young woman paled beneath her apricot-coloured foundation. She blinked, setting her long false eyelashes fluttering like trapped moths. Now she did peer at the screen, and her immaculately manicured nails clicked a few keys. She smiled nervously up at Kat.

'I'll just call her,' she whispered, as if somehow Michelle might overhear the conversation and, as Tom had predicted, do a runner.

'Hi, Michelle, it's Maya on reception. I've got two—'

Kat reached over and rapped the desk. Maya looked up, shocked. Kat shook her head violently.

Instead of saying 'two detectives', Maya thought fast and said, 'I've got to . . . update my spreadsheet. Where will you be this morning?' She frowned. 'It's a new thing, from HR. I'm just doing what I'm told.'

She nodded, pushed a button on her console and looked up at Kat.

'She's in Research. Doing a presentation in the big meeting room. Take the lift to the fifth floor and turn left when you come out. It's the door at the far end of the corridor.'

Kat thanked her and followed her pointing finger to the bank of lifts.

'Benzene!' Maya called after her.

Unsure she'd heard correctly, Kat called over her shoulder, 'We're parked in a staff space. Could you—'

Maya nodded and smiled. 'I'll tell Morgan. He's on duty today.'

Kat and Tom stepped out of the lift into a carpeted corridor decorated with framed prints of highly magnified ball-and-stick models of chemical compounds. Opposite them an open door bore the label *5.3 Chloride.*

Tom turned to Kat. 'Cute, naming their meeting rooms after chemical compounds.'

'Come on,' she said, turning left, anxious to arrest Michelle without incident.

She'd have preferred to find her alone at her desk or peering down a microscope, not making a presentation to a dozen scientists. She formulated a plan on the twenty-metre walk down the corridor, which took them past *5.2 Ethylene* and a couple of private offices behind whose closed doors she glimpsed people hunched over computer keyboards.

Kat stopped outside the door at the end of the corridor, marked *5.1 Benzene*.

'I'll go in and say I need to talk to her urgently,' Kat said. As Tom's face fell, she continued. 'Hold your horses, nobody's taking your turn. She knows me, so she'll come out nice and quiet. Then you can do the business and we'll be away.'

He nodded. Bit his lip.

'Nervous?' Kat asked.

'A little,' he agreed. 'It's true what I said before, I have arrested people. But she'll be my first murderer.'

'Your first *what*?' she asked, eyebrows elevated.

'Oh, sorry. Murder *suspect*.'

'Good boy. Ready?'

'Yup.'

'Wait here.'

Kat pushed the door handle down and stepped into the meeting room. A dozen or so people sat round a long boardroom table on which bowls of wrapped boiled sweets were scattered, along with glass decanters of water, coffee cups, laptops, phones and bits of paper. Michelle was standing at the far end of the room, arm raised, pointing at a multicoloured pie chart on a pull-down screen.

'Kat!' she said, frowning. 'I'm right in the middle of something, as you can see. I'll be finished in about ten minutes.'

Ignoring the twelve other sets of eyes that had swivelled in her direction, Kat focused on Michelle. She injected a little steel into her tone. 'It can't wait, I'm afraid. Could you just step outside with me, please, Michelle?'

It did the trick. Michelle opened her mouth to protest, glanced round the room then back at Kat, who was fixing her with a stare as hard as her voice.

'Fine. I'm sorry, everyone, I won't be a minute.'

Although her colleagues looked intrigued, irritated or even amused, half of them were already checking their phones by the time Michelle joined Kat at the door.

'What is this all about?' Michelle hissed. 'Couldn't it have waited?'

Kat nodded at the door. 'I'll explain outside.'

Where Tom was waiting for them.

Kat closed the door behind her as he spoke.

'Michelle Wilson, you are under arrest on suspicion of the murders of Jo Morris and Elise Burrluck,' he said in a clear, firm voice. 'You do not have to say anything, but it may harm your defence if you do not mention when questioned something which you later rely on in court. Do you understand the caution I have just given you?'

Michelle was blinking rapidly. Her mouth dropped open, but no words emerged. The shocked expression seemed genuine. Kat suppressed a flicker of doubt. She'd met plenty of murderers who could have won a Bafta for acting innocent. Tom repeated the question.

'What's this all about?' Michelle said. 'There must be a mistake. I haven't murdered anyone.' She turned away from Tom and reached for the door handle. 'I have to go back in there. I need to finish my presentation.'

Kat laid a firm but gentle restraining hand on Michelle's forearm. 'Can you just answer DC Gray's question, please.'

Michelle jerked her arm away. 'Well, of course I understand it. I'm not an idiot. I just don't believe it.'

'Come with us, please,' Tom said, extending an arm.

'No! This is ridiculous. I'm a research chemist, not a murderer.' She folded her arms across her chest. 'You can't just drag me out of the meeting like this. They'll wonder what's happened to me.'

'We *can* do it, Michelle. Now, I brought some handcuffs with me.' Tom brought a pair of Quick Cuffs out to show her, causing her eyes to widen further. 'But I'd rather not parade you through the building like a common criminal. So why don't you just come with us quietly and we can sort this all out at the police station?'

'Fine,' she said indignantly. 'But you're making a big mistake. I could sue you for wrongful arrest. I'll get a lawyer.'

Tom motioned for her to precede him down the corridor. 'Which is your right. And if you can't afford a lawyer, one will be provided for you. We'll also give you writing materials and more details of the reason you've been arrested. Thank you for cooperating though. It's making this a lot less awkward than it might otherwise be.'

Kat could only follow her DC, glowing with pride at the way he was handling this assertive, well-educated potential poisoner. He was using deliberately fancy language in an effort to connect with Michelle on her own level. No way would Kat ever have used a phrase like 'it might otherwise be' on some of the lowlifes she'd collared in her own police career. Poor sods probably wouldn't understand it.

In the car, Michelle lapsed into silence. She'd complained when Tom had asked for her phone, but had handed it over, nevertheless. He'd established the relationship early on and now she seemed grudgingly willing to comply with everything he asked her to do.

◆ ◆ ◆

Michelle had insisted on using her own solicitor. Which was her right, as Tom had said. But the woman wouldn't be available for two hours. While Kat waited, she called Darcy.

'We've just arrested Michelle Wilson. Can you fast-track a comparison of the prints we've just taken from her with the partials on the water bottle, please?'

'Sure. Call you as soon as we have the results?'

'Yeah. If I'm interviewing, get someone to pull me out.'

Leaving Tom to prepare for the interview, Kat drove back to Clemmows Hall. Something about the way Goneril Pickering had left her room was niggling at her. Had she really had so few possessions she could clear them *all* out? Wouldn't there be *some* trace of a woman's presence? A discarded paperback? A bit of make-up on the dressing table? Something?

Leaving her car beside the white marble nudes still expressing sisterly love in the middle of the fishpond, she rang the bell. A nun answered, her pink complexion heightened by the pale grey veil and white coif that encircled her face.

'Hi, I'm DS Ballantyne with Hertfordshire Police,' Kat said. 'I was hoping to speak to Mercy.'

The nun smiled, her cornflower-blue eyes sparkling. 'Oh, yes. I think she's playing tennis. The quickest way is round the end of the house there.'

Kat followed her pointing finger and emerged on the far side of the hedge onto a large lawn speckled with purple and yellow flowers. In the far corner, four people – two men, two women, one of whom was Black – were playing tennis on a patchy grey asphalt court. The net looked a little ragged; the white tape had parted company, leaving a long, drooping ellipse. Apparently one of the players had just volleyed a ball through the gap and they were arguing good-naturedly about whether that constituted a fault or not.

As she neared the court, and their features resolved, Kat saw that the Black woman wasn't Mercy. Kat walked over, smiling. The woman's tennis partner – a stringy guy about half her age – was scratching at his wispy beard and grinning, revealing a set of teeth even worse than Isaac's.

'Hello,' she said, 'I'm looking for Mercy. One of the nuns said she was playing tennis.'

The woman shook her head. 'Don't think so, love,' she said in a smoke-roughened voice. 'It's been me, Tim, Janey and Dan the Man all along. What did you want her for? I'm Sharon, by the way. Maybe we can help?'

Kat shrugged. Maybe she could at that. 'I was supposed to meet Goneril, I mean Alison Pickering, with Mercy earlier today. But Alison seems to have disappeared. I wondered if any of you knew where she might have gone. Did she have any close friends? Or a place she talked about a lot? Or maybe . . .'

She trailed off, feeling anxious. Sharon was looking at her with an expression of disbelief on her face. Her partner, Dan, was sniffing, and his eyes had reddened. Across the net, Tim was glaring at her, and Janey was openly weeping. What had she said?

'Are you serious?' Sharon asked. 'Where she might have *gone*? She's *dead*, isn't she?' She pointed skywards with her racket. 'That's where she's gone. If there's any justice in this world.'

Kat felt the world tilt on its axis as the case lurched off course again. *Dead? What the hell is going on with the Pickering sisters?*

'I'm sorry, dead? When? How?'

'Last April! She took her own life.'

The girl who'd been crying pushed the net down, tearing the tape away a little more, and climbed over it to stand in front of Kat. Up close, Kat could see she might once have been very pretty, but her face was puffy, from more than just crying, and broken thread veins in her cheeks pointed to alcohol abuse.

'Mercy loved Alison. We all did. Why would she lie like that?'

Why indeed? Kat realised she'd been played. By maintaining the fiction that Goneril was still alive, her two surviving sisters, aided and abetted by Mercy Kipyego, had thrown the spotlight onto a dead woman. After all, Kat herself had determined that Goneril had a potent motive for murder.

As a plan it would never have survived – at some point they would have run a database search and found Goneril on the register of deaths. But it had muddied the waters. Used up resources. Wasted time.

'Have any of you seen Mercy today?' she asked.

'I have,' the man called Tim said from the other side of the net. 'She was here all morning running group sessions, then I think she said she was going into town.'

Kat thanked them, apologised for causing them any distress, and left them to the remains of their game. She called Leah and told her to get everyone looking for Mercy Kipyego and to arrest her on sight.

'And check for Goneril Pickering, aka Alison Pickering, on the register of births, marriages and deaths.'

CHAPTER FORTY-ONE

The interview room smelled of stale coffee, staler cigarette smoke, BO and fear.

Canteen mythology held that, as a police officer, you developed immunity to the stink, but that it worked on detainees, unsettling them, playing havoc with their defences. In truth, everybody hated it. She secretly wondered whether interviewing people in a room that smelled of vanilla, or cinnamon, might yield more results. Probably not. There'd be less incentive to get out, wouldn't there?

Certainly the woman opposite her seemed in no hurry to leave. She still wore her jacket from the meeting and had somehow managed to keep her hair and make-up looking fresh and professional.

Michelle's solicitor gave them both a run for their money in a sharply tailored navy suit paired with a crisp shirt in a sprigged pattern of tiny, china-blue flowers. She'd introduced herself as Beth Sharpe, a partner in a local firm Kat knew to have the priciest criminal defence solicitors in Middlehampton.

Once the official caution had been recited, and everyone present had introduced themselves for the recorder, Kat looked at Michelle. The woman believed she held all the cards. But two of them, each marked with the name of one of her sisters, were lying face-up on the table and she didn't realise.

Kat knew she'd have to tread very carefully. Lawyers like Beth Sharpe usually advised their clients to go 'No comment'. It was the smart move. She had to rattle Michelle enough for her to disregard Sharpe's expensive advice.

'How's Judith?' she asked, a hand resting on the slender file of paperwork, including the record of Alison Pickering's death from a drugs overdose.

Michelle shrugged. 'Fine, as far as I know. I haven't spoken to her for a while. Mobile reception's terrible on that sheep station.'

'But it's OK here in Middlehampton, isn't it?'

'What's that got to do with it?'

Kat smiled. Time to try a bluff. Find out if her hunch was correct.

'Well, she isn't in Australia, is she? She's right here in town.'

'Er, I don't think so,' Michelle said, smiling.

'She booked a session with Jo Morris for Monday morning two weeks ago, using a pseudonym. I think she murdered her, possibly with your help.'

Beth laid a fine-boned hand on her client's sleeve. 'My client has just told you she believes her sister is in Australia, DS Ballantyne. Do you have any evidence to the contrary?'

It was a great question. And if she'd had more money, or the digital forensics team hadn't already been working their arses off, she could have answered more confidently.

'We're currently tracing Judith's mobile phone. We believe it will have hooked up to a mobile phone mast in Middlehampton.'

Beth made a note with her slim gold biro. She looked up at Kat. 'I see. So, in summary, at this moment in time, you do not have any evidence that Judith Pickering is in Middlehampton. Despite basing this theory of yours on just such a piece of evidence.'

The woman sounded, and looked, as though she were enjoying herself. But Kat had conducted plenty of interviews. This was a long game they were playing. And the PACE clock, though ticking, still had more than twenty-one hours left before she'd have to ask Carve-up for an extension.

'So you haven't spoken to Judith for a while, but you assume she's fine and happy down under, wrangling sheep.' Kat looked into Michelle's eyes. 'How about Goneril? When was the last time you saw her?'

Kat glanced at the solicitor, wondering how much Michelle had told her. *See*, she wanted to say, *you're not the only one who can ask an Olympic-level question.* She'd laid a trap. A 'no comment' here would sound decidedly odd. But if she gave a date after her sister had died, she'd be laying herself open to all kinds of trouble. If she went with a date before she'd died, she'd be contradicting her earlier witness testimony.

'How is this relevant?' Beth asked, rescuing her client. 'You've arrested my client on suspicion of murder. Is this a missing persons case now?'

Kat ignored her. 'Regan? When did you last see Goneril?'

'Don't call us that!' she blurted. 'I told you before. I don't use my first name. Jude doesn't. And nor did Ali.' She flushed. Bit her lip. 'Does, I mean.'

A wave of sympathy for the woman sitting opposite her engulfed Kat. Having once lost the woman she'd always regarded as closer to her than her own flesh-and-blood sibling, she knew what it felt like to have death sever that bond of sisterhood.

'Michelle,' she said in a soft voice. 'I know she's dead. And I am so sorry for your loss. Her friends at Clemmows Hall told me earlier today. And I've seen her death certificate. I know what she went through. What you all went through. It doesn't sound to me like your mum and dad were all that bothered about what happened to Ali. You three had to stick together. But then, when she died, I think everything just got too overwhelming. You decided that Jo, Elise and Hayley had to pay for what they'd done. Ali never recovered from what they did to her, did she? You blame them for her death, don't you?'

Beth passed her client a tissue, which she carefully unfolded before blowing her nose. She screwed it into a ball and squeezed it in her right fist. Looked straight into Kat's expectant eyes.

'They *were* to blame,' she said, shaking off her solicitor's hand. 'What those sadistic bitches did to her was torture. And the school did nothing. *Nothing!* They were useless. And the police! Mum, Dad, you lot, the head: none of them cared about it. Do you know what our dad said? He said it was character-building. Can you believe that? Bloody character-building! His oldest daughter was bullied so viciously she tried to kill herself and he thinks it's some sort of bloody rite of passage.'

'Did you kill them, Michelle? Did you kill Jo and Elise? For what they did to Ali? When she took her own life, was that the trigger? Did you start planning these murders?'

Michelle sniffed and cleared her throat, and leaned towards her solicitor, who had tightened her grip on her wrist.

She nodded, set her lips. Kat felt the air go out of the balloon that had been ascending with her hopes on board. She was going to go—

'No comment.'

Kat leaned back a fraction. Tom moved forward.

'Can you look at the dates I'm going to show you, please?' he asked, sliding a sheet of paper towards Michelle. 'For the tape, I am showing the suspect document AT 17/6, which has been entered into disclosure. Can you also confirm your whereabouts on those dates?'

Michelle scanned the dates on the sheet of computer-printed paper in front of her. Conferred with Beth in a whisper behind raised hands. She stared at Tom. But answered to Kat.

'On both those dates I was on video conference calls with colleagues. There'll be records, and the meetings were all recorded.'

Kat suppressed a sigh. That was that, then. Digital forensics would have some more work to do, but this time it would be working against her case, not for it. But they weren't done yet. Not quite. She and Tom had discussed the interview strategy beforehand, and she still had questions to ask. One of the techniques she'd found worked well was to circle back to earlier questions that the suspect had either refused to answer or dissembled over.

'I know this is painful, Michelle, but I'd like to ask you about Alison again, if that's OK?' She waited. Got the nod she'd been looking for. She'd have asked anyway, but having interviewees agreeing to your suggestions, however minor, was an important step in gaining their trust, and their cooperation. 'Did you go to her funeral?'

'Yes.'

'It must have been very sad. I'm sorry you had to go through it. Was Jude there, too?'

Michelle's lips parted with a click but then, just as she was about to answer, she snapped her jaw closed again.

'No comment.'

'Why did you lie to me about Ali being alive?'

'No comment.'

'Did you conspire with Mercy Kipyego to create the impression Alison was alive when she was already dead? Were you hoping we'd assume it was she who'd been committing the murders?'

A wince. 'No comment.'

'Do you know where Mercy Kipyego is at the moment?'

'No comment.'

'Do you know who killed Jo Morris?'

Michelle's eyes flicked to the ceiling and back. 'No comment.'

'Do you know who killed Elise Burrluck?'

'No comment.'

'Did you prepare the strychnine used to kill Elise Burrluck?'

'No comment.'

Kat took a breath. Time to break this pattern. 'Michelle, I am very worried at the moment. You see, I know that Hayley Edwards was the third member of the Three Sisters gang who terrorised your sister.'

She pulled up her shirt and touched the bare skin of her stomach, hoping the unusually intimate gesture in the formal confines of a police interview room might shock Michelle into answering.

'They branded her with their sign. I've seen it. I can't imagine how painful, how terrifying that must have been. How much you must have hated them for doing that unspeakable thing to Alison. Now, Jo and Elise are already dead. But Hayley's still alive. And right now, *she* is terrified. She told me she bitterly regrets what they did at school. I honestly think if she could, she would go back in time and change things so that they never happened.'

'But they *did* happen, didn't they?'

Kat ignored the interruption. 'Whatever Hayley did in the past, I can't stand back while she's murdered out of a sense of revenge, however justified you think it is. I just can't. So I'm going to ask you again, because you are already in a lot of trouble for lying about Alison. Do you know the identity of the killer? Are they planning to kill Hayley?'

Michelle leaned forwards and clasped her hands on the table. 'I don't know. But if I did know, I wouldn't tell you. All I know is, it wasn't me. And to save you the trouble, I'm not saying anything more.' She turned to face the tape recorder. 'On the advice of my legal representative, I am refusing to answer any further questions.'

She sat back, folded her arms and stared defiantly at Kat.

It wasn't ideal. But they still had time on their side. For now. But just as with Ian Morris and Tyler Bolton, eventually the PACE clock would run down. Then Kat would have to ask Carve-up to authorise a further period of detention.

And out of spite, stupidity or just sheer bloody-mindedness, he'd probably say no.

CHAPTER FORTY-TWO

Kat formally suspended the interview. Back at her desk she and Tom discussed their next move.

'She's lying, isn't she?' Tom said, stirring his coffee as though agitating it with a teaspoon might transform it into something more palatable.

'Yes. She could barely hold it together in there. I think she's been working with Judith all along. Probably with Mercy, too. I think they met up at the funeral and hatched the plan there.'

Kat called over to Leah. 'Any news on the whereabouts of Mercy Kipyego?'

'Still in the wind. She won't get far though. Soon as she uses a credit card or calls someone, we'll have her.'

'Thanks, Leah. Keep on that.'

Kat turned to see Darcy hurrying over. 'Prints on the water bottle and EpiPen don't match Michelle's, I'm afraid.'

Kat sighed resignedly. 'Bollocks! Would have been nice if they did, given she's already in custody.'

She leaned back and looked at the murder wall. Ian Morris, Mark Knight and Tyler Bolton had lines drawn through their names. Not completely exonerated – but given recent developments they had moved right down the list of potential suspects.

She got up and crossed to the whiteboard. Picked up the red marker and drew a line through Goneril Pickering's name. Of the women involved in this tangled case, Michelle, Judith and Mercy Kipyego remained.

Whoever had handled the water bottle and EpiPen, it hadn't been Michelle. That still left the other two women.

'Pity Michelle *didn't* have arsenic all over her hands,' she said dispiritedly. 'We probably could have charged her.'

'Fun fact,' Tom said, 'which I found out during my background research on her. They use arsenic to treat cancer these days. Back in the 1970s, they discovered arsenic trioxide could put certain types of leukaemia into remission. Probably worth losing your hair for.'

She had to smile. 'That *is* a fun fact, Tomski. Please tell me this sudden interest in poisons is only down to your—'

Kat frowned. The sensation was familiar. An itch inside her head. Not somewhere physical. And maybe 'itch' wasn't quite the right word. A tickle, maybe. Or just an insistent knocking from her subconscious, where she'd linked previously unrelated bits of evidence.

She closed her eyes and let the connections unspool in front of her like the central white lines on a long night-time drive. Arsenic treated cancer . . . Isaac Handy's mum had cancer . . . They were giving her chemo . . . which had made her hair fall out so she needed a wig . . . Vera Maidment's hair looked like a wig . . . Vera, who had professed not to remember details of the Three Sisters' bullying. But . . .

'What is it, Kat?'

She opened her eyes.

'When I asked Vera if she could remember any specific victims of Jo and her mates, she was really vague. But just before I left, she also said she remembered all her pupils. Surely if Goneril had been bullied to the point of attempting suicide, Vera would have remembered? What if she's hiding something? What if she's *involved*? She is a chemistry teacher, after all.'

Tom shrugged. 'Maybe. But if she's all you've got, that's that, isn't it?'

'But she isn't, Tomski! The head mentioned another teacher who was there back in the day.' She consulted her notebook. 'Nigel Jenkins, head of maths. He was on holiday, but he'll be back now.'

She called the school. Two minutes later, she was speaking to Jenkins.

◆ ◆ ◆

Kat arrived at Middlehampton College at 4.30 p.m. to be informed by the school secretary that Vera had left for the day carrying 'a Mount Everest of marking'. Kat asked for her address – a street in Bradyfield on the east side of town – and headed straight there. She parked behind a yellow VW Beetle.

Vera opened the door with a smile on her face that slid off like a fried egg from a Teflon pan when she saw who had come calling. In its place a weary expression, all the more downbeat for being painted onto such sallow skin. It was almost yellow in the sunlight and Kat had a shrewd idea why.

'Hello, Vera. Can I come in?'

'Of course.'

Kat stepped across the threshold. The house smelled of sickness. A metallic odour of drugs and a body fighting something invasive.

Vera led Kat down the hallway to a large, cluttered kitchen-dining room. Somehow the mess made it feel homely, rather than chaotic. At the eating end of the room sat a large pine table disfigured by black scorch marks. Crowding its battered surface were reels and offcuts of silver wire, bits of yellow metal Kat assumed was gold, what looked like semi-precious stones, a kitchen blowtorch, and a thick-walled white clay bowl blackened on its inner surfaces. Vera pushed the whole lot to one end; Kat glanced over as something metallic fell to the floor.

Tutting, Vera picked it up and pocketed it. She smiled.

'You'll have to forgive the mess. I make jewellery. It's just a hobby. For friends mainly, but I'm not a very tidy worker. My poor table! Tea?'

'Please.'

Vera made tea using a sleek boiling-water tap installed in the worktop.

'What can I do for you, Kat?' she asked after placing two mugs on the table.

'When we spoke before, you said you couldn't remember any particular victims of the Three Sisters.'

Vera tapped her head. 'My memory's not what it was.'

'But as I was leaving, you told me you remembered all your pupils.'

Vera smiled wistfully and sipped her tea.

'A figure of speech. Nothing more.'

Kat nodded. Tried her own tea, which was both weak and far too hot.

'The thing is, I spoke to Nigel Jenkins this afternoon. And he told me that you took Goneril Pickering under your wing. That you mentored her. She even stayed at your house a few times when she fell out with her parents.' Kat scrutinised the older woman's face. Beyond the sallow complexion she saw nothing. No tells. No guilty glances. A blank. 'So, given that Goneril attempted suicide, I'm just surprised you couldn't remember such a traumatic event for a girl you clearly cared a lot about.'

Vera shook her head. Placed her mug down carefully.

'You're right, Kat. I *do* remember Goneril. But over the years I have tried, mostly successfully, to block out that dreadful time.

It was simply too painful. I would find myself weeping halfway through a lesson. It upset the younger children and elicited derision from the older ones. I prefer not to talk about it.'

'Even to a homicide detective?'

'Even to her.'

'Vera, we have somebody in custody. I am concerned that she may have used undue influence to co-opt others into a plan to murder Jo Morris, Elise Burrluck and the third member of their gang, Hayley Edwards. If you have been contacted and forced somehow to help, you can tell me. Acting under duress, especially if you were in fear for your life, is not an offence. Has anyone contacted you or put you under any kind of pressure to help them? Did they ask you to synthesise LSD or strychnine?'

Vera sipped her tea. She glanced down at the ring she'd left on the table and frowned, before quickly replacing her mug.

'I'm afraid you have rather overestimated my skills as a chemist. I could probably knock you up a batch of laughing gas, or some fart powder. But strychnine's a little outside what Henry would probably call my "core competence". I'm a secondary school chemistry teacher, not a professional scientist. You'd need a full-blown industrial lab for that.'

Kat nodded. Michelle Wilson had access to just such a lab. So maybe the Pickering sisters hadn't needed to coerce Vera after all.

'There's something else I need to ask you. Were you aware that Alison was living at the rehab facility at Clemmows Hall?'

'The last I heard of her she'd left Middlehampton for London. I can't say I blame her.'

'She never tried to make contact with you?'

Vera sighed and shrugged her bony shoulders. 'I wish she'd felt able to. But after what happened, I just think she wanted to put as much space between her and the school as possible.'

Kat steeled herself. Though Vera wasn't anywhere near being next of kin, she'd clearly cared for Goneril Pickering. And it fell to Kat to tell her she was dead. She cleared her throat.

'I'm afraid I have some bad news for you. Goneril – Alison, I mean – died.'

Vera turned her head away and stared out of the window. She sniffed, once.

'How did it happen?'

'An overdose. We're waiting to get the medical reports.'

Now Vera did turn. She wasn't crying, but her face was twisted with grief. She cleared her throat.

'That poor, poor girl. All that potential, and she never lived to achieve any of it.'

A phone buzzed. Vera smiled. 'Sorry, that's mine. Hold on, would you?'

Kat shook her head. 'I'm done, Vera. Thanks for your time. I'll see myself out.'

She got to her feet and left Vera to her phone call, nodding and starting to rearrange her jewellery-making stuff as she listened.

Something niggled at the back of Kat's mind as she drove away. It was infuriating not to be able to remember. Was it something Vera had said or done? Was it about Judith? Did Vera know where she was? Was that who was calling her? No. That didn't feel right.

The traffic in front of her slowed, then came to a dead stop. She heard horns blaring up ahead and lifted herself off her seat with her hands to see if she could make out the cause of the trouble. It was impossible. Maybe she could use the jam creatively. She closed her eyes.

What was it about Vera's house that was ringing alarm bells?

Breathing slowly and steadily, she let the sounds from outside her car fade away. She reran the whole visit from the moment she stepped over the threshold to the moment she left and closed the front door behind her.

It was the kitchen. Something she'd seen in there. Vera had cleared some space for their teas. She'd carelessly pushed all her jewellery-making stuff down one end of the table and something had fallen off. Kat had looked down and seen it before Vera picked it up. What *was* it?

Brownish wire, too thick for jewellery, though. Curled into a question mark. The straight part twisted. Was that it? It felt right, but there was something else. Those burn marks. Vera had said she wasn't very tidy. She must have burnt the table with the blowtorch she used to make her rings and necklaces.

Kat gasped. Snapped her eyes open. A car horn blared. The cars ahead had moved off and the driver behind her had given her a few seconds' grace before making their displeasure audible.

She pulled left down a side street and brought the car to a juddering stop.

In her own experiment, before improvising the branding iron, she'd clipped the hook out of the coat hanger with a pair of cutters from the toolbox in the garage. It had left a question mark of bronze-coloured wire with a twisted end.

And that burn mark on Vera's kitchen table. The one she'd hurriedly put her mug down on. Kat had glimpsed the shape of it before the mug covered it. A crude figure of eight.

She accelerated away from her parking spot, made a U-turn and sped back towards Vera's house. When she arrived, she slewed to a stop and leapt out, running up the front garden path and hammering on the front door.

An elderly lady clipping the hedge separating the two houses called out to her. 'You've just missed her, love. Vera went off in her Beetle. Tearing hurry she was in, too. She clipped the car in front, look.'

Kat followed the neighbour's pointing finger to a black BMW, its angular rear end sporting a broad, dented scrape of gouged-in lines and bright yellow paint.

'Did she say where she was going?'

'No, dear. But she had a bag with her. Maybe she was off to the shops?'

A bag. Kat knew what it would contain. A homemade branding iron made from a bent and twisted coat hanger. A kitchen blowtorch. And a vial of poison. Maybe a hypodermic.

She raced back to the car. Called Tom.

'Get yourself over to Hayley Edwards's house pronto. I think Vera Maidment's gone over there to kill her.'

She slammed the transmission into first and pulled away from the kerb with a screech of rubber.

CHAPTER FORTY-THREE

Kat flipped the switches for the blue lights and siren.

Chaos ensued on the road ahead.

It never failed to amaze her, as she sped through the afternoon traffic, how otherwise rational, presumably skilful, drivers became incapable of controlling their cars in the presence of an emergency vehicle with its lights flashing.

People stopped dead in narrow stretches, preventing her passing them. Drove up onto the pavement so fast they almost went through shop windows. Sped up rather than slowing down, perhaps imagining they were acting as some sort of advance guard, clearing the way for the manically blaring unmarked car behind them.

Finally, she hit a relatively quiet stretch of road and put her foot flat on the floor. It took her fifteen minutes to reach North End. Despite having told Hayley she knew the address, it wasn't an area she knew well. She pulled over briefly to launch the satnav app on her phone. Masons Road was only five minutes away.

She made the final right turn and swore. Facing her across the entrance to the road were three brightly painted concrete blocks. A sign read: *Pedestrian-Friendly Street Scheme – Middlehampton Council, Working for You.*

'Well, it's not working for me!' Kat shouted.

She climbed out of her car and ran through the gap in the blocks to check the number of the first house.

'Oh, you have to be kidding me!'

The white-painted plaque bore three screwed-on numbers: 692. What the hell? Was this the longest residential street in Middlehampton?

She ran back to the car and checked the satnav. It would take her another five minutes to drive round to the next available street that would allow her access to Masons Road.

That was time she didn't have.

She locked the car and ran back between the blocks. Halfway down the street a vicious stitch pierced her side. It was like being stabbed. Wincing, she slowed to a trot for a few metres before picking up speed again. Maybe Tom was there already, using his gung-ho energy to kick the door down and save the day.

As she ran on down the road, she checked the house numbers. She was still in the mid-300s. The stitch was getting worse and as she slowed again her foot caught in an uneven paving stone and she sprawled headlong.

Arms outstretched, she broke her fall at the cost of scraping half the skin off her palms. She got to her feet again and ran on, now trying to ignore both the stitch, which felt like a red-hot arrow stuck in her rib cage, and the pain radiating up both arms from her wrists.

She hit the 200s and slowed to a trot. The road was utterly deserted. Not a car or a pedestrian in sight. She passed 100 and forced herself to run faster. Finally, lungs burning, palms dripping blood, she reached 17. No sign of Tom. But Vera Maidment's yellow Beetle was double-parked, blocking in a silver Honda Jazz. Its engine was still ticking as it cooled. Vera couldn't have been more than a few minutes ahead of Kat.

Kat ran up the garden path and rang the bell. Without thinking, she balled her right fist and hammered on the wooden strip separating the two stained-glass panels, crying out as her raw flesh met the paintwork.

'Hayley! Are you in there? Vera? It's Kat Ballantyne. It's over. Come out.'

She stood back, heart thumping in her chest, pulse roaring in her ears. Was she in time to save Hayley?

Nobody came to the door. Of course nobody came. Either Hayley was already dead, or she was following Kat's own instructions and hiding herself away.

Frantically, Kat searched the front garden for something she could use to get in. She picked up a large flower pot planted with scarlet geraniums and, wincing as its gritty surface scored her bleeding palms, hurled it at the left-hand glazed panel of the front door.

The glass shattered with a loud crash and the pot bounced backwards off the frame, smashing on the doorstep. Kat used a large, terracotta shard to scrape the remaining glass out of the putty. She reached in and twisted the door handle.

She was in.

'Hayley? Where are you? It's DS Ballantyne. We spoke on the phone. Are you OK?'

Silence.

Kat tiptoed down the hallway towards the door at the far end. If the house was built on the same lines as the thousands of other terraced houses in Middlehampton, it would lead to the kitchen.

Her pulse was still racing, and the run down Masons Road in her low-heeled boots had her drawing in ragged breaths as her screaming muscles tried to replenish the oxygen they'd burnt through.

The door wasn't shut completely. Kat leaned closer and listened at the crack between door and jamb. Nothing. She stepped back.

Took a dancing step forward and kicked out at the door, sending it swinging inwards and round to bang against the wall.

The sight that greeted her at the far end of the kitchen confirmed her worst fears.

A woman in her thirties – Hayley Edwards presumably – dressed in a powder-blue velvet hoodie and matching joggers, was leaning back against the kitchen counter, her arms limp by her sides. A dark patch had spread out from the crotch of her joggers.

Behind her generous frame, Kat saw another figure. A woman, slim to the point of being scrawny, like someone on chemo. Her face was hidden behind Hayley's head. Hayley's brown eyes were wide with terror, and tears had drawn her mascara down into smudged black streaks.

At first, Kat struggled to understand what she was seeing. Why wasn't Hayley moving? Then she saw why.

A bony hand curled around from behind her, gripping a slim-barrelled hypodermic syringe. The plastic tip was pushed up hard against Hayley's neck, denting the soft flesh of her throat. The entire needle was beneath the surface.

Vera's right hand was clasping the duct-taped handle of a thin wire, its twisted tip glowing in the blue flame jetting out from a kitchen blowtorch standing upright on the worktop.

She moved her face into view.

'Hello again, Kat.'

Fighting to keep her voice level, Kat said, 'Hello Vera. Put the branding iron down. And the syringe. Let Hayley go. It's over.'

'It's *nearly* over.'

'Please help me,' Hayley said to Kat in a voice from which terror had leached all power.

'I'm going to, Hayley, OK? I'm going to. Just keep calm.'

Vera turned her face a little and spoke directly into Hayley's right ear.

'Pull your top up, Hayley.'

'Why? What are you going to do?'

'Come now, Hayley. You know perfectly well what I'm going to do. The police didn't release the details, but you should be able to remember what you did to my poor Alison. You branded her, didn't you, with your hateful little symbol.'

'I'm going to be sick.'

'If you throw up, I'll push the plunger home and you'll be dead before you hit the floor. Now. Pull. Your. Top. UP!'

She barked out the last word and Hayley's hands jumped up from her sides, grabbed the hem of the hoodie and yanked it up, exposing her midriff.

'Please, please, please. Don't. I'm begging you. I know what we did was wrong. But it was so long ago. We were just kids. You have to forgive me.'

'Shut your mouth, you bitch!' Vera hissed. Then she glared at Kat, who'd been sliding her feet across the floor tiles, trying to close the gap between her and the tangled-up figures of the murderer and her third victim. 'Stop! One more step and she dies.'

Kat held her arms up, palms out, towards Vera. 'I'm not coming any closer. But, please, think about what you're doing. It doesn't have to end like this.'

Vera raised an eyebrow. 'Oh, really. How *does* it have to end? I've already killed the others. Do I get a lighter sentence for two murders rather than three?'

'The judge will look favourably on anything you do now to mitigate the damage you've done. Sparing Hayley would be a big move on your part.'

Vera shook her head. 'Like they spared Alison, you mean?'

'Hayley's right. They *were* young,' Kat said. 'That doesn't excuse what they did. It was vicious and cruel. Criminal. They should have been arrested and charged with grievous bodily harm. But think about what you're doing, Vera. They didn't take a life, but you have.'

'Of *course* they took a life!' Vera said. 'Maybe Alison survived her overdose back then, but they took her life from her all the same. She went to London and ended up selling herself on the streets to pay for her next fix. I thought when she got back here and we got her a place at Clemmows Hall, she might have been all right. But you know what happened.'

'Yes, she took an overdose. But you can't lay that at Hayley's door,' Kat said, fighting harder than she'd ever fought in her life to find arguments that would persuade someone not to commit a crime.

'Can't I? Remind me of the date when Alison died.'

'April twenty-first last year.'

'Have you read her medical records?'

Kat shook her head. She felt sick, suddenly, as the connection Vera was asking her to find presented itself anyway.

'We're still waiting for them.'

'They branded her on April twenty-first. She killed herself on the anniversary. Every year it was the same. Michelle or Mercy or I would sit with her all night while she wept and shook and vomited. This year, I was having chemo and neither Mercy nor Michelle could make it. We thought she'd be fine: one of her friends at the hall offered to sit up with her.'

Kat thought back to the quartet of recovering addicts who'd been playing tennis.

'Was it Janey?'

'That's right. She was distraught afterwards. She was so heavily sedated she slept for two days.'

Kat was starting to feel she might, just, be able to turn the situation around. Vera seemed more interested in talking than acting.

Although the twisted coat hanger was still glowing red-hot in the blowtorch's flame.

'Vera, why don't you let Hayley go? She can leave, and you and I can talk about Goneril.'

'Sorry, no. I need to see this through.' She brought the glowing wire out from the flame. 'Now, Hayley, hold still. This is going to hurt.'

Just then, the front door crashed back, slamming into the wall. 'Kat?'

It was Tom. She turned her head to the door behind her. Opened her mouth to shout for him to come in slowly. But the noise that made her ears ring in the confined space wasn't her own shouted instruction, but a high-pitched, agonised scream. She spun round. Caught the nauseating smell of burnt flesh. Saw the livid burn on Hayley's soft, pallid belly.

Then the velvet hoodie dropped to cover it. Eyes rolling upwards then closing, Hayley groaned and fainted, sagging in Vera's arms. As she slumped to the ground, the needle pulled free of the flesh of her neck.

Arms raised, Kat leapt towards Vera, but Vera raised her left hand again and placed the point of the needle against the side of her own neck.

'Stop!' she shouted in a commanding tone that brought Kat to a shuddering halt.

She had time to think the voice must have been useful for quelling playground disputes or classroom uproars.

Behind her she heard Tom enter the kitchen.

'Boss! Are you OK?'

'Quiet, Tom,' she said in as calm a voice as she could manage. In truth, it sounded tremulous to her ears and not at all that of an officer in control of the situation.

She sensed him moving slowly to stand beside her. As he entered her peripheral vision, she motioned for him to stay still, patting the air with her right palm.

'It's over, Vera,' she said. 'Don't do anything stupid.'

Without taking her eyes off Kat, Vera held her right hand out wide and dropped the still-glowing branding iron to the floor. It sizzled against the vinyl tile, releasing an acrid plume of whitish smoke.

'I think we're a little beyond that, don't you? You'll want to arrest me, I suppose. Take me to the police station. Read me my rights. Find me a solicitor. Interview me. Charge me. Place me on remand. Bring me to court in front of a judge and a jury of my peers.'

'It's the law, Vera. You've murdered two women and now you've attempted to murder a third.'

Her heart clenched in her chest. *And one of them was my half-sister*. She fought back tears that threatened to burst free.

Vera scowled. 'I delivered justice for Alison. Justice that should have been delivered a long time ago. But in any case, I'm not going to debate the law with you. Jo and Elise are dead, and Hayley will bear a reminder of what she did for the rest of her life. Now all that remains is for me to end my own and this whole sorry tale can finally be laid to rest.'

'Don't do it, Vera,' Tom said, taking a step forward. 'Please. You don't have to die. Listen, I studied criminology at university. Something Alison might have gone on to do if only she'd been strong enough. There's something I want to tell you. Something I learned on my course.'

Kat held her breath. He was trying something audacious, but it might just work.

'If you plead not guilty by reason of temporary insanity, I think with a good lawyer and a sympathetic jury, you might succeed. You obviously loved Alison like a daughter. That sort of loss could be shown to have knocked you for a loop.'

'That's a lovely thought. And thank you for trying . . .' Vera said with a smile, then hesitated, 'Tom, isn't it? I assume you're Kat's assistant or, what do they call them on the telly, bagman? But I'm afraid I have no more appetite for spending my remaining days in a psychiatric hospital than I do a prison – or a hospice.'

Kat's heart was pounding in her throat. Because even though she'd got her breath back, she knew what she must do. It was her only chance to stop Vera Maidment from taking her own life with whatever poison was filling the thin plastic tube extending between her fingers.

While Tom had been occupying Vera's attention, Kat had managed to slide another half-metre closer to the older woman. She'd not taken her eyes from the syringe as she was doing it and it looked as though Vera had lessened the pressure of her thumb on the plunger.

She still had to cover a distance equal to at least her own body length to reach Vera, but it had to be worth a try.

She focused all her energy on her legs, planned how she'd close the gap between them; visualised bringing her arm up and knocking the hypo clear.

Trying not to *think* the move but simply to *make* it, she launched herself across the two-metre space between them. Vera turned, saw her. Her eyes narrowed. In the slowed-down time as adrenaline propelled Kat like a dart towards Vera, Kat saw Vera's thumb tighten on the plunger. The needle beginning its short but deadly journey into the blood vessels of her neck.

Time sped up, lightning-fast. Kat swung her right arm up in a slashing backhand movement and smacked Vera's left wrist. Vera shouted hoarsely, 'No!' as the syringe flew out of her grasp and clattered harmlessly against the side wall of the kitchen.

Together, they tumbled sideways in a tangle of arms and legs. Kat landed on top of Vera and heard a loud snap.

Vera screamed again. 'My arm!'

Panting, Kat rolled clear and sat back on her haunches. In front of her, slumped against the knee-level kitchen units, Vera cradled her left arm. The hand hung at an unnatural angle. The snap had been a bone breaking.

Hayley lay a metre away, eyes still closed.

Then Tom was at Kat's side.

'You OK? Did she scratch you with the needle?'

'No, I'm fine. Quick, bag it. And don't touch it!' she shouted as Tom scuttled into the corner to retrieve the poison-filled syringe.

She turned to Vera.

'Vera Maidment, I am arresting you for the murders of Jo Morris and Elise Burrluck, and for the attempted murder of Hayley Edwards.'

She recited the caution in a monotone as shock got the better of her.

In the distance, she heard sirens.

CHAPTER FORTY-FOUR

Kat slid across the kitchen floor to where Hayley was coming round. Her eyes were fluttering open, and her mouth was twitching, as though she was trying to say something.

'Get her out of here,' she said to Tom, pointing at Vera, who was sitting perfectly still, staring at the ceiling. 'Drive her up to MGH yourself. Straight into A&E. Get her arm looked at as soon as possible then I want her booked in and in a cell, pronto. And call an ambulance for Hayley.'

While Tom lifted Vera up bodily and took her out of the kitchen, Kat sat beside Hayley and took her hand.

'Hayley, you're going to be OK. The ambulance is on its way.'

'She burnt me,' Hayley whimpered. 'It hurts so much.'

'I know. Can you manage here on your own for a second? I need to cool it down.'

Hayley nodded, her eyes full of tears.

Kat filled a large saucepan with cold water and grabbed a mug from the draining rack. She brought it all back to Hayley and laid the items out beside her. Then, as gently as she could, she lifted the hem of the hoodie, along with the loose white T-shirt beneath it.

She winced. The burn was an ugly mess of red and black flesh. The surrounding skin had reddened as Hayley's body fought to contain the damage.

Kat dipped up a mugful of the water and trickled it over the wound. Hayley cried out and squeezed Kat's hand so hard she felt a knuckle pop. With her free hand, she kept scooping up the water and maintained a steady stream over the burn. Gradually, Hayley stopped whimpering.

'What we did to Goneril?' she whispered. 'Me, Elise and Jo? It was evil.'

'Why did you do it, then? What was going on between the three of you?'

'I've asked myself that a million times. I just think we got off on the power it gave us. People were scared of us. It felt like we ran the school. But now I just think we were these little psychos. We should have been arrested for what we did.' She looked at Kat. 'What will happen to me now? Will I be charged?'

Kat blew out her cheeks. She knew no prosecutor in the country would want to take that route. But *she* did. She wanted Hayley to suffer for what she'd done.

If not for the Three Sisters' addiction to causing pain and terror in their victims, Kat might have had a chance to meet Jo while she was still alive. To build a relationship with someone who, whilst a blood relative, would have some distance from Colin-bloody-Morton and his toxic empire. But it wasn't to be. That possible future was as dead as Jo Morris.

She sighed. Pushed down her grief for her lost sister.

'Honestly, it's too long ago. Goneril's dead. There's no public interest in charging you now.'

Hayley shook her head. Kat noticed that some colour had come back into her cheeks. A relief, as it meant Hayley wasn't going into shock.

'It's gone on too long. I think I should have to pay for what we did. Not how Vera wanted me to, but all the same, I'm the only one left and it was us who started this whole thing.'

Kat heard boots clumping down the hallway. The paramedics had arrived.

'I think you've paid plenty,' Kat said. 'But if you really wanted to make amends, you could wait for a few days and then visit Mr and Mrs Pickering. I need to go and tell them one of their daughters is dead and at least one other is involved in a conspiracy to murder.'

She looked up as the paramedics entered the kitchen. It was the same pair who'd attended the scene when they'd found Elise murdered.

'Hi, Rosemah,' she said, getting to her feet. 'Ryan.'

'What have we got?' Rosemah asked as she knelt beside Hayley and said hello.

'Serious burn. She was branded with that.' Kat pointed to the crudely twisted coat hanger.

'OK, my love, can I just take a look?' Rosemah asked, peering at the burn.

Kat left them to it, telling Ryan she'd meet them at the hospital.

She arrived in A&E fifteen minutes later. Tom was sitting beside Vera on bright green plastic bucket seats in the crowded waiting area.

'We've been triaged,' Tom said. 'Not looking good. Could be hours yet.'

'How are you doing, Vera?' Kat asked, taking the seat on the woman's other side.

Vera gave a rueful smile. 'It's rather painful. But I've become used to discomfort over the last six months. I'll live. A little longer,' she added ironically.

Kat nodded. 'I'll see if I can shake things up a little.'

She went over to the harassed-looking nurse at the reception desk. She recognised the other woman. Chloe, that was her name. Cops and nurses often ended up spending time together. Sometimes in the small hours of the morning, when everybody would rather be asleep at home and not ankle-deep in blood while the walking wounded wailed, the drunk, drugged and incapable ranted and raved, and the seriously ill people lay in silence, white-faced and sunken-cheeked.

'Hi, Chloe, how's it going today?'

The nurse blew out her cheeks. 'Oh, you know, it's so calm I think I might knock off early and go for a swim in the hospital pool. Or maybe get a massage.'

Kat grinned. 'Listen, our prisoner over there. I know it's only a broken bone, but she's under arrest for two murders and we really need to get her booked in. Any chance there's a nice young doctor who can give it a quick x-ray and plaster her up?'

Chloe peered round Kat's hip. 'Her? She doesn't look like she could murder a cup of tea, let alone two people.'

'She's got cancer. In fact, does that help?'

Chloe sighed. 'Give me a second. I'll see what I can do.'

'Thanks. I owe you one.'

'Like tearing up my last parking ticket?'

'How about I pay it off for you?'

Chloe smiled. 'Don't be daft. I was only joking. But you could buy me a coffee some time.'

'Deal. You've got my card. Call me when you're off duty. We'll go somewhere nice.'

Kat felt a twinge of guilt as, five minutes later, a nurse in blue scrubs holding a clipboard called out Vera's name and took her away, Tom in attendance, to have her arm looked at. While Kat waited, Rosemah walked in with Hayley beside her. Kat was relieved to see that Hayley's complexion had returned to normal. She even managed a smile as she saw Kat.

'Could you help Hayley?' Rosemah asked. 'We've had another shout.'

'Sure. Thanks, Rosemah. See you around.' She took Hayley's arm. 'How is it?'

'It's OK. Hurts like hell, but I'll survive. You saved my life. Thank you.'

Kat nodded. 'Listen, I have to go. But I'm going to call Victim Support for you. We'll arrange for one of their people to contact you. They can help you if you need anything.'

'Thank you. I really don't deserve all this. You must hate me.'

They'd just reached the reception desk, but even so, Kat stopped dead and turned Hayley to face her. 'You're a victim of crime, Hayley. Attempted murder. My job, my *duty*, is to protect you and deal with the person who attacked you. As for what you did in the past? That's between you and your conscience.'

Hayley opened her mouth to speak but then quietly closed it. The two women maintained eye contact for another few seconds.

'Who have we got here?' Chloe asked, breaking the spell.

Kat stepped back to allow Chloe to get to work. The noise of the busy A&E department faded. Her thoughts turned inwards. What was it that had turned one girl, Hayley, into a bully while others – like Liv, like Keisha, like Goneril Pickering – had always been on the receiving end? Was it just as simple as something in their background?

As far as she could tell, Hayley had come from a comfortable middle-class family. Whereas Liv, in care since early childhood, would have presented an ideal target.

She shook her head. Too simplistic. There'd been plenty of hard-as-nails poor kids at Queen Anne's you wouldn't want to tangle with. And bullied kids with nice accents, properly fitting school uniforms, and lifts to school in BMWs and Audis.

Maybe Hayley had it right. The Three Sisters just got off on the power it gave them. But Kat saw a darker reason. One that troubled her every time she read about another force dealing with a spate of serial murders.

Some people just enjoyed inflicting pain on others. Like Hayley herself said. They were 'little psychos'.

Kat met Carve-up as she entered MCU. Even though it was the end of the day, his shimmering silver-grey suit looked as though he'd just taken it out of the dry-cleaner's polythene bag. Not a crease, not a mark, not a flake of dandruff on the shoulders.

'I hear you had a result on the Three Sisters case, DS Ballantyne. Well done.'

The words were conventionally appreciative. But Carve-up's expression and his refusal to use her name undercut the praise. A smirk, like she was walking around with her skirt tucked into her knickers.

'Thanks, Stu. She's already confessed but it was before we cautioned her. I'll be interviewing her with Tom later, as soon as she's back from A&E.'

Carver's smirk morphed into a grin. 'What, did Tom lamp her like he did that idiot Bolton?'

'I fell on top of her trying to get a syringe full of poison off her. Broke her arm.'

'Oh, great! Well done, you. Remember to complete a Use of Force form, then. Don't want Professional Standards on your case, do we?'

Even though she felt like employing a little bit of force against her superior officer there and then, Kat grudgingly had to admit he was right. There were people at Jubilee Place who would cheerfully ignore the arrest of a multiple murderer, and the saving of her intended victim's life, in order to focus on pursuing a detective for incomplete paperwork.

She made herself a coffee and went back to her desk. It was going to be a long night. She called Van.

'Hey, everything all right?' he said.

'We got her. The killer, I mean. I can't say more right now, but we'll be here till late. I'm sorry, love.'

'It's fine. And well done. I knew you'd get there in the end.'

'How's Riley?'

'Upstairs doing his homework.' He paused. 'Allegedly.'

'Got to go. There'll be a break at some point. I'll come in quietly. Can you make up the spare room?'

'Absolutely not! I want you in bed with me.'

'I'll smell of the stinky interview room.'

'Mmm, you know that always gets me going.'

She grinned. 'Ivan Ballantyne, you're dreadful! Is there anything that *doesn't* get you going?'

'Bring your handcuffs home, then you can put them on me and interrogate me to find out.' A beat. 'In your pants.'

'I'm going. I love you.'

'I love you, too.'

Still smiling, she woke up her PC. While she waited for Tom to bring Vera back, she could make a start on the damned UoF form.

CHAPTER FORTY-FIVE

Kat waited for the tape recorder to finish screeching. Opposite her and Tom, Vera, her left arm in plaster and held in a royal-blue foam sling, sat beside her solicitor. He looked relaxed. Maybe Vera had told him he wouldn't have much to do. Kat decided to proceed on that basis. She didn't think Vera wanted to make a fight out of it.

'Vera, did you murder Jo Morris and Elise Burrluck?'

'Yes.'

The solicitor made a quick note.

'Did you also intend, and attempt, to murder Hayley Edwards?'

'I did, yes. And I'd like to tell you why.' She nodded towards the tape recorder's slowly rotating spools. 'So that it's all on the record.'

Kat nodded. 'Go ahead.'

Vera sat straighter in the hard chair. 'Teaching a girl like Goneril Pickering was a privilege. I felt it gave my life meaning, those moments. I never married, but I truly loved that girl like my own daughter. Then *they* got their claws into her and tore her apart. All her self-confidence went. I saw the light start dimming in her eyes. She became withdrawn, stopped studying. Began playing truant.'

She coughed, winced, and placed a hand on her chest, high on the left side. Then reached for the plastic cup of water at her left elbow.

'How long have you had cancer?' Kat asked.

'Less than a year. It's a very aggressive form of leukaemia.'

'I'm sorry.'

'Don't be. I'm in no pain. Not yet anyway. I've no husband to reassure he'll cope when I'm gone. No kids to mourn me. Not even a cat. My best days are behind me.'

'Like when you were teaching Goneril Pickering.'

Vera nodded, smiled sadly. 'She was such a lovely girl. Bright, but not a swot. Empathetic, friendly to the younger children. Confident, but not arrogant. Just one of those special children you might only meet once in your career.' She sighed. 'I thought she might have made an excellent teacher herself. Although she could have gone on to do anything.

'Do you know what Jo said to her as they branded her?' Vera pressed the pads of her fingers against her belly, just where her tweed skirt creased at the tops of her thighs. '"You're ours now. You'll never be free of us." I think Alison thought taking her own life was the only way she ever *could* be free of them. It was only because I was keeping an eye out for her that I noticed she wasn't at school. I called her parents and told them I had this strange feeling she might be trying to hurt herself. I was right, as it turned out. They went to find her. Can I tell you something?'

'Please.'

'The parents were useless. Worse than!' she hissed. 'They just wanted the whole thing hushed up. In the end, I went to the head myself. It was this useless old fart back then. Carrick, his name was. I hope he's mouldering in the ground by now. I told him enough was enough and he had to do something, or I'd go to the police.

He tried to smooth it all over. Said since she was alive nothing too terrible had happened. And he had the reputation of the school to consider. Ha! That's a joke. Back then the only reputation the College had was for turning out poorly educated call-centre fodder.'

'What happened?'

'I followed up on my threat. But the police were worse than Carrick. They promised to look into it, but in the end, they said there was nothing they could do. Goneril wasn't dead and there was no evidence connecting the Three Sisters to what she'd done.' Vera snorted. 'No evidence! If what they did to her wasn't evidence, I'd like to know what was.

'Poor, poor Goneril. She never recovered. Not really. She finally found a kind of respite at Clemmows Hall, but all that potential, all that joy, it just went out of her like air from a child's balloon.

'When she finally took her own life I was heartbroken, but in a strange way, also relieved. She'd finally found peace. I thought I'd be able to accept it, but I came to see that it was wrong that those three should be free to walk around, enjoying life, while my Goneril was cold and in her grave.'

'So you decided to murder them?'

'Yes, I did. They deserved it. Can't you see that? They'd got away with murdering an innocent young woman. Maybe not on that day itself, but they killed her just as surely as I killed them. It just took longer. I took my time planning it. There was a lot to do.'

Uncomfortably aware that in a dark corner of her soul she could see Vera's point, Kat changed tack.

'Did you have any help?'

Vera's eyes flashed. 'None. Absolutely none at all. This entire plan was my idea. I dreamed it up, I procured the necessary equipment, and I carried it out.'

'Why poison?'

'Isn't it obvious? They were toxic. So I thought poisoning them was fitting. Let the punishment fit the crime. Rather Old Testament, don't you think?'

'You said you didn't have any help—'

'—because I didn't. This is on me.'

Kat glanced down at her files. 'I think you *did* have help. From Michelle and Judith. You're trying to protect them, which I understand. You think that as you haven't got long to live, you can take all the blame. But I think we're going to find out that Judith's in England. And that Michelle befriended Jo so she could keep tabs on her. I think Judith booked an early-morning training session with Jo, using a pseudonym beginning with R, and then you turned up in her place.'

Vera shook her head. 'You're wrong about Judith. But right about the rest. I didn't use my real name in case she recognised it. I needn't have bothered. Even when I showed up at the Three Sisters, she didn't realise who I was.'

Kat made another note.

'We found unidentified fingerprints on Jo's water bottle and EpiPen. I think by the end of the night my forensics colleagues are going to come to tell me they match yours.'

'They will, but, to reiterate, I had no help from Judith. I had no idea she was even back in England. After the session, I said I was thirsty. I offered to get Jo her water bottle and I swapped it for mine. I'd been observing her at the gym, you see, and I bought an identical bottle. Hers was full of water. Mine was laced with kiwi juice and LSD. I'm sure your forensics colleagues found traces. When she started going into anaphylactic shock, she asked me to get her EpiPen. I administered it myself, but into her vein, not her muscle. I watched her die, and then I left.'

'Where did you get the LSD? Did you have Michelle synthesise it for you?'

'I did not. I bought it from a nice young man in town.'

'Name?'

'I didn't ask.'

Kat had a horrible feeling she knew exactly who had sold Vera the LSD.

'You killed Elise Burrluck with strychnine. That's a banned substance. How did you get it? Did Michelle synthesise it for you in one of her company's labs?'

'No. I lied to you before. My abilities as a chemist are far in excess of those needed to teach chemistry at a secondary school. I made it myself. Henry would have been impressed at how far I'd expanded my so-called skillset.'

'So we'll find evidence of your home laboratory when we search your house.'

'You will not. I destroyed everything.'

'Convenient.'

'True.'

'Why use strychnine at all?'

'Oh, that's easy. The characteristic grin I'm sure you observed on her face. The *rictus sardonicus*? Elise was always giving us teachers this smug little smile when we tried to intervene. Like butter wouldn't melt. I thought, well, let's give her a smile she'll never be able to wipe off her face.'

'What was in the syringe you were going to inject into Hayley's neck?'

'Tetrodotoxin, commonly abbreviated to TTX.'

'Which is?'

'Puffer fish poison. For a puffed-up little bitch.'

'Can it be synthesised?'

'It can and I did.'

Kat frowned. She was sure Vera was stonewalling on the others' guilt.

320

'Vera, are you seriously telling me that you, as a secondary school chemistry teacher, were able to procure the ingredients and no doubt extremely expensive equipment to create strychnine and artificial puffer fish poison?'

Vera's eyes twinkled. 'Have you heard of the dark web? One can get anything one desires if one knows where to look and has sufficiently deep pockets.'

'I see. And because you used a TOR browser, we won't be able to find any trace on your computer of your searches?'

Vera merely shrugged.

'Just one more question from me, Vera. Why did you, Michelle, Judith and Mercy pretend to me that Alison was alive? Did you hope we'd think she was the murderer? That when we couldn't find her, we'd eventually run out of resources and the case would be closed?'

'A nice try, Kat. Getting me to incriminate three innocent women. I have no idea what, if anything, they said to you. As for me, yes, I admit I was trying to buy time. My aim was to kill Hayley and then take my own life. You see, during my research I also found time to plan a peaceful, painless death for myself. Before the cancer robbed me of my dignity. As the sole perpetrator, I intended to leave a confession along with my suicide note.'

Kat sat back. Tom leaned forwards and began asking questions, but although he was doing his best, she knew it was hopeless. Vera had a look on her face of a cat who'd got the cream. She'd achieved what she'd set out to achieve, or two-thirds of it, and she was determined to go down alone.

◆ ◆ ◆

Kat looked across the table at the woman she was sure had conspired with Vera Maidment, Judith Pickering and Mercy Kipyego to murder Jo, Elise and Hayley.

Michelle's face was smooth: no stress lines, no tics, no flickering glances around the room. She just held Kat's gaze as if daring her to try something.

Best start with something simple and presumably uncontroversial, then.

'Do you have access to laboratory equipment at Bohrheim, Michelle?'

Michelle didn't break eye contact. 'On the advice of my legal representative, I decline to answer that question.'

'You're a research chemist, aren't you?'

'On the advice of my legal representative, I decline to answer that question.'

Seeing now the source of Michelle's unusual calm, Kat tried a third question. Received the same, thirteen-word answer.

Michelle stuck to the same, brief script for all the others. Ten minutes later, Kat ended the interview.

It didn't matter. Carve-up was hot to have Michelle charged with conspiracy to murder, and the CPS was eager to play ball. At the very least, they could charge her with obstruction for failing to reveal that Alison was dead. He authorised a further twenty-four hours' detention. The alert was still out for Mercy Kipyego and Judith Pickering, whose phone digital forensics had finally traced to a mast in Middlehampton. It was only a matter of time before they were both picked up. It was over.

At 4.15 a.m., just as she was getting ready to leave, Tom came over to Kat's desk.

'Before you go, I just wanted to say something.'

'What is it, Tomski?'

'Well, the way you went for Vera like that, it was totally irresponsible. What if she'd stuck you with the hypo? You'd have been dead in minutes. I looked it up. There's no antidote for TTX. It was an unacceptable risk. And she'd just confessed to murder.'

'You're wrong. I couldn't just let her die like that. Not if I had a chance to save her.'

'But she's dying of cancer, anyway. Maybe it would have been kinder.'

She shook her head violently. 'Not my job to make those decisions. I told you before. We catch the bad guys, end of. Everything else's above my pay grade. Especially deciding who lives and who dies. Now go home and get a couple of hours' kip. Busy day tomorrow.'

Half an hour later, Kat herself climbed into bed beside her snoring husband. He rolled over in his sleep and mumbled something that might have been a greeting. She kissed his bristly cheek and encircled his waist with her arm.

'You're mine,' she whispered into the back of his neck, 'and don't you forget it.'

EPILOGUE

A week later, arriving at work, Kat barely had time to put her bag down before Carve-up called out to her across MCU.

'DS Ballantyne? A word.'

He retreated, closing the door behind him. One of his petty power-plays, forcing her to knock and wait to be admitted.

She squared her shoulders, straightened her jacket and went in without knocking.

Carve-up was sitting behind his desk in conversation with a rotund stranger, his thinning sandy hair swept over his scalp in a style she'd thought had died out years ago. Carve-up pointed to the second visitor chair. She sat, turning to the stranger. A bulging, pockmarked nose dominated his doughy face.

'DS Ballantyne,' she said, holding out her hand. 'Kat.'

He looked at her hand as if she might have just used it to wipe herself after going to the toilet. Disdained the offer to shake.

'DI Senior,' he lisped, offering a lipless smile.

'DI Senior's with 3C-ACU,' Carve-up said.

Her stomach flipped. Even though she had nothing to hide, the mere mention of the Three Counties Anti-Corruption Unit was enough to get any copper's pulse trotting along just that little bit faster.

'OK. Why am I here?'

Senior turned to her. 'Have you checked your bank balance today, DS Ballantyne?'

'No.'

'Would you mind doing so now for me, please?'

He had the manner of a dentist asking a nervous patient to open her mouth. Knowing what he was about to do would hurt, however much he might keep his voice calm. Except that everybody knew 3C-ACU loved causing ordinary coppers that kind of discomfort.

She opened the mobile banking app on her phone and tapped on her current account. She was about to twist the phone round to show Senior her usual, middle of the month, few-hundred-plus-a-bit balance when she stopped. Eyes wide, she had to read the digits twice. According to the small blue figures in front of her, she had £50,358.14 in her current account.

'May I see?' Senior enquired mildly. A butterfly collector requesting a look at a rare specimen in another's killing jar.

With a shaking hand, Kat turned her phone towards him. 'There must be a mistake.'

Senior's sandy eyebrows, in which flakes of dandruff sat between the unruly hairs, crept upwards.

'My, my, that is certainly a healthy balance. Remind me, DI Carver. What is the salary for a sergeant in Hertfordshire Police at the moment?'

'For pay point 1, DS Ballantyne's level, that would be £45,000.' Smirk. 'Per annum.'

Kat felt panicky, light-headed. They'd cooked up this little double act between them and were clearly enjoying themselves.

Senior repeated the amount. 'Now, if we subtract National Insurance and Income Tax, that would leave someone on that annual salary with take-home pay of £33,861.' He turned watery blue eyes on Kat. 'Would you care to explain, DS Ballantyne, how you have in your current account an amount equal to almost one and a half times your annual take-home pay?'

Kat gulped down a sudden rush of nausea. Her palms were slick with sweat, and without realising she wiped them on her thighs. She had no idea how the money had appeared in her bank account. But she knew that would cut very little ice with Senior. It was just the sort of response he presumably got all the time.

'I think before we go any further, I should have my Fed rep in here with me,' she said, annoyed at the tremor in her voice. 'I would also like to know how you knew, because you clearly did, what I was going to find. And also whether I am under formal investigation.'

Senior offered a wintry smile.

'To answer your questions in reverse order' – he turned to Carve-up – 'a bit like an awards ceremony, this. No, DS Ballantyne, you are *not* under a formal investigation by 3C-ACU. At this stage, my inquiries are entirely *informal*. How I knew about the money is confidential. It may be revealed to you later, at such time as I deem it appropriate. And finally, no need for your Fed rep. Not yet, at least. That's all for now.'

On rubbery legs, Kat left Carve-up's office and made it back to her desk before collapsing into her chair.

She'd been set up. Mind racing, she tried to identify a suspect. Who'd want to put her in trouble with the ACU? Was it Carve-up himself? He hated her enough, but where would he get that kind of money?

A bank of blinding-white floodlights illuminated her brain like the Eels' stadium for an evening cup-tie. Where would a corrupt DI like Stuart Carver get a ton of money? Where else but from the man who paid for his designer suits and his flashy Italian motor. Colin Morton.

But why? She'd done a deal with him over Jo. His silence for hers. Her dad wouldn't risk the peace he'd negotiated with Kat just to indulge his tame detective inspector's grievance against his daughter.

But if not Carve-up, then who? Surely her dad wouldn't have done it on his own account?

She looked around the bustling open-plan space. On the far side, Linda was chatting to Tom. Was it him? The stickler for the rules. Had she cut a corner somewhere and outraged his sense of propriety by suggesting he do the same? No. Surely not. She called him Tomski. They bantered. They were partners. And anyway, where would he get the money? He earned less than she did.

Maybe it wasn't a cop at all. Was it Daniela Morris? Jo's outraged mother-in-law. She had the money and maybe she felt Kat hadn't done enough to find her daughter's killer.

Kat felt panic swelling in her chest. Names rushed at her. Marnie Pryce, scheming to take Van from her. Even Liv. Did she want Kat out of the police so she could join her on the commune?

No. No. Nonononono. This wasn't right. She'd just solved a double homicide. She was a good cop. An *honest* cop.

Then Linda turned and caught Kat's eye. She wasn't smiling. Mouthed a two-word phrase.

My office.

With a dark, sickly weight poisoning her insides, Kat levered herself to her feet and crossed MCU. Felt her colleagues' collective gaze burning the back of her neck.

As hot as a brand.

ACKNOWLEDGEMENTS

I want to thank you for buying this book. I hope you enjoyed it. As an author is only part of the team of people who make a book the best it can be, this is my chance to thank the people on *my* team.

For sharing their knowledge and experience of The Job, former and current police officers Andy Booth, Ross Coombs, Jen Gibbons, Neil Lancaster, Sean Memory, Trevor Morgan, Olly Royston, Chris Saunby, Ty Tapper, Sarah Warner and Sam Yeo.

For their patience, professionalism and friendship, the fabulous publishing team at Thomas & Mercer: my editor Kasim Mohammed; development editor Russel McLean; copyeditor Jill Sawyer; and proofreader Gemma Wain. Plus the wonderful marketing team including Rebecca Hills, Hatty Stiles and Nicole Wagner. And Dominic Forbes, who, once again, really smashed the brief with another awesome cover design.

The members of my Facebook Group, The Wolfe Pack, are an incredibly supportive and also helpful bunch of people. Thank you to them, also.

And for being an inspiration and source of love and laughter, and making it all worthwhile, my family: Jo, Rory and Jacob.

Andy Maslen
Salisbury, 2024

ABOUT THE AUTHOR

Photo © 2021, Kin Ho

Andy Maslen was born in Nottingham, England. After leaving university with a degree in psychology, he worked in business for thirty years as a copywriter. In his spare time, he plays blues guitar. He lives in Wiltshire.

Follow the Author on Amazon

If you enjoyed this book, follow Andy Maslen on Amazon to be notified when the author releases a new book!
To do this, please follow these instructions:

Desktop:

1) Search for the author's name on Amazon or in the Amazon App.
2) Click on the author's name to arrive on their Amazon page.
3) Click the 'Follow' button.

Mobile and Tablet:

1) Search for the author's name on Amazon or in the Amazon App.
2) Click on one of the author's books.
3) Click on the author's name to arrive on their Amazon page.
4) Click the 'Follow' button.

Kindle eReader and Kindle App:

If you enjoyed this book on a Kindle eReader or in the Kindle App, you will find the author 'Follow' button after the last page.